N

Mary Bunyan

A Tale of
Religious Persecution
and Heroic Faith

Sallie Rochester Ford

Solid Ground Christian Books
Birmingham, Alabama USA

Solid Ground Christian Books
PO Box 660132
Birmingham, AL 35266
205-443-0311
sgcb@charter.net
http://solid-ground-books.com

Mary Bunyan
A TALE OF RELIGIOUS PERSECUTION AND HEROIC FAITH

Sallie Rochester Ford (1828-1910)

Solid Ground Classic Reprints

First printing of new edition September 2007

Cover work by Borgo Design, Tuscaloosa, AL
Contact them at borgogirl@bellsouth.net

ISBN: 1-59925-121-3

Mary Bunyan: A New Introduction

The practice of reading biography is, without a doubt, one of the most enriching habits in which the Christian mind can engage. Faith brought to life in the recorded stories of characters of the past, often communicates to our hearts more richly than faith described in mere propositions. It is only unfortunate that, in so many instances, history has been allowed to leave us only sketchy data about a character. Thus has arisen the popular value of those books dubbed "living history", popularized by G.A. Henty and other authors who wrote much of it. Using those facts and knowledge which they have been able to gather, they help us grasp something of the life and times of a character about whom we would otherwise know little. Such is the case with Miss Mary Bunyan, young daughter of the famed John Bunyan of Bedford, England.

This English preacher (1628-1688) is best known as the author of "The Pilgrim's Progress". As an unintended and unfortunate outcome, the fame of that book (Bunyan's most well-known and beloved writing) has probably obscured to many believers the fact that Bunyan wrote dozens of other books and treatises. He penned a wealth of works, all of which are worthy of the highest recommendation to the Christian reader. For the current publication of his complete works, we are indebted to the Banner of Truth Trust.

But back to the volume in your hand: Sallie Rochester Ford, the teller of Mary Bunyan's story, originally entitled the book, "Mary Bunyan, The Dreamer's Blind Daughter: A Tale of Religious Persecution." Ford's focus on this one girl and the life of her family has left us one of the most moving stories of suffering for the Christian faith ever penned. She has done a masterful job with what data she was able to find, weaving into Mary's story an accurate portrayal of the political and religious climate of times, the stance of local and national rulers, the living conditions and situation of an impoverished family in seventeenth-century England (impoverished only because the husband was unlawfully held in prison), the prevailing opposition to Baptist principles and, perhaps the most striking element of the story, rarely mentioned but ever-present in the background: the blindness with which John's daughter Mary was afflicted, while still devoting so many hours of her days to a stunning devotion to her father and a more diligent service to her family than most perfectly healthy sons render in their households today.

Bringing food to him daily in prison, making frequent pleas and appeals to the authorities for his release, and doing more than her share at home to help manage the care of the other children, Mary truly bears her cross and makes her father's suffering her own while he spends 14 years in prison. Under a trial which would have made many question their faith, father and daughter both instead grow in faith, learning to trust their Lord and Savior Jesus Christ with an implicit trust under such afflictions; all the while as God providentially uses John to write many of his worthy and instructive works which we have today.

It has been speculated in other biographies of Mary Bunyan that, perhaps the reason "The Pilgrim's Progress" is so vivid in its word-pictures (not even to mention "The Holy War", Bunyan's lesser-known allegorical volume) is because of father John's yearning to describe the realities and truths of Christian the faith to his darling sight-impaired Mary. This may well be the case. One can picture him sharing with her his latest written efforts, reading them aloud to her as his first audience, and perhaps even improving and sharpening the imagery after she departed for the night, when he could see that his first composition did not quite "reach" her mind's eye.

The latter chapters of this book also contain the delightful and nearly equally-moving story of Agnes Beaumont, the young convert to Christ in Bedford who so loyally followed her dear pastor Bunyan's teachings, even at a great cost of the loss of family favor. For further reading on Agnes' striking testimony, the small volume "Behind Mr. Bunyan" is recommended.

Mary Bunyan will leave the reader with a greater appreciation not only of those who have suffered for the faith before us, but may well catch you off guard when it stirs you on an unexpected point: to realize the devotion called for from the rest of us when one member of the body suffers. For, as the Apostle Paul wrote in 1 Cor. 12:26, when one member of the body suffers, it is fitting that all the members suffer with him. Mary Bunyan – already bearing more than enough afflictions of her own – made that choice, and made it for years. For this, the memory of her life is cherished, exemplary, unforgettable.

Dennis Gundersen
Tulsa, Oklahoma
June 2007

MARY BUNYAN.

CHAPTER I.

THE ARREST.

Two hundred years ago! Since then what changes have passed over 'Merry England.'

Two hundred years ago there stood in Bedfordshire, near Harlington, a low, thatched cottage, the dwelling of a pious husbandman. To it let us go.

It is a calm autumnal evening. The sunset sleeps upon the green hills, and twilight drops her curtain. The labors of the day are over, and around the kitchen hearth are gathered the rustics of the adjoining hamlets, awaiting in eager expectancy the coming of one who shall break to the hungry the bread of life, and speak words of cheer to the fainting.

A noble figure, clad in the peculiar garb of that age, stands at the door and knocks. It is John Bunyan.

The door is opened, and he is admitted. A kindly welcome greets him. He passes among the little company shaking the hand of each, and speaking a friendly word to all. He is about to seat himself by an aged sister, when the master of the house hurries up to him, and drawing him aside, whispers in an eager agitated voice :

'Oh Mr. Bunyan, there is a warrant out against you, and the officers are on the look-out for you. We cannot have our meeting. They are prowling around here, and if they find you they will carry you to the Justice, and he will send you to prison. You must leave.'

'What, brother,' says Bunyan, 'go away and not have the meeting ?'

'Oh yes, Mr. Bunyan, they are in search of you, and they'll have you in prison, if they can find you.'

'It is true, Mr. Bunyan, what he tells you,' said a white-haired man in the group; 'the warrant is out, and they are hunting for you now.'

'And what if they are?' says Bunyan; 'shall I dismiss the meeting for this?'

'Oh, I know of what spirit they are, and I tell you they will send you to prison.'

'What if they do? I will by no means stir, neither will I have the meeting dismissed for this.'

He spoke with the calm, decided tone of one, who, knowing what was before him, had made up his mind to meet the worst.

'But what will become of us when you are imprisoned?'

'Oh, brother,' replied Bunyan, ' come, be of good cheer ; let us not be daunted; our cause is good, we need not be ashamed of it. To preach God's word is so good a work that we shall be rewarded if we suffer for that.'

Seeing that he could not be dissuaded from his purpose, they left off their entreaties, and seated themselves amidst the restless group, whose anxious questionings attested deepest interest.

But before entering upon the meeting he 'walks out into the close seriously to consider the matter,' to lay it before God, and to ascertain his will.

The twilight is throwing its dusky shadows across the sward and over the peaceful straw-thatched homes of the villagers. He walks to and fro in the little garden in pensive soliloquy, and thus he reasons with himself :

'I have shown myself hearty and courageous in my preaching, and have made it my business to encourage others. What will my weak and newly converted brethren think if I now run away? Will they not say, ' He is not so strong in deed as in word?' And if I should run, now that there is a warrant out for me, will it not make them afraid to stand when great words only shall be spoken to them? And seeing that God has chosen me to go in this *forlorn hope* in this country—to be the first that is offered for the gospel —if I should fly, it will be a discouragement to the whole body that may follow after. And will not the world take occasion at my cowardliness to blaspheme the gospel ; will they not have some ground to suspect worse of me and my profession than I deserve? For blessed be the Lord, I know of no evil which I have said or done. I will see the utmost of what they can say and do unto me. I will not flinch if God will stand by me.'

Noble words of a noble heart! Who, but the man stayed on Israel's God, could utter them?

Willing to brave all for Him who had 'led him into his own words,' he 'comes again to the house with the *full* resolution to hold the meeting, and not to go away.

His face is radiant with the light of trust and hope as he enters the little room and approaches the stand whereon rests the Bible.

'Let us bow in prayer,' says the holy man; and each one of the little company kneels. How earnestly they supplicate the throne of mercy; how fervently they plead the promises of the God of Sabaoth! They feel their need, and as feeble, helpless creatures they venture into the presence of the great I Am. But listen to their leader, as in deep, fervid tones he sends up his cry for help. His faith is strong, and he comes 'boldly' to a throne of grace. How his zeal and trust inspire the hearts of the less resolute! Hear him say, in the full belief of what he utters, 'God will not cast away his chosen people, neither will he suffer their enemies to triumph; but with a mighty hand and an out-stretched arm he will lead them on to victory. The horse and the rider are slain, and they that work iniquity shall be consumed; but he that trusteth in the Lord shall never be confounded, world without end.'

How like a healing balm fall those words of faith on the bleeding bosoms of those whose joy had been crushed beneath the heel of the oppressor; and tears of thanksgiving stream down the face of many a bowed suppliant.

They arise. He takes the Bible from the stand, and, opening it, reads: 'Dost thou believe on the Son of God?' How searching the question, how suitable to the occasion! What a touch-stone to their faith! As Christ had asked of him whom 'they might cast out,' so would his servant ask of his people that their faith might be made manifest; and as the despised castaway had answered, so would they now, 'Lord, I believe.'

But as he reads strange voices are heard without; eager, anxious looks are bent upon the door—it opens. And there stand before them two unfamiliar forms. It needs not words to tell them they are the constable and the justice's man; and the officers have but to cast their eye over the little assembly to find the object of their search. There he sits, his eye steadily fixed upon them, with his finger pointing to the text as if he would ask them too, 'Dost thou believe on the Son of God?'

They stand before him, and producing their warrant, command him to follow them.

He remembers the apostle says, 'Let every soul be subject

to the higher powers;' so he closes the Bible and rises to
do their bidding.

We fancy we hear him exclaim with the apostle, as he looks
the officers in the face, 'I am ready, not to be bound only, but
also to die at Jerusalem for the name of the Lord Jesus.'

'Well, then, come along with us, for the justice is ready
for you.'

'Stay a moment,' says Bunyan, as he moves toward the
door. He turns round, and addresses the weeping assembly.
All is hushed to silence; even the hirelings of the law dare
not interrupt him, as he proceeds to exhort the little group
to patience and long suffering for the Master's sake.

'We are prevented you see, brethren, of an opportunity
to speak and to hear the Word of God, and are likely to
suffer for the same. But be not discouraged, my dear brethren; it is mercy to suffer on so good an account. We
might have been apprehended as thieves or murderers, or
for other wickedness; but, blessed be God, it is not so—we
suffer as Christians for well doing, and we had better be the
persecuted than the persecutors.'

'Leave off your cant and come along with us,' says the
Justice's man, interrupting him, 'this is no time for such
talk.'

He commends the little company to the care and guidance
of God, and departs with the officers.

But as it happened the Justice was not at home that
night. A friend of his engaged to bring him to the constable on the morrow morning, and he was released from
custody.

And now let us go with him to the bosom of his family,
and see the brave man there, beset on every side by persecution and affliction: there let us see what it was that
supported him amid his deep trials, and nerved his great
heart to bear without murmuring the vile accusations of
his enemies, enabling him to exclaim in the fulness of
determination, 'The Almighty God being my help and shield,
I will suffer until even the *moss shall grow on my eyebrows*,
if frail life continue so long, rather than violate my faith
and principles.' And again, on a future occasion, when he
was passing through deep water: 'Were it lawful, I would
pray for greater trouble, for the greater comfort sake."
And yet again, 'I have been able to laugh at destruction,
and to fear neither the horse nor his rider.'

Was not this an unchanging, sublime, eternal trust;
that faith which 'reaches within the veil and lays hold on
the crown?'

He separates from his friends, and slowly and thoughtfully finds his way to his cottage. He is not fearing, neither is he doubting the precious promises—only he cannot tell how to break the intelligence to his wife. With head bent and downcast eye, he walks leisurely on, while fear and hope alternate strive for victory. The light through the little front window meets his eye as he passes up the green. His heart is big with sorrow as he thinks of his faithful Elizabeth, his poor blind Mary, and the little ones—all so dependant upon him for their daily bread. How can he tell them that it may be he will go to prison? It will almost break their hearts to hear that he must be taken from them! From the depths of his soul he sends up agonizing prayer to God for direction in this matter. For though the clouds are as thick darkness around him, he has read, 'The eyes of the Lord are upon the righteous, and his ear is open to their cry.'

The simple evening meal has been eaten in the little cottage at Elstow, and the family are gathered around the winter fire. The 'faithful wife' is engaged with her sewing by the lamp which burns on the stand, whereon rests the Bible. The book is open before her; for the father is away, and she has read a chapter to the children, and bowed with them in prayer. The blind daughter is rocking the youngest child to sleep, while the other two children pursue their quiet play by their mother's side. The old high-backed chair stands vacant in the corner, waiting the return of the master.

'God will give them strength,' he says, as he pauses on the door stoop.

He enters; Mrs. Bunyan looks up surprised, and there is an expression of wonder and fear on the sightless face of the blind child, for she recognises the well-known step before a word is spoken. The children leave off their play, for they are glad to see the father back. They note not the unseasonableness of the hour.

'You are home early to-night! Did you have your meeting?' asks the wife in a tone which betrays the anxiety of her heart.

'No, the officers came and broke up our meeting, and brought me away.'

'And how did you get away from them? won't they follow you?' asks the wife eagerly, for astonishment and alarm are increasing every moment.'

'No, no; I have not fled from justice; they suffered me to come home to-night, as the Justice was away.'

He seats himself in the old chair; eagerly the wife listens while he relates his story.

'Just as we were in the midst of our meeting the constable came in with his warrant to take me, and would not give me time to finish my preaching, but hurried me away, only letting me speak a few words of counsel and encouragement to the people; and he would have brought me before the Justice, but that he was not at home to-day; so a friend engaged to bring me to them to-morrow morning, otherwise the constable must have given me to a watch or secured me in some other way; my crime is so great.'

'And must you go to-morrow to be tried?'

'Yes, for so I have promised, and I must not forfeit my word.'

'But oh, my husband, if they should send you to prison.'

'Well, Elizabeth, if the Lord wills it, we must submit. He will not put more on us than he will give us strength to bear. If we must suffer, it is in a good cause, and we must be of good cheer. It will all be right in the end.'

He speaks hopefully; but as the tears start to the eyes of the loving wife, and the sadness deepens on the *darkened* face, a sigh comes up from the heart of the brave man: 'What will become of his wife and children if he is taken from them? Who will give them food and raiment?'

'What *shall* we do,' asks the wife imploringly, 'if you have to leave us? We have but little to eat now, and when you are gone, who will give us more?'

'God will take care of his children, my Elizabeth. He feeds the sparrows, and he will feed you; and besides, they may not send me to gaol; perhaps they will let me go free after they have tried me. I cannot think they will imprison me for reading the Scriptures and explaining them to the people.'

'But the judges are so hard-hearted, my husband. They send all to prison who will not conform to the rules of the church. I heard yesterday of two who were thrown into gaol at Bedford, without having a fair trial, and they may treat you so.'

'Well, we will hope for the best, Elizabeth. God will overrule it all in righteousness—we must give it up into his hands.'

'But, my dear husband, if they should send you to prison, what shall we do? Who will give us bread?'

This is a gloomy picture even for his brave, trusting

heart—his family pinched with hunger and cold, and he
shut up in the walls of a dungeon! He bows his face in
his hands, and a groan comes up from the depths of his
soul as he contemplates it. The little boys look on with
timid wonder. 'Tis a strange sad sight to them to see
their father thus oppressed with grief.

A hand is laid on his—an arm thrown around his neck,
and a voice whispers in his ear, ' Do not be grieved, fáther,
if they do send you to prison; I will help mother to take
care of the children.'

He looks up as the gentle tones fall upon his ear. The
sightless eyes, eloquent with sympathy and love, are turned
to his.

' It is but little you can do, my poor child, with your
feeble hands and darkened eyes,' replies the father sorrowfully.

' But I can do something, father ; I can take care of the
children when mother goes out to work, and I can hoe in
the garden when summer comes.'

His eye rests on the delicate blue-veined hand fixed in
his, and then on the upturned rayless eyes, and he heaves
a deeper groan as he thinks of what hardships this poor
child must endure if he should be condemned.

' And I can bring wood for mother,' interposes Thomas,
the oldest son, ' and help sister in the garden and carry the
things to market.'

' But it will be a long time till summer, my boy, and
you must live through this cold winter ; ' and the father
strokes the white hair of the innocent boy, and thanks God
for the sympathy of his children.

' If the worst come to the worst, Elizabeth, and I must
go to prison, we must trust in the Lord for the future. He
will give us meat in due season, and grace to enable us to
keep up under all of our trials. I will speak to neighbor
Harrow, to-morrow, as I go to Bedford, and get him to
attend to you if I should not come back. He can get
together the little sums that are owing me, and this will
help you for a while; and, when this is gone, God will
provide some means of support. He has said, " No good
thing will he withhold from them that walk uprightly,"
and we must not doubt him. But I hope they will not
sentence me, seeing that I have done nothing but read the
Scriptures and explain them to the people. But if they do,
I must not flinch, but be willing to stand all manner of
persecution for the Gospel's sake.'

Thus with words of hope and trust, does his tried soul

endeavor to comfort and sustain the sinking heart of his
wife.

She is a woman of a brave heart and great fortitude, and
she leans for support on his Word who has said, 'Fear not,
I am with you.' But this trial is so sore, so sudden, the
issue so momentous, so fatal, should her husband be found
guilty, that, for the time, she can see nothing before them
but despair and death.

Thus the evening passes. The little family at Elstow
are in the wilderness; the enemy is in pursuit, the
mountains rise on either side, the sea is before them. Will
there be no rod uplifted, no hand stretched out for their
deliverance? Will there be no 'pillar of cloud' to give
them light, which shall also be a cloud and darkness to
their enemies?

'Fear not,' stricken ones, 'stand still, and see the salvation of the Lord, which he shall show you.'

The morrow comes. Bunyan is up betimes, that he may
meet his word and not keep the officer waiting. He bids
his wife and children farewell for the time, commending
them to God and bidding them 'be of good cheer,' for he
thinks he will soon come again to them. The wife parts
from him with a sorrowful, dejected heart; Mary embraces
him affectionately and turns round to weep, while the little
ones, Joseph and Sarah, kiss him and bid him 'come back
again soon.' Thomas goes with his father to Bedford to
bring home the tidings of the trial.

On the way Bunyan is joined by the friend who had
engaged for his appearance. He stops a few moments at
neighbor Harrow's to speak to him about his family's
destitution.

'I will see after their wants, friend Bunyan, if you do
not get back, but God grant that they may send you free.'

'I trust they will, but if they do not it will all be right,
brother Harrow.'

They shake hands, the neighbor committing the prisoner
to the protection of God, and wishing him a speedy return.
They part—one to offer up a silent prayer for his brother
in the Lord, who is dragged along by the cruel hand of
persecution, perhaps to a felon's death; the other to go on
his way, 'rejoicing that he is counted worthy to suffer for
his name.'

Engaged in holy conversation, he and his friend pass
along, Thomas all the time wondering how it is his father
can talk so composedly about going to gaol. The very
thought of the old prison standing on the bridge which

he has sometimes seen, with its heavy black walls and small iron-grated windows, fills his childish mind with horror. He starts as he recals its dreadful form, and yet his father says, 'Rather than give up preaching I will go to it gladly.' Strange language to his untaught heart. The mystery was solved in after years, when 'the Spirit gave him utterance,' and he too felt, while proclaiming the 'unsearchable riches of the gospel of Christ,' that, although imprisonment might await him, yet would he not cease 'to declare the whole counsel of God.'

They find the constable in waiting for them. He is eager for his work. Hastening the prisoner to court, he conducts him before the justice.

With magisterial dignity, Justice Wingate eyes him, and then turning to the constable asks, 'And where did you find him? Where were they met? And what were they doing?'

'I found him at Samsell, your honor. There were only a few met together to preach and hear the word.'

'And what had they with them?' (meaning what arms.)

'They had nothing but their Bibles, your honor; no sign of anything else; and the prisoner here was beginning to preach.'

The justice turns upon Bunyan with a frown of indignation, and in a harsh voice asks:

'And what were you doing there?'

Bunyan looks at him mildly, yet firmly, and in a firm tone that can be heard by all present replies:

'The intent of my going there and to other places is to instruct and counsel people to forsake their sins and close in with Christ, lest they miserably perish.'

'And why don't you content yourself with your calling? Don't you know that it is against the law for such as you to do as you have been doing?'

'But I can do both of these without confusion,' says the prisoner promptly. 'I can follow my calling and preach the Word also.'

'What,' says the justice, chafing with anger. 'Then I'll break the neck of your meetings, that I will.'

Bunyan unmoved answered calmly, 'It may be so.'

The Justice, losing all self-possession, exclaims, 'Produce your sureties, man, or I will send you to gaol.'

Two friends are ready as his security, and they are called in.

The bond for his appearance being made, the Justice turns to the sureties, 'You are bound to keep this man from preaching; do you hear? If you don't, your bonds are forfeited.'

'Then I shall break them,' interposes Bunyan, interrupting him, 'for I shall not leave off speaking the Word of God, nor cease to counsel, comfort, exhort, and teach the people among whom I come; for I think, sir, this work has no hurt in it, but is rather worthy of commendation than blame.'

'If you will not be so bound,' says the Justice, turning to the sureties, 'his mittimus must be made, and he shall go to gaol, to lie there till the quarter sessions.'

'Make out the mittimus,' commands the Justice, and retires.

The prisoner stands with folded hands, awaiting the order to prison.

While the mittimus is being made, there comes in Dr. Lindale, 'an old enemy to the truth,' who falls to reviling and taunting the man of God, to whom Bunyan says,

'I did not come hither to talk with you, but with the Justice.'

The 'old enemy,' supposing he had nothing to say for himself, triumphs as if he had the victory, charging and condemning him for meddling with that for which he could show no warrant.

Insolently he questions him, 'Have you taken the oaths? If you have not, it is a pity but that you should be sent to prison.'

'*Had I a mind,* I could answer any sober question you could put to me,' is the calm rejoinder.

Confident of victory the 'old enemy' asks, 'Then can you prove it is lawful for you to preach?'

'Doth not Peter say, "As every man hath received the gift, even so let him minister the same.' And the prisoner looks him steadily and fully in the face, to show that he could answer him if he listed.

'Aye,' saith the old enemy sneeringly, 'to whom is that spoken?'

'To whom? Why to every man who hath received a gift from God. Mark,' and the 'sharp quick eye' of the defendant lights up as he speaks, 'Mark,' saith the apostle, " As every man hath received a gift from God, even so let him minister the same," and again, " You may all prophecy one by one." '

Whereat the 'old enemy' is a little stopped, and goes a softlier pace; but not willing to lose the day, he begins again.

'Yea, indeed, I do remember of one Alexander a *copper-smith*, who did much oppose and disturb the apostles.' (This is a thrust at Bunyan because he is a tinker.)

'And I too have read of very many priests and pharisees that had their hands in the blood of our Lord Jesus Christ.'

'Aye, and you are one of those scribes and pharisees; for you, with a pretence, make long prayers to devour widows' houses.'

'What,' says Bunyan; 'I tell you, man, if you have got no more by preaching and praying than I have done, you would not now be so rich.'

But he remembers it is written, 'Answer not a fool according to his folly,' so after this he is sparing of his speech as he can be without prejudice to truth.

The mittimus is made out, the prisoner is committed to the constable, and hurried off to gaol. A crowd gathers around as he is borne along, some with sympathetic hearts, while others, with the spirit of the ancient persecutors, cry, 'Away with him, away with him.'

They move as rapidly onward as the crowd will permit.

'Stay, constable,' cry two of his brethren, coming up in breathless haste. At the tone of command, the officer halts.

'You must not go to gaol. We think we can prevail with the Justice to let you go at liberty. We have a friend who will intercede for you. We must back to the Justice.'

So the two men, joined by a third, hasten to the court room to speak to the Justice. They talk long with him and come running out again to the prisoner.

'Oh, if you will come to him again,' they exclaim with increased agitation, 'and say some words, he will release you.'

And what are those words? 'Speak no more in his name.' The same bait had been vainly offered his disciples sixteen hundred years before. Should it tempt him from his integrity? Hear his answer.

'I will not promise. If the words are such as can be said with a good conscience, I will say them; if they are not, I will not.'

They importune him, and he goes back with them, not believing that he shall be delivered. He knows the spirit of the minions of the law too well; they are too full of opposition to the truth to let him go unless he should in some way or in some thing dishonor his God and wound his conscience.

But he casts it all upon the Lord, wherefore as he goes along he lifts up his heart to God for light and strength to help him, that he may not do anything that would either dishonor him or wrong his own soul, or be a grief or discouragement to any that was inclining after the Lord Jesus Christ.

The Justice is awaiting his return. Another personage comes suddenly out of another room, and seeing him thus greets him—'Who is there—John Bunyan?' and with such seeming affection as if he would leap on his neck and kiss him. (A right Judas.)

This is a Mr. Foster, of Bedford. Bunyan has but little acquaintance with him; has seen him but a few times. All that he knows of him is, that he has ever been a close opposer of the ways of God, and he wonders that he should carry himself so full of love to him now. But it is soon explained. Then he remembers those sayings, 'Their tongues are smoother than oil, but their words are drawn swords.' And again, 'Beware of men.'

With feigned surprise this new busy-body asks, 'But tell me, Mr. Bunyan, how it is that you are here. I was little expecting to see you in this place.'

Ah! you 'right Judas,' do you think to deceive him now, and win him by your flattery?

Bunyan turns a full look on him for a moment, and then in a calm significant tone replies:

'I was attending a meeting of people a little way off, intending to speak a word of exhortation to them; but the Justice hearing thereof, was pleased to send his warrant to fetch me before him.'

'Ah, ah, I understand; but if you will promise to call the people no more together, you shall have your liberty to go home; for my brother is *very loth* to send you to prison if you will but be ruled,' says this 'right Judas,' coaxingly.

'Sir, pray, what do you mean by *calling the people together?* My business is not anything among them when they are come together but to exhort them to look after the salvation of their souls, that they may be saved.'

'Hist, hist!' exclaims he, putting his hand soothingly on his shoulder, 'we must not enter into explication or dispute now, Mr. Bunyan. Only say you will not call the people any more together, and you shall have your liberty; otherwise you must be sent away to prison.'

'Sir, I shall not *force or compel* any man to hear me; but if I come into any place where there are people met together, I shall to the best of my skill and wisdom, exhort and counsel them to seek after the Lord Jesus Christ for the salvation of their souls.'

'But this is none of your work,' impetuously replies the 'right Judas,' losing his self-possession, 'you must follow your *calling.* If you will leave off preaching, and follow your calling, you shall have the Justice's favor and be acquitted presently.'

'Sir, I can follow my calling and preach the word too; and I look upon it as my duty to do them both as I have opportunity.'

'But such meetings are against the law; therefore *you must leave off,* and say you will not call the people any more together.'

'I dare not,' replies the brave man, 'make any further promise; my conscience will not suffer me to do it, for I look upon it as my duty to do as much good as I can, not only in my trade, but also in communicating to all people, wheresoever I can, the best knowledge I have in the world.'

'The " *best knowledge!* " Why, you are nearer the Papists than any, and I can convince you of it immediately.'

'Wherein?' asks the confessor, boldly.

'In that you understand the Scriptures literally.'

'Those that are to be understood literally we understand so, and those that are to be understood otherwise we endeavor so to understand them,' replies the noble defender of the faith.

'Ah,' replies the old enemy, 'and which of the Scriptures do you understand *literally?* '

'This sir : "He that believes shall be saved." This is to be understood just as it is spoken. For whoever believeth in Christ shall, according to the plain and simple words of the text, be saved.'

A derisive smile curls the lip of the interlocutor—'You are ignorant, and don't understand the Scriptures. How can you understand them when you do not know the original Greek?'

'If that be your opinion, sir, that none can understand the Scriptures but those who have the original Greek, then surely but very few of the poorest sort will be saved. Yet the Scriptures saith, "That God hides these things from the wise and prudent," that is, from the learned of the world, "and reveals them to babes and sucklings." '

'But there are none that hear you but a company of foolish people.'

'You mistake yourself, sir; the wise as well as the foolish do hear me. Those that are most commonly counted foolish by the world, are the wisest before God ; for God hath rejected the wise, and mighty, and noble, and chosen the foolish and the base.'

'But, man, you make people neglect their calling. God has commanded people to work six days and serve him on the seventh.'

'Ah, sir, it is the duty of people both rich and poor to look out for their souls on these days as well as for their bodies ; and God commands his people to "exhort one another daily, while it is called to-day."'

The meddler stood confounded. The tinker showed himself an approved workman.

Breaking into a rage, he again exclaimed, 'But they are none but a company of poor, simple, ignorant people, that come to hear you.'

'The foolish and the ignorant have most need of teaching ; therefore it will be profitable for me to go on in my work.'

'But will you promise not to call the people together any more ? If you will, you may be released and go home.'

'I dare not say any more than I have said. I dare not leave off that which God has called me to.'

Then this 'right Judas' withdrew to advise with his friend the Justice. While they are in counsel several of the Justice's servants gather round the prisoner, telling him that he "stands too much on a nicety. Our master,' they say, ' is willing to let you go if you will say that you will call the people no more together. If you will but make this promise, you may have your liberty.'

He returns them the same answer—'I dare not promise.'

Presently the council being ended, in come the Justice and Mr. Foster, and urge him to promise that he will hold no more meetings. But Bunyan is not to be moved by persuasion any more than by threats and flattery. There he stands invincible, panoplied with truth.

'Then send him away to prison,' says Mr. Foster to the Justice in a rage, 'and it will be well for all the others to follow him.'

And they thus parted, the prisoner and the judges. The one to imbrue their hands yet more deeply in the blood of the saints ; the other to the gloomy dungeon which shall be made radiant by the indwelling presence of the 'Light of the World.' Even as he was going out of the doors of the public hall, he 'had much ado to forbear saying to them that he carried the peace of God along with him ;' but he keeps silent, and 'blessed be the Lord, went away to prison with God's comfort in his soul.'

CHAPTER II.

THE SHADOW ON THE HEARTH.

'How long father stays, mother! Do you think he will come back to-day?' and Mary left off her work for a moment, and turned her sightless eyes up to her mother's face sorrowfully.

'I hope so, my child! God only knows,' and the fearful wife drew a long breath, while the tears started to her eyes.

The child heard the sigh, and understood it; and she left off her questioning, and tried by little kind offices to raise from her mother's heart a portion of the care and apprehension which were pressing it so heavily.

Mrs. Bunyan had watched through the long weary morning hours for her husband's return. At first, her hope was strong and confident. She felt that they could substantiate no accusation against him worthy of imprisonment, and she could not believe they would throw him into gaol under false pretences. But as hour after hour wore by and brought no news of him, her hope by degrees grew less strong, until at last, surprised, she found herself counting 'all the cost' of his firm adherence to his principles. As we have before said, she was a brave, noble woman, one of fortitude and true courage, and she had also that hope 'which is an anchor to the soul, sure and steadfast.' And she will need it now, poor woman, for the storm is gathering black and fierce.

After the sad farewell with her husband, she had gone about her usual household duties with her wonted cheerful countenance and quick active step; and if now and then she paused listless and abstracted, it was but for a moment; she rallied her energies, and pursued her morning round.

The sun shone in through the little front window, and as it stretched its flood of golden radiance further and further along the floor, measuring the flight of the silent hours, her heart grew fainter and more faint. Often would she turn aside from her cares to look across the yard in the direction of Bedford.

The two pursued their work, each endeavouring to console and comfort the other.

Mary is now twelve years old. In thought, in feeling,

far beyond her years ! With deep, quick sympathies, and a maturity of mind attributable to the circumstances of her outer life, which caused her to think and to reason, she was a companion for her mother, who, though her senior by several years, was yet young, Bunyan having married her after the death of his first wife, and about the time she attained her majority.

' Do you think father will come home to dinner, mother ? I will set a plate for him, and I do hope he will come.'

' I hope so, my child, but I see nothing of him now,' and the mother closed the door, choked down the rising sigh, and went to work to finish little Joseph's stockings.

' Don't you think Thomas would be back before this if father wasn't coming ? '

' Yes, I think your father would have sent him to tell us how the matter ended, if he was not coming himself.'

' What are they going to put father in that old gaol for, mother ? He hasn't done anything bad, has he ? ' asked Joseph as he placed himself by his mother's side, and looked earnestly into her face.

' No, my son, he has only preached the gospel.'

' Why, that is a good work, father says. How can they put him in gaol for that ? '

' They say he disobeys the king.'

' And don't the king want anybody to preach, mother ? '

' Yes, my child, but he wants them to do it as he orders, and in no other way.'

' And why don't father preach the king's way, mother ? Then they couldn't take him away from us and put him in that old ugly gaol. I wish father would mind the king, don't you, mother ? '

' Your father must mind God, Joseph, and do what he says. He cannot preach as the king wishes, because he would not be preaching as he believes God's book teaches.'

' I wish father wouldn't preach at all, mother; then they wouldn't put him in prison, would they ? '

' No, my son : but your father thinks he ought to preach ; he thinks God has told him to do it, and you know, Joseph, the Bible says we must obey him rather than man.'

' I am glad I don't have to preach, mother. I would be afraid to go to the gaol to live there. I do hope they won't put father in, do you think they will, mother ? '

' I hope they will not, my child, but your father will not give up preaching, even if they do. He would rather live in gaol all the rest of his life than do it.'

' Why, mother, father can't preach in gaol, and I don't

see what he wants to go there for. Why won't he quit preaching, and stay at home with us?'

'I cannot tell you now, Joseph, so that you will know what I mean. When you get older, you will understand why your father would rather go to prison than disobey God.'

The little child could not comprehend it, so he turned thoughtfully from his mother's knee, and went to play with Sarah in the corner.

'We will not wait for your father any longer, Mary. The children are very hungry and we will eat. Perhaps he has stopped at neighbor Harrow's to get his dinner.'

It was the wife's last hope, and her sinking heart clung to it with the death grasp of despair. The little family seated itself around the plain simple board, and with tearful eye the mother humbly asked for God's blessing upon them while they should partake of it. It was a sad silent meal, for fear had sealed all utterance. Often before had they gathered around the frugal table when the father was away, but then they knew he would come again. Now that comforting assurance was gone, and fearful apprehension sat a dread unwelcome guest in their midst. The children hushed their innocent prattle as they saw the mother's sad face and heard her heavy sigh, and cast on each other looks of childish wonder and inquiry. Mary essayed again and again to speak words of hope to her mother, but her own heart was almost as sorrowing as hers.

The dinner hour passed, and the evening came; and yet no tidings of the father. Their only stay, now, was derived from the fact, that Thomas had not yet returned. On this they hung the faint hope, that the trial, though a long and troublesome one, would end well for the prisoner.

'Hark! mother, I think they are coming. I hear the dog barking, and that is Tom whistling, I believe.'

The mother sprung to her feet. She opened the door, and looked out in every direction. The dog was barking in front of the house, but she heard no whistle, and saw no one.

'You are mistaken, my child. I can't see anybody, and I have looked every way as far as I can see.'

She seated herself, and again took up her knitting. Disappointment, sad and despairing, marked her noble face. Mary closed her rayless eyes, and as she did so the lids turned out the scalding tears. The children kept on at hushed play, sometimes looking at their mother and sister with mute wonder, and then again forgetting everything like sorrow, they pursued their childish play mirthfully.

The door opened; all eyes were raised. Thomas stepped in. No one followed.

'Your father, Thomas, your father,' exclaimed the agitated mother, throwing aside her work and looking eagerly up to the boy. 'Where is your father, Thomas?'

'In gaol, mother,' the little fellow sobbed out, 'they have put father in gaol.' She buried her face in her hands and wept aloud. Her fortitude forsook her—her resolution gave way. Mary started from her seat and bent towards the weeping mother. The children crying, clung to her with fright and wonder. The storm had burst in its wrath over the tinker's dwelling. Was there no hand to stay its fury, no oil to calm its troubled waters, no voice heard above its roar and din, saying in tones omnipotent, 'Thus far shalt thou go and no farther?'

'In gaol, Thomas! Have they sent your father to gaol?' asked Mrs. Bunyan, her face pale with terror.

'Yes, mother, that they have. I—saw—him—go.'

Tears and sobs choked her utterance as this last answer shut out every possible ray of hope. The shadows of despair wrapped themselves closely around her, and for some minutes she could see nothing but their thick darkness. After a while a faint glimmering ray struggled through the blackness of her sorrow, and shone feebly in upon her bursting heart. 'The bruised reed he will not break. Light is sown for the righteous, and joy for the upright.' 'Whom the Lord loveth he chasteneth,' whispered the Angel of the Covenant, and as the sweet low voice stole in upon her soul she ceased her weeping; and again she heard the gentle tones, 'He shall deliver thee in six troubles, yea, in seven there shall no evil touch thee.' 'He hath torn and he will heal; he hath smitten and he will bind up. Come unto me and find rest. I, even I, am he that comforteth thee.'

Tears were streaming from her eyes, and her voice was still broken with the storm of grief that had swept through her bosom, as she looked into the sorrowing face of the boy beside her, and asked:

'Did they try your father, Thomas?'

'Yes, mother, they had him there a long time.'

'Were they harsh to him, Thomas—the judges?' and her woman's heart almost broke at the thought of the rude-ness and contempt they might have heaped upon her dear husband whom she might not again see.

'They did not strike him, mother; and they didn't speak much unkind to him, only once the man got mad and said he was going to break the meeting's neck.'

A shudder passed through the frame of the blind child as this harsh language fell upon her ear.

'Going to break the meeting's neck. What did he mean by that?'

'I don't know what; that's what he said. Father told him he must preach, and the man didn't want him to do it, and said if father would do it, then he would break the meeting's neck.'

'Who said this to your father, Thomas?'

'Mr. Wingate, the great man that sat in the big chair.'

'And they sent your father to prison because he would preach the gospel, did they? Well, thank God it was for no crime!'

'Yes, mother, they did, for soon after the man said he would break the meeting's neck, they started with father to the gaol; but they brought him back again and tried him over.'

'How was this? Did they want to insult him again?'

'I don't know. As they were going to gaol they met two men that father knew, and they would take him back with them to see if they couldn't get him off from going to gaol, and let him come home.'

'And what did they do with him after they carried how back?'

'They kept asking him if he would leave off preaching, and father said he would not. Then they said if he would not do that, he must go to prison. All the big men said so.'

'How long is he to stay in prison, Thomas?' asked the wife eagerly, her voice tremulous with emotion.

'They said till the quarter sessions. I don't know how long that is, mother—but a long time I believe.'

The wife sat as one stupefied, rendered insensible, by the suddenness and force of some mighty and unexpected blow. That which she had most feared had come upon her, and her house was left unto her desolate. What could support her under this grievous affliction? Poverty around her, four little helpless children to feed, and before the horologe should have measured many more days of sorrow, a fifth should open its eyes upon the heartless world, more than fatherless; her husband vilely cast into prison for preaching the word of God, there to be in pain and neglect till death should end the scene. Oh, how dark all these things were to her—how mysterious—she could not understand them. Had not God forgotten to be gracious? Had he not cast them off for ever? Where now was the Gentle Shepherd of Israel? The lambs of his fold were perishing—exposed to the pitiless blast, and he folded them not to his bosom, nor gently led them into green pastures. They called upon him, but he was not near, and there came no cheering voice of his to bid them ' be strong and fear not.'

Could the hand of faith have torn aside the veil, and her eye peered into the glories of the future—that glory which was to radiate with unfading beam that narrow prison-cell where the holy man of God lay incarcerated, waiting to see 'the salvation of the Lord,' and that immortality which was to gather around his name making it the watchword of religious truth and liberty through all ensuing ages until time itself shall be no more—that heart so bowed, so broken, would have looked up and taken fresh courage—yea, would have sung praises unto His name who remembers Israel in all his afflictions, who 'bringeth light out of darkness, who leadeth his people by a way they know not.'

'Mother, won't father come back any more?' asked little Joseph timidly, his eyes filled with wonder, as he again stole up to his mother's side.

'I do not know, my little one; your father is in prison now.'

'Did they put father into that old ugly gaol, mother?' and the child began to cry piteously.

'Yes, Joseph, they have put your father in the gaol, and you may never see him again.'

She could say no more. The thought of her fatherless children and her own desolate condition overpowered her, and she could not proceed any farther.

Mary removed the children from the weeping mother, and, providing them with amusement, returned to console her.

'You had better lie down and rest now, mother; you are weary; you have been busy all this day;' and she gently placed the pillow, and taking her mother's hand, led her to the bed, where the poor woman lay in a state of almost unconscious helplessness. Then remembering that Thomas had had nothing to eat since the early morning, she prepared him something warm, moving about so noiselessly and with such a dark shadow of grief upon her angel face, that could the ' unjust judge' but have seen her, his heart would surely have been moved to pity, and he would have said to the prisoner, ' Go free even for thy daughter's sake.'

Mrs. Bunyan was aroused from the troubled slumber into which she had fallen by a knock at the door. Mary opened it, and the wife of neighbor Harrow stepped in.

'How do you do, sister Bunyan? Don't get up because I have come in,' and the good woman stepped to the bedside to shake hands with the pale sufferer. 'Brother Bunyan stopped by my house a little while this morning, as he was on his way to Bedford, to see my good man, and when I saw Thomas coming back without him, I thought I would run in a minute or two and see how things had gone. You look pale. What's the matter? Are you sick?'

'Oh, sister Harrow, I am undone, undone! They have put my poor husband in prison,' and she covered her face with her hands, and bowed her head upon her bosom. She could not weep. The fountain of tears was dry.

'Have they? and what did they do that for? He's done nothing to go to gaol for, I know.'

'They put him there for preaching the gospel of our Lord Jesus Christ. This was all they could say against him.'

'Put him there for preaching? Oh, what a shame! God will punish them, I know he will. He'll not suffer his children to be treated in this way without scourging their persecutors. I feel it here.' She laid her hand on her heart, and looked up to heaven with faith and resignation.

'Oh, but sister Harrow, my husband is taken from me. What shall I do with these poor little children?'

'Be of good cheer. The Lord will not let you want. What has he promised? Don't he say I will be with you in six troubles, and the seventh shall not harm you? It looks dark now and fearful, but thank God he will bring us out of all our troubles, and make all our paths straight to our feet.'

'But who will feed these children now their father is gone?'

'Why, they have got a father left. Jesus will take care of them. Don't he say I will be a father to the fatherless? He feeds the ravens when they cry, and do you think he will let his children want for bread? Oh, no; he is too good for that—blessed be his name.! Remember Elijah in the wilderness, sister, and Daniel in the lion's den, and the Hebrew children in the fiery burning furnace, heated seven times hotter than ever it was before. Didn't he deliver all them out of their troubles, sister Bunyan, and won't he deliver you? Yes; that he will, my blessed Master. I feel it here this minute,' and she placed her hand on her bosom, while her upturned countenance glowed with the faith and trust that filled her soul.

'Trust, him, my sister, trust him; I tell you he will not deceive you. 'He is the same yesterday, to-day, and forever.' Give yourself up into his hands, and don't you trouble yourself so much about what is to come. He'll give you strength according to your trials. I tell you he will.'

'But I deserve nothing but chastening and affliction at
the hands of God. I am so forgetful of his love and mercy
to me. I stray so into forbidden paths.'

'Ah, that's what we all do. If we received what we
deserve at his hands, what would become of us poor sinful
creatures? We ought to bear our trials without murmuring, for we know they are for our good. God is merciful,
and he does not send these things on us willingly, only to
keep these poor sinful hearts from forsaking him. What
did dear old David say in all his distresses? Didn't he say,
"Before I was afflicted I went astray, but now I have kept
thy word.' How sweet brother Bunyan talked on this
very passage of Scripture when he was at my house only
last week to mend my old kettle. My old man had just
been telling me of the king's orders, and how he feared
trouble would be abroad in the land, and that all the non-
conforming preachers would have to go to gaol, or leave the
country for ever. I had been thinking about it all the
morning, and I said to myself, what will become of us if
brother Bunyan is taken away? It seemed my heart
would burst with a great burden here. I don't know
why it was I felt so. It must have been the Spirit of
God bearing witness with my spirit of this very thing. I
had been going along with a heavy heart ever since breakfast. I couldn't shake off the load that was here, sister
Bunyan; it would stick by me. I tried to pray, but it
didn't do any good. There it was. Presently brother
Bunyan stepped in with his furnace in his hand to mend
the ear of my kettle, which John snapped off the other day
against the jamb. I had just cleaned it to heat some water
in to wash up the plates, when he jerked it up to put it on
the crook, and knocked it against the rocks. What day
was it, one day l ast week? You remember I sent John—'

'Oh, sister Harrow, I can't remember now. Don't talk
to me of it. I can't bear to think of such things now,
while my poor dear husband is in gaol and I am left alone.'

'Don't talk so, sister Bunyan. You are not alone. Jesus
will be with you if you will only trust in him. I know he
will. Go to him with all your griefs, he will bind up your
broken heart. Nobody ever trusted him in vain. And he
is always willing too. Often when I have felt such a load
here, it appeared to me my heart would burst, I have just
got down on my knees in prayer, and when I was done it
was all gone; Jesus had taken it, and I was as light as air.'

'I cannot pray, sister Harrow. My words rise no higher
than my head. I can think of nothing but my husband

and these poor helpless children. I cannot pray, I cannot pray.

'Oh, you must not give up this way, Jesus is a mighty and a willing Saviour. He will not forsake you. As I was telling you, while brother John was mending my kettle that day, he kept on talking about trusting in the Lord and abiding in his strength, and it made me feel good; it lifted me up from this poor earth to hear his words, and to feel here in this heart that God would keep me safe from falling, let man do what he might. I can rest in Jesus, sister Bunyan; he is my stay and my comfort. Blessed Jesus, I will trust thee, and never fear if thou art with me. Let the adversaries do what they can, thou art my portion for ever.'

The pious servant of God, turned her exulting face to heaven as she pronounced these words, and a smile of serenest trust lighted up her full ruddy face. She had numbered fifty winters, but being endowed with a hardy constitution by nature, which had been developed by active exercise, was yet active and healthful, with a flow of spirits which nothing but a sense of sin and sorrow, because of the opposition her Saviour's cause met with in every land, could dampen. She was one of God's faithful ones; and to her 'no good thing was denied,' for she 'walked uprightly.' Whenever she met with difficulty, when disappointment appeared to hedge in her way, and all her efforts proved unsuccessful, she would say, 'I have done all I can. I will give it up to Jesus now. He will bring it to pass in his own good time.' And from the moment she was able to make this unqualified surrender of her troubles, 'her burden, which she had been carrying, was all gone,' as she expressed it.

'You must take courage, sister Bunyan, and keep your spirits up, or you will be sick. You look pale now; and she leaned over her and whispered some words into her ear which she did not wish the children to hear. 'This thing will all be straight, and you may live to see the day when you will thank God for it; and if you don't, when you get to heaven you will then understand it all. It will then be as clear to you as the shining sun. Only trust Jesus.'

The words of faith and confidence of this truly devoted child of God fell like oil upon the stricken heart of the sufferer, and she was able to compose herself so as to talk about her husband's imprisonment with some degree of calmness.

'It is not as bad as if he was dead, for as long as there

is life there is hope. How long did you say they put him in for?'

'Till the quarter sessions, Thomas says.'

'Then I suppose he will be tried again, won't he, and may be they will let him go then. How long is it till the quarter sessions, do you know?'

'I do not, but I am afraid it will be a long time. They say they are very cruel, and they will keep him in prison just as long as they can, I know.'

'Let me see,' she added, counting it upon her fingers, 'I heard my good man say this morning that the quarter sessions took place in January. He and brother Bunyan were talking about it, and this is what he said. I remember it well. This is the twelfth day of the month, and it will only be seven weeks till then, and may be they will let him go free. We will all pray to the Lord that it may go well with him.'

'Oh, it is a long time for him to stay in that cold damp prison. I know it will kill him.'

'We must trust him to Jesus, sister Bunyan; he will take care of him, and deliver him from his enemies if it be his will.'

'But what shall I do then? We have but little to eat, and when this is gone where shall we get more? There is no longer any one to make bread for us; we must starve, there is no hope.'

The sealed eye-balls were turned from the corner in the direction of the bed, and the lips moved as if to speak, but the thought came to the sensitive heart, 'She can comfort her better than I can.'

'You shall not want, sister Bunyan, you and your little ones, as long as I have a morsel; and my old man will see that you will get all that is owing to you. Brother John spoke to him about it this morning, and I heard him promise he would see to it, and you know he is always as good as his word.'

'I know brother Harrow will do all he can, but we would be too great a burden,' and as she spoke she raised her eyes to those of her kind consoler. They expressed from their sorrowing depths all the fear and hopelessness that words were too poor to utter. 'I will not complain,' she added; 'He doeth what seemeth to him best.'

'I brought you some good oaten bread and some meat in my basket outside the door. I was just baking some for myself, and I thought you would may be like a little.

Things sometimes taste better when we don't cook them ourselves.'

'Oh, that my poor husband had it! He hasn't had a mouthful of food to eat to-day, poor man, and I know he is hungry and faint, and they will not give him anything. He will starve.'

'These are perilous times, sister Bunyan, and the people of God must expect to bear afflictions. These are the troubles that are to try men's souls, and happy shall be the man who shall endure to the end. Did you hear of that poor man that was thrown into gaol the other day? I didn't hear his name. They brought him from some other part of the country, but they say it was for preaching the gospel. Oh, we are going to have dark and bloody times! Oh, that Jesus will give us strength to prove ourselves good soldiers, and bear any burden for his sake.'

'I feel I could bear anything but this; if they had just left my dear husband to me, I would not murmur; but to snatch him up, and put him in gaol, and leave me alone with these poor little helpless children. It seems to me I cannot stand it. It is so hard, so hard!' and the poor woman sobbed convulsively.

'Remember the promise, sister Bunyan, "As thy day so shall thy strength be." Don't forget this. It is a most precious promise. Cling to it. Go to Jesus with all your troubles, and he will give you peace. Do not be down-cast; our enemies will reproach us, and it will bring shame on our Saviour's cause. "I will trust him though he slay me," that is the confidence, that is the faith. You must pray to God to give it to you.'

'Oh, I wish that I could, but how can I? You have never known what it is to be placed in my situation. Your husband has never been torn from you and cast into a horrid prison, and you left with four little starving children.'

'Come, my dear woman, do not cry so, you will make yourself sick. You haven't had a morsel to eat since breakfast, have you? You are weak and faint for the want of something. I will call Mary, and let her make you a little broth, and you can eat some of that bread I brought you.'

She stepped to the back-door of the kitchen and called the child, but there came no answer.

'I cannot make Mary hear me,' she said, as she closed the door after her, 'so I will do it myself,' and she hastened to make ready the pot for the broth.

'The poor little creatures have got to the basket as it

stood outside the door. See, the bread is almost all gone,
and the meat too.'

The tears started afresh in the mother's eyes. 'They are
so hungry, poor little helpless things.'

'But they shall not starve. Your neighbors will not let
them want for something to eat. But Mary stays a long
while. I'll just step out and call her, sister Bunyan. You
keep entirely still while I am gone. You look so pale and
sick.'

'Here, Tommy, my son, leave off your play a little
while, and run towards the spring, and see if your sister
Mary's there, and tell her to come here directly, I want to
see her. Come here, Sarah, and stay with me, while brother's
gone. Come along, and we will go where mother is. Come,
child, I'm waiting for you.'

Little Sarah left off her play very reluctantly, for it was
not very often that she was so highly favored as to have
Thomas for a playmate.

'Run on, Sarah, mother wants you,' and the boy bounded
over the stile in the direction of the spring while Mrs.
Harrow, leading 'Baby Sarah' by the hand, hastened to
Mrs. Bunyan's room.

'I can't find sister anywhere, mother. I've called her
and called her. She's not at the spring, and I don't know
where she is, unless she and Joseph have gone over to neighbor Whiteman's. I saw her with her bonnet on a little
while ago, and Joseph was with her.'

'And which way did she go ?' asked the sufferer feebly.

'I don't know, mother. I didn't look which way she
went. I was playing with Sarah, and did not see, and had
forgot all about it till Mrs. Harrow called her.'

'How long since you saw your sister, Thomas ? She
would not go to neighbor Whiteman's without telling me
of it. She must be about the house somewhere. I'll get
up and call her myself.'

'Oh, pray don't, you are too sick. She will be in directly.
Come, be still, my good woman, you will faint if you leave
this pillow.'

'I am better now, and would like to sit up awhile.'

She made the attempt to rise, fainted and fell back. In
the endeavor to restore her to consciousness, Mary was forgotten for the time. Let us follow her!

Her mother's words, 'And he has had nothing to eat
to-day, and is now in that cold damp prison,' fell like burning coals upon her heart. She could not rest while her dear
father was cold and hungry. Her resolution was formed,

and quietly she proceeded to accomplish her purpose. It was an easy task to gain Joseph's company. She had but to tell him she was going to see father. The little fellow caught the idea in a moment, and with that sense of importance and responsibility which a child always feels when you entrust to it a secret, and ask its assistance, he joined his sister, and the two proceeded on their journey. Mary knew part of the way, and she could ask the rest. She placed a basket of provisions on her arm and set out with the child in the direction of Bedford. Let us follow her.

CHAPTER III.

MARY AND JOSEPH VISIT THEIR FATHER IN PRISON.

THE declining sun throws its rays more faintly over the russet landscape. The air is damp and chilling. Clouds gather in the heavens; but the sealed eyes see not the beauty around her, nòr the light airy forms of the gathering clouds above. She unconsciously *feels* it all; but there is a deeper feeling in her bosom which swallows it up, and it makes no impression on her busy mind. The black-bird and the song-thrush warble their sweet notes amid the withering verdure of the wayside hedges, and where in spring time innumerable insects made the air murmurous with their low ceaseless hum, now bursts forth in snatches the melody of the finch. But nought of music now arrests the quick ear, all unattuned to sweet sounds. On, on, the little feet go, now and then pausing for a moment to rest their weariness.

'Is this the way to Bedford, sir?' the timid voice asks, while the face is averted. It may be some one she knows, and she would avoid discovery.

'Yes, that's the road—keep straight on;' and the countryman hurries by, and gives not another thought to the two little ones, who, for aught he knows or cares, are homeless and without an earthly friend.

'Oh, it's such a long way to where father is, Mary! Do you think we will ever get there? I'm so tired:' and little Joseph clasps more tightly his sister's delicate hand and quickens the pace of his little weary limbs.

'We will get there after a while, Joseph, and then we will see father. Won't you be glad to see father?'

'Yes, that I will; but I am so tired, Mary,' and the little fellow stopped as if he wanted to sit down.

'There, sit down and rest awhile, we'll soon be there.'

A horseman swept up. 'Ask the man, Mary, how far father is from here?'

'Hush, hush, child! he may not know.'

'Don't everybody know father, Mary?'

'Don't you know our father, sir,' and the boy looked inquiringly up into the face of the rider, 'please tell us how far is he from here?'

The horseman galloped on, and the little fellow was ready to cry as he saw that his mighty effort had been thrown away on the unheeding traveller.

'It cannot be far now, Joseph, and father will be so glad to see us. Come, jump up, and let's go on.'

'Won't father come home to us any more, Mary?'

'I don't know, my dear. They have put him in the old dark prison.'

'He can steal out and come back, can't he? I'm going to tell him to do it, and we'll bring him home with us.'

'They have locked him up and he cannot get out. The walls are so thick and strong, and the door is so heavy, father can't get through. But I hope they will let him out after awhile, and never put him in that ugly old gaol again.'

Her voice trembled, and the tears glistened in her darkened eyes; but she must not cry; for the little fellow's sake she must bear up.

On, on, hand in hand, the two little wanderers go—weary, but not discouraged. They are going to see their father. This buoys up their little hearts, and soothes the pains of the aching limbs.

The little boy prattles of the houses and the birds and laborers in the fields by the way. He dreams not of danger. There is no fear in that guileless heart. The sister holds his hand in hers.

Surely they are almost here. She has been once or twice before, but it was with her father, and his strong hand and kindly words made the way seem short. She asks a footman—

'How far is it to Bedford, sir?'

'It's just before you, little girl. Don't you see it yonder?'

'I see it! I see it! Mary; the houses and the river, and everything. Oh, I'm so glad we are there. I'm going to tell father how tired I am, and how mother cried when brother came home,' and the little fellow bounded away from his sister, and ran on crying out, 'Come on, Mary, come on, I'm going to see father.'

'Will you please show us the way to the gaol? I am lost, and don't know where to go.'

'And what do you want to go to gaol for, you little vagabond?' asked the fierce man grimly.

'We are going to see father. Will you please tell us the way?'

'You couldn't find it if I was to. Who is your father?'

She trembled beneath the severity of his tone, but she drove back her tears and replied as well as she could:

'Preacher Bunyan, sir! They put him in prison to-day because he would preach the gospel.'

'You had better say because he wouldn't obey the laws of the land, the vile offender. He deserves his fate. But how are you going to find the gaol? You can't see what you are about.'

At any other time the sensitive child would have been overcome by such cruel language, but now she felt that she could endure anything, however hard, if she could but find her father.

'Come along with me and I'll show you where the gaol is, where they put all such rebels as your father. Come along, will you? I have no time to wait.'

Mary pressed Joseph's hand in hers, as if to crave protection and sympathy, and obeyed the stranger's bidding. Taking her along that street, and then turning to the right, he led her to a point from whence the bridge 'whereon the gaol stood' could be seen.

Halting suddenly, and pointing with his coarse rough hand towards the prison, he said:

'See that bridge yonder, and that house on it? Well, that's the goal. Go there and knock at the first door you come to, and ask for the gaoler. Maybe he'll let you in. Do you see, say?'

'I can't see, sir, I'm blind.'

'I see it! I see it! I'll show Mary the way,' said Joseph. 'Come on, Mary, we'll find father now.'

With quickened step they passed along the street to the gaol. They forgot their weariness in the joy they felt at so soon seeing their dear father, and being clasped to his bosom.

'Where is the door, Joseph?'

'I don't see any. The man told us wrong, Mary. We can't find father now, and we will have to go back without him,' and the poor little boy, whose heart had borne up so nobly under the fatigue of the great journey to him, was about to give up, and sit down to cry, when a man made his appearance on the bridge in front of the gaol. The children did not hear him until he stood before them.

'What do you want, children? You poor, little shivering things, what are you doing here this cold day?'

'If you please, sir, we want to go in the prison to see Preacher Bunyan,' replied Mary, almost overcome by the remembrance of the vulgar man whom she had last spoken to.

'He is our father, sir, and we have come all the way from home to bring him something to eat. Mother said he was so hungry, and there was no one to give him any bread, and we have brought him some. Please, sir, let us see him,' and she turned upon him her rayless eyes, all eloquent with entreaty.

'You can't go into the prison. It is against the rules.'

'Oh, if you please, sir, let us see father,' and the tears ran down the imploring cheeks.

'We won't take him away with us, let me and Mary see him. We want to give him this bread we have brought all the way for his supper.'

'I cannot break the rules. You cannot go into the prison.'

'Oh, can't we see father, sir?' and the child, no longer able to contain herself, burst into loud sobs. 'Just, if you please, let him come out that we may speak to him, and we will go away and not trouble you any more. Please, sir, let him come.'

The gaoler's heart was touched.

'You may talk to him, but you cannot go where he is;' and unlocking the huge front door, he admitted them into the court-yard, where he left them standing, while he went within.

He unlocked the prisoner's cell.

'Two little children want to see you in the court-yard, one of them a little blind girl. You can come out and see them for a minute.'

'Their mother has sent them, bless the dear woman,' and he arose from his seat and followed the gaoler to the grated door.

'You can come no farther now. You may talk to them through the grate.' So saying he passed into the court and locked the door after him.

Bunyan's great heart was melted. He who had stood before the judges and received the sentence of imprisonment without dismay, but rather with 'blessing the Lord,' and had gone to the gloomy cell with God's comfort in his soul, now wept as his eye rested on the shivering forms of his half-clothed children, and he realised that their love for him had nerved their little timid hearts to brave the dangers of an unknown way to spare him the pangs of hunger.

Oh, how he longed to press them to his heart, and kiss their cold pinched cheeks, but iron grates intervene, and he must be content with words.

Joseph sees his father, and stretches up his little hands to reach him, and Mary puts forth hers. They strike against the cold dull iron. Shudderingly she withdraws them, while an expression of horror passes over her raised face. The father sees it and sighs—not for himself; no, he can endure all things for his Master's sake—but for the effect upon the guiltless heart of his innocent child.

'God bless you, my poor little ones. I cannot reach you,' he said as soon as he could find utterance. 'You have had a long weary way of it to find me. Did your mother send you?'

'No, father, mother's sick,' answered little Joseph quietly. 'We come to bring you some supper. Here it is.' And he lifted Mary's covering, and took from her the roll of bread and meat, and handed it to his father.

'God bless you, my little boy. I cannot take it. The man will give it to me when he comes. So your mother's sick, my daughter?'

'She took it so hard when Thomas told her of you, father, that she had to go to bed.'

'My poor wife,' sighs Bunyan. 'The Lord keep her from danger. Did you leave her by herself, my child?'

'No, father, aunt Harrow was with her. She made mother go to bed and she tried to comfort her,'

'Father, won't you go home with us to see mother? She's so sick.'

'I cannot go, my little Joseph. I cannot get through these great iron bars.'

'Won't the man unlock the door, father, and let you go home to see mother? Oh, you don't know how sick she is.'

'No, my boy, you must take care of your mother. I can't come now.'

'When will you go home, father?' and the tears rolled down from the clear blue eyes as he felt that his father could not go.

'When they let me out of this dark prison, then I'll come home to see you all.'

'Can't I stay with you, father?' and the little fellow put up his hands beseechingly.

'No, Joseph, you must go home with Mary. Who would take care of her?'

'These children must leave and you must go back to your cell,' said the gaoler, gruffly, appearing in the narrow court.

A word of farewell and blessing, and the little ones are driven through the door to find their way home alone and unprotected, a distance of more than three miles, in the gathering darkness of a November evening.

The Omniscient Eye watches every step of the weary way; the Omnipotent Hand protects them from every danger.

Bunyan trusts as seeing 'Him who is invisible,' and goes back to his cell to pray.

CHAPTER IV.

THE SHADOW DEEPENS.

'The blast swept by, and on its wing
   Death's pale dread form was borne.
The mother bowed low—sorrowing—
   For a robe of darkness did he fling
   About that infant form.'

THERE is a coffin there! Tread softly!

The Angel of Death has swept his dark wing over the tinker's dwelling, and put out the little life of the new-born babe. And the mother takes up the voice of lamentation and weeping over the loss of her first-born. Ah, 'tis a dark—dark hour! When will the light come?

The little one opened its eyes on the cold friendless world, shut them, and went home. The bud of paradise could not unfold in the gloomy, chill atmosphere of grief; so the Father kindly transplanted it to his own garden, to bloom perennially.

He chasteneth, but in love. And the gleamings from his radiant throne, lighting up the darkest way, bid us press on, not fainting, nor weary.

Shroud the little form—fold the, tiny hands gently over the pure still bosom—close the pale, cold lips—seal the unwaking eyes. They shall never again need the light of the sun, nor of the moon; nor yet of the pale solemn stars. For they shall drink in the light of the Lamb eternally.

Shut out the sunlight! Let not its garishness fall on the grave stamped features! It would but mock with its glorious smile the heart-broken mother. Rather let the twilight softness enshroud the painful scene! Hush every noise! No harmony now hath the stricken heart with earthly voices. How gratingly the faintest echo falls upon the grief-attuned ear.

'Tis a bitter cup the mother is drinking now! Will it ever pass from her? Were the father but at home, it would be some slight solace. But he is in the dark, drear prison, and his voice of love and sympathy cannot reach her. His eyes shall never gaze on the form of his child, nor his lips kiss its pale, cold cheek. ' Dust to dust, ashes to ashes,'—many a day will the little one slumber on in the graveyard before its father's face shall again light up the darkened dwelling. Why, oh why, is the hand of chastening laid so heavily upon her? Hath the Father forgotten to be gracious? He seeth it best; his covenant remaineth unbroken; his hand holdeth the rod, but the eye of faith cannot see it; the clouds are so thick and dark.

The children gather around in childish wonder, their young hearts touched by the sight of their mother's distress. Death, even to their untutored minds, is a dread, dark mystery—an awful presence, which they fear, yet cannot understand. The poor blind one cannot see it, but she *feels* it in the clayey coldness of the tiny hand, the touch of the icy cheek, the dread stillness of the breathless air. She hears it in the low deep sob of the mother's bursting heart, as she learns from the tremulous lips of neighbor Harrow that her child is gone, and the despairing moans ever rising from that mother's throbbing bosom pierce like barbed arrows her sympathetic soul. She strives with neighbor Harrow to soothe her mother's bursting heart; but she feels that every effort is vain, yea, more than vain: and she goes away alone in the little back kitchen to pray. She is not yet herself a child of God, but she has heard her father talk so much about the efficacy of prayer that she thinks she will try it now, that God would comfort her mother and send her father home.

With many little acts of kindness, and with words of heavenly truth, 'Goody Harrow,' as she was familiarly called in the neighborhood, endeavored to console and cheer the desponding woman. She had stayed with her through the night to administer to her wants and provide for her such comforts as the exigency of the case demanded.

'Try to be calm, sister Bunyan; try to cheer up. The little creature is gone, but it is taken from the evil to come. No pain and sorrow for it now. It is in the Saviour's bosom. It is all God's doing, and it is all for the best. His ways are past finding out, they look very dark and mysterious; and so they are! But he never forgets his children; he never casts away his people; no, no, he is too good for that. He will hear their cries, and in his own good time he will deliver them. Many a time in my life I've been so cast down with trouble I didn't know which way to look. My heart was so full I couldn't do anything. It appeared as if there was a great load dragging me down to the very earth, and I've tried to read, and to think, and to pray, but in vain. Then I would think God had cast me off, and I was no child of his. And I would think this thing and that; and at last, after I had tried everything else, I have had to come to Jesus and say, "Here I am, my blessed Saviour, a poor, weak, sinful, blind creature; do with me what thou seest is best. Take from me this great trouble if it is thy will; but if I must bear it, only give me thy grace. I want thy will to be done, not mine." And I tell you, sister Bunyan, just as soon as I would do this— just as soon as I could come to Jesus and look to him, my burden would all be gone, and I could praise his holy name. My heart would be as light as a feather; no more trouble, no more sorrow. All was joy and peace. Jesus is good, sister Bunyan. He is kind; trust him. Jesus, Master, thou art good and kind to thy children. Many a time has this poor heart felt it,' and she laid her hand upon her bosom to witness the truth of what she had just uttered, and turned her eyes reverently upwards. 'Trust him, sister Bunyan, trust him; he will give you peace.'

'I know I ought to trust him, sister Harrow, and I do trust him some. He is all the hope I have. But I am so encompassed with sorrow that I know not which way to turn. If my dear husband was here I think I could bear this better. But it breaks my heart to think the little one must be buried, and he shall never see it. If he could just look on its little face once, it would do me so much good; it would not be so awful as it is now. Poor little thing, it has no father, and ——'

'Do not cry so, sister Bunyan. It wants no earthly father, and it has gone to its heavenly one, who can do everything for it. Don't cry so, my good woman, you will kill yourself, and it will do no good. God has promised to be a husband to the widow, and a father to the fatherless—and can't you trust him for his promises? What did Job say in all his distresses?—"I will trust him though he slay me." Try to feel like Job. Try to get nearer to the Cross, then you will be comforted ; then all your sorrows will be gone.'

'Pray for me, sister Harrow, I cannot pray for myself. God, it seems, will not hear my prayer. Oh, ask him to remember me in all my afflictions, and bind up my broken heart, if it is his will.'

The dear old disciple of Christ knelt by the bedside of the sick woman, and in agony and tears made supplication that she might be made submissive to the will of God ; that she might be enabled to praise him in the midst of her afflictions. With streaming eyes and quivering lip she asked God to bless his servant, who was willing to testify to his name, even with his life ; to strengthen and console him in the dreary prison, and to give him grace to bear all manner of shame and reproach for his truth's sake.

God does not turn a deaf ear to the earnest beseechings of faith. He hears even before his children ask ; and he is ever ready to bestow every good and needed gift.

The Comforter came in his sweet invisible agency to the tried heart to impart peace to it, even while the words of supplication were ascending from the faithful, earnest soul of this poor, untaught follower of the Saviour—untaught in the wisdom of the world, but truly learned in the school of Christ.

As she arose from her knees, her face lighted up with the beams of inner glory, one, to have seen her, would have said, 'Truly, she hath peace and joy in believing.' Like Moses, after he had been upon the Mount, her face shone with unearthly lustre. She had been with Christ.

Thomas was dispatched for the good man, Harrow, to give assistance in the duties before them.

'Send the children to their father, that he may know my sad bereavement,' besought the mother.

'Oh, it will distress him so, sister Bunyan, and do no good. And he has as much to bear now as he can get along with.'

'But we can send him something to eat. I know they will let him starve, for they have no pity on prisoners. Let them take him some bread—but—' and she heaved a heavy sigh—'there is but little bread in the house, and nothing to buy more—God have mercy!' she exclaimed, while a piercing groan escaped her.

' " Are not two sparrows sold for a farthing? and one of them shall not fall to the ground without your Fathers notice." This is what our Master himself says, sister Bunyan; and he tells us not to fear, for we are of more worth than many sparrows. But we are such poor, short-sighted worms of the dust, we cannot see one step ahead of us; and we are so unbelieving, that we won't trust unless we can see. It's a wonder God don't cut us off for our un-belief. But thanks be to his great and glorious name, " he is long suffering and full of mercy." Can't you trust him, sister Bunyan?'

' Yes, I can say I trust him some; I wish I could trust him more. I know he will do what is right, but it is very hard to be afflicted as I am. I cannot see my way through it.'

' It was just so with the children of Israel when they got to the Red Sea; they couldn't see how they were to get across, but God brought them through. And when they were in the wilderness, don't you remember how he gave them bread and water, and delivered them from their ene-mies? He makes all the crooked paths straight. All these things are given to us for our instruction. We ought to heed them all, sister Bunyan. I remember last spring, when George got his foot hurt by jumping off that old back porch at his grandfather's. I thought what a dreadful thing it was that he should hurt himself just at the very time that Elizabeth was going to be married, because we wanted to have some of the neighbors in; but you see, when——'

' But the passing of the children of Israel through the sea, and their being fed in the wilderness, were miracles, sister Harrow, and we can't look for any such help now. If God should work a miracle, how easy it would be for me to believe; but when everything seems to strive against me—my husband in prison, and my poor little one lying there ready for the grave—how can I see any light; how can any good be in store for me? Ah! no, there can't come anything out of this but trouble and sorrow.'

' Well, shall we receive good at his hand and not evil? But what has he promised, sister Bunyan? Don't he say that all things shall work together for our good? Think of this. He don't say some things, or most things, but all things. And if we are his children, we will believe what he says; we will not doubt his word; we cannot. Look how he brought his poor old Job through all his afflictions, and made his last days his best ones. Your troubles are not equal to his; he had everything taken from him— houses, lands, children, camels, and all his servants—and you know he had a good many, for he was a rich man. And then he was afflicted in his own body—all covered with boils—the sorest things in the world. I remember I had one last spring on my hand, just here in this very place; see, it has left its mark, and it had like to have run me crazy. I couldn't do any work for a whole week. How often I thought of poor old Job, and wondered how he lived with them all over him, from head to foot. Just think of him in all his distresses, and how God brought him through them all. And then you will be willing to trust him for yourself. He was given to us as an example to follow.'

'But Job was an upright man, sister Harrow, and I'm a poor, weak, sinful creature. I don't deserve any good at God's hands. I am so prone to forget him. I don't love him as I ought to. I don't serve him as I should. He ought to scourge me, I am so wicked.'

'Ah, sister Bunyan, you don't think any body deserves any good thing from God, do you? Oh no; it is not for our good works that he loves us; it is all his own sovereign love and mercy. Oh, I tell you we have nothing to commend us to his favor, as your dear good man said the last time he spoke at my house; and we can't do anything. So much sin—so much sin always here in the heart—that God can't find anything in us to love us for. It is only for Jesu's sake—only because he died. There's our hope, sister Bunyan—nowhere else—no, no, nowhere else. Jesus is all, all, sister Bunyan. No merit but his. Yes, blessed Jesus! thou art all, and in all; the beginning and the end; I feel it here in this poor heart, which every day bears its load of sin, but it loves thee, thou blessed Master,' and she looked upwards, while her hand pressed her bosom, as if beseeching God to witness what she had said. 'But you must keep quiet now, sister Bunyan, or it will be the worse for you. Think of these things and try to trust in God. He will take care of you; rest assured he never forgets his children.'

'I long for unshaken truth in the promises, sister Harrow, but my faith is so weak.'

'Let the children go to their father—Mary and Joseph. He must know this thing. Maybe they will let him come home to see me. Would to God they would. But if they don't, I will feel better satisfied for him to know it all. Send them here to me, and I will tell them what to say.'

' I'll look after that, sister Bunyan. Calm yourself to
sleep now. Rest will do you good—you need it. Leave
everything to me. I'll see that all goes straight. There,
get to sleep. I can't let anybody come in to disturb you
now.'

' Let them tell their father I am better. It will be a
sore distress to him to know it all. God give him strength
to bear it, poor man. Don't forget the food—the food,
sister Harrow. He must be almost starved.'

' Be still now, be still, while I make Joseph ready to go.
Here, Mary, give your mother this warm tea. It will
strengthen her and make her sleep better ; ' and the kind old
woman lifting up her heart in prayer to God for his presence
amid the dark scene, went to find the two younger children
who had quietly stolen away from the chamber of sorrow
and death to pursue their merry play, where the shadow
could not fling its dark folds over their innocent hearts.

Is not the midnight of sorrow enshrouding the tinker's
humble dwelling? Ah, and throughout the land from how
many other hearth-stones, by the decree of wickedness in
high places, is going up to heaven the cry to stay the
tyrant's hand? The children of darkness are exalted on
high for a season, and they drink, with insatiate thirst, the
blood of the saints. Hellish cruelty stalks unimpeded
through the land, revealing, through its tattered garments
of false religion, its own hideous deformity ; and on the
right hand and the left—in God's sanctuary, and among
his chosen ones by their own peaceful firesides, with reeking
hand,it deals death and imprisonment until from thousands
of anguished hearts, in cell, in cave, and mountain height,
there goes up one long, loud, piercing cry, ' How long, O
Lord, how long ! '

CHAPTER V.

THE CHILDREN VISIT THEIR FATHER.

EIGHT days have passed since the massive prison-door
clanked heavily, as it shut in from the world the man who
courted the hard cold pillow of a felon's cell, and the fœtid
breath of the narrow court-yard with its hundred occupants,
rather than give up the preaching of the glorious gospel of
the Son of God. Courageous man! thou hast acquitted
thyself like a man, yea, rather like a saint of God. Thy

reward is on high. The cross here, the immortal crown hereafter.

At the mother's earnest solicitations, the children were made ready to visit their father. A basket was prepared and filled with everything edible the house afforded, and the children set out for Bedford. Their little hearts were full of gratitude and joy, poor little innocent creatures, that they were permitted to carry their father this simple token of love; they forgot that their breakfast was but a scant supply of cold oaten mush and dry bread in their great happiness at being able to take their father something palatable.

'Father will be so glad to see us, won't he, Mary?' and Joseph's face brightened up with the great joy it would be to him to see his father once more, even if it was within the dark prison he so much dreaded.

Could the poor blind eyes but have seen his bright buoyant expression, as he turned his face to hers, it would have chased away some shade of sorrow from the sad face, and some portion of pain from the throbbing heart. The gloom of the picture he had left behind had faded from his mind like darkness before the rising sun.

Children dwell not on sad remembrances; and well it is for them they do not. Did they, with their incipient judgment to decide on every case, treasure up their ills, real and imaginary, how miserable their little lives would be.

'Where are you going, children?' asked neighbor Lawrence of them as he passed them on the highway.

'We are going to Bedford to the gaol, to take this dinner to our father, and to tell him our mother is sick,' answered Mary, in a sweet timid voice.

'And how is your mother, Mary?'

'She says she is better now.'

'Has she been much sick, child?'

'Oh yes, sir; she has been very sick ever since they put father in prison.'

'And the baby's dead,' added little Joseph, while the tears rushed to his large blue eyes.

Instantly the truth flashed through the mind of kind neighbor Lawrence, and, bidding the little ones good morning, he hastened home to tell his wife the sad story, that she might go to the aid of the poor suffering woman.

'Father will be sorry to hear mother is sick. But she is better now, ain't she, Mary?'

'Yes, Joseph, Goody Harrow said so, and told us to tell father so.'

'Do you think mother will die, Mary, like the baby?' he asked in a tremulous voice, and his fresh chubby face wore a sorrowing look as the dark sad scene rose up before his young mind. The darkened room so hushed, so still, the pale wan look of the mother, the sober face of Goody Harrow, and the silent tears following each other very fast down the calm quiet face of his poor blind sister; and, above all, the little clay-cold form, shrouded in white, lying on the settee in the corner of the room, recollections of all this filled his childish heart with mysterious awe.

'Is mother going to die, Mary?' he asked a second time.

'I hope not, Joseph. Mother is better now.'

'Yes, Goody Harrow said so; but Mary, if she should die like the baby, then we would have no father nor mother.'

'But we would have a heavenly Father, Joseph, who would care for us, and give us our daily bread. Don't you know father always tells us this?'

'Yes, Mary, but God is up always in heaven, and maybe he'll forget little children like us.'

'No, no, Joseph, he will never forget us if we love him and pray to him as he tells us. Don't you remember father read to us the last Sunday evening before he was put in prison, that God never forgets his promises to his children, and then he has said he will give them each day their daily bread.'

'But heaven is so far from here, Mary, and there are so many people in the world, God might not think about us little children one day, and then what would we do?'

'God is not so far off, Joseph. He is here with us, and hears all you say about him. He knows everything we do; and he will take care of us if we are his children.'

'I wish I could see God, Mary. Don't you?'

'You will see him when you die if you go to heaven. Father says we will all see him then.'

'Will you see him, Mary, like me and father.'

The tears gathered in her eyes and rolled slowly down her face as she answered in a subdued tone—

'If I get to heaven, Joseph, I will. Father says I shall see him for myself, and not another for me.'

He bent his head thoughtfully. He was busy endeavoring to look into the mysteries of what he had just heard. Questionings were awakened in his young mind, which only the ages of eternity can answer to any of us.

'Are you tired, Joseph?' asked Mary, seeing that he lagged somewhat behind her.

'I am not much tired, but my feet are sore;' and the little fellow stooped down to pick the stones from his worn-out shoes.

'Come, let us hurry on with father's dinner. He is hungry I expect.'

'And don't they give father anything to eat?—the people at the gaol.'

'Yes, they give him coarse, rough victuals; and father can't eat much. He will be so glad to get something from home.'

'Will we have to bring his dinner to him every day, Mary? I can carry the basket.'

'Oh no, Joseph, I reckon not. We may not have any for ourselves.'

'Why, didn't you say God would give us our bread every day?'

'Yes, he will, Joseph, if we love him and trust him. But come, hurry on, I think we will soon be there.'

'Yonder's the bridge, Mary; and the gaol too—I see them both,' he exclaimed, as they gained the eminence that overlooked Bedford, and the 'lilied Ouse.' 'We'll soon be there,' and he grasped more firmly his side of the little basket, and quickened his pace almost to a run.

Could the tyrant king, as he sat on his throne of blood, but have seen those two little faithful children—Bunyan's blind Mary, and Joseph, her brother—braving everything because of their love to their father, would not his obdurate heart have softened? Would he not have released the holy prisoner, even for his children's sake? And this is but one instance of thousands where his hand of death has made the wives and children of the servants of God widows and orphans, with broken, bursting hearts, and sad forsaken homesteads. And will not God avenge the death of his elect—his chosen ones, which crieth unto him day and night, from the scaffold, the dungeon, and the flame?

'What are you children doing here?' said the gruff assistant gaoler to Mary and Joseph, as they presented themselves in front of the prison door.

He was a man naturally of a fierce, hard heart, and the prayer which had just reached his ear from the prisoner's cell, as he passed by, had stirred up all the brutality of his nature. 'The canting deceiver,' ne exclaimed to himself, 'he'd better let praying alone and go back to his family.'

The blind child let go her hold on the basket, and, turning fearfully in the direction of the harsh voice, said— 'We want to see our father, sir. We have brought him a little food in our basket for his dinner.'

'Your father gets enough to eat here. We don't want any children in the gaol, so get you back home with your basket, and don't trouble me any more,' and he waved them off with his rough sinewy hand.

'If you please, sir,' ventured Mary, stooping in pleading dread before him, 'let us see our father. Our mother is sick at home, and ——'

'Begone, girl, I tell you begone! both of you. You couldn't see your father if he was before you, with your blind eyes. Go home this minute, I have no time to be bothered with children.'

Joseph, who had been standing behind Mary, holding her bonnet in one hand, while the basket rested on the other arm, stepped to her side, and, looking into the dark angry face of the man, spoke —

'Please, sir, let Mary and me go in! Mother is so sick at home, and we want to tell father about it. And the baby's dead, too, and father don't know it. Please, sir, let us go in to see our father; we won't take him away with us, and we won't stay long, either.'

'And who is your father?'

'Mister Bunyan, the poor man they put in here because he would preach the gospel,' answered the trembling child.

'Yes, the vile ranter, and it's the place for him. I just this minute heard one of his devilish prayers.'

Mary felt like sinking beneath those hard, wicked words, but she knew it was no time for weakness and tears, so she commanded herself as well as she could, and, turning her sightless eyes up to his face with a look of pleading earnestness, and, reaching out her hands in a supplicating manner, she said, with all the eloquence of her bursting soul:

'Oh, please, sir, let us in a little while. We want to see our father and tell him our mother is sick—'

'And the baby is dead, too, and father don't know anything about it, and we want to tell him. Goody Harrow said we must. Oh do let us in now, sir,' interfered Joseph eagerly.

'Begone from here, I tell you, you vagabonds. What do I care for your sick mother and dead baby?' and he clenched his left hand and assumed a most threatening attitude.

The poor blind child could see nothing of this, but trembled as she heard the clanking keys at the gaoler's side, and his harsh voice of denial filled her with dread. Joseph clung to his sister, overcome by fear.

'Can't we see our father, sir?' said Mary in broken accents, making one more effort to succeed in her undertaking.

The request seemed to enrage the gaoler. He placed his broad hand on her slender arm, and turning her round, bade her begone, and not come back to trouble him again.

With streaming eyes and breaking hearts the children turned from the door. As they were passing the bridge, they met the principal gaoler, who, recognising them, asked, 'What, here again to see your father?' Mary remembered the voice, and a ray of hope darted through her bosom. Turning her streaming face to his she answered, 'Yes, sir, we have brought father some dinner in our basket, but the man with the keys would not let us in.'

'He drove us away, and said we should not see father,' added little Joseph, stepping up to the man, whose pleasant countenance reassured him.

'Well, give your basket to me, and I will take it to your father; he is Bunyan, the preacher, ain't he? Here, child, give me your basket.'

'Oh, if you please, sir, let us see our father,' interrupted Mary, beseechingly; 'mother is sick, and we want to tell him about it.'

'And the baby is dead, too, sir, and father don't know anything about it. Please, sir, let Mary and me see father a little while.'

It would have required a harder heart than the gaoler possessed to refuse the sad, sorrowful entreaty of the weeping blind girl, and the simple, earnest appeal of little Joseph. So, telling them to follow him, he led the way to the prison door, and, unlocking it, conducted them to Bunyan's cell.

The prayer was finished that had fallen on the ears of the cruel-hearted turnkey, and Bunyan was sitting meditatively by his narrow, grated window, that overlooked the 'lilied Ouse,' whose clear bright waters rippled gently round the piers of the old bridge, and then floated peacefully on towards the sea, reflecting in golden light from their crimpled bosom the November noon-day sun. He started as the key turned in the lock. His nerves were unstrung by his entire relaxation from labor, and the noisome humidity of his narrow cell, which was always damp enough to make 'moss grow upon the eyebrows' of the prisoners, built as it was on one of the piers of the bridge, and overhanging the river; and he who quailed not for a moment before iron-hearted judges, nor shrank from the dungeon's gloomy walls, 'often started, as it were, at nothing else than his own shadow.'

The children entered. He recognised them by the dim light of the cell, and catching them in his arms, pressed them to his bosom. His thoughts had been of his family, of his wife and little ones, and now his great heart melted with a father's love, and tears of mingled thankfulness and sorrow coursed down his manly cheek.

The gaoler was moved by the touching scene. From that day until Bunyan's release, he regarded him with a degree of consideration and respect above any other prisoner.

How powerful is the influence of holy love! The gaoler felt it, and retired.

And now the father is left alone with his children. He seats himself, and gathering them about his knees, he asks them of their mother, and Thomas, and Sarah. In her own sweet, simple way, Mary tells him all that has transpired. The tears fall faster; his bosom heaves, and a deep groan swells up from his tried soul. The clouds of sorrow dim the eye of faith for the time, and even Bunyan feels that the Lord has cast him off for ever. But the darkness lasts but for a moment. It is the passage of the desires of the carnal heart over the ever-shining Sun of Righteousness, which eclipses his rays for a season. But the transit is made! And there are the glorious life-giving beams to penetrate every recess of his soul, imparting life, and warmth, and joy, and he feels that, as the sufferings of Christ abound in him, so his consolation also abounds in Christ. He remembers that He, on whom he trusted, hath said, 'Leave thy fatherless children, I will preserve them alive, and let thy widow trust in me;' and again, 'The Lord said, Verily, it shall go well with thy remnant; verily, I will cause the enemy to entreat them well in the time of evil, and in the time of affliction.'

Trust on, thou brave, noble heart! Faint not, though the cross burden thee to the earth. God notes thy patience and 'labor of love.' The mansion and the crown await thee. Look up, and press on!

The time is rapidly passing. The basket is emptied of its contents. The children tell their tale of sorrow. The holy man hears it with a bursting heart. Messages of sympathy and love are delivered them for their mother, and words of affectionate advice and encouragement are spoken to themselves. A hand is laid on each head, and a prayer sent up to God for their protection and guidance. Fifteen minutes have passed. The gaoler enters. The children must leave their father's tender caresses and words of love. Longer stay is impossible. The prisoner is a black offender, and but little favor must be shown him. He kisses their tearful faces, and commends them again to God. The gaoler takes them by the hand, leads them out, and locks the door.

The prisoner is alone with his God and his heavy anguish.

CHAPTER VI.

BUNYAN IN PRISON.

'Take all, great God! I will not grieve,
But still will wish that I had still to give.'

NORRIS OF BEMERTON.

THUS exclaimed Bunyan, as the dark cloud, which enveloped him in his prison, 'with beams of light from the inner glory, was stricken through.'

But the resplendence of the 'inner glory' did not always shine upon him; the dark cloud would oftentimes shut it out, and he was again left in the black night of disappointment and despair. His was a chequered experience—alternate hope and fear, joy and sorrow; now a look by faith into the glories of the Heavenly Jerusalem, and then the fearful groping in the thick darkness of doubt and dread. The Arch Fiend, who formerly would have him believe he had sold his Saviour, and thus caused him to fall, 'as a bird that is shot from the top of a tree, into great guilt and despair,' would now bring before his racked mind all the horrors and distress of death, and tell him this should be his fate, and paint to him in the most frightful colors the gloom and distress of his suffering family.

What, but the grace of God, and that abundantly bestowed, can keep even his strong heart from bursting amid such trials? Poor man! he is reaping the earthly reward of following Jesus! But though he is encompassed by infirmities, and the way is dark and rough, he must not give up. It is just as the Master had told him, ' In the world ye shall have tribulation.'

Earthly hope he has none. For the merciless tyrant, restored to the throne of his forefathers, is meting out, with unsparing hand death and destruction to all Nonconformists. His fierce, dark will is inexorable. His victims may starve to death in their loathsome cells, or shriek in unpitied anguish from the horrid rack, or hang soddening in the summer's sun from the roadside gibbets, the scorn and jeer of his pleasure-besotted minions—and what cares he? His voluptuous court moves on, and revelry and music shut out the long loud wail of the perishing ones, down-trodden by the iron heel of relentless hate. Wickedness sits on high, and the earth mourns. Will not the Lord arise in his anger and awake unto judgment, that the just may be established and the righteous rescued from the net of the fowler?

Weeks have passed since Bunyan has received any intelligence from his helpless family. The children have come with their little basket of provision, but the hard-hearted assistant gaoler would not let them in, but drove them from the door with jibes and bitter taunts. Their entreaties were in vain. Their pleading words and looks served only to exasperate his brutal nature, and with the big tears of disappointment rolling down their tender cheeks, they turned away with broken hearts to tell their sad tale to their mother.

It is a cold winter's evening in January. Bunyan, through the livelong day, has been sitting by his little grated window looking at the dull, leaden clouds, as slowly they marched their dark battalions through the murky sky. He has been busy with his own thoughts, for to-morrow he is to stand before his judges. The evening draws to a close. Availing himself of the privilege of the prison regulations, he leaves his cell and walks into the narrow court-yard in front of the gaol. He finds his health giving way beneath the continued confinement and wearing suspense, so that at times he starts at his own shadow. Dark, fearful thoughts are revolving through his mind, and a pensiveness shades his face such as he is not wont to wear. The apprehension of coming evil is visible in his agitated features, and he bears himself as one weighed down by heavy care. He is under the cloud.

Entering, from the inner prison the court-yard, which was scarce fourteen feet square, he observes, pacing to and fro, with a slow, irregular step, a man of middle age, with sad worn countenance, and arms folded in the hopelessness of despair. His once dark hair is now quite grey. Sorrow and anxiety, more than years, have done this work. As he approaches, Bunyan regards him with steadfast look. There is something in his appearance attractive, which bespeaks him above the common felon. Bunyan thinks he may be a prisoner for conscience' sake.

As the man reaches him, he looks up. Their eyes meet. Sorrow is keen-sighted, and readily understands. They read in a moment their mutual suffering in the same great cause.

Bunyan was the first to speak. He was not a man for ceremony or mincing words.

'A sufferer for conscience' sake,' he says, looking at the bowed form and sorrowful face before him.

'For preaching the gospel of our blessed Redeemer,' is the answer.

'And I am here for the same,' he replies, 'but I thank God that he has given me grace to suffer for his name.'

'John Bunyan, of Elstow?' replies the prisoner, interrogatively.

'The same.'

'And I am Dorset, of Newburg.'

The two seat themselves on some stones which project from the foundation wall of the gaol, and enter into conversation.

'Ah, these are dark times for the servants of the Most High. They are smitten from the rising to the going down of the sun, and there is no uplifted arm to stay the hand of these bloody Amalekites,' opens Dorset, despondingly.

'But the Lord hath sworn to preserve his people, and in his own good time he will bring them deliverance. Let us wait on him, for hath he not sworn that he will utterly put out the remembrance of Amalek from under heaven? Let us be strong, and of a good courage, for the Lord himself will be with us; he will never fail nor forsake. And his people shall yet ride in the high places of the earth, and eat of the increase of the fields.'

'Ah, but he hath hidden his face from them, and hath forsaken them, and they are devoured from off the face of the earth, because his anger is kindled against them,' responds Dorset.

'Do not vengeance and recompense belong to him? And the Lord himself will judge his people, and repent himself for his servants when he seeth that their favor is gone, answered the holy man of God.

'But the blood of his slaughtered people crieth daily unto him from the ground, but the heavens are as brass, and they walk like blind men, and their blood is poured out like dust, and there is no healing of their grievous wounds,' and Dorset of Newburg shook his head seriously.

'But he will avenge the blood of his servants, and will render vengeance to his adversaries, and will be mindful unto his land and unto his people ; and he will bring them out of the places where they have been scattered, the cells, and the dungeons, and the caves ; and will lead them in green pastures, and upon high mountains, and will bind up that which was broken, and strengthen that which was faint. And they shall no more be a prey of the violent man, neither shall the wicked devour them ; but they shall dwell in safety, and none shall make them afraid, for the Lord God hath spoken it.'

How eloquent with trust was the face of Bunyan as he repeated these praises of his God!

'The promises of God are true and mighty, I know, brother Bunyan, but my way seems so hedged in. My wife and children are left desolate, and to-morrow I am to be tried, and if I do not recant, death, or imprisonment, perhaps for life, will be my lot. Why is it that the people of God are thus scattered and peeled, meted out and trodden down ?'

'God is trying the faith of his people, my brother, even his own elect, but in due time he will succor and save them. We should let none of these things move us, but always be ready, not only to be bound, but also to suffer death, if need be, for the furtherance of the glorious gospel of the Son of God.'

'Hard, hard!' said the prisoner, sighing deeply, and fixing his eyes to the ground. 'Unless God gives me grace, I do not see how I am to live in this miserable, loathsome confinement, if this should be my doom.'

'And his grace will be vouchsafed to you, my brother, if you have built on the sure word of promise. Mighty and willing is he to do all for his chosen ones that he has said. I never had in all my life so great an *inlet* into the word of God as now. Those scriptures, that I saw *nothing* in before, are made in this place and state to *shine* upon me. Jesus Christ, also, was never more real and apparent than now; here I have seen and felt him indeed. Oh, that word!—"We have not preached unto you cunningly devised fables;" and that other, "God raised Christ from the dead, and gave him glory, that our faith and hope might be in God," are blessed words unto me in this my imprisoned condition.'

'I pray that he may stand by me and uphold me, if it is his will to send me to this horrid place.' A shudder passed over the frame of the man, as if the thought of the darkness and dreariness of the prison house was more than he could bear.

'Feed upon his word, my brother, look to him and you need not fear. His words are sweet and precious. These three or four scriptures have been great refreshments to me in my sad condition, and they may be so to you if you will but lay hold of them by faith. "Let not your heart be troubled; ye believe in God, believe also in me. In my Father's house are many mansions; if it were not so, I would have told you. I go to prepare a place for you. And if I go and prepare a place for you, I will come again and receive you to myself, that where I am ye may be also. These things I have spoken unto you, that in me ye might have peace. In the world ye shall have tribulation, but be of good cheer, I have overcome the world. For ye are dead, and your life is hid with Christ in God; when Christ, who is our life, shall appear, then shall ye also appear with him in glory. But ye are come to Mount Zion, and unto the city of the living God—the heavenly Jerusalem—and to an innumerable company of angels—to the general assembly and churches of the first born which are written in heaven, and to God, the Judge of all; and to the spirits of just men made perfect; and to the blood of sprinkling, that speaketh better things than that of Abel." Sometimes when I have been able to enjoy the savor of these precious words, I have been able to "laugh at destruction," and to fear neither the horse nor his rider. I have had sweet sights of the forgiveness of my sins in this place, and of my being with Jesus in another world. Oh! the Mount Zion, the heavenly Jerusalem, the innumerable company of angels, and God the Judge of all, and the spirits of just men made perfect, and Jesus have been sweet unto me in this place. I have seen that here, that I am persuaded I shall never, while in this world, be *able* to express. I have seen a *truth* in this scripture, "Whom having not seen, ye love," in whom, though now you see him not, yet believing, ye rejoice with joy unspeakable and full of glory.'

'Hath Satan never tempted you to doubt and fear, **my**

brother?' and as the man questioned, he looked into Bunyan's face with surprise and wonder at his words.

'Oh, yes; I have not escaped the assaults of the Wicked One; but I never knew what it was for God to stand by me at all times, and at every offer of Satan to afflict me, as I have found him since I came hither; for whenever fears have presented themselves, so have supports and encouragements; yea, when I have started, even, as it were, at nothing else but my *shadow*, yet God has been very tender of me, hath not suffered me to be molested, but would, with one scripture or another, strengthen me against all, insomuch that I have often said, "Were it lawful, I could pray for *greater* trouble, for the greater comfort's sake."'

'Has the Lord always thus been unto you a tower of salvation—a shield and rock of defence, so that the darts of the adversary have been turned aside from thee, my brother?'

'Oh, no. Fear has been upon me, and trembling, which made all my bones to shake. Before I came to prison I saw what was *coming*, and had especially two considerations warm upon my heart. The first was, "How to be able to encounter death, should that be here my portion." For the first of these, that scripture was of great information to me, namely: to pray to God "to be strengthened with all might according to his glorious power unto all patience and long suffering with joyfulness." I could seldom go to prayer before I was imprisoned for not so little as a year together, but this sentence or sweet petition would, as it were, *thrust* itself into my mind, and persuade me, that if ever I would go through long suffering, I must have patience, especially if I would endure it joyfully. And this, also, was of great use to me when I thought of having to die here in this goal—"But we had the sentence of death in ourselves, that we might not trust in ourselves, but in God that raised the dead." By this scripture I was made to see, that, if ever I would suffer rightly I must first pass a sentence of death upon everything that can properly be called a thing of *this* life, even to reckon myself, my wife, my children, my *health*, my enjoyments, and all as *dead* to me, and *myself* as dead to them.'

The listener moaned. The fear of pain and death was heavily upon him. If Bunyan, whose courage and fortitude at his trial had been, as it were, the watchword of all the persecuted throughout Bedfordshire and the neighboring counties, stirring them up to stedfastness and zeal in the great cause of man's redemption—if he had been so overtaken by the Tempter, and sore broken by his malignant assaults, how should *he* stand when the conflict was fierce upon him—when wicked men should make haste to shed his blood?

'My soul is among lions. And I lie even among them that are set on fire, even the sons of men, whose teeth are spears and arrows, and their tongues a sharp sword,' he repeats slowly to himself, as his eyes rest on the ground.

'But God shall send from heaven and save his people from the reproach of them that would swallow them up. He will not suffer the righteous to be moved, but will redeem their soul from violence and deceit, and will deliver them from from the hand of their enemies. I find, my brother, the best way to go through suffering is to trust in God, through Christ, as touching the world to come; and as touching this world, " to count the grave my home, to make my bed in darkness ; to say to corruption, Thou art my father; and to the worm, Thou art my mother and sister." '

A shudder passed through the frame of the prisoner as this dark picture falls from the lips of the speaker. He has not fully learned to trust the Lord, though he slay him.

The turnkey comes to order the prisoners to their cells. One goes away with the light of God burning in his soul, the other is treading a path in which there is no light.

But scarcely is Bunyan alone in his cell before the Tempter comes, and he who but a few minutes before was strong in the Lord and in the power of his might, finds himself now encompassed with fears and dark forebodings, ' so that he was like a broken vessel, driven and tossed on wild, tumultuous seas.'

It was when Job was hedged about, himself and his house, when the Lord had blessed the work of his hands, and his substance was increased in the land, that Satan put forth his hand and touched all that he had. It was just after Peter had eaten bread with his Lord that he heard these fearful words, ' Simon, Simon, behold Satan hath desired to have you, that he may sift you as wheat.' And thus oftentimes it is, when the Christian is on the Nebo of his hopes, that he is commanded by the Arch Fiend to come down and die to all present enjoyment and future bliss.

Bunyan rests on his stool beside the little window, with his head buried in his hands. The flowing river, and leaden cloud, and sweeping winds without, have no attraction or interest for him now. His thoughts are turned painfully within. The morrow is his trial day, and death may await him. His family will be left without a protector or supporter. Who will stand by them in their need? He starts from his seat and paces his narrow cell in agony. Poor man! the Tempter is hard upon him. The rending thoughts of his bosom form themselves into words, as back and forth he goes in almost frenzied desperation; " Oh! the parting with my wife and children is as the *pulling* of the flesh from my bones. What hardships, and miseries, and wants, my poor family are likely to meet with, if I am taken from them; especially my *poor blind child*, who is nearer to my heart than all beside. Oh! the hardships this poor blind one will have to undergo will break my heart to pieces!'

And then, as if the blind eyes were turned upward to his, with their dark imploring gentleness, and he felt the resting of the thin, frail hand in his, he exclaims, 'Poor child! what sorrow thou art like to have for thy portion in this world. Thou must be beaten, must beg, suffer hunger, cold, nakedness, and a thousand calamities, though I cannot now endure the wind should blow upon thee. But I must venture you with God, though it goeth to the quick to leave you.'

He wipes away the big tears rolling from his earnest eyes.

' Oh! I am as a man who is *pulling* down his house upon the *head* of his wife and children,' and he stops suddenly, as if overcome by the horror of the thought. 'But I *must* do it—I MUST do it,' he exclaims with energy, as he again dashes forward.

' I will give you back to your family,' whispers Satan— ' to your wife and helpless children; you shall be free, and have long life and comfort, if you will but promise. You have but to say that you will *call* these meetings no more together, and you are at liberty. And surely there can be no harm in this. Can't you do this without compromising the truth? It is an easy matter to let this alone. For the sake of your wife and children you can submit to the law this much. And think what will be the end in this matter if you don't. Your name will be cast out as a reproach, and your wife and children will be left to die. You surely are not foolish enough to do this.'

' Oh! I *must* do it—I *must* do it. No compromise for me. I must bear torturing, if need be, unto death. God tells me, " Leave thy fatherless children, I will preserve

them alive; and let thy widow trust in me;" and again,
"Verily, it shall go well with thy remnant; verily, I will
cause the enemy to treat them well in the time of evil, and
in the time of affliction."'

'But how do you know this is required at your hands?
and how do you know God will fulfil these promises to
you?' suggests Satan.

'If I venture all for God,' he answers to himself, 'I
engage God to take care of my concernments. But if I
forsake him in his ways for fear of any trouble that shall
come to me or mine, then I shall not only falsify my profession, but shall admit that my concernments are not so
sure as if left at God's feet while I stand to and for his
name, as they would be if they were under my care, though
with the denial of the way of God.'

'But how do you know you will be able to do these
things?' whispers Satan. 'How, if when you have made
hard *shift* to clamber up the ladder, you should with
quaking, or fainting, or some other symptom of fear, give
occasion to the enemy to *reproach* the way of God and his
people for their timorousness.'

'But if I can but speak to the multitude which shall
come to see me die, and if God will but convert *one* soul by
my last words, I shall not count my life thrown away nor
lost.'

Faith is gaining the ascendency over doubt and dread,
and the prisoner's face lights up with hope, and bidding
Satan get behind him, he seats himself with something like
composure to contemplate with joy of testifying to the truth,
even unto death, when the Wicked One sounds in his ear
so loud that he again rushed to his feet.

'But whither must you go when you die? What will
become of you? Where will you be found in another
world? What evidence have you for heaven and glory,
and an inheritance among them that are sanctified?'

Ah, these are searching questions that dart through his
soul, causing his frame to quiver with the energy of despair. Hear him as he answers, 'I *must go on* and venture
my eternal state with Christ, whether I have comfort or
not. If God does not come in, I will leap off the ladder,
even *blindfold*, into eternity—sink or swim—come heaven,
come hell. Lord Jesus, if thou wilt catch me, *do;*—if not,
I *will venture* for thy name.'

Thus the weary night-watches wear on, spent by the
prisoner in self-examination, reflection, and prayer, and
the gray morning finds him ready to be offered. Faith has

triumphed over fear. Hope has conquered doubt; Christ
has slain the Evil One. His shield has withstood and
broken the fiery darts of hell.

CHAPTER VII.

BUNYAN BEFORE HIS JUDGES.

IT is a cold, piercing morning in January, 1661. Everything in Bedford is astir betimes, for it is the meeting of
the Quarter Sessions, and it has been noised throughout the
whole country that Bunyan is to be tried that day. Friends
and foes are eager to hear his defence, for his fame has
gone to every hamlet and farm-station, and awakened in
every breast a desire to hear the man who had so nobly
withstood the Justice and '*that right Judas.*'

The court-room is a scene of eager expectancy. The
crowd is partly assembled. The prisoner is expected every
moment. The Justices, seated in all their consequential
dignity, prepared to enter with zest on the work before
them. There are five of them—Keeling, Blundale, Leechir,
Chester, and Snagg. Little do they think, vain, insolent,
minions of a tyrant king, that the prisoner, whom they
now await with chafed indignation, is to hand down their
names to posterity covered with opprobrium! That this
day's proceedings is to fix upon them everlasting disgrace!
—to enter them as '*red*-letter names for ever, in the
Almanac of Persecution.'

The felon is brought in by the gaoler, and placed in the
prisoner's box. All attention is directed to him. He
bears himself calmly and unmoved. No earthly hand
is there to support him. But he finds support; he is
leaning on the Arm Omnipotent.

They bid him rise up. He stands; his eyes fixed
unwaveringly on his judges. The indictment is produced.
The Clerk of the Sessions rises and reads it.

'John Bunyan, of the town of Bedford, laborer, doth
devilishly and perniciously abstain from coming to church
to hear divine service, and is a common upholder of
several unlawful meetings and conventicles, to the great
disturbance and distraction of the good subjects of this
kingdom, contrary to the laws of our sovereign lord, the
King.'

The clerk pauses for a moment, and looks the prisoner

BUNYAN BEFORE HIS JUDGES.

steadily in the face. The look is met by one equally as fixed.

'Prisoner, what say you to this?' he asks in a voice which indicates his rage and contempt.

The prisoner answers calmly and unflinchingly:

'As to the first part of it, I am a common frequenter of the church of God. And I am also, by grace, a member of the people over whom Christ is the head.'

The blood mounts to the face of Justice Keeling, who acts as judge on the occasion. He is enraged that a prisoner, and he a *tinker*, should dare thus to reply in the presence of the officers of the crown. He is a vindictive man, ready at all times to deal vengeance upon those who dare to oppose the civil laws of which he is the insolent representative.

Assuming such importance as he can, he addresses the prisoner imperatively.

'Do you come to church, you know what I mean—to the *parish* church—to hear divine service?'

'No I do not,' is the firm reply.

'And why don't you?'

'Because I cannot find it commanded in the word of God,' answers the noble confessor right boldly.

'We are commanded to pray.'

'But not by the common prayer-book.'

'How then, will you tell me, you insolent one?'

'With the Spirit. As the apostle saith, "I will pray with the Spirit and the understanding."'

'Well, we can pray with the Spirit and with the understanding, and with the common prayer-book too,' and the judge stamps his foot with rage.

'The prayers in the common prayer-book are such as are made by other men, and not by the motion of the Holy Ghost within our hearts. The apostle saith he will pray with the *Spirit* and the *understanding*, and *not* with the common prayer-book.'

Well done, thou noble defender of the truth as it is in Christ Jesus! Stand firm and *contend* for thy faith, though the odds be against you. Fear not what man can do. He who holds the scale of justice in his own hand will himself mete out your reward. Put thy trust in God; so shalt thou inherit the land, and possess the holy mountain. The Lord hath spoken it.

'What do you *count* prayer?' questions Justice Chester, rising from his seat, and chafing under Bunyan's calm collected answers. 'Do you think it is to say a few words over before, or among, a people?'

'No, not so, sir; men may have many elegant, yea, excellent words, and yet not pray at all.'

'But how do we know that you do not *write* out your prayers first, and then *read* them afterwards to the people?' asks Justice Blundale derisively. This is a hard-hearted, narrow-minded bigot, who 'could *cudgel* Nonconformists as well as question, insult, and fine them.' To this jeering, scornful question, Bunyan calmly answers:

'It is no use, sir, to take a pen and paper and write a few words thereon, and then go and read it over to a company of people.'

'But how shall we know this?'

'Sir, it is none of our custom.'

Then says Keeling—

'But it is lawful to use the common prayer-book and such like forms, for Christ taught his disciples to pray, as John also taught his disciples. Cannot one man teach another to pray? Faith comes by hearing, and one man may convince another of sin; and therefore prayers made by men and read over are good to teach and help men to pray.'

'But, sir, the Scriptures saith, that it is " the Spirit that helpeth our infirmities, for we know not what we should pray for as we ought, but the Spirit itself maketh intercession for us with groanings that cannot be uttered." Mark, it doth not say that the common prayer-book teacheth us how to pray, but the Spirit. And "it is the *Spirit* that helpeth our infirmities," saith the apostle; he doth not say it is the common *prayer-book.* And as to the Lord's prayer, although it be an easy thing to say, "Our Father," etc. with the mouth, yet there are very few that can, in the spirit, say the two first words in that prayer, that is, can call God their Father as *knowing* what it is to be born again, and as having experienced that they are begotten of the Spirit of God, which, if they do not, all is but babbling.'

'This is a truth. But what have you *against* the common prayer-book?' asks the judge warmly.

'If you will hear me, sir, I will lay down my reasons against it.'

'You shall have liberty. But first I will give you one caution. Take heed of speaking *irreverently* of the common prayer-book; for if you do so, you will bring *great damage* upon yourself.'

'My first reason, sir, is that it is not *commanded* in the word of God, and therefore *I cannot* use it.'

'And where do you find it commanded in the Scripture that you shall go to Elstow or to Bedford, and yet it is lawful for you to go to either of them, is it not?' asks Justice Snagg, rising to his feet, and looking scornfully on the prisoner.

'To go to Elstow or to Bedford is a *civil* thing and not material, though not commanded. But to pray is a part of the divine worship of God, and it ought, therefore, to be done according to the *rule* of God's word.'

'He will do harm, he will do harm; let him speak no further!' exclaims Chester, in a loud voice.

But Judge Keeling interrupts.

'No, no, never fear him ; we are better *established* than that ; he can do no harm ; we *know* the common prayer-book hath been ever since the APOSTLES' time, and it is lawful for it to be used in the church.'

But the defender wants a higher authority than that, so he demands—

'Show me the place in the epistles where the common prayer-book is written, or *one* of scripture that commands me to read it. Notwithstanding, they that have a mind to use it have their liberty ; I would not keep them from it. But for our parts we can pray to God without it, blessed be his name.'

'Who is your God, Beelzebub? You seem possessed of the spirit of delusion and of the devil,' and Justice Leechir shakes his head in the madness of his rage. The prisoner regards him with a steady, firm look, but answers not to his vile accusations.

'Blessed be the .Lord,' he says, when their words are over, 'we are encouraged to meet together and to pray, and to exhort one another, for we have had the comfortable presence of God among us, for ever blessed be his holy name.'

'All this is *pedlar's* French! leave off your canting!' and Judge Keeling, no longer able to contain himself, starts from his seat, and shakes his head menacingly at the prisoner.

'By what authority do you preach? You have no right to do it!' he exclaims in the same infuriated tone.

'I can prove to you, sir, if you will hear me, that it is lawful for me, and such as I am, to preach the word of God.'

'By what scripture, tell me?'

'By that in the first epistle of Peter, the fourth chapter and eleventh verse, and Acts, the eighteenth chapter, with other scriptures, and——'

'Hold, hold! not so many! Which is the first?' asks the Judge in a low voice.

'It is this,' replies the prisoner calmly: ' "As every man hath received the gift, even so let him minister the same unto another, as good stewards of the manifold grace of God; if any man speak, let him speak as the oracles of God." '

'Hold there; let me explain that scripture to you. "As every man hath received the gift," that means, I say, as every man hath received a *trade*, so let him follow it. If any man hath received the gift of *tinkering*, as *thou* hast done, let him follow his tinkering, and so other men their trades, and the divine his calling.'

'Nay, sir, but it is most clear that the apostle speaks here of *preaching* the word; if you do but compare both the verses together, the next verse explains this gift, *what* it is, saying, "If any man speak, let him speak as the oracles of God." So that it is plain that the Holy Ghost doth not so much in this place exhort to *civil* callings, as to the exercise of those gifts that we have received from God.'

'This you may do in your *family*, but nowhere else.'

'But, sir, if it is lawful to do good to some, is it not lawful to do good to more? If it is a good duty to exhort our families, it is good to exhort others. But, sir, if you hold it a sin to meet together to seek the face of God, and to exhort one another to follow Christ, then I shall *sin still*, for so I shall do,' and the man of God looks the infuriate Justices stedfastly in the face.

'Hold, hold! I will not dispute with you. We cannot wait on you any longer. You confess to the indictment, do you?'

'This I confess: We have had many meetings together, both to pray to God and to exhort one another; and we have had the sweet, comforting presence of the Lord among us for encouragement, blessed be his name; therefore I confess myself guilty, and not otherwise. And——'

'Stop, stop,' exclaims the Judge, 'you confess yourself guilty, do you? Then hear your judgment: You must be had back again to prison, and there lie for three months following; and at three months' end, if you do not submit to go to *church* to hear divine service, and leave *your preaching*, you must be banished the realm; and if, after such a day as shall be appointed you to be gone, you shall be found in this realm, or be found to come over again without special license from the king, you *must stretch by the neck for it*, I tell you plainly.'

The prisoner looks the Judge unflinchingly in the face, as he answers:

'As to this matter, sir, I am at a *point* with you, for if I were out of prison to-day, by the help of God I would preach the gospel again *to-morrow !* '

'Away with him, away with him!' vociferates the Judge, and the Justices join in the cry, 'Away with him, away with him!' The gaoler seizes upon him and hurries him to the gaol.

Well done, thou good and noble confessor! Thou zealous contender for the faith, great shall be thy reward when the Lord God shall come to make up his jewels. Thou hast borne good testimony before men, and thou shalt stand approved of Him before men and angels at the great day of final accounts. Oh, that thy spirit were now in every Christian bosom! Then should one chase a thousand, and two put ten thousand to flight. Then should Zion awake to put on her strength, and 'go forth conquering and to conquer.'

Oh, spirit of the living God, breathe upon the children of the Most High! quicken them from their stupor and death, that they may gird on the *whole* gospel armor, and go forth to fight valiantly the battles of the Lord.

CHAPTER VIII.

THE PRAYER MEETING.

IT is a cold, cheerless, January evening. The stars have hid themselves behind the thick, dull clouds. The rain falls chill and penetrating. The wind roars through the leafless branches of the trees, and wails through the desolate streets. All nature, animate and inanimate, seems benumbed by the cold bleak air.

In a small room of an humble dwelling, situated just without the town of Bedford, a company of men and women are assembled.

What is it that has brought old men and women, young men and maidens, from their homes such a fearful night as this? Surely their hearts are warm in some cause. Surely their desires must be ardent. 'We will not let thee go until thou bless us,' seems to have been the determination which nerved them to dare the pitiless blast and the fast falling rain.

It is a Prayer-meeting.

The little church at Bedford have set apart this night for earnest prayer to God in behalf of themselves and of their beloved brother Bunyan. The women are there 'whom Bunyan saw sitting in the sun at the doorside, and who had directed him to the Lamb of God who taketh away the sin of the world.' It is a momentous time. Each heart shares the burden which has fallen on the little congregation. A solemn air pervades the small assembly; and anxious fears prevail lest the worst is not yet. A sigh steals out from an overburdened heart, and is answered by another, another, and another from hearts less pressed down beneath a weight of sorrow.

The holy man enters with a slow, calm step, and is greeted by a kindly look from every eye. He shakes hands with two or three of the aged brethren as he seats himself near the stand on which rests the Bible. All is still as death, save when some troubled heart sends up a silent petition in groanings that cannot be uttered.

Another enters and falls into a vacant seat — then another, and another, until the room is well nigh filled.

The aged man arises and opens the old worn Bible.

'Let not your hearts be troubled; ye believe in God, believe also in me,' falls in soft full strains from his lips. With feeling he reads through that beautiful chapter, the fourteenth of John, so rich with consolation to the tried heart. 'In the world ye shall have tribulation, my brethren, but in Christ ye shall have peace. Let us pray.'

The whole company kneel, and, while the man of God sends up a fervent petition to the Most High that his Almighty arm shall work out deliverance for his children, a silent 'amen' is going up from each bowed heart. 'Oh, deliver thy servant from the hand of the persecutor, and grant, oh God, that the guidance and strength of thy Holy Spirit may be vouchsafed to thy people, that they may be enabled to acquit themselves like men. Oh, may they be endued with power from on high to bear testimony to the unsearchable riches of the glorious gospel of the Son of God; and, if need be, to seal that testimony with their blood. Give unto them that faith which overcometh the world. And if imprisonment await us, as it has done our brother, let us be sustained and strengthened, that we may endure hardness as good soldiers of our Lord Jesus Christ. Oh, eternal God, be our refuge, place beneath us thine everlasting arms of love. Thrust out the enemy from before us, tread upon their high places and destroy them, that they may vex thy people no more. And say unto thy people, "Fear thou not, for I am with thee; be not dismayed, for I am thy God: I will strengthen thee, yea, I will help thee. I will uphold thee with the right hand of my righteousness," for thou, oh Lord God, givest power to the faint, and to them that have no might thou increasest strength. Oh, make then for us a way in the sea, a path in the mighty waters, that the floods may not overwhelm us, that we may pass through dry shod from the hands of our enemies.'

The stillness of death is upon that little assembly, broken only by the supplicant's earnest voice, and now and then a groan which forces its way from some surcharged bosom. Each heart is melted, and there is much of self-examination; and many a fervent, unuttered prayer ascends to the throne of sovereign love for grace to meet the darkest hour, for strength to triumph over all foes, and that support might be vouchsafed to him, who for the gospel's sake had been assaulted, derided, and cast into prison.

They rise from their knees and sing a song of praise to God. Another prayer is offered, another song sung, and aged brother Landon rises to talk awhile to the little band. He is one who has been on the pilgrimage many a long, weary year. He has fought some hot battles with the world, the flesh, and the devil, always conquering through grace. Every one present knows him, and his words fall like sweet music on their listening ears. His long gray hair flows over his shoulders, his form is stooped under the burden of life's journey, and his thin hand trembles as he lifts it to wipe the tears from his dimmed eyes. But over his face there shines a look of radiant love, which tells us he has been with Jesus.

He wipes the tears from his face and looks upwards, then placing his hands quietly behind him says: 'Dearly beloved brethren and sisters in the Lord, I once was young, but now I am old, yet have I never seen the righteous forsaken nor his seed begging bread, for the Lord is his portion, and hath sworn unto him the sure mercies of David. Did not God himself destroy the foes of Israel, even all that did vex and pursue them? Did he not triumph gloriously over the hosts of Egypt, and cast the the horse and the rider into the sea? Did he not cut off the enemies of his people in the wilderness and bring them safely into the promised land? Has he not been with them that fear him in all generations a hedge round about them, so that the enemy could not come near to hurt them? Did

he not turn the rock into standing water, the flint into a
fountain of waters? Did he not say, "I have created thee,
O Jacob, and have formed thee, O Israel; fear not for I
have redeemed thee. I have called thee by thy name,
thou art mine?" Oh, my brethren, hearken to his promises,
and let your soul rest on his word; for he is true, and
he will bring it to pass; he is mighty, and he will deliver.
He himself will shield us from our enemies and give us
power to overcome, will hedge us in on the right hand and
the left, and provide for us a way of escape. "For although
the fig-tree shall not blossom, neither shall fruits be on
the vines, the labor of the olive shall fail, and the fields
yield no meat, the flocks be cut off from the fold, and there
shall be no herd in the stalls, yet will I rejoice in the
Lord, I will joy in the God of my salvation." Let us
not grow weary then, nor faint by the way. Thanks to
his high and holy name, he hath brought me thus far on
my journey, and here again I set up my Ebenezer in the
presence of you, my brethren, and of witnessing angels, and
inscribe thereon, "Unto him who hath loved me and washed
me from my sins in his own blood, and hath made me a
king and a priest unto God, to him be glory and dominion
and power for ever and for ever. Amen."'

'Amen and Amen,' responds every heart in that weeping
assembly as the old man takes his seat.

Another brother rises on the opposite side of the room to
bear his testimony to the goodness and love of God. He is
a younger soldier than Brother Landon, but he, too, has
been in the thickest of the fight, and his scars testify how
valiantly he has fought the battles of the Lord. And thus
he tells of his warfare:

'My brethren, when Moses held up his hand Israel prevailed, and when he let down his hand Amalek prevailed;
and so it is with us throughout our earthly warfare. Whenever we trust in God, and send up, from unfeigned lips, a
cry to him for his help, then his own right hand doth get
for us the victory over all our foes. Then are the Amalekites
that would destroy us discomforted with the edge of the
sword; then can we build our altars and call them
Jehovah-nissi.

'But, my brethren, we must not faint by the way, for,
if we do, Amalek will prevail. We must hold up our
hands. We must pray the prayer of faith; then shall one
chase a thousand, and two put ten thousand to flight. The
times are dark around us; the enemy besets us on every
side. The people of God are insulted, and imprisoned, and

slain. They have become a hissing among the nations, a by-word and term of reproach to all people; they are scattered and peeled ; they are smitten with the rod of the Assyrian, and the Philistine is hard upon them. But their cry has gone up before the Lord of hosts, and he will have respect unto all their troubles. The Lord will have mercy on Jacob, and will yet choose Israel, and the day shall come when the Lord shall give his people rest from all their sorrows, and from the hard bondage wherein they are made to serve ; for he shall break the staff of the wicked and the sceptre of the rulers ; and the enemies of his people shall be chased as the chaff of the mountains before the wind, and like a rolling thing before the whirlwind. This shall be the portion of them that spoil us, and the lot of them that rob us.

'Let us trust in the Lord, my brethren, and he will bring us out of all our troubles. Let us pray earnestly for our brother who has been called upon to bear his testimony before men, and has been condemned to suffering for the sake of the gospel of our blessed Master. Let us pray that grace may be given him equal to his day, and that he may be able to praise the Lord in his chains and in the dark dungeon. And if he and we shall be called upon to witness to the world that God is true, let us acquit ourselves like men, and be willing to suffer, even to the offering up of ourselves, that his love and his goodness may be known, and his truth preserved in the earth. And here this night let us renew our covenant vows to the Lord and to one another, and wrestle with God for a blessing as did Jacob of old, that we may have power with God and with men, and prevail over our enemies. And may this be unto us a Bethel, where the Lord shall answer us in the day of our distresses ; '—and he knelt in the midst of them and with David prayed :

'How long wilt though forget us, oh Lord? For ever? How long wilt thou hide thy face from us ? How long shall we take counsel in our souls, having sorrow in our hearts daily ? How long shall our enemies be exalted over us ? Deliver us from our enemies, oh God. Defend us from them that rise up against us; deliver us from the workers of iniquity, and save us from bloody men. They hate us without a cause ; they lie in wait for us. We are poor and needy. Make haste, O God, to help us ; for thou art our help and our deliverer. O Lord, make no tarrying ; we trust in thee and not in man ; we put confidence in thee, and not in princes. Surely the righteous shall give thanks

unto thy name; the upright shall dwell in thy presence.
Guide us through life, and afterwards receive us into glory,
and to thy name and thine alone, Father, Son, and Eternal
Spirit, be everlasting praise. Amen.'

Another and another speaks and prays. Their hearts are
knit together in bonds of Christian affection. And the groan,
and sigh, and falling tear attest that love which says, ' For
one is your Master, even Christ, and all ye are brethren.'

Thus the time passes in prayer and praise and exhortation until the night is far spent. No petition has been
offered that did not bear up before a throne of pitying love
that faithful brother whom chains held to the earth
because he *would preach the gospel of the Lord Jesus
Christ.* Their hearts are bound to his by cords of holy love.
They are afflicted in his afflictions, and are partakers of
his shame.

The aged pastor once more arises to speak to them.

It is John Gifford, ' that holy man of God,' as Bunyan is
wont to call him. He is the under shepherd over the little
flock at Bedford. He goes in and out before them dispensing
unto them the bread of life, giving unto each his portion
in due season, even as the Holy Spirit gave him guidance.

He wipes the streaming tears from his wrinkled face, and
with an effort, subdues his swelling emotion. Composing
himself, he speaks in a voice full of love and gratitude:

' My dearly beloved brethren and sisters in the Lord, the
purchase of Christ's blood and the seal of his redemption, I
would speak to you this night words of encouragement
that you may be built up and strengthened, made perfect
men and women in our Lord Jesus Christ. And girded
about with his salvation, and relying on his sure word of
promise which can never fail, for it is yea and amen for
ever, I would exhort you to all patience and long suffering,
that ye may acquit yourselves men and women in the Lord,
and be a light to the world in the midst of this crooked
and perverse generation. God's ways towards his people
are oftentimes dark and mysterious, my brethren, and were
it not for that increase of faith being granted to us for
which the apostle prayed, we could not bear up under the
trials which beset our pilgrimage through this world of sin
and sorrow. Amid the storms and billows of this life,
when the fierce blasts of persecution sweep over us, and
forked lightnings of man's wrath threaten to strike us
through, we should certainly make shipwreck of all our
hopes and expectations, did not God give unto us an increased measure of his all-supporting grace. My grace

shall be sufficient for thee, he tells us, and we believe it. Thanks to his holy name that he has given us this blessed promise, which is an anchor to the soul both sure and sted-fast. " My grace is sufficient." To this we moor and are safe. Let the storm rage with dreadful power and the fierce winds howl in wildest fury, we will not fear, for the Captain of our salvation is at the helm, and he will guide us safely through the passage, and land us at last in the haven of eternal safty and rest.

' The clouds and storm are black round about us now, my brethren, and the fierce winds of persecution howl about our ears. Our dearly beloved brother Bunyan has been seized upon by the relentless grasp of the tyrant's law, and has been borne from our midst to a noisome cell, from which he may be dragged to meet an ignominious death, or he may lay there long weary years, dragging out a life of wretched captivity. Our hearts are sorrowful even unto death. But, my brethren, the hand of God is in it. These things are not of chance, neither do they rise up out of the ground. They are sent by the hand of Him who ruleth the universe. They are designed to teach us an important lesson, to try our faith, to prove whether we are really sons and daughters of God, or whether we are deceived ; and it is our duty now, as dear children of God, to walk worthy of the vocation wherewith we are called, examining ourselves daily to see if we be in the faith, and ever ready to testify for God, though we know bonds and imprisonment await us.

' Brother Bunyan is in prison, but it is for the gospel's sake. Let us sympathise with him and his suffering family, but let us not complain against Jehovah that he hath done this thing. His wisdom hath directed it. Oh, I know well the darkness and gloom of the damp rayless cell. I have been there myself, my brethren, but it was not as a witness of the glorious truth of our Lord and Master. Oh, no, I had no such honor and joy as this in my dark captivity. Would to God I had had ! I was a slave of sin ! In bondage to the prince of the power of the air, that spirit which worketh in the children of disobedi-ence. I had borne arms against the people of the Most High to support a royalty which gloated in the blood of the saints. I had bid defiance to the Lord of Glory, and had taken league with the enemy of the King of Heaven. But thanks to his marvellous love, he snatched me from the jaws of hell, he rescued me from everlasting burnings.'

The old man pauses, he cannot proceed. He thinks of the exceeding love of God, and his heart is broken within

him. Oh, how much he loves, for he has had much forgiven! Surely he, above all others, is a miracle of grace.

Wiping the flowing tears from his face, and controlling
his voice he proceeds.

'Sentence of death had been passed upon me, and I and
seven others were to be hung for our allegiance to the
dethroned king. We lay groaning in the prison. The
last night had come, and I sat heartless and stupid in my
cell, knowing that the morning would bring my execution.
Oh, what a power does Satan gain over the souls of men.
I was to die. I knew it. A few hours more and I should
be in eternity, before the bar of God, and yet I defied death
and eternity, and thought, with bitter cursings, on what
I had been, what I then was, and what was before me in
the future. Oh, my brethren, my heart was besotted with
sin. The light of reason had been darkened by the evil one,
and I was a willing captive to the arch enemy of my soul.
But God, even the great and holy God, had intentions of
mercy towards me, the chief of sinners.'

The old man's words are choked by tears. Tears are in
the eye of every listener. All is breathless silence.

'It was past the hour of midnight,' he resumes, as soon
as he can command himself sufficiently to proceed, 'and I
sat, as I tell you, cursing my fate. I cursed the hour I
was born, the course I had pursued, the justice that had
overtaken, and the doom that awaited me. I would not
listen to the monitions of conscience that told me I alone
was the culpable one. I bade conscience be still, and
cursed on. My sister entered the prison and stood before
me. It seemed the presence of an angel. I could scarcely
trust my vision. She spoke to me, and urged me to fly.
I heeded not her words. She repeated her importunities
with increased vehemence. I told her "it was impossible,
I could not escape; the guards were on the watch and it
was folly to attempt to pass them." "Fear not this," she
answered, "the guards are fast asleep without, and your
fellow-prisoners are dead drunk within, and there is no one
to give alarm. Make haste! make haste! my brother!
fly from these dreadful walls. Fly, I beseech thee, fly."

'Scarcely conscious of what I did, and with but little
hope of succeeding in my attempt, I suffered myself to be
led by my sister whithersoever she chose. We gained the
outer prison, and in safety passed the sleeping guards.
The hand of God guided us beyond danger, and I was
saved! Saved from death, saved from hell. Oh, what
abundant reason have I, my brethren, to be thankful to

God, and to trust his holy word. How manifest was his hand in my deliverance from death. But he had also delivered me from the curse of sin, under which I was so long a time in bondage. Herein is his love manifest, that he gave his Son for us, the just for the unjust, that we might be reconciled to him through the blood of atonement, and escape the awful doom under which fallen sinners rest because of sin and disobedience. Oh, wondrous love! Oh, infinite condescension! God bowed the heavens and came down to raise us from our low estate, when there was no eye to pity, and no arm to save. Let us, my brethren, praise his glorious name. Let us sing praises unto the Most High God that he hath delivered us from everlasting death, and hath given us inheritance with the saints in light—an inheritance incorruptible and undefiled, and which passeth not away. Oh, let us trust his gracious promises now that all these things seem to be against us, for we know that he is both able and willing to preserve his people from the hands of their enemies, and that he will deliver Israel from the land of bondage. " Glory and honor, and power, and dominion to Him that sitteth on the throne, and to the Lamb for ever and ever."

' Let us not fear, my brethren and sisters, what man can do unto us ; for no weapon turned against the righteous shall prosper, for the mischief of the wicked shall return upon his own head, and his violent dealings shall come down upon his own pate. Let us be encouraged by the example of those, who, through faith, have overcome and have entered into the promised rest. They had trials of cruel mockings and scourgings, yea, moreover of bonds and imprisonments. They were stoned, they were sawn asunder, were tempted, were slain with the sword. They wandered about in sheep-skins, and in goat-skins, being destitute, afflicted, tormented. These obtained a good report through faith, though they received not the promise. But God hath provided some better things for us ; and seeing that we are compassed about with so great a cloud of witnesses, my brethren, let us lay aside every weight, and the sin which doth so easily beset us, and let us run with patience the race set before us, looking unto Jesus, the author and finisher of our faith, who, for us laid aside the glory of heaven, and became a man of sorrow, bearing infamy, and shame, and buffetings, that we, through his sufferings and distress, might be made heirs of eternal bliss at God's right hand. Let us then, my brethren, take up the cross, despising the shame.

'The Lord himself will come to avenge his people, and our enemies shall have confusion of face; they shall lick the dust, their lofty looks shall be humbled, and their haughtiness shall be bowed down. "For behold the day cometh that shall burn as an oven, and all the proud, and all that do wickedly shall be stubble, and the day that cometh shall burn them up, that it shall leave neither root nor branch. The Lord of Hosts himself hath spoken it. But unto them that fear his name shall the Sun of Righteousness arise with healing on his wings." Let us then, my brethren, trust in the Lord, knowing there are yet some in Israel that have not bowed their knee to Baal. The Lord God Omnipotent reigneth, and Zion shall awake to put on her strength, and Jerusalem the holy city, shall arise, shake herself from the dust, and put on her beautiful garments; for the Lord will make bare his holy arm in the eyes of all the nations, and all the ends of the earth shall see the salvation of our God."

The pastor seats himself, overcome by the intensity of his feelings. Tears stream down his wrinkled cheek. His face is lighted up with the radiance of prophetic vision. His soul is stayed on the promises of God. What can he fear? I AM THAT I AM hath spoken, he cannot doubt. He knows that the Lord's hand is not shortened that it cannot save, but that his own right hand and holy arm shall get to him an everlasting victory.

Each heart takes fresh courage as his words of hope and consolation sink deep into every bosom; and, when he has commended them to God, each one goes forth from that little assembly, feeling, as did Paul when he thought of Jerusalem, 'ready to be offered for the gospel's sake.'

CHAPTER IX.

THE TRUE WIFE.

How dark, oftentimes, and mysterious are the providences of God in his dealings with his people. When after the counsel of his own mind he leads them by a way they know not, and makes them, like his servant of old, 'weary' and to desire the grave, they are made to *feel*, as well as to utter, 'How unsearchable are his judgments, and his ways past finding out.'

Only faith, firm and steadfast, can bear them up under

the crushing difficulties through which, in his wisdom and love, he sometimes calls them to pass. Philosophy cannot do it, reason is of no avail, the smile of the world is vanity, and friends prove 'miserable comforters.' Only faith in the omnipotent arm of the Lord God Jehovah can support them when 'the enemy is round about,' and only that arm omnipotent can work out for them sure deliverance.

Oftentimes, like Abraham of old, we are commanded to take the wood of the burnt offering and lay it upon our only son Isaac. And we take the fire in one hand, and a knife, and we move onward to the place of sacrifice : and as we journey along with timid, fearful hearts, we hear a voice say, ' *Offer him up, thy son, thine only son, Isaac.*' Then the heart stands still, and dark clouds of distrust gather, and great swelling words of murmuring are ready to burst from doubting lips ; but still the voice rings through our ear, 'thy son, thine only son, Isaac, offer him up as I have commanded thee.' And we ask, ' Wherefore, Lord ! hast thou not established thy covenant with Isaac ? ' The answer comes back, ' Get up and do as I have told thee.'

We dare not disobey the voice of the angel of the Lord, so we hasten onward to do his bidding.

And as we journey on, Isaac looks up into our face and innocently says : ' My father, behold the fire and the wood, but where is a lamb for a burnt offering ? ' Ah, does our faith fail then ? and do we murmur, ' How great this trial —surely I am above all others afflicted and oppressed ? Or do we, with the old patriarch's unflinching faith, say, ' My son, God will provide himself a lamb for a burnt-offering ? ' and so go on as the Lord hath commanded us ? If so, how great the reward ; for the same voice that bade us offer up Isaac says to us in love, ' Lay not thy hand upon the lad, neither do thou anything unto him, for now I know that thou fearest God, seeing that thou hast not withheld thy son, thine only son, from me.'

Bunyan was an innocent man ! This he knew—this his friends knew—this his vile persecutors knew ; yet he was kept in prison as a *convicted* person. What was his innocency to those bent upon his ruin ? Nothing ! He *could not* submit to their forms and errors—their prayer-books and liturgies ; his conscience would not suffer him to do it, and he must be punished—imprisoned ! It was a hard fate ; but God had a purpose in his having to bear it. The 'Pilgrim's Progress' was to be written, and John Bunyan had to write it. But, in order to write it, he must have the necessary preparation of mind and of soul. And

God saw that Bedford gaol was the place for this preparation. He was put there by those, who, under the cloak of religion, used every means to persecute and destroy the children of the Most High. 'God makes even the wrath of man to praise him.' But he also visits destruction upon the evil ones, who, to subserve their own purposes of ambition and hate, lay in wait for the righteous man, that they may ensnare him.

Charles had been crowned April 23rd, 1661. Bunyan was committed to prison in November, 1661, five months after the return of the king from his long exile in France and Holland.

It was customary, at the coronation of a king, to release certain prisoners—those who had not been convicted of capital offence—by virtue of the coronation. Bunyan had hoped, by this means, to secure his liberty, until they should pronounce the sentence of banishment or hanging; and then he knew he would be regarded as a *convicted* person, and the only privilege the coronation conferred upon him was a grant of twelve months' time to sue out a pardon. No sentence could be executed until twelve months after the coronation, and he determined to use every effort to effect his release before the expiration of that time.

The family of Bunyan had lived since his imprisonment amid trials, and hopes, and fears. Twice had he been summoned from the gaol to stand before the judges. Each time his Elizabeth had hoped that he would be set at liberty. But each time he had been remanded to gaol with the weight of the sentence increased. The poor wife's heart was almost broken. Her health, left very feeble by her sickness, had been so worn upon by alternate hope, fear, and disappointment, that now her kind neighbors feared that she could not overcome the shock. It was a touching sight to see her go on, day by day, with her sad face and failing form, to provide for and support her poor little fatherless children.

The neighbors were very kind to her to supply such wants as it was in their power to do from their own scanty stores, and speaking, whenever opportunity offered, kind and sympathising words.

The children sometimes went to see their father, to carry him some little token of love and remembrance; and sometimes, too, the wife would go. But the meeting with her husband, and the sight of his wasting form, and sunken eye, and of the cold, damp cell, so touched her loving heart, that the time of her stay was spent in tears and sobs ; and when the parting came, her grief was so deep and heart-rending that even the iron-hearted turnkey was moved to compassion. Under her own individual sufferings she bore up with a fortitude astonishing to all, even to those who knew most fully the strength of her womanly nature. But to see her husband wearing away, day by day, under what she knew to be an unrighteous sentence ; his manhood's strength wasted in a felon's cell ; his talents, which she knew and appreciated, buried within the walls of a loathsome dungeon—this was more than her soul could endure, and she felt, amid her overwhelming sorrow, that surely, surely, the Lord had forgotten to be gracious, and his mercy was clean gone for ever.

And when she would, with bleeding heart, sore pressed, find her way from the gaol to her forsaken home, all there seemed so dark and forbidding, that it was days before she could recover sufficiently from her sadness to pursue her accustomed duties. It was at such times as these that Mary stepped forth from her childish reserve and timidity, and gave manifestations of that judgment and determination of will which in after years she so prominently displayed, and which enabled her, child as she was, to take her mother's place, when that mother, oppressed by grief and worn out by hope deferred, gave way, for the time, beneath the weighty burden.

Her gentle words of affection and sympathy, uttered in her sweet, mild voice, fell like healing balsam on that mother's despairing heart, and oftentimes persuaded, as it were, that heart to lay aside its sorrows and rest upon God. And then, too, in her own blind way, she would look after the duties of the house, and take care of Joseph and Sarah, when it became necessary for her mother to seek employment from home. The younger children regarded her with reverential love. Her blindness threw a charm around her and an awe, so that they respected while they loved.

Bunyan had determined to obtain his release from gaol if it were possible to do so. Whereupon he decided to make himself heard at the next Assizes, which were to take place in August. How to effect this was a question which gave him much thought and anxiety. He could not go in person —his gaoler had no power to grant him such liberty—and he knew of no one who would undertake the matter for him that would be likely to accomplish his purpose. He thought of neighbor Harrow, and of those brethren who had befriended him at the time of his first trial, but he feared to entrust his case to their hands, lest they, not

understanding how to proceed, should defeat the very aim
of their efforts.

He at length decided, after much prayer and reflection,
to write out a petition, and present it by his wife to the
judges. He sent for her to come to see him, and opened
the matter to her. Most willingly she undertook the office
of advocate for him before the Lord Chief Justice of the
kingdom.

The Midsummer Assizes were drawing near. Bunyan
wrote out his petition, in which he besought 'that he might
be heard, that they would impartially take his case into
consideration.' He gave it to his wife, and commended her
to God. His hope was bright, for he felt that surely the
judges would not turn a deaf ear to a wife's pleadings for
her husband. He felt that the hardest heart must melt at
the sight of that delicate form, and that sad, earnest face.
His Elizabeth took the petition, and they knelt within the
narrow cell to pray that God would prosper her according to
the dictates of his own immutable will.

As she wended her way homeward, accompanied by little
Joseph, her mind was busy with various thoughts, and her
heart agitated by conflicting emotions. The prattle of the
child reached her ear, but could not distract her attention
from the one mighty consideration which occupied her
mind. 'Shall I be successful in obtaining my husband's
freedom ?' was the question ever before her. Her soul sank
within her at the thought of failure, but she rallied her
courage again, for it could not be possible that they would
refuse to hear her ; and surely she could convince them all
that her husband was innocent. 'But what if her courage
should fail when she comes to confront the august assemblage of judges. Then how will it go with her cause ?'
She cast the thought from her ere it was half formed. How
can she falter when her husband's life is at stake ? No,
no ; she could face judges and justices, kings and courtiers
—yea, the assembled world, to plead for her innocent husband.

Woman's heart is fearless when actuated by love, and a
consciousness of right. She rises from her modest reserve
and natural timidity to the sublime heights of guardian and
defender of her heart's cherished treasures.

On her return home Mrs. Bunyan called at neighbor
Harrow's to spend a few moments in rest, and to get his
advice as to the best way of proceeding in the execution of
her undertaking. The old man was not at home, having
gone out among the neighbors to see what could be done to

replenish the almost exhausted supplies of the destitute family. 'God suffereth not his children to want,' Mrs. Bunyan said to herself, as 'Goody Harrow' replied to her interrogation respecting her husband, and silently the tears of grateful thankfulness gathered in her eyes and rolled down her face.

'What makes you cry, sister Bunyan? Don't it fare so well with you these days? You mustn't give up. God is faithful.'

The words which the good old woman intended for consolation only served to call up fresh tears. The fountain was full, ready to overflow; only the touch of one emotion to trouble the waters, and they gushed forth abundantly. The weeping woman could make no answer. Little Joseph, with childish wonder and sympathy, clung closely to his mother.

'What makes you cry so, sister Bunyan?' said the kind old woman in her plain, blunt style. 'Is brother Bunyan sick? or are they going to do anything with him? You mustn't distress yourself so. These things will all come right after awhile. All the followers of Jesus must have their troubles and trials here below. Evil men will torment and persecute them, and say all manner of evil against them. Didn't he tell us so? Didn't Jesus say it? It is our inheritance in the wilderness world, sister Bunyan, and we have to take it whether we want it or not. It's mighty hard to bear it when we know that wicked men do wrong us so, and that, too, under the cloak of religion. It's bad, it's bad, sister Bunyan, but we must bear it like good soldiers. God himself will bring it to an end after a while. He won't suffer the wicked to go unpunished; for the wickedness of the wicked shall come to an end. This is what David, that good old man, said, sister Bunyan, and can't you believe it? Things were sometimes so dark around him that he could see no way of escape, but God always opened up a way, and he walked through all his troubles leaning on the arm of the Lord. Can't you do like David, sister Bunyan?'

'Oh I am sore distressed, sister Harrow, to see my husband wasting away in that cold, damp prison, but I was not crying for that. I was thinking how kind God is to me and my poor little ones, always to provide something for us to eat. He has never left us to suffer yet. He always raises up some friend to help us even in the darkest moment. It was the thought of his goodness that overcame me, and I could not hide my feelings.'

'The seed of the righteous shall never beg bread, sister Bunyan. Don't David tell us that? and don't he say, too, "Cast thy burden upon the Lord and he shall sustain thee, he shall never suffer the righteous to be moved?" Ah, I tell you, sister Bunyan, these have been sweet words to me—like manna in the wilderness. Often, sister Bunyan, I have borne my burden here on this poor heart'—and as she spoke the good old woman placed her hand upon her bosom and turned her eyes trustingly to heaven—'until I was forced down to the very earth. It seemed to me that I couldn't find comfort anywhere. I'd go to preaching, and I'd talk to my old man, and I'd study about my troubles, but it all didn't do any good—the trouble was still here, and I'd go on, day by day, bearing the burden. I couldn't do anything but to ask Jesus to give me his grace to bear it, and when it was his will to give peace to my poor troubled soul. And I tell you, sister Bunyan, when the right time came he did give me peace, yes, and joy too. He took away my heavy load, and left me as light as a feather. Yes, sister Bunyan, Jesus will do it for us, but we must wait his own good time. Blessed Master, thou wilt not forget thy poor distressed servants. Thou wilt hear their cries and bring them out of all their troubles! Trust him, sister Bunyan, trust him; he will deliver you out of six troubles, and in seven he won't forsake you. Hasn't he always been kind to you?'

The weeping woman hesitated to reply. She scarce knew how to answer. If she looked at one side of the picture it was very dark, but if at the other she could see all along her way the hand of God stretched forth towards her in unceasing love and mercy. The words of the good old faithful servant of Jesus had fallen soothingly upon her wounded soul, and she felt comforted.

'I could bear all my trials, sister Harrow,' she replied after a pause in which she partially subdued her emotion and wiped the tears from her face, 'if my dear husband was not dying in that miserable cell. I could get along with my own trouble if I did not know that he was suffering. But it almost breaks my heart to see him wasting away as he is, and I do not know that he will ever be released.'

The poor wife was again overcome by the thought of her husband's sufferings, and she burst into tears.

'It's a mighty hard trial, sister Bunyan. I know it is, and my heart feels for you. You must bear it as well as you can. It can't be helped. God has some purpose in it. He will glorify his own great name in brother Bunyan's trials. I am sure of that—I know it is his own work, and he just suffers evil men to have their way for a little time to show his power, and he'll cut them off suddenly, and that without remedy. You needn't give yourself any trouble about the end of all these things. God will make it straight after a while. All you've got to do is to go along and do what's right and look to Jesus. He'll work it out in his own good time, and then you'll see it is all as clear as the shining sun. Just have patience and trust to our blessed Master, he'll take care of you and it.'

'But I must do something to try and get my husband out of that dreadful dungeon. He cannot live if he stays there.'

'Oh, yes; if you could do anything, sister Bunyan, it would be well enough. But what can you do, poor woman? They won't listen to you, these men here at Bedford.'

'I have been thinking of going to London, sister Harrow, to see if I cannot be heard there. My husband has written out this paper which I have in my hand. It is his petition, and I am going to take it with me and get it handed to the king or to the lords.'

'You going to London, sister Bunyan?' exclaimed the old woman, almost rising from the settee on which she had been seated during the conversation. 'You go to London by yourself? Why, what will you do when you get there? Why, you'll be lost I tell you in that great big city. They tell me it is a world in itself, and you'll never find your way to the king and the great men.'

'I think I shall be able to do something, sister Harrow; if I can do anything I must. I cannot see my husband suffering as he is without making some attempt to get him out of that horrid place. My heart is wrung to see him pining in that narrow cell when I know he has done nothing sinful in the sight of God or man. I can't understand—it's very, very, dark.'

'And are you going to London sure enough, sister Bunyan?' asked the old lady in surprise. She had never in all her life been so far from home, and the idea of a lone woman going to London to present a petition for her husband's life before the king and the lords filled the honest soul of the poor old woman with great consternation. 'Why, won't you be afraid, sister Bunyan?' she added, as she drew her settee nearer the weeping woman. 'And how will you go?'

'It was to find this out that I came by to see brother Harrow. I thought he could tell me. Mr. Bunyan said he would arrange the matter for me, and help me to get off.

'To be sure he will, sister Bunyan. My good man will help you all he can if you must go. And I think you ought to if you can do any good. How long before you will start?'

'I must go next week. The assizes begin the week after next, and I want to be in time.'

'And who will go with you to look after you, sister Bunyan, and what will you do when you get there? Oh, me, it is a great undertaking for you. But it is for your good husband, and you ought to do it. May the Lord help you on your way. He can bring you off in safety.'

'Nobody will go with me, and I don't know how I shall go. When I get there I am going to stay with an old friend of my husband, a Mr. Strudwick, on Snow Hill.'

'Well, sister Bunyan, I hope you will get your wish. I pray that God will go with you and watch over you, and make the king and the great men see their wickedness, that their hearts may be opened to do what's right. Poor sinful creatures, how will they be able to stand at the last day?'

'The poor undone creatures! Oh, 'tis dreadful, sister Bunyan, to think of the everlasting torments they must meet.'

'A fearful thing, sister Harrow. May the Lord, in his infinite mercy, give them repentance before they die. They have imprisoned my husband and left me a widow and my children fatherless, and for all this I believe God himself will punish them in this world; but I have to pray that he will open their eyes before it is everlastingly too late, and give them to repent the wickedness of their hearts that they may be saved. But I must be getting home; it is getting late and the children are by themselves. Tell your good man I would like to see him and get his advice.'

'Yes, he will be over to see you to-morrow. He told me before he went away that he was going to your house to-morrow to carry you some things. Now don't be troubled about this thing, sister Bunyan, it will all work together for good. Only trust God, he won't deceive you. He'll make you triumph over all your enemies, for he has a strong arm, and you know, sister Bunyan, none can hinder him. I hope God will be with you on your way, and give you sweet consolation, and give you strength to go before the king and the great men, and that he will incline their hearts to grant you your request. Keep in good spirits, Jesus is your friend. I will come over to-morrow with my old man, and when you go down to London you must leave the children with me.'

The afflicted wife pressed the hand of the kind old woman in grateful assent, and departed. Little Joseph clung closely to his mother. The conversation between his mother and Goody Harrow had confused and frightened him. He could not unravel it. He understood that his mother was going to London, which seemed to him a most wonderful thing, and that, too, to see the king. He could scarcely credit his own ears when he heard this—his mother going to see the king, that great man, whom his childish imagination had pictured so far above all other men, and whom his untaught veneration had made an object of idolatrous worship. He could not understand it. It was something about his father and the gaol, and what it all meant was beyond his comprehension. So he walked along silently beside his mother, pondering over all he had heard, and trying, with all the reasoning powers of his little mind, to overcome all difficulties, and make the different parts of the story harmonize with each other. He wanted to tell it to Sarah when he got home, but he wished first to understand it well himself. He longed to ask his mother all about it, but, with that intuition which children oftentimes possess, he saw clearly that his mother's mind was deeply occupied; so he walked quietly along, with his thoughtful eyes fixed on the ground, trying to solve his difficult problem. Suddenly he looked up into his mother's face and asked:

'Mother, are you going to see the king?'

'I do not know, Joseph, whether I shall see him or not,' was his mother's abstracted reply.

He was again silent for some moments more. But he could not satisfy himself, and his curiosity must be gratified, so he seized his mother's hand, as it hung lifeless at her side, and asked:

'Mother, mother, will they let father out of that old dark dungeon?'

'Who, Joseph?'

'Why them big men in London that you are going to see. Will they let father out of gaol? I do hope they will.'

'I cannot tell whether they will or not, Joseph,' answered the mother, pursuing her train of thought.

'Well, you are going to ask them when you go to London, ain't you, mother?'

'Yes, Joseph. They had no right to put your father in gaol, and I think they ought to let him out that he may come home to see us.'

'I think so, too, mother. Father didn't do anything bad, did he, mother?'

'No, Joseph. Your father did not do anything to be put in prison for. Bad men put him there without a cause.'

'But the big men in London will let him out when you ask them, won't they, mother? and then father will come home and stay with us like he used to do. He won't preach any more either, and then they can't put him in the ugly old gaol again.'

The mother knew she could not explain the causes of doubt respecting the father's releasement so that the child could understand, and so she made no answer. Joseph's questions had brought before her mind with great vividness the difficulties of her proposed undertaking. She pictured herself in the streets of London, a lone, unprotected woman, whose name could have no influence upon those who heard it, except to bring down contempt and insolence upon her own head. If her husband was known at all, it was as John Bunyan, in Bedford gaol for disobedience to the laws of the land. When she thought of the judges, with their stern faces, and the laughs, and jeers, and gibes of those who might hear her business, she shuddered. And then, horrid picture! there came up to her mind the refusal of her petition, while the judges turned a cold look upon her, and unfeeling ones stood by, laughing at her anguish and disappointment.

Her tears began again to flow as this most fearful finale presented itself to her overtaxed mind; but she wiped them hastily away, and choked down her emotion. She was almost home, and she did not wish to appear unusually troubled before the sensitive child, whom she knew awaited her with eager, anxious heart.

After the evening meal was over, the two youngest children were sent out to play, and Mrs. Bunyan then unfolded to Mary the plan before her, and the probable result of the undertaking.

'Oh if dear father could get out of that frightful gaol and come home to us once more, how glad I would be, mother!' and the poor blind child turned her darkened eyes towards her mother with such an expression of solicitude on her sweet, sad face, as made the mother's heart ache.

'Do you think they will let him out, mother?'

'I cannot tell, Mary. God will attend to that. I must do what is my duty in the case, and leave the result with him. If it is his will he shall be set at liberty, it will be done. But if he sees fit to keep your father in prison, we must try to submit, and say, ' Not our will, but thine, oh, Lord, be done ; "' and the poor woman heaved a deep long-drawn sigh, which told to Mary's heart how faintly the mother was able to pray the dying Saviour's words.

How often we utter with our lips truths which the heart has not yet been made subject to. We desire to feel, we pray to feel that submission which our lips utter, but ' grace sufficient' has not yet been given, and, while the words flow, the heart beats in fearful apprehension.

'I cannot tell, my child, how this matter will end,' resumed the mother after a pause, ' but it is our only hope, and if God shall bless my efforts your father will be pardoned. If not—' and she shook her head despairingly, as the unfinished sentence died on her quivering lips.

While the mother and Mary had been discussing the matter on the front stoop, Joseph, with all the intensity of his nature assisted by his excited imagination, had been pouring into the ear of little Sarah his wonderful story of his mother's intended journey to London. The poor little Sarah caught her brother's enthusiasm, and her reddened cheek and agitated manner, as she earnestly listened to his strange words, fully betrayed the excitement and fear of her timid heart. And when Thomas came home bringing up the cow, the little ones took him aside and disclosed to him the wonderful tale.

'Twas a night of silent sorrow in the little homestead at Elstow. Burdened hearts dared not speak their agony, and, while silence sealed the lips, the fountain swelled higher and higher its bitter waters. Oh, God, thou alone canst be a father to these fatherless ones, a stay to their widowed mother's heart. Speak some words of consolation to her soul, and protect the children of thy servant. They are in thy hand. Oh, lead them gently! They are lambs of thy fold, let not the enemy devour.

The mother knelt with her four helpless ones round the deserted hearth-stone, over which dark, deep shadows brooded! Shall these shadows ever be supplanted by the light of happiness, or shall they deepen—deepen—until the darkness becomes settled, rayless gloom? God alone knows. The issues are in his hands. He worketh, and none can hinder; he speaketh, and it is done! And as the stricken soul of the desolate wife poured forth her simple,

fervent petition, she realised in all its fearful sublimity
that God 'doeth according to his will in the army of
heaven, and among the inhabitants of the earth, and none
can stay his hand, or say unto him, 'What doest thou?'
By faith having triumphed over the fear and anxiety of
time, she laid hold on the promises of eternal life, and was
enabled to feed on the hidden manna of God's own precious
word, realising that he who had called her to follow him
would guide and protect her the journey through.

> 'Alas! a deeper test of faith
> Than prison cell, or martyr's stake,
> The soft abasing watchfulness
> Of silent prayer may make.'

The next day, as was promised, neighbor Harrow came
to present the little stores he had gathered together from
sympathising friends, and to see about preparations for the
journey to London. It was decided that Mrs. Bunyan
should go in a public conveyance, as being the speediest
and most prudent way of travelling. She was to leave on
the following Monday, so that, if possible, she might return
to her little family before the Sabbath day. The old man
guaranteed that she should be furnished with every thing
necessary, and, as he took her by the hand to bid her good-
by, he recommended her to the care and guidance of God.
The few intervening days passed by. The wife made such
arrangements as the circumstances required at her hands.
The mission was one of fearful import. Upon its result
depended her weal or woe. She pondered the matter well.
Could she have seen her husband once more before leaving,
what a consolation this would have been, what strength
would it have imparted! But this was impossible. She
had just made him a visit, and she knew full well that the
gaoler would not admit her again for weeks to come. There
were many things respecting which she wished to advise
with her husband, many points upon which she needed his
instruction. But it was too late. She must entrust herself
to God, and go forward in the path of duty.

What will not a woman brave for the sake of an innocent
husband? — one that she knows and feels is innocent—
stands clear in the sight of God, however much persecuting
enemies may seek to destroy him, and to cast out his name
as evil. She will dare the highest heights, and pierce the
deepest depths—will bear contumely, reproach, the gibes
and sneers of fiends in human form—will remain firm and
immoveable when all else forsake, and trusting to God and

in the might of truth to prevail, will stand defender
of his rights till life itself shall end. This is woman's
love.

Monday came. The mother set out on her journey.
How sorrowfully her eyes rested on the dark, gloomy form
of the heavy gaol, as it stood there in its forbidding loneliness on the old bridge. Her heart's treasure was there
sealed in from her sight by heavy time-stained stones and
massive bars of iron. The evil spirit of persecution had
torn him from her bosom. The evil spirit of persecution, under the borrowed cloak of religion, had
placed him there, and there kept him in weary chains
from day to day, while his strength and manhood wasted
fast away.

Her feelings as she journeyed on we will not make an
attempt to describe. No words of ours could do them
justice. Neither could those who have never been called to
pass through the deep waters of persecution for righteousness' sake understand them, though they were portrayed in
characters of living light. There are certain bitter expe-
riences of the heart which no language can speak—a
sorrow which no tongue can describe—it fills the soul,
but seals the lips. It wastes its very life, but oh, how
silently !

Owing to detentions, the journey, though only about
thirty miles, was not completed until the next day. About
noon of Tuesday the great city burst upon the view of the
daring wife. For a moment she shuddered with a feeling
of dread and wonder ; but it was only for a moment. ' It
is for my husband that I brave all this,' she said to herself, ' and I must not falter now, and what I do must be
done quickly.'

She descends from the diligence, and, taking from her
bosom the petition written by her husband, with throbbing
heart she wends her way towards the House of Lords. She
prays as she walks along that God himself will interfere
for her, and grant her success. On, on, she bends her steps,
inquiring as she goes, until at last the magnificent
building, wherein are assembled the nobility and wealth of
England, bursts upon her view. She stops suddenly, overcome by a fearful feeling of apprehension. How shall she
ever be able to make known her desires ? ' God will open up
a way for me,' she says to herself as she again moves on.
' I go to plead for his poor innocent persecuted servant, and
he will give me strength according to my trials.' As she
was approaching the door of the House of Lords, a noble-

man, with kind, benignant face, perceived her, and thus accosted her:

'My poor woman, what is your desire? Have you any business to be attended to?'

Her heart revived as she heard the gentle words and remarked the compassionate expression of the nobleman's face, and presenting to him the petition which she held in her hand, she said:

'I have come, my lord, to see if I can get my husband's liberty. He has been falsely accused and thrown into prison, and I have come to the city to see if he cannot be set free.'

'And this is your petition, is it, my woman? Who wrote it for you?'

'My husband himself did, my lord; he is a preacher, as you will see from that, and they have thrown him into prison because he will not promise to quit preaching.'

'Well, well, we must look into this matter. Come along with me, and I will see what can be done for you;' and Lord Barkwood passed through the doorway, followed by the trembling steps of the faithful wife.

He motioned her to a stand, where she remained in fearful suspense, while he presented her petition to various members of the House, and spoke with them respecting it.

'*We* cannot release him,' each replied. 'The matter must be handed over to the *Judges* at the coming Assizes, and they must decide upon the case.' The kind-hearted lord felt this was too true. It was not a part of their business, and they could take no action upon it, except to commit it to the Judges, which was done.

He reached her as she stood anxiously watching every movement and expression, and explained to her their inability to decide the matter.

She was sorely disappointed, and her whole frame shook tremulously. The great man spoke kindly to her. 'They could not,' he said, 'release him.' He advised her how to proceed at the coming Assizes, which were to take place in Bedford the following week, and, wishing her success, he pointed her to the door and left her.

And thus all her expectations were blasted. The House of Lords could not give liberty to her husband, and her journey to London had proved fruitless. Yet there was the shadow of hope left her. She was not altogether overwhelmed in despair. It might be that the Judges at the Assizes would hear her petition. She would hasten to communicate this intelligence to her husband. But how was she to get out of the city? How should she find the diligence? She met a boy in the street of whom she inquired. He promised to show her to the place for a shilling. On they went through the streets, until they reached an inn, which was the starting-point of the Bedford mail. The diligence was waiting at the door. She stepped into it, and in a few minutes was on her way from the great city, hurrying back to bear the sad tidings of her failure to her husband and children.

Bunyan's was not a heart to despair ; and when he heard from his blind child the result of his wife's visit to London, he determined within himself to again make an effort through his wife to obtain his liberty. He wrote out several petitions, which she was to present to Judge Hale and the Justices during the following week, when the Assizes would be in session in Bedford, and sent them to her, with all necessary instructions, by the hand of his daughter.

CHAPTER X.

THE WIFE BEFORE JUDGE HALE AND THE JUSTICES.

It is the second day· of the Assize Court. The Audience Chamber is filled to overflowing. Judge Hale, in his robes magisterial, sits in silent dignity to receive petitions and hear the pleadings of the petitioners. There is a pause in the business of the Assizes, and a woman, clad in a coarse black dress, with a cap of snow white shading her pale, sad face, rises from the crowd at the back of the room, and passes up the aisle with dignified but modest step. She approaches the Lord Chief Justice and presents a petition. Her hand trembles and her cheek flushes, yet she betrays no farther emotion, as the Justice at the right rises, and, receiving her petition, hands it to Judge Hale. The Judge reads it ; remains silent for a moment ; then, turning very mildly upon her, he says :

' My poor woman, I will do the best good for you and your husband that I can, but I fear that I can do none.'

He extends to her her petition, telling her that he will look at it again. Her heart throbs, her head bows, tears gather in her eyes, and a sigh such as only the sorely disappointed heart can know escapes her bosom. An old man, with trembling step, comes forward, holding in his hand a paper. She steps aside, and is lost amid the crowd.

A handsome equipage halts in front of the Swan Chamber. On its luxurious cushions reclines a Judge, in all the nonchalance of undisturbed complacency. He knows nothing of the deep griefs that rend the human bosom, and he decides the weal or woe of bursting hearts with as much indifference as a judge at a cattle show determines the relative grades of the sleek dumb brutes. The footman is in the act of opening the door, when a pale woman, in the garb of mourning, steps to the carriage and hands him a paper. With a look of annoyance at being thus detained, Judge Twisdon glances over the petition, and, turning upon her with an angry look, 'snaps her off,' telling her that her husband is a *convicted* person, and cannot be released unless he will promise to preach no more. She *cannot promise this for him*, so she receives again the petition, and turns away with sorrowful heart, while the Judge, with an air of pompous pride, passes into the hall, and seats himself in his chair of state.

Is justice clean gone for ever? Has the Lord forgotten righteousness, that his humble follower should thus be turned aside to weep in bitter anguish, while the heartless wretch who tramples on the rights of bleeding, suffering humanity, steps on high, followed by the admiring gaze of obsequious thousands? Wait yet a little while and see. The wicked shall be cut off suddenly, and that without remedy. He shall not live out half his days. But the righteous shall flourish.

'Cast down but not destroyed,' the faithful wife determined to make another attempt to procure her husband's liberty. Directing a silent, fervent prayer to God for strength and wisdom, with faltering step and trembling heart she again entered the court-room, and presented her petition to Judge Hale as he sat upon the bench. He recognized her as the pale, sad supplicant of the previous day. His heart was moved, and, as he looked kindly upon her, and spoke a few words of encouragement, her soul beat high with hope and gratitude.

'God had at last heard her prayer, and was about to answer her fervent requests in granting to her the liberty of her husband.' Oh, how light seemed all her previous troubles! They were all swallowed up in the joy of the present moment. All she had endured, all she had suffered, was not worthy to be compared with her present happiness. She trembled almost to falling with the intensity of her feelings.

But stop! a Justice steps forward and speaks to the Judge. Her eager ear catches the words :

'He is a troublesome fellow, your lordship, and ought not to be set at liberty. Moreover, he was convicted in court, and is a hot spirited fellow that will do harm, and ought to be kept in gaol.'

The Judge paused for a moment and looked upon the floor. It was a moment of heart-rending suspense to the unfortunate wife. What could be his decision? What—oh—what?

He turned his eyes pityingly upon her, handed her her petition, and waved her from him. She staggered to the door, and passed out. Not a word escaped her lips ; but those words of the Psalmist were in her heart ; 'Why standest thou afar off, oh Lord? Why hidest thou thyself in times of trouble? The wicked in his pride doth persecute the poor. Let them be taken in the devices they have imagined.'

'They that wait upon the Lord shall renew their strength ; they shall mount up with wings as eagles ; they shall run and not be weary, and they shall walk and not faint.' How fully did the faithful wife realise the truth of this most glorious promise of the Lord God of Israel, as with trembling step she pressed her way along the aisle, while eager, curious eyes were riveted upon her, to present, for the third time, her petition for her husband's release.

The Swan Chamber was crowded—judges, justices, and gentry were there. But she feared neither the frown of the one, nor the contemptuous gaze of the other. Unfalteringly she walked the crowded room, until she stood before the Judge and Justices. Directing herself to Judge Hale, she said :

'My lord, I make bold to come again to your lordship to know what may be done with my husband.'

All eyes were fixed upon her as she spoke, and eager ears bent forward from every part of that large audience to catch her words. There she stood, a poor, frail woman, pleading before the assembled dignity of the realm, for the life of her husband. Was ever sight more sublime—was ever a scene more touching?

The Judge turned upon her. He hesitated, then answered in a tone of mingled confusion and decision :

' Woman, I told thee before I could do thee no good. They have taken for a *conviction* what thy husband spoke at the sessions, and, unless there be something done to *undo* that, I can do thee no good.'

Hear her as she replies :

' My lord, he is *unlawfully* kept in prison : they clapped him in prison before there were any proclamations against the meetings. The indictment also is *false*. Besides they never asked him whether he was guilty or no. Neither did he confess the indictment.'

' He was lawfully convicted, woman,' interfered one of the Judges, chafing at her words.

She turned a look upon him. He was one whom she did not know. Addressing Judge Hale, she replied, with the true courage of a noble soul :

' My lord, it is false ! For when they said to him, " Do you confess the indictment ? " he said only this, that he had been at several meetings, both where there was preaching the word and prayer, and that they had God's presence among them.'

' What, woman, do you think we can do as we list ? ' interfered Judge Twisdon, in a loud, angry tone. ' Your husband is a breaker of the peace, and is convicted by the law.'

' Bring the statute book,' demanded Judge Hale, ' and we will see for ourselves.'

' He was not *lawfully convicted*, my lord,' said the brave woman, as she looked upon Judge Twisdon.

' He was lawfully convicted,' interrupted Judge Chester, raving with madness that his act (his was one of the five red letter names that sent Bunyan to prison) and his word should be called in question.

' It is false,' she said calmly, ' it was but a word of discourse that they took for a conviction.'

' It is recorded, woman ; it is recorded, I tell you,' vociferated Chester, as if he would silence her by the power of his voice if he could not by argument.

' It is false if it is,' and she looked him unflinchingly in the face.

' He is *convicted* and it is *recorded*,' repeated Chester. ' What more do you want ? '

' My lord,' said the fearless wife to Judge Hale, ' I was a little while since in London to see if I could get my husband's liberty, and there I spoke with my lord Barkwood, one of the House of Lords, to whom I delivered a petition, who took it from me and presented it to some of the rest of the House of Lords, for my husband's releasement, who, when they had seen it, they said that *they* could not *release* him, but *committed* his releasement to the Judges at the next Assizes.   This *he* told me, and now I am come to you to see if anything can be done in this business, and *you* give neither releasement nor relief.'

The Judge made no answer.

'He is convicted and it is recorded,' reiterated the infuriated Chester.

'If it be it is false,' repeated the heroic woman.

'He is a *pestilent* fellow, my lord.   There is not such a fellow in the country,' exclaims Chester turning to Judge Hale.

'Will your husband leave off preaching, woman?   If he will do so, send for him, and let him answer here for himself,' spake out Judge Twisdon, almost as much exasperated as was Chester.

'My lord,' the Christian woman said, 'my husband *dares* not leave preaching as long as he can speak.'

'See here!   see here!' vociferates Twisdon, rising from his seat, and striking the bench with his clenched fist, 'why should we talk any more about such a fellow?   Must *he* do what he *lists?*   He is a breaker of the peace.'

The brave woman noticed him not.   Keeping her eyes steadily fixed upon Judge Hale, she said:

'My husband desires to live peaceably and to follow his calling, that his family may be maintained.   Moreover, my lord, I have *four small children* that cannot help themselves, and one of them is *blind*, and we have nothing to live upon but the charity of good people.'

The eyes of the Judge bent in pity upon her.

'Hast thou four children?' he said kindly.   'Thou art but a young woman to have four children.'

'I am but mother-in-law to them, my lord, not having been married to him yet two full years.   Indeed, I was with child when my husband was first apprehended, but being young and unaccustomed to such things, I, being *smayed* at the news, fell into labor, and so continued for eight days, and then was delivered, but my child died.'

'*Alas, poor woman!*' said the kind Judge, as she finished her touching story.

'You make poverty your cloak, woman,' broke in Twisdon, 'and I hear your husband is better maintained by running up and down a-preaching than by following his calling.'

'What is his calling?' asked Judge Hale of her.

'A *tinker*, my lord, a *tinker*,' answered some one standing by.

'Yes, my lord, and because he is a tinker, and a poor man, he is despised and cannot have justice.'

'Since it is thus, my poor woman,' said the Judge mildly, 'that they have taken what thy husband spake for conviction, thou must either apply thyself to the king, or sue out his pardon, or get a writ of error.'

At the mention of a writ of error, Chester chafed, and was highly offended, and exclaimed:

'This man will preach, my lord, and do what he pleases.'

'He preaches nothing but the word of God,' fearlessly spoke out the true wife.

'He preach the word of God!' repeated Twisdon, with a bitter sneer, turning towards her as if he would have struck her, 'he runs up and down the country and does harm.'

'No, my lord, it is not so; God hath owned him and done much good by him.'

'God!' repeated Twisdon sneeringly, 'his doctrine is the doctrine of the devil.'

'My lord,' she said, 'when the righteous Judge shall appear, it will be known that his doctrine is not the doctrine of the devil.'

'Do not mind her, Judge, but send her away,' exclaimed Twisdon, seeing that he could not intimidate her.

'I am sorry, my poor woman, that I can do thee no good,' said Judge Hale compassionately. 'Thou must do one of these three things aforesaid, namely, either apply thyself to the king, or sue out his pardon, or get a writ of error;—but a *writ of error* will be cheapest.'

At the second mention of a writ of error, Chester was in a great rage, and took off his hat and scratched his head for anger.

'Though I was somewhat *timorous* at my first entrance into the Chamber,' says Mrs. Bunyan in her account of this most wonderful and heroic defence of her husband, 'yet before I went out I could not but break forth into tears, not so much because they were so hard-hearted against me and my husband, but to think what a *sad account* such poor creatures will have to give at the coming of the Lord, when they shall there answer for all things whatsoever they have done in the body, whether it be good or whether it be bad.

'So, when I departed from them, the book of statutes was brought, but what they said of it I know nothing at all, neither did I hear any more from them.'

CHAPTER XI.

DISAPPOINTMENT.

'HATH God forgotten to be merciful? hath He in anger shut up his tender mercies?'

The prisoner sat, his head low bent upon his bosom. He was struggling with great, weighty thoughts, too deep for him. He had read the truths and promises of God's holy book; he had meditated thereon; he had prayed in the burning words of the forsaken Son of God—'Father, if it be possible, let this cup pass from me,'——'yet not my will, but thine be done.' Oh, how he had wrestled with God! With what consuming desire had he groaned forth his supplications! He read of the purposes of God, fixed and immutable. 'He doeth all things according to the counsel of his own will, and none can hinder.' And his mind kept reaching—reaching—after the infinite, until he found himself lost amid the grandeur and sublimity of his thoughts.

'Who can by searching find out God?' 'As the heavens are higher than the earth, so are my ways higher than your ways, and my thoughts than your thoughts.'

Mrs. Bunyan was pleading before the Judges while her husband was thus communing with the Infinite.

But the scene is ended, she has been in the presence-chamber. Threading her way along the streets, she reached the bridge, passed the outer door, and stood within the narrow enclosure. Poor disappointed woman. Her hair, escaped from the plain white cap, fell loosely over her face, swollen with weeping, and bearing the plain, deep lines of sorrow—that sorrow, which, with cold iron hand, writes itself upon the hopeless heart, and traces itself in time-defying characters on the despairing countenance. She passed her hand slowly over her throbbing brow, as if to wipe out the painful recollection of her cruel repulse. Her brain reeled; her limbs trembled. She paused, and looked irresolutely towards the narrow door, with its heavy iron gates.

She had stood before the assembled multitude, judges, justices, nobility, and gentry; and her courage had never forsaken her. Prying looks had peered with disgusting curiosity into her still calm face, but her eye had quailed not under their insulting gaze. Taunts and sneers had been heaped upon her as she passed along the aisle of that crowded court-room, but her heart, nerved by undying love to her husband, and full consciousness of his innocence, had never for a moment feared, neither had her step faltered. With truth and right shielding her as a helmet, what had she to fear ?

But her petition had been disregarded ; .her entreaties set at naught ; her earnest supplication been made the butt of ridicule and laughter, and while pride and wickedness sat exalted on high, she, the worn and sorrowing wife, follower of the suffering Jesus, had been spurned aside as unworthy of consideration.

How could she proceed ? How could she tell her husband that all her endeavors had been abortive ? What could she say to him under this grievous disappointment that could give consolation ? Her own heart was without a ray of hope. She could see nothing but darkness whichever way she turned. She felt with David when he said, ' Reproach hath broken my heart, and I am full of heaviness. And I looked for some to take pity, but there was none ; and for comforters, but I found none.' And she stood and gazed wildly around, scarce knowing what she did. The assistant turnkey, as he threw wide open the grating door, turned to her and bade her enter. She mechanically obeyed his command.

She trod the dark and narrow passage with unsteady step. What a world of agony there was pent up in that throbbing heart! She paused a moment before reaching the cell door of her husband to gain composure. She must nerve herself to meet him. She could not add to the trials of his heart by manifesting her own. She adjusted her hair beneath her cap, and folded her neckerchief. Silently she breathed a prayer for divine assistance. She endeavored to look calm, that her appearance might not break the intelligence of her defeat too suddenly to him she loved.

The turnkey opened the narrow door to the cell and stepped aside that she might enter. The light of evening came in through the small window that overlooked the river, and fell in sombre shade on the bare walls and the meagre couch of the prisoner. In one corner of the cell, by the low settee, knelt Bunyan, his Bible beside him.

He arose, and his eye, accustomed to the dim light of his cell, took in at a moment's glance the sad, pale countenance of his wife, and in it he read enough to fill him with apprehension.

She seated herself on the couch. He sat beside her.

For a few moments not a word was spoken. Thoughts and fears could not voice themselves in words. The prisoner looked his wife steadily in the face to read the result of her effort. He saw she had been unsuccessful; disappointment and grief had worn themselves in upon that full countenance in ineffaceable lines.

At length Bunyan turned to his wife and said :

'I fear, my Elizabeth, it has gone ill with your plea. I see it in your face. My persecutors and they that hate me are set in their hearts to ruin me. The Lord forgive them ; they know not what they do. But tell me, why did they refuse to hear you ? Tell me all, Elizabeth, all.'

The poor heart-broken woman essayed to answer her husband's question; but all she could answer was :

'I tried, my husband, to persuade them to send for you, but they would not.'

'And what did they say, when you asked them to let me be sent for?'

'Some answered one thing, and some another. One said that you were a pestilent fellow ; another said that you were a breaker of the peace. Some said that you were lawfully convicted, and others that you run up and down and do harm.'

'And won't they grant my release ?'

She threw her arms about his neck and leaning on his bosom sobbed out, 'The Lord is against us, my husband, and the rulers hearts' are stone. They heeded not my petition, but turned cruelly from me. They will not let you go. And you must die here in this cold dark prison, away from me and the children.' And the despairing wife clung more closely to her husband and wept most sorely.

Ah, what a sad defeat to the prisoner ! He had hoped, had prayed ; but there was no longer any hope : yet he could still pray, and his full soul found utterance in the following sublime petition :

'Lord, thou hast been our dwelling place in all generations. Before the mountains were brought forth, or ever thou hadst formed the earth and the world, even from everlasting to everlasting, thou art God. Save me, oh God, for the waters are come into my soul. I sink deep in mire where there is no standing. I am come into deep waters where the floods overwhelm me. They that hate me without a cause are more than the hairs of mine head ; they that would destroy me, being mine enemies wrongfully, are mighty. Draw nigh unto my soul and redeem it. Deliver me, because of mine enemies.

'My soul is among lions; and I lie even among them that are set on fire: even the sons of men whose teeth are spears and arrows, and their tongue a sharp sword. Reproach hath broken my heart, and I am full of heaviness; and I looked for some to take pity, and there was none; and for comforters, but I found none. They gave me also gall for meat, and to my thirst they gave me vinegar to drink. But I will cry unto thee, oh, God Most High, unto thee that performeth all things for me, and thou wilt send from heaven and save me from the reproach of him that would swallow me up. Deliver me, O God, from the workers of iniquity, and save me from bloody men, for they lie in wait for my soul. The mighty are gathered against me, but not for my transgression, nor for my sin, O God. Pour out thy indignation upon them, and let thy wrathful anger take hold upon them. But I am poor and needy; make haste unto me, O God; thou art my help and my deliverer. O Lord, make no tarrying, but help me. For my soul trusteth in thee.'

It was a fervent petition that the poor man uttered in the hopelessness of his bitter disappointment.

'But tell me, Elizabeth, did Judge Hale give you no encouragement? Surely he would not turn you away unanswered.'

'He said he could do me no good,' replied the still sobbing wife.

'And did he say that *nothing* could be done? surely there is some resource left me. It cannot be possible that I must die unjustly.'

'He told me that one of three things must be done, seeing that they had taken for a conviction what you spoke at the sessions.'

'And what are they, Elizabeth?' asked the prisoner eagerly.

'Either that I must apply myself to the king, or sue out your pardon, or get a writ of error.'

The prisoner heaved a long, deep groan. For the first time he realised that nothing could be done. He felt that death was just before him. From the inexorable decree, he saw no way of escape. The dealings of God with him were so mysterious, so deep, that for a moment he was staggered. His expectations had perished; his faith was eclipsed, and darkness, thick darkness, was round about him. He looked for help, and there was none, and he prayed for deliverance, but his way remained hedged up about him.

God sometimes leaves us, as it were, to ourselves, on

purpose to show us how weak we are. We devise and arrange, and fondly imagine that it will all be fulfilled according to our desires. Have we not purposed, and shall we be defeated? Ah, no! And as we stand gazing, the picture unfolds charmingly before our eyes. Not one mar or blemish anywhere to be seen. All is beautiful and bright as heart could wish. Then we admire the work of our own hands, and dwell with delight in the accomplishment of our own purposes. And we say to ourselves, now, surely, all will be well with me, I shall have the full desire of my eyes. Then our hearts begin to swell with pride; and we forget God. His name is on our lips, and his image is on our souls; but we pronounce the one coldly and the other is shut out from our view by the superstructure of our own hands. Then God, who is a jealous God, comes suddenly, and dashes out with a stroke the charms and fair proportions on which we so much delighted to dwell, and we hear his voice, 'Have I not said, "Thou shalt have no other God beside *me*?" " "Repent and turn yourselves from your idols, and turn away your faces from all your abominations, and worship *me* only." ' Then we are at our wits' ends; and we cry unto the Lord. And he saveth us from all our troubles.

Bunyan sat without speaking. He was stunned by his wife's information. Either of the three things proposed by the Lord Chief Justice seemed impracticable, and he felt to be a doomed man. Then came up before his mind thoughts of his suffering wife and children, and his little flock of humble believers through the country scattered for want of a shepherd.

Oh! how his soul was burdened in view of these things. He felt for a moment that God had withdrawn his presence from him, and he was left to himself to grope his way in darkness where there was no light.

'And am I to die a death of ignominy,' he exclaimed, 'or must I wear out my days in this narrow cell? O Lord, my times are in thy hands! Unto thee belongeth mercy, that thou mayest be feared.'

'Tell me all you have done, my Elizabeth, that I may see if there is any hope. Come, dry your tears. God will reveal himself a helper in our time of need,' he said consolingly to the weeping woman. 'Let us never doubt the God of Israel, our God, Elizabeth, for his promises are sure and steadfast, and he will have mercy and not sacrifice. His loving kindness endureth for ever, and his tender mercies are over all his children.'

Encouraged by the kind and confident tones of her husband, Mrs. Bunyan suppressed her tears, and entered upon the recital of her narrative. The prisoner watched her eagerly, and his heart swelled with emotion as she portrayed to him her repulses by the Judges, and her mental sufferings in consequence.

'And Chief Justice Hale did turn you away without hearing your petition?'

'The first time I went to him he told me he would do the best good for me and for you he could; but he feared he could do none. I then threw one of the petitions into Judge Twisdon's carriage, hoping he might be disposed to grant my request, and intercede with the Lord Chief Justice. But he frowned upon me, and snapt me up, and said, "you were a convicted person, and could not be set at liberty unless you would promise to preach no more," which I knew you would not do; so I took back my petition, and he did not notice me any more. I went a second time to Judge Hale—'

'And what did he do?' anxiously asked the prisoner.

'He read my paper, and looked at me. Then one of the Justices went up to his side and told him you were a troublesome fellow, and did not deserve to be set at liberty. Moreover, they said you were convicted in court, and was a hot-spirited fellow, that would do harm, and ought to be kept in gaol. After all this had been told him he turned upon me with pity in his face, and handed me back my petition, and motioned me away. I thought my heart would break, my husband, as I staggered out. But nobody cared for me.'

'God cared for you, my Elizabeth. He was watching over you for good. His hand is in this thing. We must wait until it shall please him to make crooked paths straight. I am glad they did not insult or ill-treat you.'

'But this is not all. I was determined to leave nothing undone, my husband, to effect your liberty: and although I had been twice repulsed, I resolved to go again and see if I could not move the heart of the Lord Chief Justice in your favor. And the next day of the Assizes I went. I prayed earnestly to God to speed me on my way, for I felt that I could not bear to be again refused. I went praying, and when I got before the Judge, I lifted up my heart in prayer, that he would look upon my petition with favor, and grant my plea. And I believe he would have done so, but Judge Twisdon said you were a troublesome fellow, and had been convicted, and that it was recorded against you.'

'The Lord help!' groaned the injured man.

Tears started afresh to the eyes of the disconsolate wife. She relied on the brave heart of her husband, and as long as his courage remained undaunted she felt strengthened. But just as soon as he gave way, her fears and doubts prevailed, and she was ready to give up all in despair.

'Go on, my Elizabeth, and tell me all,' he added after a minute's reflection. 'I would hear it all, and the Lord of grace give me strength to bear it. Did they give you any other reason for not putting me at liberty?'

'They said you were a breaker of the peace, and a pestilent fellow. Twisdon said you would run up and down the country and do harm: and that your doctrine was of the devil. They called you a tinker, my husband, and said you had better be following your calling than running up and down preaching. I told them because you were a tinker and a poor man that you were despised, and could not have justice done you; and that when the righteous Judge shall appear, it will then be known that your doctrine is not the doctrine of the devil. I also told them that God had owned you, and done much good by you.'

A sigh, long and deep, was the prisoner's only reply.

'I tried to move their hearts. I told them about my little children, and my poor, blind Mary; and that we have nothing to live upon but the charity of kind people. I told them you dared not to leave off preaching while you could speak. But Chester and Twisdon laughed at my words, and stirred up the Chief Justice against me. If they had kept silent, I believe I should have succeeded;' and the poor woman wept bitterly as she thought of all the cruel taunting and contradiction she had endured at the hands of the heartless Judges.

'Do not cry now, my Elizabeth; it is all over. The Lord has directed it according to his own pleasure, and it will work out for us an exceeding great reward, if we trust in him and remember his promises. "Vengeance is mine, I will repay," saith the Lord. "Our enemies shall be confounded and put to shame; and all they that persecute the children of the Most High God, shall be cut off suddenly, and that without remedy." Let us trust in the God of Israel, who brought his children up out of Egypt, and led them through the wilderness into the promised land. "He poureth contempt upon princes, and causeth them to wander in the wilderness where there is no way. Yet setteth he the poor on high from affliction, and maketh him families like a flock." We must not forget that he doeth all things according to the counsel of his own will, and he will accomplish his purposes in us and through us. We will not fear what man can do unto us, for the very hairs of our heads are numbered, and our enemies cannot go further than God sees is best for us. Let us trust him for all coming time, feeling confident that our grace will be sufficient to our day. The more he multiplies our trials and afflictions, the greater measures of his Holy Spirit will he impart to us; and if we are called to pass through the fire, even there we will praise him. Dry your tears, Elizabeth, and try to console yourself with his promises.'

' But, my husband, what will become of me and the children if you are taken from us, or left here to die in this miserable dungeon? Oh, we shall starve to death! There will be nobody to care for us when you are gone. It is so dreadful to think of, my husband. Our poor blind Mary; I am more distressed about her than any of the rest. She is so feeble now, and since you have come to this horrible gaol, she looks so sad. She is almost ready for the grave herself. Oh, it is so hard, so hard!'

' "I will be a father to the fatherless and the widow's stay." "I once was young, and now I am old, yet I have not seen the righteous forsaken, nor his seed begging bread. Trust in the Lord, and do good, and verily shalt thou inherit the land, and thy seed shall be fed." Our poor dear blind one will be taken care of, my Elizabeth, and none of you shall want. I desire to praise God in my death as well as in my life, and if it is his will that I shall go to the stake, and burn there for the glory of his cause, amen, I am in his hands. Let him do with me what seemeth to him best. Pray for an exceeding abundant share of grace, my poor wife, to help you along on your thorny way. Teach the children to look to God and to rely on him. And may our God bring them all to a knowledge of the truth as it is in Christ Jesus our Lord. It is a hard task, my poor Elizabeth; but God will be with you to direct and support you, and he can do much more for you and our little ones than I could. If he takes me from you and them, he will raise up some one in my stead to give them food and raiment. Go on, then, trusting in him, and do the best you can. It will all be well in the end. The psalmist tells us that light is sown for the righteous and gladness for the upright in heart, and we will not fear what man can do unto us; for though the earth be removed, and the mountains be carried in the midst of the sea, yet will we not fear, for the Lord is our light and our salvation; the Lord is the strength of our life.'

'But, it may be,' interposed the fond wife, 'that if you would give up preaching for a little while, just while these troublous times are upon us, you could go free, and then after awhile you could preach again. I cannot believe that God is going to chastise his children always. He will have mercy, and remember their cries and tears.'

It was a powerful appeal. The strong man wavered for a moment. Things would soon change, and then he could preach again. Would it not be best? Would it not be for the glory of God and the advancement of his cause on earth?

It was a moment of intense interest. What weighty consequences hung on the decision about to be made. 'Take up thy cross, take up thy cross, and follow me,' 'through evil as well as good report,' came thundering through his conscience. 'He that loveth his life shall lose it.' 'Whosoever shall be ashamed of me, and of my words, of him shall the Son of Man be ashamed when he shall come in his own glory, and in his Father's, and of the holy angels,' followed upon the heels of the other dreadful warning. 'It will be but a little while,' whispered Satan: 'your poor wife and children, what will they do without you?' 'Every one that hath forsaken wife or child for my name's sake shall receive a hundred fold, and shall inherit eternal life,' the Spirit answered.

A heavy step was heard approaching the cell.

A moment, and the turnkey opened the door, and told the wife that she must leave. Throwing her arms about her husband's neck, she bade him farewell amid sobs and tears.

'God be with you, my Elizabeth, and take care of you and my poor little ones.'

The door closed. The prisoner was alone with God. He prayed for grace, for direction, for patience, and strength to do his Master's will. He was 'passing through the valley of Baca.'

Could he make it a well?

CHAPTER XII.

FAITH TRIUMPHS.

THE grief-stricken wife passed the bridge and gained the field. Her heart was almost breaking. Scalding tears rolled down her cheeks. All hope was gone. The world seemed to her shrouded in gloom. There was no more light nor pity for her; nothing before her but darkness and despair. Oh, that she knew what to do. No earthly adviser, and forsaken by God!

She sat down by the hedge-row, for she could proceed no farther. It was a fearful hour to the anguished bosom of the disconsolate woman. Those who have been sorely tried can sympathise with her in her anguish. She tried to pray. Bewildered, she could not. Her head was reeling with the intensity of her emotion—her heart was faint from its burden of anguish. She arose and proceeded on her way. The winds fanned her parched cheek and dried up her scalding tears. Her frame trembled as onward she went— onward—onward—towards her forsaken home, and her fatherless children crying for bread.

As she was passing neighbor Harrow's the good old woman espied her, and, calling unto her, bade her come in and rest awhile. But she heeded her not.

' Go, David, and overtake sister Bunyan, and tell her to come in a little while. Run, child, or you won't catch her.'

'Mother says come back,' said the boy as he breathlessly gained her side. 'She wants you to come in and rest, and tell her about Mr. Bunyan.'

The poor woman had no will to resist, although she knew the hour was late, and her children were all alone. She turned round and went towards the house. Goody Harrow met her at the door, and in kindly tones asked her for her husband.

' There is no hope,' was all she could reply.

' Oh, I have been bearing a mighty burden here on this poor old heart, sister Bunyan, for these two or three days. I have felt that things were mighty perilous. But we must trust in God, sister Bunyan. That's all we can do. I have been down upon my knees praying for you and brother Bunyan most all this morning. My heart has been sore pressed. I can't tell what will come of it all. I have been thinking it all over, and I can't make much out of it, but I know God is in it. His hand is there, if we can't see it, and in his own good time won't he work it all out so clear? I tell you he will. We needn't fear God, sister Bunyan. He is faithful to the end. I have tried him and I know it. When my poor daughter died I thought it would have killed me. It seemed to me I could never be comforted. I prayed, and I cried, and I went to preaching, I did everything I could to get rid of my grief. But I couldn't do it. Then I began to feel rebellious against God. I thought he ought to give me his Holy Spirit to comfort me, and I got to be quite disconsolate and murmuring. And so I went on day by day, and found no peace. It appeared to me my heart would break, there was such a weight upon it. I could not tell what to do or what to say, and I thought nobody had trouble like to me. Oh, I tell you, it was a dark way and a heavy burden that I bore here on this heart, and I believed I should never in this world get over my sorrows. But after awhile, in his own good time, Jesus did speak peace and joy to my poor troubled soul. He took from me my dear old mother; and just before she died, she opened her eyes and looked upon us, and told us she saw my poor dear Martha in heaven with Jesus and the angels. She told us she was going up to meet them there, and we mustn't grieve after her. And she died. It gave me such joy to hear her talk as she did, that I could not shed a tear, but kept praising Jesus for his love and goodness. And I have been praising him ever since, to think of his wonderful love to me.

'I sometimes long to go to heaven, but I must wait patiently till my dear Saviour comes. He'll send for me when he gets ready. My mansion is not yet prepared for me. When he gets it done, he will send his messenger for me. A few more days of toil and tears, and then I shall enter into everlasting joy. Blessed Jesus, what hast thou done for me! My lips will continually praise thee.' And the dear old woman, as was her wont, placed her hand on her breast, and looked reverently up to heaven.

'Can't you trust God, sister Bunyan? He has never forsaken his children. Look at his people of old, how he led them and fed them. Whenever they wanted anything, it just came down from heaven. He let them have every good thing, and in his own time he brought them into the promised land. And so he will do with you, sister Bunyan? Now, can't you trust him?'

'I ought to trust him, sister Harrow, but the way before me is so dark, and I can't expect God to work any miracles for me.'

'Well, trust him, any how, sister Bunyan. I tell you he won't fail you. This thing will all come right after awhile. You'll live to see it, I expect, and if you die, you'll know all about it in heaven. God has something for your husband to do, and brother Bunyan will have to do it. He can't run round it, and he can't jump over it. It has to be done, and the more willingly you submit to his will the better it will be for you.'

'I know what you say is all true, sister Harrow, and I wish I could feel as you do about this thing. But I can't. I can't see through it at all. I am blind, blind!'

'The more need you have to rest on Jesus, sister Bunyan. He is our light in darkness, our strength in weakness, and our comfort in affliction. He is not going to give you a greater burden than you can bear. It may be very heavy; it may weigh you almost to the ground. You may stagger, and stumble, and get almost down. But he won't let you fall. Why, what does he say, sister Bunyan? "He will give his angels charge concerning thee, lest at any time thou dash thy foot against a stone." You must not give out by the way. His children must endure to the end. They must fight like good soldiers. Jesus is the Captain of our salvation, and he will bring us off conquerors over death, hell, and the grave. Love him, sister Bunyan. Trust him, sister Bunyan. We please our blessed Master when we believe what he has commanded us to do. Bear up under your burden; look to Jesus, and he will support and comfort you under all your trials.'

The precious words of the old woman fell soothingly on the ear of the despairing wife and mother. But she could not be entirely consoled.

'It is all true that you have said, sister Harrow, and I pray that God will enable me to bear up under all my troubles, and to praise his holy name for all his loving kindness and tender mercies towards me. But I am sorely grieved. I do not know what is before me. And if——'

' "Sufficient for the day is the evil thereof," sister Bunyan. You can't make things any better by grieving. They will have to come just as God has planned them.'

'My children will starve for bread if they keep my husband in that horrid prison. We have nothing much to eat now, and the neighbors are tired of being troubled with us.'

'You do wrong to talk so, sister Bunyan. It was only the day before yesterday I heard Brother Laman say that he intended to send you a good store of things soon. And he said, too, he was glad God had put it in his power to do something for you. And old sister Westerby said the same thing at meeting last week; and so did Deacon Drury, and many others spoke in the same way about you. They said it was a shame for them to keep your husband in prison, and let you and your little ones starve; but they would see you did not suffer for anything to eat as long as they had a mouthful for themselves. Don't you see now that God is raising up friends for you everywhere? You and your little ones will not be left to want.'

'God is good, indeed, sister Harrow, and I'll try to trust him, and never again to complain. I am a poor unthankful creature, always forgetting all the mercies God has favored me with. I must go home now, and when my soul is bowed down within me, try to feed on these sure promises.'

'Don't forget, sister Bunyan,' said the good old woman, as she walked by the side of the afflicted wife, 'don't forget that "God giveth liberally, and upbraideth not." "Ask, and ye shall receive." Ah! precious promises, my soul would feed for ever upon them. Brother Bunyan will be set free if it is the will of God; but if it is not, you must learn to submit, knowing that our Father doeth all things well. I hope he will comfort you in your troubles, and give you his Holy Spirit to bear you up. I will run over to see you to-morrow. I hope you'll be better by then.'

The weeping woman pressed her hand in grateful acknowledgment. 'Pray for me, sister Harrow,' was all she could say.

'Yes, that I will, sister Bunyan, and my old man will pray for you, and brother Bunyan, and the children too; we will not forget you when we go to the throne of sovereign grace.'

In silence the troubled woman pursued her way. She reviewed as well as she could the whole ground. She turned upon the past, she dwelt upon the present, looked into the future, endeavored to fathom the mysteries which seemed thickening around her path. She was endeavoring to understand why it was God was dealing so heavily with her; why his afflicting hand was laid upon her rather than others? She revolved the matter in her own mind, and scanned it in all its phases. It was an inscrutable Providence. She would have murmured, but she dared not.

'Fear not; stand still and see the salvation of the Lord.' This command of the leader of all hosts fell upon her ear— 'Stand still.' She was convinced that she had erred in attempting to work out what was not in accordance with the purposes of Jehovah. Her business was to 'stand still,' not to move to the right nor the left; neither look back, nor yet to try to proceed! 'Stand still' and see the salvation of the Lord. She prayed for grace to acquiesce.

The little ones met her in the close, and asked many

questions about their father. The blind child awaited her at
the door with a sweet, sad look.

The scanty meal was ready, and the widow and fatherless ones gathered around the humble board. As they sat
there, they appeared forsaken of God and neglected of man.
A few Irish potatoes, some oatmeal cakes, and a bowl of
broth was all they had for five hungry mouths. The
mother asked a blessing on their scanty fare, and then the
two youngest, Joseph and Sarah, commenced to ask questions about their poor father, shut up in the 'big old gaol.'

The evening passed on, and night came. The widow's
mite was gone. 'He will be a father to the fatherless,
and the widow's stay,' repeated Mrs. Bunyan to herself, as
she looked at the low fire, and thought of the empty cup-
board and remembered the coming morrow.

She gathered her children around her, and Mary repeated
in a sweet, low, solemn voice, the ninetieth Psalm. How
replete with consolation fell the first lines upon the wounded spirit: 'Lord, thou hast been our dwelling-place in all
generations. Before the mountains were brought forth, or
ever thou hadst formed the earth and the world, even from
everlasting to everlasting, thou art God.'

The last words of the sweet psalm had died away from
the ears of the charmed listeners. The mother bowed with
her forsaken ones to supplicate the blessing of the Most
High God upon them and her, and upon him who, for the
gospel's sake, lay languishing in a dungeon. Her simple,
fervent prayer was borne by the angel of the covenant to
the throne of God. The Father, well pleased, heard the
humble petition. 'For thus saith the high and lofty One
that inhabiteth eternity, whose name is holy, I dwell in
the high and holy place; with him also that is of a contrite and humble spirit, to revive the spirit of the humble,
and to revive the heart of the contrite ones.'

The little family arose from their knees. The good-
night kisses were given; and there reposed on humble cots
weary limbs and stilled hearts, while angels kept watch
over the abode of God's chosen ones.

'Thou wilt keep him in perfect peace whose mind is
stayed on thee, because he trusteth in thee.'

CHAPTER XIII.

'Mrs. Gaunt, do you think they would admit me to the gaol in Bedford?'

'I can't say, William! But why, my boy, do you ask me this question?'

'Because I want to go up to see my poor old father. Mother told me when I left home that I must go to see him as soon as I could, and send her word how he was doing, and whether she could see him if she were to go there. And I must go. Maybe I may not get in, but I'll go anyhow and try.'

The speaker was a tall, noble-looking youth of eighteen. His handsome manly countenance spoke forth the high and honorable feelings of his heart, while the fiery expression of his clear blue eye told plainly the enthusiasm of his nature. His was a face to be admired—so full of generosity and noble daring. His dark auburn hair, parted in the middle, formed a wavy outline to his high jutting forehead, and fell, after the fashion of those days, in rich luxuriance over his broad shoulders. Habitually his mouth wore a pleasing smile, but whenever his mind was set to do a thing, the smile gave way to a compression of the lips, expressive of a firmness of purpose not likely to yield before anything but impossibility; and then his eye assumed a steady look, indicative of settled determination.

Thus he now appeared as he stood leaning against the fire-place, gazing earnestly at the female seated in front of him. She cast her eyes upward from the Bible that rested on her lap to the face of the speaker. It wore that expression of decision which so peculiarly characterised it. She had known him but a few months, yet she had learned to read the thoughts of his mind and the feelings of his soul in his speaking countenance. She saw now that his determination was fixed, and she felt that any effort on her part to dissuade him from the accomplishment of his purpose, even were she disposed to do so, would be useless entirely. But she had no desire to do so. She was gratified at the expression of filial love in her young friend.

'Yes, that I will go,' he resumed, his lips compressing more tightly, and the steady expression of his eye deepening. 'I will go to see my poor dear old father. God knows it is a shameful thing for him to lie wearing away in that hateful dungeon; the poor old man that never in his life harmed a living creature. It is a wretched thing, Mrs. Gaunt;' and a tear ran down his flushed cheek as he thought of the wrong his father had endured at the hands of those who professed to be zealous for the honor of the Most High God.

'He doeth all things after the counsel of his own will, William, and as the mountains are round about Jerusalem, so is the Lord round about his people. Do you think that your father suffers in vain? No, no. His trials, and those of all God's afflicted children here on earth, will redound to the honor and glory of the cause of our blessed Lord. He maketh the wrath of man to praise him, and the vile persecutors of his children are working out his own eternal immutable purposes; and his poor, down-trodden Zion, which is now the prey of the wolves and the devourer, will awake, and put on her strength, and her beautiful garments, and the waste places shall break forth into singing, and all the nations of the earth shall see it. They that rule over the Lord's heritage, do make his people to howl now. But it will not always be so. They that afflict the righteous shall be blown like chaff before the wind of destruction. They shall be utterly consumed from off the face of the earth, for he shall cut off the spirit of princes. He is terrible to the kings of the earth.'

The woman spoke with enthusiasm—like one ready to seal her testimony with blood. And in after years, she proved that she counted not her life dear, for she finished her course with joy amid the flames kindled by the hands of the children of the 'Mother of Harlots;' attesting to the last her belief in the doctrines of the Scriptures, and her love for their great and glorious Author.

The youth sighed and shook his head doubtfully.

'What you say may be so, Mrs. Gaunt, but I cannot believe it. I cannot see that what you tell me can ever come to pass. There is no hope for our poor, unhappy blood-stained country. The heel of the oppressor will trample her into the dust, and she will be abased never to rise again.'

'Say not so, William. God hath spoken by the mouth of his holy prophet, "that from one new moon to another, and from one Sabbath to another, shall all flesh come to worship before me!" "They shall sit, every man under his vine, and under his fig tree, and none shall make them afraid. The mouth of the Lord of Hosts hath spoken it, and he cannot lie."'

'Oh, that that time had come, Mrs. Gaunt. Would that this oppression and tyranny throughout the land might cease.'

'In God's own good time it shall, William. Be content in that thought.'

'It will be a long time first, Mrs. Gaunt, I tell you. Iniquity abounds everywhere. Oh, it is dreadful!— the sufferings which the poor prisoners endure in the horrid gaols and dungeons. I cannot bear to think of it. Oh, that I could but avenge their wrongs ——'

'That is a wicked desire, William. "They that take the sword shall perish by the sword," said Jesus. You must learn to bear patiently. God will avenge his elect when he seeth fit. Leave it to him. Wait and see his glory.'

'How can I wait, Mrs. Gaunt, when my father is rotting in prison, placed there by the cruelty of deceitful men? How can I wait when my mother's heart is breaking? No, no. The blood leaps in my veins when I think of it. I am driven to fury, and if there was any hope, I would raise a war-cry which shall echo and re-echo throughout this land. I would down with the vile wretches who persecute the poor, and put them to reproach.

'Hush, hush, William, God will hold you accountable for such words. You sin against him. "Vengeance is mine, I will repay," saith he. Leave the matter in his hands, and trust him. He will not deceive. He will not lie. His words are sure and steadfast, and he will bring it to pass when he seeth the time has come.'

'Well, I am going to Bedford to see father, and I will get him out of that hole if I can. He ought to promise to quit preaching, if they will not release him on any other condition. What is the use of his threatening to preach, if it only keeps him in gaol. He can't preach there, and he had better regain his liberty than lie there wasting away.'

'The curse of God will rest upon you, William, if you undertake such a course. His children can preach louder by their sufferings and trials, if they bear them with patience, than they can in words. Be content to wait for the manifestations of the power of God. He could bring your father out of prison as he did Paul and Silas, if he saw proper, but it is his own good pleasure that he should stay there for a season. Could the enemy triumph unless the Lord Jehovah permitted it? No; I tell you the horse and the rider should be slain, and the persecutors should flee away like chaff before the strong wind, if the Lord of Israel saw fit to smite them with the breath of his power.'

The young man stood silent. The sublime truths of God's word impressed his heart. He had heard them oftentimes from the lips of his father, as he sat around his fireside, telling of the dealings of God with him; or expounded the sacred oracles to the villagers assembled in their hidden meetings; but now they fell with double weight. The Holy Spirit was sending them home with power to his heart.

'I will go with you to see your father, William,' the woman said, after a pause of a few moments. 'It is a year since I have seen the faithful old man, who, through the grace of God was the means of bringing me to a knowledge of the truth. Ah, that was a blessed time, a time of praise and rejoicing,' she said, as if speaking to herself, 'when the Lord took my feet out of an horrible pit, and placed them on a rock, even Christ Jesus, and put a new song in my mouth, even praises to the Lamb. "What shall I render unto God for all his mercies shown? I will take the cup of salvation, and call upon the name of the Lord; yea, I will praise him continually, for he hath blotted out my transgressions, and washed me from mine iniquity, and cleansed me from my sin."

'Yes, William, I will go with you. I hear that Bedford gaol is filled with witnesses for the truth. You know that man of God, John Bunyan, is there. It will do my soul good to listen to the words of heavenly wisdom from the mouth of such a man. I will go with you, and we will start to-morrow.'

'I am glad you are going with me, Mrs. Gaunt,' the youth answered enthusiastically, 'for maybe you can help me to hit upon some plan for my father's escape, and——'

'I can do nothing, William, but what will be right before God, and honorable in the sight of men.'

The young man sighed deeply. The impetuosity of his nature could not bear any opposition to his cherished hope. The thoughts of his poor old father's imprisonment had preyed upon him night and day, but he had never yet seen any feasibility in any plan that had suggested itself to his mind. His hope now was in Mrs. Gaunt's superior wisdom, and her influence, which, although but little, for she was but an obscure woman, would yet be something if brought to bear in his favor.

'It will be a long tiresome walk for you,' said William,

as he seated himself on the settee by the side of the kind woman.

'It is only thirty miles, William, and maybe we can get into a waggon and ride part of the way. I don't fear the weariness of the journey; I am stout, and you are young and strong. I must go now to the gaol, and try to comfort the poor, distressed disciples of my Master, who lie therein languishing for the truth. You make ready for your journey, for we will, God willing, set out early on the morrow.'

'Be careful, Mrs. Gaunt, and do not show yourself too much in your visits of charity. The spies of the Church are abroad, and they scent the righteous, even from afar.'

'My ways and times are in the hands of the Lord, William. Why need I fear what man can do unto me?'

The good woman put on her hat, and taking up a basket of provision, set out on her daily mission of charity. She visited the sick, and those that were in prison. She clothed the naked and fed the hungry, and to the thirsty she gave drink.

Long before the sun gilded the turrets and spires of the sin-cursed city, the two travellers were on their way. It was a cold, crisp morning in November. The sun, rising from a bed of clouds, threw its mellowed beams over the sere autumnal landscape. The ploughman was in the field, turning over the fallow ground. And fieldfares and starlings followed on his steady steps, and gathered the food sent them by the all-bountiful One. While from the hedgerows by the wayside the blackbird and song thrush warbled forth sweet praises to the Maker of the glorious heavens and the glad earth.

The travellers journeyed on, discoursing on the beauties of the day, which were springing up before them. And with thankfulness did the woman speak of the goodness of God, whose love is ever over his people, and whose hand is open to supply their wants. High noon came, and they sat themselves down by the roadside, and partook of the provisions prepared by the careful hand of Mrs. Gaunt, and then, refreshing themselves from a spring by the way, which sent a little rivulet to dance and sparkle through the copse-wood, they resumed their journey.

They were on a noble mission—sublimer far than that of ambassadors and princes, who look only to the things that are seen. Yet the world heeded them not. The passer-by saw in them only two plain pedestrians, weary with the toil of the way. But the eye of God rested on the scene approvingly, and 'Well done' was the seal set by the Hand omnipotent to that humble, unpretending mission.

Wonderful power of the glorious gospel of the Son of God, that invests the barefoot journey of the faithful disciple of Jesus with an interest and grandeur far exceeding the pomp and show of earth's most illustrious cavalcades. Stupendous love and condescension, which looks down from the throne of the universe to support and cheer the fainting heart of the weary and worn pilgrim!

The travellers had passed more than half their journey. The woman's pace was languid and slow.

'William,' she said, 'I must stop and rest.'

'I see a waggon,' said he, 'coming on our steps. I will get the driver to let us ride.'

The waggon was going several miles in the direction of Bedford. The driver, a staid yeoman, with a big heart and a kind face, was glad to help them on their journey.

As they drove on, the woman spoke to him of religion. She soon learned that he was a child of God; and as they rode along they held sweet converse. He too belonged to the persecuted flock of the despised ones, but the hand of persecution had not yet fallen on their little band.

The shades of night came on. They yet wanted five miles of Bedford. Because of the woman's fatigue, they decided to stop at a farm house by the wayside. William was eager to proceed. He felt no weariness in the pursuit of his father. 'But if I should not get there to-night,' he said to himself, 'the gaol would be shut, and I could not get in; so I will content myself to rest here.'

CHAPTER XIV.

THE REPULSE.

'No, I tell you, you can't go in!'

'And why not?'

'The prisoners haven't had their breakfast, and nobody can get in so soon.'

The answers were given in a rough, harsh voice, and the turnkey bent a look of scowling severity upon the applicants. He grasped tightly the ponderous keys which depended from his leathern girdle, and raising his great, coarse hand, motioned them away.

'When can we get in, tell us?' asked the youth impatiently, aroused by the insulting manner of the assistant

THE BLIND GIRL AND HER BROTHER REFUSED BY THE JAILER.

gaoler. The blood was in his cheek, the flash in his eye, but judgment told him to be still.

'I don't know, sometime to-day.'

'We will go away, William,' spoke the woman soothingly. She saw that he was excited, and might say something that would end seriously. 'Come, we will go now, and come some other time,' and suiting the action to the word, she turned from the door, and walked towards the end of the bridge. The youth hesitated a moment, keeping his eyes fixed steadily on the turnkey, who wavered beneath their gaze. Then, as if suddenly recollecting himself, he wheeled, and followed the woman.

'We will go to the inn, William, and rest awhile. They may let us in when we come again. God incline their hearts to grant us this favor.'

'The wretch!' exclaimed the aroused youth, 'how dare he refuse to let me see my father! It's tyranny, wherever you turn. Oh, it is too hard to bear. When will these things end! I will be revenged!'

He spoke with the energy of a man bent on some desperate purpose. His frame trembled with the intensity of his emotion, and the blood mounted higher and higher on his cheek, until it suffused his vein-marked temples. The lips were fearfully compressed.

'William, William,' said the woman reprovingly, 'how can you do this! Don't you fear to sin against God? He worketh and none can hinder. See his hand in all this, and be still. Shall not the man of great wrath suffer punishment? Calm yourself and sin not.'

A deep groan was the only reply he made, while the right hand involuntarily clenched. The young man felt that it was foolishness to fight against the words of wisdom; but the enmity of the heart was not overcome, only the lips were bridled.

THE VISIT TO THE GAOL.

The mother mused as she pursued with heavy, flagging step, her way across the meadow. Her soul was burdened with a heavy weight. Her heart was filled with fear. Unfathomable were the dealings of God with her. When would he reveal himself a God of love? Surely, his hand was laid upon her in anger, and deliverance would never come. Each day that dawned but added new cares to her already overwhelming burden, and she felt to strive against her destiny was but a foolish mockery. Each day increased the certainty of her husband's doom; each day brought more and more domestic trouble, for the children were crying for bread, and their tattered garments and bare feet, now pinched by the chill November, spoke in mute appeal to the bleeding tenderness of her stricken heart. She was in a deep, dark valley; mountains of trouble and difficulty reared themselves all around, so that the beaming of hope was for ever shut out. No flickering ray of light betokened the coming day. All was night, incessant night, wherever she looked.

Poor, desolate, tried woman. She was indeed passing through 'deep waters,' and was ready to perish.

She pondered her condition as she walked slowly along, while tears streamed down her wasted cheeks. Little Joseph was by her side with his basket. There had been but a scant breakfast that morning in the forsaken household. The father must have something from home, and there was none to spare, save the offerings-up of self-denial, prompted by love.

' I must bear up and try to be cheerful for his sake,' said the poor afflicted woman to herself, as the dark mouldy walls of the old gaol burst upon her view.

' Yea, for his sake I would do anything, bear anything ; He is my all on earth. O my God, deliver him out of the power of the tormentor ; bid the prisoner go free. Save him ! save him from the hands of cruel men, and from them that seek after him for his hurt.' Her tears fell rapidly.

' Is any little baby dead, mother ?' said Joseph, timidly, as he walked by his mother's side.

' No, my little boy ; what made you ask me that question ?'

He paused for a moment, as if unwilling to give his reason. Then looking up into his mother's face, his large blue eyes full of innocence, he replied :

' Because you cry so, mother, just like you and Mary did when our little baby died.'

The fountain of a mother's love was stirred, and the tears fell more bitterly. Her Heavenly Father's chastenings were more than she could bear. She clasped her hands in agony. Her soul was rent with sorrow. There was no consolation, no hope ! Surely she was sinking in the deep mire where there was *no* standing. She had come into deep waters, where the floods overwhelmed her.

But she looked to the Lord from the midst of her troubles, and in the words of the afflicted king of Israel, she cried, 'Give ear to my prayer, O Lord, and hide not thyself from my supplication. Attend unto me, and hear me. I murmur in my complaint, and make a great noise. Because of the voice of the enemy, because of the oppression of the wicked ; for they cast iniquity upon me, and in wrath they hate me.'

'My heart is sore pained within me, and the terrors of death are fallen upon me. Fearfulness and trembling are come upon me, and horror hath overwhelmed me.'

' Oh, that I had wings like a dove, then would I fly away and be at rest. I would hasten my escape from the windy storm and tempest.'

' Be merciful unto me, O God, be merciful unto me. My soul is among lions.' ·

'For his sake, dearer to me than life, I must be calm,' she repeated to herself, as the little window, at which she thought he might be writing, became visible. She quickened her dragging steps, stilled the fountain of her grief, wiped away the tears from her face, and tried to look cheerful.

' We will soon see father, won't we, mother!' ventured little Joseph, as he saw his mother's changed appearance.

' Yes, my boy, we will soon see your poor father once more. It may be for the last time.'

' Why, what are they going to do with father, mother ? They won't kill him, will they ?' and the child's face assumed a look sad to see.

' Ah! I don't know, Joseph, what they will do with him. I can't tell.'

The women eyed each other closely as they met at the door of the prison. It was evident to each that they were on a similar mission. The turnkey seemed fretted by their application for admission, and with dark, vengeful countenance, he stood fumbling over his keys, as if undecided whether to grant them entrance.

Mrs. Gaunt said to the other, 'You come to see a prisoner ?'

' My husband,' was the reply.

' Does he suffer for the sake of the Master ?' asked the first speaker.

' Even so. For preaching the gospel of the Lord Jesus Christ.'

She understood instantly, and replied with increased animation :

' John Bunyan, of Elstow, a glorious martyr for the truth as it is in Christ Jesus ?'

'The same,' and Mrs. Bunyan gazed on her with surprise.

The heavy grating door flew open. The applicants were admitted into the narrow court. The prisoners, some of them, were out for morning exercise, if the walking about in a miserable court-yard, fourteen feet wide, and but little more than that in length, could be called exercise.

William looked eagerly around on the faces nearest him, but he saw not his father. 'I may be mistaken,' he said to himself. 'My father may be so changed.' He viewed their faces a second time more minutely. Shaking his head, he stepped on a little farther. His attention was arrested by a noise as of a woman weeping in the farther end of the court. He paused and looked. It was the woman he had met at the outer door, leaning on the bosom of one of the prisoners. A man was standing near them. an old, gray-headed man. He looked again. It was his father. A moment more, and they were locked in each other's arms. Tears of joy streamed down the pallid cheek of the old man, and sobs burst from the heaving breast of the son.

'My son, my William! thank God, I see you once more, my boy!' and the old man strained him to his heart. 'And your mother, William, and my dear Nancy—when did you hear from them?'

'Well, father,' was all the son could say.

'Thank God! thank God!' exclaimed the old man, gazing on the son with delight.

'Do you know me, father Dormer?'

The old man wiped the tears from his eyes with the back of his hand, and gazed upon the new speaker. After a long look, he shook his head slowly.

'No, my good woman, I never saw you before.'

'God made you the means of turning me from my sins. You baptised me.'

The old man's face brightened. 'One seal to my ministry,' whispered the old man to himself.

'You know me now!' the woman exclaimed, as she saw the old man's face light up.

The man smiled faintly.

'I am old now, my daughter,' he said, 'and my eyes are dim, and my mind is frail. The names and faces of my youth have passed from me, and I cannot bring them back.'

'Elizabeth Shirley, father Dormer, you remember her?'

'My cousin Henry's child?'

'Yes.'

'I know you now, my child!' he said, and he threw his arms around her and wept afresh.

'The Lord is merciful to me in sending you and my boy to see me. I had never hoped to see again on earth the faces of those I have known and loved. My race is almost run, my daughter; a few days, and my Master will send for me to go up, *up*,' he exclaimed, turning his eyes heavenward, 'to the mansion he is preparing for me. No prisons there; no weeping there; no suffering there. Friends will never more be parted. The husband shall not be torn from the wife, nor the father from the children. The hand of the violent man shall no longer oppress, and the persecutor shall not destroy. And I will soon be there, my child. My sinning will be done, my weeping will be done. I shall be for ever at rest. Oh, that we may all meet there at last—our troubles all ended.'

The old man sank to the ground. The little party gathered around him.

'This is our brother in the Lord, John Bunyan, and his wife,' said the old man. 'We are all children of the Most High God, and we are journeying on amid our trials and besetments towards the celestial city, whose builder and maker is God. How is it with thee, my son? Has God begun a new work in your poor heart, my dear William? Have you laid down your arms of rebellion against the King of kings, and become submissive to the peaceful reign of the Prince Immanuel? My poor child, have you turned to God?'

The young man shook his head.

'May the Lord quicken you by his Holy Spirit, and create within you a clean heart, my boy.'

'Amen! Amen!' repeated the little company.

And shall not the prayer of faith be answered?

'We pass through tribulation and sore vexation in this world, sister,' said Bunyan, turning to Mrs. Gaunt.

'Yes, brother Bunyan; but the grace of God will bring his children off conquerors over the flesh, the world, and the devil,' she answered.

'His grace is all-sufficient, my sister, and we should ever be ready to say with the apostle Paul, "I am now ready to be offered, and the time of my departure is at hand. I have fought a good fight; I have finished my course; I have kept the faith. Henceforth there is laid up for me a crown of righteousness, which the Lord, the Righteous Judge, shall give me at that day; and not to me only, but to all them, also, that love his appearing." These are

perilous times, and we cannot tell what a day may bring
forth. The hand of the Lord is stretched abroad over the
earth, and his anger is kindled against the sons of men.
He hath laid the vine waste, and barked the fig-tree; he
hath made it clean bare, and cast it away. The branches
thereof are made white.'

'But he will cause the waste cities to be built up, brother
Bunyan. He will plant again the vineyard, and the fig-
tree shall blossom. For yet a little while and his anger
shall be overpast, and the Lord will come again to visit
Zion, and to execute judgment on her persecutors.'

'Her persecutors are as ravening wolves, my sister, as
howling beasts of pray; they tear and rend her in pieces;
they scourge and devour her.'

'Zion mourneth, I know, my brother, because of her
enemies. But they shall lick the dust like a serpent; they
shall move out of their hills like worms of the earth;
they shall lay their hand upon their mouth; their ears shall
be deaf. Neither their silver nor their gold shall be able to
deliver them in the day of the Lord's wrath; but the
whole land shall be devoured by the fire of his jealousy;
for he shall make even a speedy riddance of all them that
dwell in the land. For God is a jealous God, and the Lord
avengeth, and is furious. The Lord will take vengeance
on his adversaries, and he reserveth wrath for his enemies.'

'The words of Elizabeth are true, brother Bunyan,'
added the old man. 'What did the prophet Habakkuk
say?—"Art thou not from everlasting, O Lord my God,
my Holy One?" We shall not die. O Lord, thou hast
ordained them for judgment; and O mighty God, thou
hast established them for correction. Thou art of purer
eyes than to behold evil, and canst not look on iniquity;
and the cry shall go forth, "Howl, ye inhabitants of Mak-
tesh, for all the merchant people are cut down; all they
that bear silver are cut off;" and then shall his people
hear the glad shout, "Sing, O daughter of Zion, shout, O
Israel! be glad, and rejoice with all the heart, O daughter
of Jerusalem; for the Lord hath taken away thy judgments; he hath cast out thine enemy. The King of Israel,
even the Lord, is in the midst of thee; thou shalt not see
evil any more. For the Lord thy God in the midst of thee,
is mighty. He will save, he will rejoice over thee with
joy; he will rest in his love; he will rejoice over thee with
singing. Behold, at that time I will undo all that afflict
thee; and I will save her that halteth, and gather her that
was driven out. And I will get them praise and fame in

every land where they have been put to shame.   For I will
make you a name and a praise among all people of the
earth when I turn back your captivity before your eyes,
saith the Lord."   The Lord God hath spoken this through
his Holy Spirit, my brother, and his word shall stand fast.'

'Yea, and forever,' replied Bunyan. 'May God give us
strength to bear our afflictions, and patience to await his
coming.'

Bunyan and his wife arose and repaired to his cell.   She
had something to say to him which she wished no stranger
to hear.   Little Joseph followed with his basket of pro‹
vision.   The old man, William, and Mrs. Gaunt were left
alone.

'When William talked of coming to see you, father
Dormer, I felt that I must come too.   I have nothing to do
now but go about and attend to the children of my Master.'

'Are you not married, child?'

'I was married, soon after I went down to London to
work, to John Gaunt, a godly man, and I lived with him
three of the happiest years I shall ever see in this life ; but
God took him to himself, and left me alone in this world,
childless and friendless, and since his death I have given
my time, and much of my little store, to clothe the naked,
and feed the hungry of my Father's children.'

'A blessed work, my daughter,' replied the old man, as
he set gazing upon the changed features of one who had
often gathered with his children, now in heaven, around
the frugal board, and sported with them through the
meadows. "Whosoever shall give to drink unto one of these
little ones a cup of cold water only, in the name of a disciple, verily, I say unto you he shall in no wise lose his
reward." These, my child, are the words of our blessed
Lord and Master, who shall reward us at the last day
according to the deeds done in the body.'

'How did you fall in with my poor William, Elizabeth?'
he added, looking with a fond father's love upon his son,
who sat listening intently to every word.

'I met William in the street one day as I was going from
one of the gaols to my humble home. He asked me if I
could tell him of any one that could gave him work. His
manner and voice seemed so like something I had known
long years gone by, I asked him who he was.

'"I am the son of David Dormer," he answered.

'"David Dormer, the old Baptist preacher that used to
live in Lincolnshire?" I said in haste. "That's my father,"
he answered. Then I asked where you were. He told me

in Bedford gaol. I made him understand who I was, and took him home with me, where he has been living ever since. And he shall stay with me as long as he wants to.'

'The Lord of heaven and earth be praised for directing the feet of my poor· wandering boy to your door. Be a mother to him, Elizabeth, and may he reward you with a son's love and obedience. Here, William, I give you to this woman. She will be to you a mother. You be to her a son, my boy, and may God make you a help to each other.'

'Now tell me, Elizabeth, how the poor saints come on in London. I hear they are persecuted there as well as here. It seems that Satan is loosed on earth, and is set to destroy the saints of the Most High.'

'The times are very fearful there. Ah! they are fearful throughout the land, father Dormer. The hand of vengeance is upon the children of God; and their cries go up from every dungeon in the kingdom into the ears of the Lord of Sabaoth. And he will come to avenge his people speedily. He delayeth his coming that his people may feel their dependance on his almighty arm. But when he doth come, then will he make requisition of blood, and all the earth shall know the Lord God omnipotent reigneth.'

'These things are very wonderful, my child. The great God is moving in a mysterious way. He is performing his purposes through marvellous means, but I know it is all right, though it is so hard to understand. I will trust the God of Jacob though he slay me. But oh, my child, what must be the terrible recompense that he will visit on the heads of his enemies! It will be a consuming fire from heaven, which shall burn up all that despise him. They shall be consumed in wrath, they shall be slain with the sword. They shall all utterly perish. For God will avenge and succor his people when the time of his visitation has come.'

'It is true, it is true, father Dormer. The Lord our God will be a refuge for the oppressed, a refuge in time of trouble. The cause of his people he will maintain. He sitteth on the throne of the heavens judging right, and the needy shall not always be forgotten; the expectations of the poor shall not perish for ever. For the righteous Lord loveth righteousness. "The Lord is in his holy temple. The Lord's throne is in heaven; his eyes behold, his eyelids try the children of men."'

Thus, these two faithful children of God sat encouraging each other, until the keeper warned them that it was time for the visitors to depart. Mrs. Bunyan came forth from her husband's cell with a more cheerful countenance. The faith and confidence of her husband had inspired her heart with a faint hope. It is good for the children of God to wait on him in faith. Their strength shall be renewed thereby.

Mrs. Bunyan invited the young woman and the young man home with her to stay through the night. Her husband had told her to do so. And she did so to comply with his wish, but her heart misgave her, for she remembered there was nothing to eat, and there was no money to buy food. She had told her husband this as she had parted with him in the cell, but he answered :

'My Elizabeth, will not the Lord provide? I have never seen the righteous forsaken nor his seed begging bread. "Trust in the Lord and do good, and thou shalt dwell in the land, and surely thou shalt be fed." Is not this promise enough to calm your fears, and to stay your heart, my wife?'

She saw that this ought to be sufficient, but she scarcely felt that it was.

Could we, under every dispensation of providence, exercise that degree of faith in the promises of God which it is our privilege to do, there would be but little sorrow to the child of God. He would then realise feelingly that all things are working together for his good. Sin has robbed us of the ability. The spirit is willing, but, alas! the flesh is weak.

Like a true woman, Mrs. Bunyan hid her uneasiness from her new friends. 'I can do something,' she said to herself, 'and maybe God will provide for me. He has never yet left me to starve, though he has suffered me to be driven to my wit's ends to get a morsel for my famishing children.'

As Mrs. Bunyan and her friends approached the door, little Sarah, overjoyed, ran out to meet her mother.

'Oh, mother, mother, something to eat, in a great big basket!' she exclaimed, as she got within speaking distance of her mother, entirely regardless of the presence of the strangers.

'Let us be thankful for it, my child,' was the mother's answer, her heart melting with grateful emotions, while, at the same time, her conscience reproached her for her unbelief. 'It is our heavenly Father who has sent it to us.'

'No, mother, Goody Harrow told Thomas that the neighbors sent it to us.'

The mother smiled at the child's reply, and told her how God must have put it into the minds of the neighbors to do it. She then turned to the woman and the young man, and explained to them her circumstances.

Mary stood at the door to meet her mother on her return. The house was as tidy as neatness and care could make it. The blood rushed to her soft, delicate cheek at the mention of the strangers' names; but with unaffected modesty she extended her hand to welcome them, smiling, and bidding them enter, in a voice so sweet, that Mrs. Gaunt, who observed such things but little, stopped to take a second look at the placid sightless face.

And the child of thirteen years was a picture of more than earthly loveliness, as she stood there, with an angelic smile lighting up her delicate features and pale cheek. Her dark hair was combed from her transparent forehead, her neck was covered with a plain white handkerchief, crossed over her breast, and tied behind. Her plain, blue stuff dress hung scantily, it is true, around her beautifully moulded form, but it was clean; her shoes and stockings, though of the coarsest kind, were as clean as her dress and handkerchief, and her manner was as gentle and easy as though she had been reared in the court of the Plantagenets.

Thus she appeared to William Dormer, as he gazed on her with pity and admiration; and as she moved quietly and meekly around the household, assisting her mother in every preparation with so much readiness, and at the same time, so much grace, he felt his interest in the blind girl constantly increasing. Her sweet voice charmed him, and whenever she spoke to him, with her soft clear tones, he felt his heart throb faster, and an unusual feeling of delight thrilled his bosom. They were the opposite in appearance and character. He, brave and fiery in disposition, excitable, and somewhat resentful. She, timid and gentle, full of fortitude and forgiveness. Yet they were both possessed of a high tone of moral principle.

This was the first meeting of the youth and the blind girl. They met often in after years; sometimes under pleasant circumstances, at others under scenes the most trying. Thus it is in life—alternate pleasure and pain. Well would it be for us if we could be grateful for the one, and patient under the other.

Almost two hundred years ago!

A group is gathered around the fireside of a poor, despised man, imprisoned by the laws of his land. They are the offscouring of the earth, unnoticed by the rich and great. They have nothing to attract the attention of the proud or noble. Who shall ever know them beyond the circle of their own little village? Surely no one. Shall not their names perish with them, as those of their fathers before them have done? Ah,—no! They were called upon by the Master to suffer for righteousness' sake, and their sufferings have made them immortal. They have passed from earth to their reward above—one from the midst of the burning faggot; but they have left a name on earth which can never perish.

CHAPTER XV.

SUNLIGHT IN THE CELL—THE ANGEL CHILD.

THE life of the daughter is so intimately connected with that of the father, it is impossible to separate them. The father watched over the daughter with ever constant care until he was sent to prison, and then the daughter administered to his wants, soothed and caressed him through the twelve long weary years of his confinement. She was his prison-companion. The early morning found her at the gate of the dungeon awaiting admittance. The peaceful evening found her standing beside him, while he, with uplifted hand, invoked the blessing of God on his poor, unprotected child. He felt for her a deeper, tenderer love, than that cherished for any of the four children, because of the great affliction which was to brood over her through life. She was his first-born. There is much in that. As early impressions are the most lasting, so the parental love first called into exercise by the being of the first-born, is deeper, more sacred, than any love of after years. As there is but one first-born, so there is but one such love as the first-born receives.

In infancy he had looked into the sealed eyes, which in their darkness, gave no answering look, and wept because of the eternal blindness, even while his weeping heart uttered, 'It is the Lord; he hath done what seemed good to him.' He had knelt with her mother, the chosen of his young affections, and consecrated their child to God Most High, before her infant lips could lisp her Maker's name. He had seen those darkened eyes weep tears of childish sorrow when the mother bade her loved ones farewell in death. And then he had clasped her to his heart, his earthly solace and support in his dark and trying hour. Year after year he had watched with a father's love the beautiful unfoldings of that meek and gentle spirit, which was peculiarly hers, and which gave to her in after life a graceful and winning manner, that made her beloved by all who knew her. Hers was not a weak nature, because amiable ; nor an unfeeling heart, because so patient. She had inherited much of her father's will and judgment, and at the same time much of her mother's patience and affection. These characteristics combined, enabled her to exercise self-control and self-reliance remarkable in one so young.

At the time of which we are now writing (the fall of 1661), Bunyan was in his thirty-fourth year, and Mary, so far as we are able to gather up from incident (there is no reliable date of her birth given), was about thirteen years old. From her childhood her father had bestowed upon her untiring care and attention. It was his delight to take her upon his knee and tell her scripture tales, or read to her scripture lessons. These truths made an indelible impression upon her mind. And while other children of Elstow were at play on the village green, or rambling through the meadows, she was dwelling upon what she had heard from her father's lips. The seed had fallen into good ground, and it was taking deep root. In after years it produced abundantly the 'peaceable fruits of righteousness.'

The family of Bunyan were in need. Pinching poverty had been tightening her grasp, until at last her lean long hands were pressing out the life of wife and children. The neighbors were kind, but they were poor, they had given and given, until they could give but little more. Mrs. Bunyan had managed and economized, even stinted herself, to make the cruise of oil hold out, but there was no prophet to say to her, ' Fear not. For thus saith the Lord God of Israel, The barrel of meal shall not waste, neither shall the cruise of oil fail,' but there was a small, still voice, whispering to her fainting heart these precious words : ' Trust in the Lord, and do good ; so shalt thou dwell in the land, and verily thou shalt be fed.' ' Shalt be fed,' she repeated to herself. ' The Lord himself hath spoken it, why should I doubt ? The heavens and earth may pass away, but one jot or tittle of God's promises to his people shall not be left unfulfilled. I cannot see how it is to be done. But did he not divide

the Red Sea? and did he not give his people quails and
manna in the wilderness, and streams of water from the
solid rock? He will not forsake me.' ' Thus would faith
lay hold on the promises, and feel secure, though the fig-
tree did not blossom, nor was there fruit on the vine.

But then the tempter would come, and faith affrighted
hid herself, and the Evil One reasoned thus with her: ' The
children do perish with hunger, and there is no hand to
give them bread. Their father is dying in prison, placed
there by the hatred of the enemies of God, and there is
none to deliver him. The heavens above me are as brass,
the earth beneath me is as iron. The Lord turneth a deaf
ear to my supplications. There is no eye to pity, there is
no arm to save. Surely, the Lord has forsaken and his
tender mercies are clean gone for ever.' Thus was her
bosom the battle-ground of alternate hope and fear.

The words of the children often added to her anguish.
They complained, they murmured sorely—all, save Mary.
No breathing of repining or sorrow ever fell from her lips.
On she went, from day to day, with her same sweet, gentle
manner; and the only visible evidence of her inward grief
was the shadowings that crept over that sweet, sad face.
She did much to assist her mother in bearing her burden of
care and responsibility. Her assiduities were untiring.
Her watchfulness over little Joseph and Sarah were unceasing. And her frequent smile and words of kindly
comfort were as healing balm to the mother's heart.

Mrs. Bunyan and Mary hid their distresses from the
prisoner with the most sedulous care, lest they should add
to his trials, which, together with the dampness of his cell
and the protracted confinement, were wearing very much
upon his health. The old garments were mended and
darned, washed and smoothed, and made to present the
best appearance possible. Little delicacies sent in by the
neighbors were prepared with the greatest care, and borne
by loving hands to the dark cell. And bright faces carried
sunshine there whenever the will could master the feelings.
But darn upon darn, and mend upon mend, soon attracted
the notice of the husband and father, and he felt that he
must lay aside his books, and do something to earn a penny
to meet the wants of his family. But what could he do?
What in that narrow, dark cell? His furnace and moulds
were useless now. He knew nothing else. The *tinker* had
to become a *thinker*. The purposes of the Infinite were
beginning to unfold. They were, it is true, the cloud ' no
bigger then a man's hand,' which only the eye of the

prophet could discern. But their gradual development and their effects have been the wonder of all succeeding ages, and thousands throughout eternity will sing praises to God for his goodness in making John Bunyan a prisoner for the ' *truth's* sake.'

Could we but see now as we shall see, when the ' vail is rent,' and the ' inner glory ' shall burst upon us, we would ' rejoice in afflictions,' and joy in persecutions.

John Bunyan looked around him to see if there was anything he could do that would bring him any gain. He plainly saw that his imprisonment would not soon end. Indeed, he must now wait months before there would be even an opportunity for him to make another effort for his release.

He racked his brain to devise some employment which might add to the scanty store of his little family. Day by day he thought of it; night after night it haunted his brain.

At last an idea struck him. Whether it grew out of his former occupation or not is not for me to decide. I have thought it was an invention of his own great brain, which, in its power and comprehensiveness, could take heed of even the smallest things, and turn them to account. His imagination and ingenuity were wonderful. This all know, who have read his ' Holy War ' and ' Pilgrim's Progress.' And although there is no record of incidents to show us that these two faculties were brought to bear on the every-day affairs of life, yet we are not therefore to suppose that they were not called into requisition there, as well as in his authorship. I have no doubt but that they aided him much in turning to useful purposes many little odds and ends which would have been wasted in the hands of other men under similar circumstances.

He found, at last, an occupation compatible with his narrow cell, and still narrower means. And what was it? What could the tinker-preacher do under such forlorn circumstances? Hear his reply: ' I can tag laces, and thereby make a penny for my poor wife and little ones.' And tag laces he did, day by day, from morn till night. It required but little outlay of capital, for the braid cost but a mere trifle, and the bits of wires he had gathered up while he was a tinker, would tip many a yard of braid. It was the blind daughter's business to dispose of these laces when thus made. She would go about the streets of Bedford, and through the suburbs, with her little basket to sell her father's work, that her mother and the children might not want for bread. Oftentimes she met with rebuffs, for there were some in Bedford violent opposers of her father, and she soon became known about the place as 'John Bunyan's blind Mary.' Those favorable to her father's cause treated her kindly, pitying her hard lot, compassionating her sad misfortune. And oftentimes a stray penny found its way into the thin hand extended to receive the trifle for her little store.

It is Saturday morning. The week's provision is almost exhausted. Watchful care and frugality have conducted the inner arrangements of the cottage home at Elstow, and economy has presided at the board. But friends have partaken of the homely fare, and it is running short.

Elizabeth Gaunt and William Dormer have left the night before to go to Bedford, on their return home. Mrs. Bunyan finds her barrel and cruise almost empty.

'I will go and see father to-day, mother. I know he has got more laces done, and maybe I can sell some and get money to buy us bread.'

'You must do this, Mary, or we will have to beg. Take Joseph with you to show you along. And may God put it into the hearts of the people to help you, my poor child; if he don't, we must starve.'

Mary went about her preparation. Little Joseph put on his cleanly washed suit. But he had neither hat nor shoes.

'My hat's all gone, mother, and I can't get a thing to put on my head to go with Mary.'

Thomas will lend you his hat, and he can wear yours about the house.'

'And I haven't got any shoes, either, and it's so cold this morning,' said he, despairingly, as he poked his little bare red feet close to the smouldering fire, and seemed every moment ready to cry.

'You can walk fast, Joseph, and you won't get very cold. It will be warm after awhile. Would you let Mary go by herself to get you bread?'

The little fellow stooped down to rub his feet with his hands, as if to see whether he could protect his sister at the expense of his own comfort.

At length he looked up into his mother's face and answered pleasantly, 'I don't want Mary to go by herself, but it is so cold. But maybe the frost won't bite my feet.'

'You will go with Mary, then, Joseph, to take care of her, and see your father.'

'I want to see father, but I'm afraid of that old gaoler.

I mean that one that opens the doors, and locks them again with the big keys at his side. He scares me most to death, he looks so ugly.'

'Who watches over little children when their fathers are in prison, Joseph, and takes care of them, so that not a hair of their heads is hurt?'

'God does, mother, when the little boys are at home with their mothers; but I don't think he can get into that old gaol, they keep the doors locked so tight. When I go, it's as much as I can do to squeeze in, the old man holds the door so close. I don't think God could get through the little crack.'

'God is everywhere, Joseph,' said the mother, smiling at the child's reply. 'He does not ask the gaoler to let him in. He goes wherever he pleases.'

The child made no answer. The thought was too much for his infant mind.

Mary soon made her appearance, ready to set out on her errand of love. Her attire was very scant, yet faultlessly clean. She had outgrown the dark stuff dress, whose sleeves, mended and darned, showed the mother's care. The old worsted cloak, with its hood of the same, which had been a family relic for years, and bore the evident marks of usage, hung lightly over her shoulders. On her arm hung the little basket, which was to bear her store from house to house. A clean white cloth covered it. Beneath the cloth there was a dainty bit for the father, which loving hands had hid away there from the scant allowance of the morning meal.

Her face was radiant with the high and holy purposes of her heart. And she who was usually so timid, so shrinking, now appeared strong in her noble determination.

'Are you ready to go with me now, Joseph?' she asked sweetly of the little boy, as he stood warming his toes.

'You must wear my shoes, Mary, yours are too poor,' said the kind mother, as she looked on the old shoes and the delicate form before her. 'Here, put them on, child; they don't fit you, but you can tie them tight, and they won't slip off. I can make out with yours to-day about the house.'

As she stooped to put the old shoes on her feet, the mother let fall a tear. The blind one could not see it, but with that wonderful sensitiveness which the blind possess, she felt it as it fell. The bright and joyous expression of her face changed instantly to one of sympathetic sadness. She could not speak a word of cheer to her mother, although her heart was bursting to do it. She knew not what to say. So she took little Joseph by the hand, and bidding her mother good morning, set out on her walk.

The morning was cold and frosty. Joseph complained of his feet. She endeavored to divert his mind from his trouble by telling him how glad their father would be to see him, and how he should go with her through the streets of Bedford, and see all the sights to be seen.

' But I don't want to go, Mary. I will stay at the gaol.'

' No, no, Joseph, you must go with me. You know I can't see, and you must go with me that I may not get lost.'

' No, I am going to stay in the gaol all the day,' replied the little fellow with that perverseness which characterises all children.

' You have gone many times by yourself, Mary, and why can't you do it to-day ? '

' Oh, I want you to go with me, Joseph, because I am going to many places where I have never been before, and I am afraid I'll get hurt.'

' But I am not going with you. I am going to stay with father in the gaol all this day.'

Mary saw it was best to let him have his own way. Resistance or entreaty but increased his opposition. So she only said timidly, ' Well, then, I'll go by myself.'

They stepped briskly along, and soon gained the eminence which overlooked the old bridge with its gaol. Mary's mind had been filled with busy thoughts. A new life was about to dawn upon her. The first faint beams were just beginning to tinge her horizon. She knew her feelings, but could not understand them. They were not ideas, which could shape themselves into words. They were emotions that thrilled the heart—the being—with strange, mysterious raptures, which could not be expressed, which she could not define to herself. The power was there, but from whence it came, or to what it would lead, she knew not.

' What, here again so soon, you children you ? You'll bother me to death,' said the surly turnkey, as Mary and Joseph applied for admittance. ' I wish they'd send your father home to stay with you, and keep you away from here ; you are so troublesome.'

Mary's heart was very tender, and at these unfeeling words of the turnkey, she began to cry. Joseph, on the contrary, felt quite heroic, and his fast walk made him more than usually animated. He looked up into the face of the assistant as he growled out his words, and when he was through, he replied with his most independent air,

'I wish they would send father home. Then we could get to see him all the time, and we wouldn't have to ask you either.'

'Hush up, you brat you!' said the turnkey, as he took the child by the arm and forced him through the outer gate. 'You had better not speak to me in that way again.'

Just at this moment the gaoler came up, on his way to Bunyan's cell, and seeing the angry looks of the turnkey, and hearing his harsh words, asked what was wrong.

'These children here, of that prisoner, John Bunyan, trouble me to death. They are always here, wanting to see him.'

'Let them come with me,' said the gaoler, rather reprovingly, to the turnkey, 'I'll take care of them. What's your name, child?' said he to Joseph. 'I know your sister's name. Come, Mary, follow me.'

'My name is Joseph,' replied the little child, looking up much pleased, into the kind face of the gaoler. 'I don't like that old man. He ain't good to little boys. I wish I was big.'

'What for, Joseph?' asked the gaoler, half divining the cause of the wish.

'Then I'd make that old ugly man know what he was about, and I wouldn't let him make Mary cry.'

'Never mind, my little fellow, we are going to see your father,' and the man led him through the narrow court, then along the narrow passage, and then through the narrow opening that conducted to Bunyan's cell.

'This is the one!' exclaimed little Joseph, as they reached the door of the cell. 'Father's in here, ain't he? I wish you'd let him come home to stay with us. He's so tired here, in this old gaol.'

'I wish I could let your father go home with you to stay,' replied the kind-hearted man, as he took the key from his pocket and unlocked the door.

'Oh, can't you, sir, can't you let father out?' asked Mary, breathlessly.

'No, child; the laws of the land forbid me to do it.'

The door opened. There sat the prisoner beneath the little window; his pincers in his hand, and his stay laces on his knee; the bits of brass, out of which he made the 'tags,' or tips, were in a small box by his side. His Bible and Concordance, and his Book of Martyrs (the only three books he ever had in prison), were on a stool near him. His rose-bush, whose memory, because connected with his most pleasing prison associations, he has perpetuated in the following lines, stood near the little window:

> 'This homely bush doth to mine eyes expose
> A very fair, yea, comely, ruddy rose,
> This rose doth always bow its head to me,
> Saying, "Come, pluck me; I thy rose will be."'

But it seems that when he wished to accept the *blushing* invitation of his coy companion, she offered to his eager fingers her pricking thorns, for which abuse of his admiration he playfully reprimands her:

> 'Yet, offer I to gather rose or bud
> 'Tis ten to one that bush will have my blood.
> Bush, why dost bear a rose, if none must have it?
> Why thus expose it, yet claw those who crave it?
> Art become freakish? Dost the Wanton play?
> Or doth thy testy humor tend this way?
> This looks like a trepan or a decoy,
> To offer, and yet snap who would enjoy.'

Bunyan raised his head. His children were before him. Putting his pincers and laces aside, he drew them to him, and placing little Joseph on his knee, while Mary found a seat on a settle beside him, he asked about their mother, and Thomas, and Sarah.

The gaoler looked at the prisoner. His noble brow was expanded with the happiness that filled his overflowing heart. Tears moistened his eyes. The gaoler's heart was troubled. He had always been very kind to Bunyan, allowing him many privileges which he did not extend to other prisoners. He often sought his cell to converse with him, for Bunyan's fine common sense and his general information made him a pleasant companion. He was a favorite with all the prisoners, except the most abandoned.

The gaoler had come to converse with him this morning. He loved to listen to the truths of Revelation, as made clear by the prisoner in his own quaint style, and to get his advice on many points of duty; for Bunyan's good sense and staunch integrity made him a safe adviser. But the children claimed the father's attention, and the gaoler bid his prisoner good morning, and retired.

'And how do all things work at home, Mary?' asked Bunyan of his blind child when the gaoler had left.

Mary tried to look cheerful as she replied, 'We get on very well, father.'

'Thank God for that, my child. I have been sore pressed, thinking of you all, fearing you would suffer for bread. But your store has held out, has it?'

'We ain't got anything to eat, father,' spoke up Joseph before Mary could answer—his murmuring spirit, because of his barefooted walk, not having yet fully subsided. 'And I haven't got any shoes to put on my feet, and my feet are so cold.'

The prisoner paused and sighed. Little Joseph, perceiving the effect upon his father, continued his complaint.

'And we haven't got any clothes hardly, just two or three old rags, that mother keeps sewing up and sewing up. And Mary's got no shoes, neither. She's got on mother's shoes now, and I had to wear Thomas's hat. My old hat is so torn to pieces, mother made Tom lend me his. It's very hard times at our house, father. Mary won't tell you all about it. I do wish you would come home to give us something to eat, and some clothes to wear too.'

It was a dark time for Bunyan's faith. Let any affectionate Christian father imagine his situation. The night was dark, the wilderness pathless, enemies were on every side, the 'pillar of fire' was scarcely to be seen.

But God *must* be trusted, though he slay. He remembered the Israelites at the banks of the sea. He brought to mind the people of God in the wilderness, where there was no bread. He thought of the chosen ones, as they stood famishing for water in the desert, with nought but the flinty rock before them. He recalled the promises, and though he was passing through the valley of Baca, yet he made for himself a well of consolation and of hope.

'I can't come home to stay with you, Joseph. And you must——'

'And why can't you, father?' interrupted the child.

'The king won't let me. God says we must obey the king, and the king says I must stay here; and if I disobey him, I will disobey God too. Don't you see that, child?'

Joseph had never before understood why his father would go back to gaol, instead of staying at home, when he was there. He was quite puzzled for an answer to his father's question, because he perceived the reason so clearly, and still was unwilling to admit the king's right to keep his father away from his family.

'You see why I come back to gaol now, don't you, Joseph?'

'Yes, father,' he said hesitatingly, 'but won't you never get out here, and come home and stay with us ? '

'I cannot tell, Joseph. It is just as God orders it.'

'Well, we won't have a thing to eat if you don't, father. I don't think God ought to keep you here, and not give us bread.'

'God will give you bread, my son. He feeds the ravens when they cry, and he will feed you.'

'And will he give Mary shoes, too, father ? If he would, then I could take her old ones.'

'Yes, he will give Mary shoes, too, if it is best for her to have them. But you don't want shoes, Joseph. You must run about, and keep your feet warm. Did you come to get laces to sell, my daughter ? '

Bunyan spoke in a tone of tenderness to his 'poor blind child ' that he never used in addressing any one else. His natural manner savored somewhat of bluntness, oftentimes of severity.

'Yes, father, I have ; if I don't sell something to buy bread with, we will have nothing to eat soon. Our meal is nearly out.'

'Well, I have got a good parcel for you, my child, and may God bless you to-day. I have worked hard since your mother was here. Here,' said he, putting Joseph from his knee, and going to the other end of his cell and feeling about for a few moments. 'There, see, I have made all of these, and there are some on that chair there that I have finished this morning. I worked hard all day yesterday, even when Mrs. Gaunt and William Dormer were in.'

At the mention of these names, a slight agitation crept over the face of the blind girl. The father did not observe it. He was too busily engaged in sorting out and arranging his week's work.

'Give me your basket, my child. Here, Joseph, don't you upset that stool and spill the things on it. I will put this little morsel in the basket for you to eat.'

'Oh, no, father, we brought that for you. I have got some bread here for me and Joseph,' and she took out from under her cloak a little roll, and showed him. 'You must eat that yourself.'

'I don't want to go with Mary, father. I want to stay with you,' broke in little Joseph, as he heard his sister making provision for his evening meal.

'I would like to have you to stay with me, Joseph ; but you must go with Mary, and show her the way.'

'I don't know the way myself, father.   I don't want to go with Mary,' answered the child pettishly.

'You don't want to stay in this dark place all day, do you, child?'

'I don't want to go with Mary.   I want to play in the river, under the bridge.'

'But you will be colder there, than if you were with Mary; and you might fall in the river and get drowned.'

The child hung his head.

'You must go with Mary, Joseph,' said the father in a tone of kind command. 'Mary wants you to keep her out of danger.'

The child felt he must obey; so he took up his hat, and, looking up at his father, said: 'Well, I must come back to see you again before I go home.'

'Yes, you and Mary must come back this evening, and let me see what you have done.   You must not run away from her, but walk along by her side, and show her the way.   God loves good children,' and he placed his hand caressingly on the child's head.

Every feeling of unwillingness was gone.   Kindness had conquered all opposition.

'Come after your day's work is done, and let me see how you have prospered.   God speed you on your way, and give the people hearts of kindness towards you, my children.'

Mary received the basket from her father's hands, filled with the results of his week's labor.   Joseph took up his hat and placed it upon his head.   As he did so, he began to cry.

'What ails you, child?' said his father, stooping over and taking hold of him.

'The people will laugh at me 'cause Tom's hat is so big.'

The father well understood now the ground of the little fellow's opposition to going with his sister.

'There, don't cry, my little boy.   I will make the hat fit you.   See, I'll take one of these laces and draw it up until you can wear it very well.'

He took one of the unfinished ones from the settee, and bound it round the hat, then fitted it to his head, and tied it.

'Now it looks well.   Dry your tears, and go with Mary. And if anybody laughs at you, you mus'n't mind it.   Be a man.'

The little boy stepped on after Mary, feeling that his father knew better than he did, to be sure, but not altogether satisfied that the hat was as becoming as it should be. And the turnkey had scarcely closed the inner door of the gaol, before he took it off, and holding it up in his hand, examined it minutely. He replaced it again with a half-satisfied air, and taking Mary's hand, the two passed the bridge, and sought the town.

It is a sad, yet intensely interesting picture, to see these two unfortunate children, the one blind and timid as a fawn, the other a little boy scarcely six years old, barefooted, and but thinly clad, wandering from house to house with the little basket of stay-laces, which was all the means of support for a mother and four children.

'Will you buy some of these laces, if you please, sir?' asked a gentle voice of a man, as he stood in the door of his shop, gazing into the street.

He looked upon the applicant a moment, and then muttered to himself, 'That pestilent fellow Bunyan's daughter,' and answered sharply:

'No, go on; I want none of your laces.'

The blood rushed to the pale brow and cheek of the girl, and tears gathered in her eyes. She clasped her brother's hand closely, and was about to pass on, as commanded. But little Joseph was not so easily intimidated; and looking at the man as he stood there, rubbing his hands together to keep them warm, he said:

'But we want bread, sir. We haven't got anything to eat at home, all of us—mother, and Tom, and Sarah and us. And if you don't buy Mary's laces, all of us will starve, sir.'

The man eyed the child closely and hesitated to reply. He thought of his four little ones at home, his Mary and Sarah; and although bitter against the nonconformists, willing at any time, in his party zeal, to see their heads cut off, yet the affections of a father were strong in his bosom, and triumphed over sectarian hatred; so he bade the blind girl hand him her basket that he might look at her laces.

As she reached out her basket, she turned her face to him. He had a full sight of it from under her blue bonnet. He had never seen anything so delicately beautiful, so pensively sad. It was the first time he had ever had a full view of her countenance, though he had often seen her passing through the streets, and had learned that she was the blind child of John Bunyan, whom he hated intensely. Her sweet, sorrowful look touched his heart, and pity for the child gained for the moment the ascendency over hatred for the father.

'What is your price for a bunch of these, child?'

'A penny, sir, for the small bunches, and twopence for the large ones,' she answered modestly, yet cheerfully.

The kind tones of the speaker had animated her heart, and filled it with hope. It was the first application she had made, and she was delighted with her success. She thought of her father's earnest request, and she felt that God would answer that prayer.

'Take as many of them as you please, sir,' she ventured to say, as the man was casting over the bunches. 'I want to sell them all to-day, for my mother and the children have no bread.'

'Here, child, I will take these six small bunches, and these three large ones.'

Mary's heart leaped with joy, as she thought of the money she was about to receive.

He walked into his store to get it.

'Didn't he take many?' said Joseph smiling, and looking up into his sister's face. 'We'll have bread now, won't we, Mary?'

'Yes, Joseph; didn't father tell you God would give us bread?'

'God ain't going to give us this bread, Mary; mother's going to buy it.'

She began to explain, but the step of the shopkeeper arrested her.

'Here, little blind girl, is your money,' and he placed in her hand a new bright shilling.

Her heart leaped with delight, as she felt the beautiful, new coin. She knew from the feeling of it that it was a pretty thing, and her highly cultivated imagination, together with that exquisite sensitiveness which the blind all possess, invested it with a thousand unknown charms. She felt like flying to the prison, to show it to her father. She pictured to herself the joy of her mother, when she should see it. She had never before, in all her selling, received so much at once. The only thought that marred her intense happiness was, that now the kind shop-keeper had so many he would never want any more.

'Good morning, sir,' she said to the shopkeeper, as she gathered her basket and proceeded on her way. Joseph, in his joy, forgot to speak.

As soon as he was far enough from the door not to be heard by the man, he said in an ecstacy of delight:

'Oh, Mary, Mary, I am so glad I came with you! I told the man to buy your laces, didn't I? I told him we had no bread at home, and we would all starve if he didn't do it. I'm coming with you every time to help you sell.'

'I want you to come with me, Joseph, but you must feel that it was God who put it into the heart of that man to treat us so kindly.'

'Well, but I got him to buy the laces, Mary. You know he didn't look at them till I told him we would starve. God made him good to us, but I made him buy the laces.'

'No, no, Joseph, you couldn't make him do anything; it was God. He made him kind to us, for he makes all men——'

'Here Mary, here is another shop; and the man is in the door. You see if I don't make him buy too.'

'Where, Joseph? take me to him, and may God make him kind to us.'

'Yes, and I'll make him buy the laces. Then we'll have two big pieces of money to take to father. Won't he be glad?'

'Good morning, sir,' said Joseph, leaving Mary's side, so eager was he to show his power. 'Won't you buy some laces, sir?'

'Buy what?' said the man in a harsh tone, drawing down his brow in a heavy frown.

'Some laces, sir,' replied Joseph, so quickly as to prevent Mary from answering.

'Laces, sir, laces. Father made them.'

'And who is your father?' growled the man.

'His name is John Bunyan, sir. Don't you know him, sir? They put him in gaol because he would preach.'

'Yes, and they ought to keep him there. He is a vile disturber of the peace.'

Mary felt keenly the unkindness of the man's words and voice, and would fain have passed on. But Joseph, although his ardor was somewhat damped, was determined not to yield so readily. So he took the basket from Mary, and going up to the man, he said boldly, 'Here they are, sir, won't you buy some?'

'No, I don't want any of your laces.'

'Joseph,' whispered Mary. But the little fellow, all eager to prove the truth of his boast, heeded not the softly-spoken words.

'We've got no bread at home, and mother and us children will starve if you don't buy Mary's laces,' and the little fellow looked up into his face triumphantly, feeling assured this speech would effect his purpose.

' It would be a good thing if you did. You and your father, and all such trash, and then we should have peace in the kingdom. I want none of your laces. If your father was hung, it would be a good thing for the people.'

The little fellow was confounded. He could say no more, but burst into tears. Silent tears were streaming down the flushed cheek of the blind child. She took her brother by the hand, and they walked away weeping—the two poor, suffering, insulted children. The heartless man looked after them, muttering between his teeth imprecations on them and their father. They passed into a side street, and wandered to the outskirts of the city, where a few poor Baptists lived.

'You see, Joseph,' said Mary, as they walked along, ' that it was God who made the man kind to us.'

He was convinced, yet unwilling to acknowledge his conviction. No words could ever have presented so strong an argument; and he learned a lesson that day which he never forgot in after years. It was to him a proof of the sovereignty of God and his special providence, which no logic of after-life could ever gainsay.

They went from house to house in the suburbs of the town, disposing of their little store wherever they could find a purchaser. They wandered on from place to place—sometimes receiving a penny for their laces, at other times only a kind refusal—until the day was well spent. Then they set them down on the step of an old untenanted house, and ate their dry bread.

'If Tom was big like that young man from London, he could work and make us bread, couldn't he, Mary?' said Joseph to his sister, as they set on the rickety doorstep of the old house.

Mary's countenance instantly brightened, and a gentle blush spread over her pale cheek.

'Yes,' answered the blind girl, letting fall on her lap the delicate hand that held the crust of bread. 'He could make us bread, but we must trust in God to give it to us until Tom is large enough.'

Mary spoke the words almost mechanically, for her mind was absorbed with another idea. She was trying to think just how large the young man from London was, and how he appeared. She had never gazed upon his face, but she knew he must be what the world calls handsome, for his voice was so musical, and there was in his tread that which gave to her a certainty that he was noble. She had pictured him to herself, his every feature, his every expression, his every change of countenance. But how should she be sure she was right? She would ask Joseph.

'How does that young man from London look, Joseph? Is he tall, and what is the color of his hair and eyes? I wish I could see him,' she said to herself. But her spirit answered 'Never, never.'

'Oh, he is a big man, Mary,' replied Joseph enthusiastically, for William Dormer's attention to him during his visit had served to enlist his heart and win his warmest admiration. 'Broad, like father, and so pretty.'

'You mean fine-looking, Joseph,' replied Mary, smiling at the child's earnestness.

'Yes, he looks very fine. And I love him too.'

'And his eyes and hair, how do they look?'

'Oh, he has blue eyes, very blue eyes, and hair like father's. It is blacker than father's, but ain't as black as mother's.'

Mary caught the idea in a moment. It was just as she had supposed. With these certain outlines, she could fill up the picture, and she did it, making it as perfect as her own brilliant imagination could do.

This is one advantage the blind have over those who have sight. We see imperfection everywhere, know things as they are really. They live in a world of their own creation, and its beings are either angels or demons. The latter they drive out from their purview; they only flit across their horizon like a frightful phantom, and are gone for ever, while the angels ever remain, filling with glory and gladness the ideal land which they have created.

The image was written on Mary's soul. It never departed.

Their meal, if so it could be denominated, was finished, and the children resumed their labor. On they went, until their limbs ached, and their hearts became discouraged. Thoughts of the approving smile and kind words of the father, and the happiness and gratitude of the mother, had nerved them to their labor when they were well-nigh ready to faint.

'See, Mary,' said Joseph, as he dragged his weary limbs along, 'the sun is almost down. I want to go home. I am so tired.'

'We will go and tell father what we have done. I wish we had sold all the laces. He will be so pleased.'

'We've sold most of them, Mary, you and me, haven't we?'

The blind girl passed her hands rapidly over the contents of the basket.

'Yes, only four large bunches and six small ones.'

'And we've got a good deal of money, haven't we, Mary?'

'Yes, Joseph, we can have some bread now.'

'And can't you get me a new hat and some new shoes, and you some too?'

'Oh, no, not now. We must wait for these things. For mother's sake, and little Sarah's; can't you?'

The little fellow hung his head. It was quite a struggle. He wished so much for the new hat.

'Yes,' he answered slowly, 'but we'll come again soon, and father will have a basket full of laces; and it may be, we'll sell them all and get plenty of money.'

'I hope so,' was the doubting reply.

The father smiled, as the children told him of their success; but his heart was pierced sorely as Joseph repeated to him the cruel words of the heartless shopkeeper.

'God bless you, my poor children,' said he, as he pressed them to his bosom and kissed them.

The children passed the outer gate, and hastened, angels of mercy as they were, to throw light and joy around the hearthstone of the cottage at Elstow.

'Will you go to London, Mr. Bunyan?' asked the gaoler of him as they sat conversing together in the evening twilight. 'You have spoken of it so often, and you remember you told me yesterday you thought you would go and see what could be done for your cause.'

'Yes, I shall go. I must leave nothing unturned that promises success. My family can't live without me. My wife and children will starve for bread.'

'Well, whenever you want to go, let me know, and I will see you get out of gaol. I will risk the laws of the land in this.'

'There can be nothing wrong in it, sir. I am unlawfully put here and kept here; and it is my duty to do all I can to obtain my release. I am going next week.'

'Well, I hope you will have success,' replied the gaoler, as he drew together the door of the cell, leaving it unlocked. 'If I can help you I will as much as is in my power. Good night.'

'Good night,' said Bunyan, as he turned to the little window, to gaze out on the noiseless heavens with their setting of pale solemn stars.

CHAPTER XVI.

THE BLIND GIRL'S DREAM.

THE stars are keeping their silent vigils in the midnight heavens. The moon, as from a full urn, pours a flood of clear, cold radiance over the hushed earth. The earth, gently reposes in the flood of silver light, which from a thousand hills and heights, is reflected back into the cold, crisp air.

The little village of Elstow is sunk in unbroken stillness. Not a sound steals out to disturb the deep, dread silence. From every hamlet and homestead the voice of busy life has gradually died away, the angel of sleep has moved on, sealing for his own silent domain those, who, through the day just closed, have hoped, and feared, and toiled, and sighed. And now the noiselessness of death presides over every hearthstone.

'Neath the uncurtained window, just where the moonbeams revealed her delicate form and angel face, the blind girl lies sleeping. The truckle-bed in which she rests, like the window, is all uncurtained. The moonlight sweeps in through the window, and falls in showers of silver glory over the tired form of the sleeper, and on across the uncarpeted floor, and steals up the farther wall, higher and higher, until it lights up with its brilliant beams the whole room. In the quiet cottage room the good man's family rest. They have committed themselves to the guardian care of the great Shepherd of Israel, who watcheth over all. They sleep sweetly, for toil makessweet their still repose.

Beside the sister lies the little Joseph. They have trudged through a weary round during the livelong day to procure means of subsistence for the mother and children, and now together they rest their aching limbs on the same narrow bed. A beautiful picture for the guardian angels to look upon.

The blind girl dreams. A smile of ineffable beauty steals over her worn features. Her lips move as if speaking. She is conversing with the angels. One there is amid that throng moving in panoramic vision, clad in garments of light, that arrests and fixes her gaze. She smiles; her lips move again; she pronounces his name—it is William Dormer.

All day she has entertained his image, a welcome guest;

and now that she rests, he comes to her in dreams, and the
eyes of her spirit gaze upon him enraptured. She could
not see him by day. The body held in subjection the soul.
But now sleep has come, and unfettered the spirit, and it
soars untrammeled through the limitless extent of the
universe, and dwells at will upon the ravishing scenes
spread out before it. Time and space are annihilated, and
the sealed eyes are unsealed.

She is no longer a child, but side by side they wander
through shaded walks, and by gently murmuring streams,
while visions of enchanting loveliness burst at every turn
upon their ecstatic view. The prison is gone, and hunger
and famine are fled for ever. Her father is free, and the
mother and the children regale themselves on delicious
viands. In the far-off vista is the cottage at Elstow, draped
in the most beautiful surroundings. She is in another
realm, where all is joy and happiness. Pain, and trial, and
suffering, shall no more be hers, but everlasting peace and
gladness. Surely she is blest now. Intense bliss fills her
being. The vision is too enrapturing; she awakes—to find
herself the prisoner's poor blind Mary—a child of sorrow,
nestled in her low truckle-bed, beside her little weary
brother.

The pale, silent moon looks coldly down. The face is
changed in its expression. The angelic smile is gone; the
heavenly beauty has faded out from the pale face, and
sorrow and disappointment mark the care-worn features.
Tears, silent, painful, gather in the darkened eyes, and
course unmarked, save by the guardian angel, adown her
thin, pale cheeks.

Oh, how exquisitely painful is it thus to be snatched from
the very pavilions of heaven back to the dull, deep misery
of earth! Fain would we put off mortality, to escape the
trial.

Long, weary hours—almost till the day-dawn—the poor
child lies there, living over in memory the beautiful vision.
She dwells upon it with exquisite delight. Shall she ever
realise it? She asks herself the question again and again.
There comes to her only a vague unsatisfactory answer.
She is now but a child—a poor blind child—and her father
is in prison. She has heard that in heaven the blind see,
and I'll go by and by. ' I must wait until I get there,' she
says to herself.

CHAPTER XVII.

BUNYAN VISITS HIS FAMILY.

BUNYAN was permitted by his gaoler, 'in whose sight he found favor,' not only to go occasionally among his flock, and to visit his family, but also to go to London, to solicit aid from the Baptists there, in view of his coming trial, which was to take place at the Assizes in 1662.

In thus permitting Bunyan to go about, often at option, the gaoler certainly exceeded the limits of the law, and made himself amenable thereto. He seems to have been driven to his leniency by the great injustice and severity of the Judges. They had violated their prerogative by insulting Bunyan and imprisoning him without a fair trial. He violated his by granting him privileges which were not legally in his power to confer. But he erred on the side of mercy. Charles had issued proclamations in favor of the Nonconformists, and the Judges, in the face of these proclamations, had pronounced sentence on Bunyan. In showing favors to him, therefore, the gaoler was only manifesting his confidence in the king, and respect for his promises. The words of the king and the acts of the Judges were contradictory. The gaoler preferred to show his loyalty by following the former, even while it subjected him to the hatred and persecution of the latter. He had entire reliance in his prisoner's integrity. Indeed, he looked upon him with almost superstitious awe, which was increased by the following incident.

'It was known to some of the persecuting prelates,' says Ivimey, the historian of Bunyan, 'that he was often out of prison,' through the leniency of the gaoler. So they determined to send down an officer to see about the matter, and to talk with the gaoler about this dereliction of duty; and in order the better to entrap him, the officer was commanded to reach Bedford in the middle of the night. That night Bunyan had gone home to his family. But he could not sleep; something seemed to tell him to go back to his cell. He rose, and told his wife 'he must return immediately.' She protested, but he insisted, and departed. 'The gaoler blamed him for coming in at so unseasonable an hour.' The day had scarcely dawned before the messenger sent by the prelates arrived, and asked—

'Are all the prisoners safe?'

'Yes,' answered the gaoler, while a slight shudder passed over him at the thought of his narrow escape from danger.

'Is John Bunyan safe?' asked the messenger, hoping to catch the gaoler in neglect of duty.

'Yes,' replied the gaoler, wondering at the providence that led Bunyan back to gaol at midnight.

But the messenger is not satisfied. 'Let me see him,' said he, hoping he could not be produced. But he *was* produced, and all was well.

The messenger left disappointed. When he was gone the gaoler turned to Bunyan and said:

'Well, you may go out again when you think proper, for you know when to return better than I can tell you.'

This incident, so well calculated to impress the mind of the gaoler with a belief in the supernatural guidance which directed John Bunyan, occurred, as we gather from the records, before his trip to London. Indeed, it would seem very reasonable to suppose that such an occurrence would have had great influence in inducing the gaoler to extend his grant of privilege.

Preparatory to his setting out for London, Bunyan goes home to spend the night with his wife and children. Let us follow him thither. He has oftentimes, in the silence and loneliness of his cell, committed his way to God, beseeching his guidance and blessing on the undertaking before him, and he would now kneel down with his Elizabeth and his four helpless children, that they may together supplicate the throne of mercy and of love. He goes for their sakes as well as his own; therefore he would send up a united prayer for success in his effort. Besides, he wanted the advice of his wife, on whose judgment he greatly leaned. She had been there before him, and although she had been unsuccessful, yet he could profit by her experience.

The declining sun saw Bunyan treading the meadows between Bedford and Elstow, with earnest, thoughtful face. All the day he had been hard at work tagging laces. His mind had been filled with pressing thoughts while his fingers had plied his daily toil. He had brought the results of his labor with him, that the blind child might dispose of them in and around the village of Elstow.

He had trod these same meadows and the narrow lane, when wrapped in his cloak of self-righteousness; and, strengthened by his repentance and promises to God to do better, 'he pleased God,' so he thought, 'as well as any man in England.' He was a 'brisk talker' in matters of religion then, he himself tells us. But alas! he was only a talker. He had never tasted of the grace of God, which makes wise unto salvation. He was a Pharisee, and despised the cross of the Lord Jesus Christ. On reviewing this period of his life in after years, when the Spirit of God had given him a new heart, he pronounces against himself in this wise, 'As yet I was nothing but a poor, painted hypocrite, yet I loved to be talked of as one that was truly godly. I was proud of my godliness, and, indeed, did all I could to be seen or well spoken of by men. Poor wretch as I was, I was all this while ignorant of Jesus Christ, and going about to establish my own right-eousness, and had perished therein had not God in his mercy showed me my state by nature.'

And he had wended his way over these same meadows when the voice of Sinai thundered in his ears, and guilt lay heavy upon his soul. When the conversation of the 'three or four women of Bedford sitting at a door in the sun talking about a new birth,' had fixed deep in his heart the arrows of conviction, so that 'he made it his busi-ness to be going again and again into the company of these four women

'Knitting in the sun,'

for he could not stay away,' until his mind was so fixed on eternity, and on the things of the kingdom of heaven, that neither pleasures, nor profits, nor persuasions, nor threats could loose it, or make it let go its hold. And here he had experienced that great joy that made him desire to speak of the love of God, and his mercy to him, even to the very crows that sat in the ploughed lands before him.

These meadows and the lane had witnessed many of his severest struggles, his joyous and joyless reveries. Tra-velling along this little lane one day, 'the temptation is put' upon him to say to the puddles in the horse pad, 'Be dry,' and to the dry places, 'Be ye puddles.' This is to test his faith; he must needs work a miracle to prove to him whether or not he *has* faith. But, just as he is about to give the command, the thought comes into his mind, 'but go under yonder hedge and pray first that God would make you able.' But he pauses for a moment, for another thought 'comes hot' upon him: 'What if I pray and try to do it, and yet do nothing notwithstanding; then to be sure, I have no *faith*, but am a castaway and am lost.'

All these trials and temptations pass in rapid review before him as he walks along, and he sees in them the work of the devil, who in times past has beset him most sorely. He has journeyed beyond the Slough of Despond now, but he has not been perfected through sufferings. Other trials are hard upon him. His faith is not yet sufficiently matured to lay hold of the exceeding great and sure promises, and make them his own. A veil will interpose itself. The hand of God is manifested to him, but his purpose is hidden.

He reaches the little close in front of the cottage just as the sun sinks in the western horizon. The children see him and run out to meet him. His Elizabeth comes also, but her step is more sober than that of the children; not that her heart is less warm, but she has a graver way of manifesting her love. Her face is sober too, as well as her step. Her daily cares weigh heavily upon her, and sorrow saps her joy. Kindly greetings and affectionate words are exchanged. The meal is spread and they together partake of the homely food. The good man sees the board is scantily supplied; his heart is pained, but he takes no notice of it. They gather round the fire-side, little Sarah on one knee and Joseph on the other. The blind girl sits near him with her hand resting on his shoulder, and her sightless eyes turned to his face, while her ears drink in eagerly his every word. He sees that the expression of her face, too, is changed; her manner is more subdued than ever. He ascribes it to her troubles. He cannot read the many thoughts *that* dream has given rise to. His faithful Elizabeth is on the other side, her industrious fingers employed in work for the little family. Tom sits in the corner where he can see them all. His father's words have a charm for him, and he never wearies of asking him questions. The children grow sleepy at last, and must be put to bed; but, before they go, the father kneels in their midst, and asks the blessing of God upon his household. After a while Thomas gets drowsy, and Mary feels that the father and mother wish to be alone, so she quietly steals away to her little truckle bed, where little Joseph is sleeping—and the two are left to arrange their plans for the future.

'I am going to London to-morrow, Elizabeth. I must see if I cannot get my liberty. I think if I could be there I might induce the Baptists to intercede for me. I want to show the king that I have been dealt unfairly by, and it may be God will put it into his heart to release me, or to make the Judges give a new trial. They won't give me a hearing at the next Assizes, if I do not look after my own case. They will do me injustice again.'

The wife sighed as she thought of her fruitless effort. But she believed her husband could be more successful than she had been, and she advised him to go.

'The Lord prosper you, my husband,' she said, as he made an end of unfolding his plans to her, 'and give the king mercy towards you. These cruel men have no mercy. They would take your life from you to gratify their spite. You can't hope for any good at their hands, and if the king's heart is not moved with pity, they will leave you to rot in that old gaol.'

'But we must make up our minds, under the grace of God, to bear the worst, Elizabeth, in all things enduring hardness as good soldiers of the Lord Jesus Christ. These are heavy trials we are passing through, but He who knows best puts them upon us. We cannot fathom his wisdom, but we know that his love is as deep as it is. I feel hopeful in this matter, but I would not deceive myself. Let us take joyfully what the Lord sends.'

CHAPTER XVIII.

BUNYAN'S VISIT TO LONDON.

THE day-dawn had scarcely gilded the eastern horizon, before Bunyan set off on his journey. He had no time to lose. A great work was before him. Much of the way was spent in prayer to God for the direction of His Spirit, and a blessing on his undertaking. A few who met him in the road, near Bedford, knew him. They were surprised to see him at liberty; but in him they saw only poor John Bunyan, the *tinker*, imprisoned for preaching the gospel. They never dreamed that there walked a man whom future generations would rise up and call blessed; one whose fame would go out to all the world, and his mighty deeds to the end of the earth. The pious of them no doubt turned their eyes reverently to heaven while they sent up a prayer of thanksgiving and praise that their lot was so much better than that of the poor prisoner; while the wicked scoffed and turned away from one who was called by them a '*pestilent fellow*,' and a '*poor mad tinker*.' But he was a glorious martyr for the truth as it is in Christ Jesus. He knew why he suffered, and his is now the reward 'of

patient continuance in well doing,'—even eternal life—
' and he shall shine as the stars for ever and ever,' for hath
he not turned many to righteousness ?

On reaching London, Bunyan first found out Elizabeth
Gaunt and William Dormer. By her he was introduced to
many of the Baptists of the city, who afterwards became
his personal friends, giving him all the assistance in their
power, not only as a suppliant for mercy before the king's
bench, but as an author. Through Mrs. Gaunt, he became
acquainted with Henry Jessee, ' a man whose talents,
learning, and philanthropy, would have given additional
weight to any good cause. He had prepared a new trans-
lation of the Scriptures, and was an almoner of the poor
Jews in Jerusalem, as well as the most influential minister
of the denomination.

' We are glad to see you, brother Bunyan,' said this
truthful minister, as he shook the hand of the prisoner.
' Your trials and sufferings for the sake of the truth
have reached our ears, and we rejoice that you have been
enabled by the grace of God to possess your soul in patience,
and thereby attest his love and goodness : you suffer in a
good cause.'

' God has most wonderfully stayed me up under my trials,
thanks be to his holy name,' replied Bunyan. ' Had it not
been for his all-abounding grace, which has strengthened
and supported me, I should long ago have failed under my
burden.'

' We have this comfortable assurance, brother Bunyan,
that as our day so shall our strength be; you have found it
so ; I know you have, for it is the promise of God, and
cannot fail. These are perilous times to this nation, for
men have become fierce despisers of those that are good,
having a form of godliness, but denying the power thereof.
Iniquity is enthroned in high places, and the people of God
are made to murmur because of the oppressor. The prisons
are filled with witnesses for the truth, and the hand of persecution is laid upon those who would live uprightly in the
midst of this wicked and perverse generation. How long
this state of things will last, God alone can tell. He is
purging his people ; he is causing them to walk through the
furnace, that he may bare his mighty arm in their rescue
from the flames. But his scourging is grievous, and we are
made to cry out, "How long, oh Lord, how long before
thou wilt come for our deliverance ? " '

' We are told, brother Jessee, that ' all who will live
godly in Christ Jesus, shall suffer persecutions, and evil

men shall wax worse, deceiving and being deceived.' These things have been foretold, therefore we must not wonder that they have come to pass.'

'Well, how is the state of things with you, brother Bunyan? Have you any hope that you will find mercy in the sight of the king?'

'I have some hope, but it is faint. I have come to London to see what can be done towards obtaining my liberty. I was unjustly put to prison, God knows I was. My enemies snatched me up and clapped me in gaol. They would give me no chance for my freedom; and when my wife went before them to plead for me, they heaped harsh words upon her, and would not listen to her.'

'How are the saints getting on in the country, brother Bunyan? We hear fearful accounts of the treatment they receive at the hands of their enemies.'

'But little do I know of how the times fare with them. The gaol at Bedford is filled with our brethren, who have cried aloud against the sins of the mother of harlots and of her offspring.'

'The times are fearful here, in this sinful city, my brother. Commotions and strifes and fiendish treachery and malice reign among those who are in power, and the righteous are trodden down, and there is none to redress their wrongs. The king is playing the part of juggler to the Dissenters. Our Mayor is harassing our people in every way that his hellish ingenuity can invent. It seems that Satan is let loose to destroy the children of God, and bring contempt on the heritage of the Lord.'

'And can no one lift up a voice in defence of God's own elect, when blood crieth from the ground. Is there none to avenge them? Oh, when will these things come to an end!'

'Our Mayor is fierce and cruel, my brother. His delight is to torment the children of God. He pursues them as a lion does his prey. He seeks them in their homes, and in the by-ways, and brings them to a speedy trial. They can find no refuge from his bloody vengeance and his determined hatred. He gloats over the blood of the saints, for his desire is to cut them off from the earth. His name has become a by-word for cruelty even among those who despise the Nonconformists. They say the "devil has ceased to be black and has become BROWN."'

'And does no one lift up a hand to stay the current of iniquity? Surely God's people should stand up when his enemies came in as a flood. O God, raise up some standard bearer that will carry the word of truth and righteousness into the domain of the man of sin.'

'There is a brother, Henry Adis, who is preparing a thunderbolt for this Brown, together with the other magistrates of the city. He calls it "Thunder to Brown the Mayor, by one of the sons of Zion become a Boanerges."'

'And will this bring about any good? Will the magistrates heed it?'

'I cannot tell. The Lord grant that it may do much good in opening the eyes of this people, to see the great wrongs which do shame this land. But they are so besotted in sin there is but little hope. God have mercy, God have mercy on them.' And the old minister's face lighted up with the intensity of the emotion that filled his bosom.

'I would see this brother before I leave; God speed him in his work, and may it be effectual in upsetting the plans of all who would bring to naught the truth as it is in Jesus.'

'Amen, amen! Will you see the king about your case before you leave, brother Bunyan?'

'I do greatly desire to do so, if it will but promote my cause. I would leave nothing untried to secure my liberty. My wife and four little ones do perish for bread, while I lay housed up in that cold damp gaol—put there and kept there by the enemies of God. But I would have your opinion about it. I came here to consult my brethren. I want to use the best means. I am in a strait. I don't know how to go on.'

'If you can obtain audience of the king, then it may be well. But this godless monarch is so given up to his sports and his vices, that he has lost all care for his kingdom. He feels that his fish, in the lakes and ponds, are of infinitely more value than the souls of Dissenters and Nonconformists. And he would not lose one hour from tennis if the interest of his whole realm were at stake. His entire indifference to the affairs of state is shameful and fearful.'

'Then you think there is but little hope in making application to his Majesty?'

'You can but try. The thing is uncertain. Albeit it cannot make your condition worse. I will go with you to consult our wisest brethren, and whatsoever is best we must do.'

From house to house the two men went, that they might obtain the opinions and views of those calculated to advise. It was deemed prudent, after close consultation, to present a petition to the king, through two of Bunyan's friends. It was feared lest his presence might stir up feelings of opposition, seeing that he had left the gaol without permission, and come down to London.

Some of the Baptists of the city were to be guarded against. Suspicion rested upon them, and therefore, it became necessary for Bunyan to become very circumspect in his movements, and not to be known as associated with them, or to be in any way connected with them. Unfortunately a few of them were ' Fifth Monarchy men,' and, of course, detested by the court and cabinet. They also placed under suspicion the whole denomination, whose movements were watched with lynx eyes by the enemies of the Nonconformists.

Bunyan was soon convinced, from his associations with his brethren, and from such information as he could casually pick up, that the court was in such a state of profligacy, and there was also such hatred to all who did not subscribe to the prevailing religion, that it would be useless for him to apply, in person, for change or mitigation of the sentence under which he was suffering. He had no influence at court. Indeed, his presence there would, it was supposed, act unfavorably to his cause. He would be looked upon as one who disregarded all law, and set at defiance the acts of those in rule. Charles was by no means a stickler for law or order, but, being the dupe of designing men, and the slave of his own whims, it was feared lest the presence of Bunyan should give rise to some caprice, by which his object would be entirely frustrated.

Bunyan felt dreadfully disappointed at the seemingly necessary result of his mission. He was so fully possessed with a sense of the justice of his cause, that he had come to believe that if he could only have an opportunity of presenting his own case, the result must be all that could be desired. He, in this, shows his ignorance of the then existing state of affairs of the realm. He had only read Charles's ' Proclamation.' He knew nothing of that man as he really was—given up to the indulgence of every passion, rioting in an excess, disgusting and destroying.

After much consultation and prayer, it was decided that William Kiffin and Richard Pilgrim should present a suitable petition to the king, at such a time as seemed most likely to secure success to their cause. William Kiffin was a Baptist minister, a man of wealth and influence, and highly respected by all classes. He was instrumental in obtaining a reprieve for twelve persons, who had been sentenced to death at Aylesbury. It was, therefore, supposed that a request from him would be regarded. Richard Pilgrim, though of the Millenarian party, was yet too obscure to arouse any suspicion. He was a man of fine sense and pleasing address, and was, therefore, selected to accompany Mr. Kiffin.

' How has the Lord prospered your cause to-day, brother Bunyan?' asked Mrs. Gaunt, as he came in, after a very hard day's labor. 'Has your petition gone before the king yet?'

'No. The brethren have concluded to wait for a more favorable opportunity than the present. The king is so engaged with his routs and plays, and wanton exercises, as to have no time for other matters.'

' You will not go home till you see what will come of it then, will you?'

'I must go to-morrow. My time is at an end.'

' What, go back, brother Bunyan, and nothing done? You ought to make one attempt, if no more.'

'The brethren tell me it would not do to present myself before the king. It would only chafe him.'

'And will you do nothing at all to obtain your freedom?'

'I have done all I could. I must trust the rest to brother Kiffin and Richard Pilgrim.'

'And so you go back as you came? What sad news it will be to your poor wife and children!'

'We must trust in God, sister Gaunt. These things are all in his hands. If he sees fit to keep me in gaol, it is for some wise purpose. If bonds and imprisonments are my lot, I must learn to rejoice in afflictions. I am a man encompassed by infirmities, and sometimes my faith grows weak, but the Spirit enables me to build myself up in the promises, until at last I get a comfortable assurance of the hand of God in all my afflictions, and then all is well with me, so long as this confidence lasts.'

' But you will not go back to prison when you go home, brother Bunyan? You will wait until this matter is settled for you?'

'I will go back to prison and stay there until the question is decided. I must not bring in danger the kind gaoler, who granted me the liberty to come to London.'

'And you will go back? Well, that's right. We must be willing to seal our testimony with our blood. The Lord give you grace to follow him in all his ways.'

The prisoner's heart was very heavy as he wended his way from the metropolis; from an elevation on the road, he paused to look back upon the city, the seat of sin and iniquity, of every uncleanness and enormity. Bitter reflections filled his mind and stirred up his blood, as he thought of the shame and suffering, the contumely and reproach, the children of God were day by day exposed to, to gratify the cruel hatred and the unrestrained iniquity of a profligate king and his heartless courtiers. 'How long, O Lord, how long,' he exclaimed, 'shall the evil one reign triumphant! How long shall the mother of harlots and her iniquitous offspring drink up the blood of the saints? Make haste, O Lord, to deliver us! Make bare thine arm in the eyes of the nation! Oh, be pleased to help us, and that right speedily! Oh, rescue thy chosen from the hands of the oppressor! Deliver thy darling from destruction!'

Bunyan was sorely disappointed; and his great heart, usually so brave, so full of fortitude and of daring, sunk within him. His physical strength was impaired. Close confinement and unhealthy diet had made great inroads on his naturally vigorous constitution. The hope that buoyed up his drooping spirits so long, was completely wrecked. All the rigors of a winter's confinement were staring him in the face, and the suffering and exposure to which his family must be subjected, filled up to the very brim the bitter cup, which he must now drain to the dregs.

There was a gleam of light that came glancing athwart the gloom. Kiffin and Pilgrim might succeed with the petition; if so, he would rejoice in his past trials, for he felt that they had wrought a good work in him, having added to his temperance patience, and to patience godliness— so that, in the knowledge of our Lord Jesus Christ, he was neither barren nor unfruitful. He weighed carefully all the probabilities against the improbabilities, and finally concluded that his prospect was still a fair one. He knew his own innocence so well, that he felt it was impossible that the king should not be convinced of the great wrong done him.

How often we reason thus, but how fallacious the reasoning! Bunyan did not know Charles; and he relied on the favorable proclamations he had issued; he did not realise that these provisions were made only for the purpose of establishing their false giver the more securely in power.

The road appeared long and weary to the traveller. He carried in his heart the burden of sore disappointment. When he reached his house, his faithful wife read in his countenance the failure of his mission. She made every endeavor to soothe and comfort him. While her own soul was pierced as with a thousand arrows, she strove to speak words of cheer to her despairing husband.

The next day Bunyan went back to the gaol. As he reached the outer gate, he met his gaoler. Their eyes met. Each read in the countenance of the other a tale of distress. The gaoler handed him a document; he paused and looked over it.

'God knows it is a slander that I went to London to make or plot an insurrection, or to sow divisions.'

'Yes, that is false, Mr. Bunyan, I know it is,' said the sympathising gaoler. 'But you see what they say here in these directions, "He must no longer look out at the door." If I disobey them now, my life will be the forfeit.'

The gailor spoke in the tones of the deepest compassion. He loved and respected the prisoner, and fain would have granted him his liberty.

'There is but one hope left,' exclaimed Bunyan, with a sorrow he had never before felt—it was for the moment almost despair—'and that is to get my name in the calendar of felons for the next Assizes, that I may get a hearing. This is all that is left me now.' And this effort to be heard before the Assizes of 1662 was the last attempt Bunyan made to extricate himself from the unjust sentence of his heartless Judges.

CHAPTER XIX.

THE BLIND GIRL IN LONDON.

THE prison doors have been closed, and the seal of tyranny placed thereon. Bunyan can no longer visit his family, or mingle privily among his brethren in their meetings of prayer. Ten long, lonely years must roll their weary round, before he shall again come forth from his dark, chill cell, to liberty and to joy.

'Hard fate!' we exclaim. But God in wisdom ordered it. His decrees are immutable, and he works all things 'according to the counsel of his own will.' What matters it, then, where we are, or what we suffer, if we are found in Christ Jesus? All things, however calamitous, are working for our good. We are fulfilling the behests of Him who knoweth the end from the beginning, and is hastening on, through his children as feeble instrumentalities, that glorious time, 'when the kingdoms of this world shall become the kingdoms of the Lord and of his Christ, and he shall reign for ever and ever.' 'Let all, therefore, who suffer persecution and trial, possess their souls in patience, yea, rejoice in afflictions, watching and praying, looking for and hasting unto the coming of the day of God.' 'Blessed is he that watcheth,' and he that endureth temptation, for when he is tried, he shall receive the crown of life, which the Lord hath promised to them that love him.

We must, for a time, bid farewell to Bunyan. We shall come again to look at him in his noisome cell, there to find him engaged in writing that book, which, next to the Bible, has instructed all succeeding generations in the things pertaining to eternal life.

It is 1665. Charles has been seated five years on the throne of his fathers. These five years have witnessed cruelties, outrages, and profligacies unparalleled in all the preceding history of the kingdom. The court, following the example of the dissolute monarch, has given itself up to unlimited indulgence in vice and crime. Pleasure is goddess of the realm, and reigns supreme. Her votaries throng the palace and the parliament, and govern every class of society. London is crowded with those, who, eager to follow the example of a popular monarch, have congregated together to yield themselves up to whatever vicious amusement his prestige has rendered noted. He has but to speak, and thousands catch up his words to echo them through the land. Never had there been before, never has there been since, a monarch so puissant in his weakness, so arbitrary in all neglect of rule, as was Charles II. of England. Never has the world seen a court and nation so given over to excess, lascivious folly, and vice, as was the court of St. James and the English nation, during his reign.

It is London—London with its teeming myriads, its wealth and poverty, its joy and misery, its worship and its crowded thoroughfares, where magnificence moves in royal trappings, and its low, damp alleys of crime, where want, and wretchedness dwell, familiar inmates of many a hovel.

The stirring sounds of busy life and activity ever go up from the numberless thousands who throng its streets and crowd its myriad haunts.

The blind girl pauses, as the din of the mighty city falls upon her delicately attuned ear. She cannot see it, but she feels it—its power and vastness overwhelm her soul. It is the very spot on which her mother stood three years before, to cast a last look upon the city, wherein dwelt those who had locked the prison doors upon her husband, and refused to open them because he was a proclaimer of the gospel of the Son of God.

The blind girl is a child no longer. The blush of womanhood is upon her cheek, and its presence may be seen in her rounded form, and tall, graceful figure. The feeble delicateness of childhood had given way to the strength and symmetry of riper years; and the excessive sensitiveness, which caused her to shrink from every touch, has been gradually supplanted by a consciousness of her own powers and responsibilities. But she is shrinking still. And as she feels the vast metropolis before her, she stops suddenly, and grasps tightly the hand of the countryman by her side. With an expression of wonder, mingled with fear, she turns her sightless face to his. But no sound escapes her partly opened lips.

Neighbor Harrow speaks words of soothing kindness to calm her excited bosom. She holds his hand more firmly, and presses more nearly to him. Her closely fitting bonnet shuts out from the eyes of the passers-by her beautiful face with its ever-varying color. Her kerchief is of snow-white, and the nobleman who dashes by, turns his head to look on that symmetrical form, so plainly, yet so chastely clad, which, with modest, lady-like air, keeps pace with the rough countryman at her side.

The sun shines softly down from the western sky, and throws a golden light over the landscape, as the weary travellers descend the long hill which leads to the suburbs of the mighty city. The evening breeze sweeps gently by, and fans with grateful coolness the flushed cheek of the blind maiden. The scene is one of loveliness. Mary feels its beauty, but she is too much excited to dwell upon it. Neighbor Harrow has but little taste for such things. He has seen the sun shine so often, has beheld so many landscapes, over which the god of day poured in boundless magnificence his flood of golden glory, that his heart is altogether untouched by the view around him. He is thinking of London, not of nature and her charms. It has been many a long year since his feet trod the streets of the great capital, and he is wondering at the changes which have been made, since, with the elasticity and ardor of youth, he had made his way through her principal thoroughfares. His step is no longer buoyant; his heart feels the chill of time, and an indistinct sensation of the great change in himself passes through his bosom. He entertains it but for a moment. He is a matter-of-fact old man, and can find no time for fancies and old remembrances.

An hour more and our travellers are in London, inquiring the way to William Kiffin's, the preacher. Mary presses close to the side of neighbor Harrow, as they tread the busy marts of trade. Her wardrobe is tied up in a square cloth, which, during the journey, she had sometimes carried to relieve the kind old man who acted as her guardian.

After much inquiry and great difficulty, the street is found, and the two travellers, dusty and worn, stand before one of the best houses in London. There the passers-by look upon them as supplicants for charity, but they are not. They feel that they have claims on the good man whose presence they seek. They belong to the same great brotherhood with him, and because of this connection, they regard themselves as entitled to his attention. They know but little about the conventionalisms of society, of the distinction which mere wealth makes. They know that William Kiffin is not a king, nor a lord, but a Baptist preacher, like John Bunyan, who has long been incarcerated in the gaol at Bedford.

They see the great and good Kiffin, who receives them with expressions of the warmest friendship, and presses upon them to make his house their home.

But they cannot accede to his kind wishes. They must find Elizabeth Gaunt, for Mrs. Bunyan has told Mary this must be her home while she stays in London. The good man's carriage is at the door. He gets into it, and accompanies them in search of Mrs. Gaunt. He knows her well, as a humble, true disciple of their Lord and Master. She is a member of a church to which he sometimes preaches, and her seat in the house of God is never vacant, save when sickness keeps her away. And he has met her oftentimes, too, in his visits to the poor and distressed of the Baptist brotherhood. Her deeds of charity and love are well known to him, and her praise is on his lips.

At last they find her in her little home, plain and poor, in Drury Lane. They are directed there by one who has for a long time been a recipient of her kindness, of her words of hope and encouragement. It is a poor Baptist brother, whose family, sick and friendless have been watched over and provided for by the untiring efforts and attention of this excellent woman, who ' careth for the things of the Lord.'

She knows the good Mr. Kiffin, and is very glad to see him. She does not recognise Mary, for it has been three years since they have met, and in that time the girl has grown to be a young woman. Her appearance is much changed, but the same sweet, sad smile, lights up the darkened face. This Mrs. Gaunt recalls in a moment, as the young girl is introduced to her by the minister. The two are received with every mark of affection and kindness. The hours pass on and tea time arrives. Mary has been momently expecting the entrance of William Dormer.

For three long years his image has been enshrined in the secret temple of her heart. Her lips have but rarely pronounced his name; but her being has thrilled when that name has fallen upon her ear from other lips. His voice, full and clear, has made rich music to her soul. And the farewell pressure—ah! she has felt it on that thin frail hand through every moment of their separation. She has seen him through every waking moment since he first stood in the cottage door at Elstow a guest of its humble roof. Need we ask what thought had been uppermost in her mind since her father had requested her to go to London and see the king in his behalf? Even the great object of her mission was sometimes lost sight of in the one feeling that possessed her soul—that of hearing again the voice of William Dormer.

A step as of a man is heard on the door-step. She starts and listens intensely. She trembles with blissful expectation. A moment more and she will hear that voice pronounce her name. Agitated she turns in the direction of the open door. It is only the baker's boy come with the bread for the evening meal.

Ah, cruel disappointment! Yet there is a ray of hope; he may come yet. How she longs to hear Mrs. Gaunt pronounce his name, and yet she fears it too. He may be dead. He may be absent from the city, gone home to his mother and sister. How gnawing is suspense, yet it is sometimes better than hopeless certainty. She would ask for herself, but she could not trust her lips to use his name; they would betray her secret. She wondered that neighbor Harrow did not inquire for him.

Neighbor Harrow and Mrs. Gaunt keep up a continued conversation about things pertaining to the Redeemer's kingdom in their different localities. Mary answers agitatedly to the questions which Mrs. Guant asks about her father, her mother, and the children.

Tea is ready. The young man does not appear; his

name has not been mentioned. Mary can eat but little.
Her kind friend insists that she shall partake more freely
of her frugal meal; but she must refuse—she cannot eat.

Weary and depressed, Mary retires to rest. Sleep has
fled from her eyelids; her heart is weighed down under a
burden of bitter disappointment. She feels so lonely too;
away from home and in the midst of strangers, and the bright
hope that nerved her soul to the fearful undertaking, and
buoyed her up under the fatigues of the journey, is gone.
Where can she look for strength and support? Then rose
before her the dark, cold cell, and the form of her dear
father, now pale and worn by five years' confinement in the
prison: and then the home picture—her mother, and
brothers, and little Sarah drudging on from day to day amid
poverty and suffering. She feels she must overcome all
obstacles and fulfill her mission. The night is far advanced
before she falls asleep, and then hideous dreams disturb and
fright her.

She awakes on the morning to find herself still weary
and excitable. After breakfast she unfolds her plans to
Mrs. Gaunt, who promises to assist her in her undertaking
to see the king. But they decide to wait a more favorable
opportunity than the present. They wish also to consult
Mr. Kiffin as to the best course to pursue. Mary's instruction from her father is 'to stay with Mrs. Gaunt until she
can see the king and present her petition.'

Neighbor Harrow attends to his little business, and makes
ready to return to Bedford. Mary bids him farewell with
throbbing heart. She loves Mrs. Gaunt, but she has never
been from home before, and a feeling of loneliness comes
over her as she holds the hand of the good old man who
has nursed her in her infancy, and watched over her and the
household with such love and solicitude since their father
has been taken from them. She gives him many messages
to bear back to Bedford. 'But tell father,' she says in conclusion, 'that I will do all I can, and I hope the king will
hear me.'

The good old man commends her to the guidance of God,
and grasping her hand warmly in his, bids her good-bye.
Then, gathering up his little packages, he turns towards his
home.

CHAPTER XX.

THE BLIND GIRL'S APPLICATION TO THE KING.

'Tis a calm summer evening. The sun, which through the day has been pouring its heated rays over the city, calling into life noisome vapors and death-dealing exhalations, now declining in the west, lights up each spire and turret. Through her many winding streets the tide of busy life rushes on continuously, and from her countless workshops goes up unceasingly the sound of the artizan's hammer and the weaver's shuttle. Man in the busy engagements of every day life, has forgotten there is a higher and holier life.

The king and court have been engaged in a continual round of pleasure throughout the day. Mirth, and wine, and jests, and ribald songs have occupied their time and minds. How debased is human nature under the curse of sin. No outward circumstances, no extraneous influences, can change it. Men may have all the world can bestow of wealth and honor, yea, may be greatly gifted intellectually, and yet, what are they without the power of the grace of God to direct and control them? Let the court of Charles II. of England, answer.

The king has amused himself to surfeiting amid the beauties of his court. His wantonness, which had now become popularised, had been as unrestrained as it was disgraceful and corrupting. Cloyed with the excess which met him everywhere, he had sought respite from it in the grounds surrounding the palace, one of his favorite amusements being the feeding of ducks and geese and other aquatic birds, which he had domesticated in the ponds of the palace grounds.

The king is not alone. A lovely being leans on his arm. It is the Lady Castlemaine—that woman of such peerless beauty and infamous celebrity.' Charles gazes up into the imperious face, and hangs on the word of command with as much servility as though he were her page. The tall figure, in garments loosely flowing, is drawn up to its full height, and the left hand is raised as if to give more emphasis to the words she is speaking. She is beseeching, or rather *commanding* the king with regard to a settlement upon her of a large estate which she claims at his hands. He has objected because of its enormity, at which the lady has fallen into a temper, and is be-rating him as a close mean fellow, and too poor to do a handsome thing. From beneath the drooping lids, with their long silken lashes, her brilliant eyes speak the fierce determination of her soul. Her nostrils are distended, and her lips curled with disdain. She will not brook a refusal. The king sees that denial is useless. The demand must be met before peace can be restored, for the imperious beauty is inexorable.

The king gives consent; he dares not withhold. Instantly a smile overspreads the exquisitely chiseled features, and an air of soft languor pervades that form which but a moment before was as commanding as Bellona. The rich red lips, so late curled in arrogance, are now as sweet and wooing as a summer rose.

They approach a small pond overshadowed by a clump of old trees, which now, that the sun is sinking in the western sky, throw their lengthened shadows across the smooth still waters and beyond on to the green sward, which like a soft green carpet, spreads itself around. They lean on the slight enclosure, and the king pours words of love into the ears of his fair mistress. She receives his protestations kindly, for he has just granted her a magnificent request. A page comes with bread, which the king takes, and while he whispers soft low accents in the seared heart of the Lady Castlemaine, he carelessly throws food to the eager birds, who vie with each other in partaking of his bounty. The lady looks languidly into his face, and smiles upon him most sweetly, and answers him in words of deep affection. Thus they while the time away in dalliance soft, until the king, ' ever changing, yet ever weary,' proposes to return. The imperial beauty accedes to his proposal, and gathering up the gauzy scarf that has fallen from shoulders of alabaster whiteness, and throwing from a Juno brow the soft dark wavy hair, she leans fondly on his arm, and the two turn towards the palace.

They pass from beneath the shadows of the old trees, and wend their way noiselessly along. As they near the palace, groups of gallant lords and gay ladies pass before them in various parts of the grounds. Not wishing to be interrupted, they turn their steps toward a less frequented part of the park. As they turn an angle and emerge from the cover of a clump of shrubbery, they are encountered by two female figures.

The king and Lady Castlemaine are about to pass on,

unheeding the pair, when the eldest steps a little forward, and says :

'Will your Majesty grant to listen to us a moment?'

'And what may be your wish, woman?' replied the king, impatiently.

'This poor blind girl wants to beseech you for her father, sire.'

Mary trembled from head to foot as she heard herself mentioned. The king's voice fell gratingly upon her ears. She moved to Mrs. Gaunt's side, and nestled close to her. The change brought her face to face with the king. Charles, who was always influenced by beauty, paused, as his eye rested on the sweet, pensive face before him. The mellow rays of the evening sun lent a fresh loveliness to the pale face, which it did not always wear. The eyes were drooped, and shaded by the long lashes, so that the king did not at first perceive that she was blind.

'And what is the matter with your father, my lassie?' asks Charles, in that familiar tone, so disgusting to those accustomed to court scenes, but which, to poor, trembling Mary Bunyan, sounds like the very embodiment of kindness. Her heart is instantly re-assured. Taking the petition from her bosom, she presents it to the king.

'Bunyan, is it?' says the king, looking at the petition, 'John Bunyan! Are you Bunyan's daughter, lassie?'

'I am, please your Majesty,' replies the trembling girl, without raising her eyes to the face of the king.

'Odds, fish! and what is the matter with your father, lassie?' exclaims Charles, vainly endeavoring to decipher Bunyan's handwriting.

'He is in prison,' replies Mary with trembling voice. 'They put him in prison for preaching, and they have kept him there for almost five years. Won't you let him come out, sire?—he does nobody any harm.'

'And what does he preach, lassie?'

'He preaches nothing but the gospel, sire.'

'What gospel?' asks the king, charmed with the modest manner and sweet voice of the girl.

'The Bible gospel, sire. The gospel of the Lord Jesus Christ,' answers Mary, growing more and more bold under the kind voice of the king.

'Do not waste words on the country girl,' whispered the Lady Castlemaine, piqued that Charles should manifest so much interest in a peasant girl. She motions to leave, but the king stands firm. A dark scowl gathers on the face of the regal beauty. She does not wish to hear anything

"Will your Majesty grant to listen to us a moment?"

about the Lord Jesus Christ. He is not a welcome guest.

'Odds, fish! Don't keep your eyes fixed on the ground. A pretty girl like you can afford to look up. Come, look up!' and the king holds out his hand encouragingly.

'I am blind, sire,' replies Mary, in a low agitated tone. 'I cannot see, sire.'

'*Blind*, eh?' repeats the king, and he hands the petition to Mrs. Gaunt, and motions to turn away.

Mary understands the movement.

'My father, my father, sire! can't he come out of the dungeon?' gasps the fearful girl eagerly, as she clings to Mrs. Gaunt for support.

'Well, I'll see about it, lassie,' and the king turns from her.

'My father, oh, my father, sire? Tell me, may he come out of gaol! He has been in gaol now five years, and my mother and the children are starving for bread. May he come out—oh, may he come out?' cries Mary convulsively, endeavoring to make her words reach the king.

Her efforts are in vain. The besotted monarch moves on to scenes of worldly pleasure, and leaves the girl to weep.

CHAPTER XXI.

THE PLAGUE.

THE year 1665 is noted in the history of England as being the period of two of the most dreadful calamities that ever befel London—the Plague and the Great Fire. The one destroyed about seventy thousand lives; the other, every tenement to be found on four hundred and thirty-six acres of ground. It seemed that God, angry with the creatures that every day provoked him and blasphemed his name, was pouring out the vials of his wrath and fiery indignation. The nation was made to mourn; for death, in its most terrible form, was ravaging the length and breadth of the land. The iniquities of a dissolute king and his licentious court had gone up before the throne of God, and the cries and groans of the elect, whom persecution and tyranny trampled daily under foot, had reached the ear of Infinite Justice. And now the measure that had been meted out by the oppressors and tormentors of the saints, was, in turn, to be meted out to them.

Who is able to stand before the terrible vengeance of an angry God? With him the nations of the earth are but as the small dust of the balance, and he taketh up the isles as a very little thing. Let man beware how he rebel against the Most High God. Let him, rather, 'kiss the Son, lest he be angry, and ye perish from the way when his wrath is kindled but a little.'

Men's hearts have waxed proud and rebellious. The fear of God is not before their eyes. They laugh, and jeer, and talk, and wanton in the ways of pleasure. Sensual and debased, amid luxurious magnificence, they riot in excesses, disregarding all social claims, and the yet higher claims of religion. Then 'the pestilence that walketh in darkness, and the destruction that wasteth at noon-day,' comes suddenly upon them, and cries of wailing and mourning go up from palace and hovel, for the angel of death is abroad to strike down, not only the firstborn of the household, but all ages, ranks, and conditions.

The cup of indignation is full. The time of retribution is at hand.

The atmosphere, like a leaden pall, envelopes the city. The air is motionless. The lurid rays of the noontide sun struggle sickly through the mantle of gloom which envelopes the earth. Men's hearts sink within them as they look fearfully around them and above. Horrid forebodings seize them as they gaze on the unmistakeable omens.

Suddenly there start out on the still, heavy air, the piercing shrieks of agony. Men tremble, and their hearts wax faint as they go about the streets, asking the cause of the lamentation.

It is the plague!

The monster is in their midst, mowing down with his death-scythe men, youths, maidens, and those of hoary hairs. The whole city is in breathless horror. '*The plague! the plague!*' is given from lip to lip, while every heart stands still with fearful consternation.

The distress deepens. Each new day but adds fresh terror to the already frightful ravages of the epidemic. Hundreds are dying hourly. Everything betokens horror and distress. Those who have sympathy for suffering humanity are taxed to the utmost. From every part of the great metropolis there come forth the lamentations of the sick and the dying.

Mrs. Gaunt scarce rests from her toil, day or night. Amid scenes of wretchedness, where the dead await the cry of the cartman, or the dying call out in vain for relief for their torturing pain; where the mother weeps over the dead child, or famishing infant lips press the breast of the mother whose heart is stilled in death—everywhere, where aid can be bestowed, she was found an angel of love and mercy, giving all the assistance her scanty means would afford. Her few acquaintances beseech her to take care of herself, lest she, too, may fall a victim to the dreadful scourge.

' " For me to live, is Christ; and to die, is gain," ' she would answer. ' A cup of cold water in the name of my Master— 'tis all I can do. I will give it, and leave the result with God.'

Mary has been told that the king is going from the city. She decides within herself to make another attempt for her father's liberty; but how will she get to the palace is the question. She does not wish to trouble Mrs. Gaunt, poor woman; who is almost ready to sink now under her pressing duties. She cannot go alone.

A thought strikes her. There is a girl living next door who has told her a great deal about London; she will ask her to go with her. She thinks now that the king is so frightened about the plague he will surely hear and grant her request. Poor girl! she does not know that the coward king has long since fled from the scene of danger to a secure asylum, where distress and suffering cannot interrupt his round of sensual enjoyment.

She will ask Margaret Purdy to go with her; this is her conclusion as she sits in the little street-room alone, waiting for Mrs. Gaunt to come back.

She will step in and see Margaret now; then she can set out for White Hall as soon as Mrs. Gaunt goes out again, which Mary knows she will do as soon as she has eaten a morsel of food.

' Yes, that I will go with you to see the king. He will let your father out of prison now. I know the way well, and there is no plague out in that direction.'

' Will your mother let you go, Margaret ? '

' Oh yes, I know she will. She told me this morning I must go out walking somewhere; she says I will die if I sit in the house so much. We can go down to the Strand, then up White Hall street, and we won't go where the plague is at all. But when will you go, Mary ? '

When Mrs. Gaunt goes out again.'

Mrs. Gaunt returned home from her round weary and sick at heart. During her morning walk she had encountered scenes more horrid than any she had previously met. The plague was increasing fearfully.

'You must rest this evening,' said Mary, as the tired woman threw herself into a chair.

'No, my child, I cannot rest; there is too much to be done. The sick and dying are on every hand. The plague is raging to-day more violently than ever. I'll take a cup of tea and some bread, and then I will go and see Mr. Cromey's family; they are Baptists, and I hear the dreadful enemy has come into their house.'

Mary shuddered as she heard of the extended ravages of the fearful scourge. Living as she did in Drury Lane, then pretty nearly on the outskirts of the city, (for the time of which we are writing was two hundred years ago,) she had not fully realised the horrors of the fearful scourge which was every day pushing its way westward towards White Hall and Westminster.

Mrs. Gaunt partook of some simple refreshments and again set out on her labor of love.

The two girls prepared themselves for their walk to White Hall.

They passed along the Strand with quick and eager step. Soon they reached Charing Cross, and were wending their way up White Hall street to the palace.

'Where are you going, children?' asked an old man, whom they encountered just after they had crossed Pall-Mall.

'We are going to White Hall,' answered Mary, timidly. 'We wish to see the king.'

'Ah, poor child, you cannot see the king there; he has been gone to the country for days; he could not face the plague. You children had better go home as soon as you can. Do you see that group of houses yonder?' and the old man pointed his finger to a clump of ordinary buildings near by, 'the plague is broken out there, and men, and women, and children are dying every hour.'

The two girls were almost terrified with fright; they turned to retrace their steps. Just at this moment a cart rolled by, and the driver, stopping before one of the houses with the fearful red cross upon it, cried out in a sepulchral voice, 'Bring out your dead.'

A cold shudder shook the form of Mary as these dreadful words fell upon her ear. She could not see the frightful red cross on the doors of the closed tenements, nor the wild stare of those who brought the livid corpse to the door, nor the despairing look of the mother as she saw the uncoffined form of her dear son heaved into the death-cart, the first of a number of bodies who were to share the same fate in the loathsome burying-ground; but she felt it all; and her exquisite sensibility pictured the horrid scene even more vividly, if it were possible, than natural vision beheld it.

Margaret grew pale with terror, and grasping tightly the thin pale hand of Mary, now cold and trembling with fear, the two hastened towards the city.

On they went up the Strand, unconscious of all things but the desire to get to a place of safety. Suddenly they encounter a death-cart, from which proceeds the most noisome exhalations.

'Where are we, where are we?' cried Mary, convulsively grasping the hand of her companion.

'Bring out your dead,' calls out in a hollow tone the voice of the driver, as the death-cart halts before a dwelling on which the red cross had just been placed.

'Hush, Mary,' cried Margaret, as the horrid sound rung in upon her soul. 'Hush, and come along, Mary, we are almost home.'

'Oh! I am so glad,' gasped out the blind girl.

On, on, the two girls hasten, the dreadful cry still ringing in their ears.

Margaret stopped suddenly.

'We are lost, we are lost, Mary; and yonder is the death-cart coming towards us.' Margaret spoke with the wildness of despair.

As the vehicle of death rolled by, they grasped each other the more closely, and pressed forward. They dared not stop anywhere, for the death sign was on every door. On, on, they rush with trembling limbs and fainting hearts.

'Stand here, Mary,' and Margaret loosed herself from the blind girl. Mary threw her hand out to catch her. It was too late. The two were separated. They never again met. In twenty-four hours the death-cart stopped before a house in the old Drury. 'Bring out your dead,' cried the driver as he saw the new red cross sign on an old building. The door opened, and the cold body of Margaret, marked with the plague-spot, was handed out, and deposited with others from the same building, and the cart rolled on.

Mary seated herself on a door-step, waiting in dreadful terror for some relief; but none came. 'I must die,' she said to herself. 'I shall never see home again; oh Lord, have mercy, have mercy on me.'

The evening came on; there she sat.   Death-carts rattled through the otherwise deserted streets.

'I shall surely die here,' she said, and with that instinctive shrinking from loneliness which haunts the bosom of all, she rose, places her hand on the door knob, and enters.   She stretches forth her hand; it rests on the cold face of a corpse; shrieking, she turns and flies to the street.

On she goes—faster, faster, she knows not whither her steps tend.

Faint and fatigued, she rests herself on the curb-stone; her heart has almost ceased to beat.   A deep loud wail rings out from some house near by, 'Oh, my son, my son!' this is all she can hear.

She starts again to her feet, and as she drives forward, hears again and again the cry, 'Bring out your dead; bring out your dead.'

The Lord help thee, poor child! He alone can succor thee now.

CHAPTER XXII.

A FRIEND IN NEED.

IN our last chapter we left Mary forsaken and in despair, wandering in wild frenzy up Ludgate Hill, towards St. Paul's, while the hideous cry, 'Bring out your dead! bring out your dead!' fell on her ear, and rung in horrid peal through her sinking soul.   Death-carts still rattled through the streets, and the sound of human voices was heard only in the dreadful summons of the cartman, and the wailing shrieks of a mother, or sister, or wife, as they gave up into his keeping the now loathsome remains of those who but a few hours before had been their joy and pride.

Mary pressed on, she knew not whither — indeed, she scarcely cared, so great was her fright.   She knew it was certain death to remain where she was.   She felt the fœtid atmosphere, as, filled with the seeds of the plague, it moved heavily over her.   It seemed to her that the wing of the Angel of death had put in motion the thick suffocating air, which stifled and weighed her down.

'I shall die, and my father will never know what has become of me,' she said to herself, as she groped her way along the street, vainly endeavoring to do something for her relief.

She was hurrying on with her hands thrown wildly out before her, and her bonnet falling from her shoulders, while her face wore the pallor of death, when suddenly she struck her foot against a stone and fell prostrate. She shrieked with terror. She could not rise—fright had rendered her powerless.

'I must die here; I must die. O God! my poor father! my dear father! and my mother, and the children! I must leave them all! O God, pity me!' she exclaimed, as she lay unable to rise.

A hand touched her arm. She started and screamed. 'I am not dead,' she gasped convulsively. She thought it was the death-man.

'I see you are not dead, but you soon will be if you stay here,' replied the man, in a full hard voice. 'Get up, get up; do you want to be thrown into the cart?' She shuddered from head to foot as she heard the words. 'Haven't you got any home? where does your mother live? Tell me, and I'll take you home.'

'Mrs. Gaunt, in the Drury,' stammered out Mary, incoherently.

'Well, get up and come along; we'll soon be there.'

Mary, electrified with the thought of so soon being freed from danger, sprang to her feet, and clutched the hand of the man, which rested on her arm. But he had mistaken her words. He understood her to say Jewry, and, instead of bearing her to Mrs. Gaunt's in Drury Lane, which at that time of the plague, was comparatively free from the pestilence, he hurried her along towards the Old Jewry, where it was raging in the wildest fury.

As the blind girl strode on, holding with a death grip to the man's hand, she sobbed aloud with emotions of thankfulness at her deliverance.

On, on they went, in the gathering gloom of the twilight, Mary weeping aloud, and the man hurrying her forward towards the Old Jewry.

'What is the matter, poor child?' asked a kind voice.

Mary could not reply.

'She has lost her way, and I am taking her home,' replied the man quickly.

'And where is your home, child?' asked the old man who interrupted them. There was something in his tone, so gentle and so kind, that re-assured Mary's heart, and gave her hope. Her sobbings were hushed, and she was able to reply with some calmness—

'I live in Elstow, sir. I am staying now with Mrs. Gaunt, who lives in Drury Lane.'

'Drury Lane, girl,' said her conductor in astonishment. 'I thought you told me you lived in the Jewry. I have been bringing you away from home instead of carrying you to it. Why didn't you tell me? Couldn't you see I was taking you wrong?'

'I cannot see, sir; I am blind,' she answered timidly, as if unwilling to tell of her misfortune to a stranger.

'Blind! live in Elstow?' repeated the old man, in a low voice, as if talking to himself. 'And what is your name child?' asked he eagerly.

'Mary Bunyan, sir; my father is in the Bedford gaol.'

'The Lord be praised!' exclaimed the old man fervently. 'Come with me, child. I will take care of you for your father's sake. He is suffering for the testimony of Jesus, and his child shall never suffer as long as I can protect her. But we must hurry away from this dreadful place. The plague is raging here with great violence. Come, quick, give me your hand.'

The man was glad to get rid of his charge when he found he was taking her the-wrong way, so he bade them a hasty good evening, and, turning on his steps, hurried back towards St. Paul's.

'Bring out your dead!' rung out in wild hollow tones on the still, loathsome air. Mary shuddered as she heard the cartman's dread call. Involuntarily she pressed more closely to the old man's side.

'Come, my child,' said the old man to her, as he placed on her bonnet and grasped her hand. 'Come, we have got a good walk before us, and it is late; but you cannot see it, poor child,' he added, in a tone of pity, as he remembered she had said she was blind.

The two hurried forward towards Gracechurch street. Not a word was spoken until they reached London bridge.

'This is the bridge,' said the old man to Mary, as they entered upon it from the street. 'I live in Southwark, and we have to cross the river.'

Mary could not see the ponderous old bridge, as it threw itself across the sluggish Thames, with its carriage-way and foot-ways, but she felt a fearfulness creep over her, as there arose the dead hollow sound from the footsteps of those who, from compulsion, were crossing at this hour. The lamps gave out a sickly glare, as the old man and the blind girl hastened on.

'There is the daughter of our dear brother Bunyan, of

Bedford, Jane,' said the old man to his wife, as he entered their door, in Southwark, leading Mary by the hand. The good wife started up dismayed.

'Is brother Bunyan in London, Mr. Brown? Where did you find the poor child? Come, child, take a seat. Poor thing, you look pale and scared. Where did he find you? Do tell me, Mr. Brown, where did you cross this child of our dear brother Bunyan?'

'In the street, Jane—knowing not whither she was going. The Lord directed me to her. A few steps more, and she would have turned, and I should have missed her entirely. It was a kind providence to send me along that way, before she got into the Jewry.'

'Oh, heavens! was she going there? Are you staying there, in that miserable place, my poor child, where the dreadful pestilence is so fearful?'

'No, ma'am. The man did not know what I said to him. I told him Drury, and he thought I said Jewry, and I could not see the way to tell him any better.'

'Oh, yes; it was so dark, you could not see, and you were so scared. Yes, yes—I know how it is; you were so far from home, too.'

'I cannot see,' said Mary, turning to the good woman. 'I am blind.'

'Ah, poor child! that is it, is it? He was leading you into death, and you did not know it. Thank God, he delivered you in his own good way.'

'There, take off your bonnet, child, and drink this glass of ale; it will do you good after your long walk. The good Lord be praised, that he has sent you to us. And where have you been staying in the city, child?'

'I have been with Elizabeth Gaunt, who was once at my mother's house, at Elstow.'

'Oh, yes; a dear good woman, my child, sister Gaunt is. She does a great deal of good for the poor and suffering of Christ's kingdom. She goes about like our dear Master —always doing good. And you have been staying with her here. I'm glad to hear you had so good a friend.'

'Yes, ma'am, ever since I have been in the city.'

'And where does this good woman live? I have seen her at brother Kiffin's church sometimes, and once or twice I have seen her in an old sister's, just this side of the bridge in High Street, but I never heard where she lived.'

'She lives somewhere in Drury Lane, it is called; but I do not know where.'

'And she was up by St. Paul's, Mr. Brown? Oh, poor child! how did you wander so far from home?'

Mary told the good woman all. How she had determined to see the king a second time in behalf of her father, and to do this without troubling Mrs. Gaunt; how she and Margaret had set out alone; of the great fright they had received, as they reached Charing Cross; of their turning back and hurrying on until Margaret found that they were lost; of her being left alone in the street, and trying to find some one to take her home; how she had entered the house and placed her hand on the dead man's face. Then of her despair, until the man spoke to her as she lay prostrate in the street, expecting to perish.

'Poor child!' said the kind-hearted woman as she wiped her eyes, and looked upon the pale, innocent face before her with an expression of sincere compassion. 'The Lord himself did deliver you.'

'And your dear father! how does he bear his long, weary life in the gaol; he has been there now five years.'

'Do you know father?' asked Mary eagerly.

'Oh, yes; and we know of his great sufferings, and of the distress of his family, and of the cruelty of the persecutor. But the Lord himself will avenge his innocent children, who bear all things for his name's sake. He was in London, some years ago, to see the king. He wanted then to get himself out of gaol. He was in our house. Oh, how we loved him! He told us about you; your name is Mary; and he called you his dear blind child; and he told us of your mother, and your brothers, and the baby— little Sarah, I think he called her name. Oh, his heart was most broke when he found he could do nothing with the king. His Majesty is so frivolous. He will never take time to right the wrongs of his subjects. The Lord only knows what will become of us. We are cruelly treated by those who rule over us. You don't understand all these things now, dear child, but you will by and by. Lord, when wilt thou come to avenge us?'

'In his own good time he will come, Jane, to bring light out of darkness—and that time is near at hand, even at the door. What is the meaning of this terrible pestilence? Is it not making straight the paths of the Lord—preparing his ways, as saith the prophet: 'Wrath and destruction must be poured on his enemies, even upon Antichrist, and the woman who rideth on the beast. The measure of her iniquities is almost full. Then will the Lord come in power and great glory to destroy the Wicked One with the brightness of his coming, and give to us, who long for his appearing, a new heaven and a new earth, wherein dwelleth righteousness.' We are pressing on towards that time. It is not far before us, thank God. 'Then shall the living be changed in the twinkling of an eye, and the righteous dead shall be raised to reign with him for ever and ever. The Lord himself hath spoken it."'

'Yes, bless the Lord,' interfered the old woman enthusiastically; 'we are looking for and trusting in his coming.'

'When my poor John died, ten years ago,' she resumed after a few moments' pause—'John was my only child, Mary, and I loved him very dear—when he died, I was sorely grieved. It did seem to me I could not live. The world was all so hollow and so dark. I wondered why it was God had afflicted me so. I felt it was very hard, because I had only the one, and oh! how I loved him, but I see now it was all well. John might have been in prison this day instead of being in heaven. John might have been suffering, and tortured, and tormented; but now, thank God, he is happy—my poor tongue cannot tell it, and he is ever before the throne of God and the Lamb to praise them for ever and ever; and I shall soon meet him, and my Saviour in the clouds of heaven. Thank God! for the exceeding great and precious promises of the gospel of our Lord and Saviour Jesus Christ!'

'Amen and amen!' responded the old man fervently.

'My child,' said Mrs. Brown to Mary, in a voice of most motherly affection, 'you are weak and tired. Here, lay down on this little bed, and rest you until you get something to eat.'

Mary heeded her bidding, and was soon wrapt in unbroken slumber.

Mrs. Brown busied herself to prepare something for her husband and Mary to eat.

'How sweet the poor girl looks,' said the wife to the old man, as she pointed to Mary, who lay sleeping with head reclined on one thin frail hand, while the other rested gently on the table by her side. Her hair fell partially over her pale, sad face, showing in broken outline the calm features. The lips were slightly parted, for she slept with the heaviness of intense weariness both of body and mind. Her white kerchief, partly opened, revealed a neck of snowy whiteness and delicate proportions. Her respiration was deep and slow. The tired frame sought to recover itself.

'She is a sweet, pretty child,' replied the old man,

gazing at her earnestly. 'I wish we had such a girl, Jane.'

'Would you want her blind too ?'

'Yes, Jane—just as this dear child of brother Bunyan is. She is so innocent and so kind. I would be willing to nurse her and tend her all the days of my life. She is so gentle and so pretty.'

'What will we do about going to meeting to-night, John ? we can't leave this child here alone, and she will be too tired to go with us.'

'When she wakes up we will tell her how it is, and if she can't go, we can send for Ellen Carter to stay with her.'

Mrs. Brown went to the kitchen to see about the tea. The old gentleman sat by the doorway, and gave himself up to thought. He sat where he could see the sleeping girl, and ever and anon his look rested upon the pale, calm face, while his eyes grew moist, and then the big tears would course slowly down his wrinkled face.

CHAPTER XXIII.

GOD'S HIDDEN ONES—THE SMALL UPPER ROOM.

WHILE persecution raged, the Nonconformists were driven to seek private places for worship, lest the insatiable enemy should spy them out, and report them to the law. They were also compelled to hold their meetings at *such times* as the eye of hate could not discover them. An obscure upper room, a barn loft, the midnight depths of the forest, an humble unobtrusive homestead, the midnight hour, the early morning dawn — these were the places and times where and when the hunted, down-trodden children of God met together to call upon his name, and to encourage the fainting hearts of each other as they journeyed along the thorny path of duty.

Bunyan, before the rigorous sentence was passed that 'he should not go beyond the prison walls,' was oftentimes compelled to disguise himself as a cartman, and appear with a cartman's whip in his hand, that he might be able to assemble himself with the little flock and break unto them the bread of eternal life ; and oftentimes he had to enter through the back door, and escape by the same way, that he might elude the vigilance of the blood-hounds who were ever on his track.

In London, the 'Fifth Monarchy men,' or those who were looking for the immediate coming of Christ, had rendered themselves particularly odious to both state and church. They were compelled to meet under the cover of night, and to use every precaution that would insure profound secresy. Their steps were dogged by officers of the law, intent on bringing 'these vile miscreants to justice;' and, when discovered, as they sometimes were by these Argus-eyed pursuers, they had to hide their Bibles in secret places, provided for that purpose, and let themselves down through trap-doors; or, like the apostle Paul, make their escape through windows, that they might not meet the vengeance of the persecutors.

We, who live in the present age of religious toleration and freedom from ecclesiastical jurisdiction, can form but faint conception of the trials and sufferings of those of our forefathers in the faith, who stood as witnesses for the truth, when the bloody hand of persecution marked all such out for the prison, the stake, or the gibbet.

Nearly two hundred years ago, in an upper room of the old building in Southwark, a small company of men and women had assembled to worship God. The house stood very near the present site of the New Park Street Chapel. It is a memorable locality to Baptists.

Here, more than a century later than the time of which we write, did John Gill, that man of God, stand as a witness for those truths for which Bunyan, and the Hewlings, and Elizabeth Gaunt, and many others, suffered imprisonment and death. And now, on the same spot, Spurgeon stands, to proclaim and defend these same immutable gospel truths. God has never left himself without a witness in Southwark.

The beginning was small; a few persons gathered together in his name, in a small upper room of an old building — defamed, pursued, maltreated. Now, there stands very near the same spot a handsome edifice, where thousands gather from Sabbath to Sabbath, to listen to the everlasting gospel. And should we not, in view of these facts, pray with increased faith for the ushering in of that glorious period, when 'the kingdoms of this world are to become the kingdoms of our Lord and of his Christ, and he shall reign for ever and ever?'

The night was quite advanced. The noise and activity of the past day were hushed to silence. In the small upper room of the old building we have mentioned, a little company of disciples had come together for the purpose of prayer. They had met thus late that they might escape the eye of the detecter. It was a plain, untenanted room, situated at the head of the stairway which communicated with the street, through a narrow, dark alley, into which no lantern flung its sickly glare.

One by one the few brethren and sisters had gathered together to explain the Scriptures and to pray. There were old and young man, hoary-headed matrons and maidens—all moved by the same spirit, actuated by the same motives, and pressing on towards the same goal, even everlasting life at God's right hand. It was a touching scene, thus to see these disciples of the Saviour assembled at the midnight hour in this small upper room, that they might worship God as they thought acceptable to him— that they might in security and in truth follow him in the ways of his own appointment. Let us look at them.

In one corner of the room, into which the feeble lamp scarce throws its sickly light, sits the blind girl, between her aged friends. Her face, so pale but a little while ago, is flushed now with excitement. But no one observes her, and even if they did, it would matter but little to her. Her sealed eyes would bring no intelligence of it to her sensitive shrinking heart. No one notices that she is a stranger. The attention of all present is directed to a middle-aged man, who sits near one of the lamps, with a Bible in his hand. One of the company present goes to the door, listens a moment, then shuts it carefully, and fastening it securely from within, returns and takes his seat. They are compelled to use every precaution.

The middle-aged man rises and addresses the little assembly. His words are full of brotherly love and encouragement. He repeats the blessed words of our Saviour: 'Let not your hearts be troubled: ye believe in God, believe also in me,' etc. In a deep, earnest tone he reads the 14th chapter of John, commenting as he proceeds. His remarks fell with soothing effect on the listening part of the pious assembly.

The little company kneel, and a fervent prayer ascends to God for his presence in their midst, for his guidance and support in the trying difficulties and oppression which now surround them, and for victory over the flesh, the world, and the devil. A song is sung, then a brother rises to exhort those present to doubling of their diligence, that they may make their calling and election sure, and to patient continuance in well-doing, that they may inherit eternal life. He speaks of his conflicts, of foes within and foes without, and then, in tones of melting tenderness, he dwells on the love of God—the compassion of our Lord Jesus Christ who, for our sakes, became poor—of the joys of heaven—of the certainty of the promises, until every heart is moved, and each face is bathed in tears.

Mary's heart is troubled. She feels as she has never felt before. Tears are streaming from her sightless eyes—but they are not tears of joy; they are not tears of repentance. The Spirit is at work about her heart. She has sinned against the high and holy God, and these sins, 'red as crimson,' now stand in dreadful array before her. No one heeds her; each is so engaged with matters pertaining to himself, that the unobtrusive girl escapes unobserved. She strives to suppress her tears—endeavors to conceal her sorrow. Satan is contesting every inch of territory. He will not be vanquished. But he 'who worketh and none can hinder,' hath commissioned his Holy Spirit to go forth to convict of sin. Which shall have the mastery?

One, and another, and another rises to bear testimony for Jesus. It is a time of confession and of supplication. Enemies are abroad and the enemy is within. The dreadful pestilence walketh at noon-day. Friends and acquaintances are falling on every side. The times are perilous! When will succor come?

In song, and prayer, and confession, the time is spent. A poor sister, one of the faithful of the Lord, rises to ask prayer for her unconverted son. He wanders day by day in the paths of the wicked one, and sets aside all counsel, and heeds no reproof. But she remembers the promises of God are 'yea and amen in Christ Jesus,' and she will trust. Another sister has a husband ungodly and unconcerned: 'Pray for my dear husband,' she cries, 'that he may not go down to eternal burnings.'

'Remember my father,' entreats a maiden; 'pray God that he may not be cut off in his sins. He is a bold blasphemer. O Lord, have mercy upon him,' she exclaims, while her heart almost breaks with anguish.

'And pray for me,' said Mary, rising to her feet. 'I am a poor, lost sinner. Oh, ask God to pardon me.' Her voice, low and sweet, is broken by her sobs. Her eyes are streaming with tears, and her hands are held beseechingly out.

This is brother Bunyan's daughter,' said old brother Brown—rising to his feet, and grasping the hand of Mary. 'I found her in the streets of London, when it was almost night, wandering without any home, and now God has

sent his Spirit to call back her soul from the paths of sin.
Blessed be his holy name. Let us beseech God, my brethren, in her behalf. Oh, let us thank him that he doth
manifest himself to his children, as he doth not to the
world. Glory to his holy name! He is mighty and willing
to save.'

'Bless his dear name — the precious name of Jesus,'
exclaims sister Brown, as she throws her arms around
Mary, and kneels by her side.

The old man cries unto the Lord for his mercy on the
dear child. 'I will not let thee go until thou bless me,' is
the spirit of his prayer. Each case is remembered before
the throne of grace—the son, the husband, the father, the
poor blind child of the suffering brother, and for each
ascends a deep, heart-burdened petition. The cry goes up
to the ear of the God of Sabaoth, who hears and answers
whenever his children cry to him in faith.

And now the little company is about to disperse. They
have assembled themselves together in the name of their
blessed Lord and Master, and he has been in their midst.
'Happy are the people whose God is the Lord; they shall
be continually praising him.'

They all gather round Mary. She is the daughter of
Bunyan, of whom they have heard. They love her for
her father's sake, and they want to point her to the Lamb
of God, who takes away the sin of the world.

'Look to Christ, my child, our blessed Lord and Saviour,
who died that sinners might live. Seek pardon through
his blood. He is willing and able. He has saved thousands
of sinners, my child, as vile and wretched as you are, and
he can save you. Don't fear to come to him; he will not
cast you out. He came into this world to seek and to save
that which was lost. Trust in him. Oh, thou blessed
Saviour—thou Jesus of Nazareth—who died for perishing
sinners, have mercy on this poor child, and forgive her
sins. Oh, that my son would come to Jesus! oh, that he
could feel himself a sinner before God'; and the poor old
woman, almost exhausted by her tears and cries, clasps
her hands in agony, and offers up a prayer, interrupted by
tears and sighs, for Mary, and her erring son.

It is the mother of William Dormer. William has not
yet turned to God. Day after day, night after night, has
the heart of the mother gone up in fervent prayer, that
God would have mercy on her son. He is her only hope
now. Her daughters are all dead. They departed in the
faith of the gospel. The father is still in prison, and she

has come to Southwark, that she may be with her son. She desires to spend the remnant of her days on earth, watching over him, and praying for him.

The little company sing a hymn in a low, subdued voice, and then the servant of God pronounces the benediction.

'This is our dear brother Bunyan's daughter, sister Dormer,' says old sister Brown to the dear old woman who has just prayed.

Mary starts at the sound of her name.

'Your husband is in the same prison with her father—the old gaol at Bedford'—resumes Mrs. Brown, not observing Mary's agitation.

'Yes, my poor old man is there, because he would preach the gospel of Christ. And this is really brother Bunyan's daughter? Poor, dear child; how did you come down to this place—and blind, too. Poor child!'

Mrs. Brown explains the matter to her.

'Ah, dear child, the Lord has been with you. He alone could have rescued you, and sent you here where his Spirit has come, to knock at your heart. Do not grieve that Spirit, but invite him to come in and be a guest. Never give up seeking, my child, until you find Christ precious to your soul. Oh, that my poor William may be led, like you, to see himself a sinner.'

'I want to go to Mrs. Gaunt,' she said to Mrs. Brown with childish simplicity, as they reached the door. 'She will be wondering why I don't come home; won't somebody take me to her?'

'You cannot go to-night, my child,' replied the old man tenderly. 'We do not know where sister Gaunt lives.'

'She lives in Drury Lane,' interrupted Mary eagerly.

'But we could not find her now, and, besides, it is a long walk. You cannot go to-night.'

'Will anybody take me to-morrow?' she asks beseechingly. 'I must go, she will be so distressed about me.'

'If we can find the way, child; you cannot see to tell us, you know. Brother Dorrow,' said the old man, addressing the preacher, 'do you know where sister Gaunt lives—sister Elizabeth Gaunt, the woman who does so much for the poor and needy?'

'No, brother Brown, I do not; I have heard a great deal of sister Gaunt, and have seen her two or three times, but I do not know where she lives.'

The question was asked of all those of the little company there convened, but no one knew where she resided. The only individual, widow Dormer, who could have given any information, had left. Poor child, it seemed that disappointment awaited her on every hand. She longed to fly to Mrs. Gaunt that she might tell her all she felt. She could not speak her feelings freely to strangers. She believed that Mrs. Gaunt could direct her to the Saviour. Could she but unbosom herself to her own dear father—could she but tell him all she suffered, and ask him to pray for her, it seemed her burden of guilt would be removed, and she be able to rejoice in the pardon of her sins.

She must do something to recommend herself to God; something whereby to secure his favor, and make him willing to forgive her. Such was the temptation Satan was now besieging her with.

Alas! how many in all ages of the world have had to wage war against the same wiles of the devil, do something to merit divine favor, when all we can do is to feel we can do *nothing*, and to fall into the outstretched arms of our great Redeemer.

Mary believed she or Mrs. Gaunt, or her father, must do something before she could be reconciled to God; something to fit her for adoption into the family of the Most High. She could not see that 'all the fitness he requireth is to feel our need of him.' The eyes of her understanding were not opened; the enemy of souls was plying hard his wiles to keep her from a true knowledge of the way. She could not yet say—

> 'Nothing in my hand I bring,
> Simply to thy cross I cling.'

The remainder of the night was spent by the blind girl in fervent prayer and meditation. She was seeking Jesus, he of whom ' Moses in the law and the prophets did write; ' he who is to his people all in all, and to the sinner 'born again,' ' the chiefest among ten thousand and altogether lovely.'

The morning dawn found Mary troubled and anxious. She endeavored to suppress and conceal her feelings, but she *could not*. This was another suggestion of the adversary of her soul; he was appealing to the pride of her heart.

The threatenings of Sinai sounded through the awakened conscience of Mary the death-knell of all her hope. She had broken the law which was ' holy, just, and good,' and ' whosoever shall offend in one point is guilty of all.' How could she escape the penalty annexed to all transgression,

even eternal death. 'Cursed is every one that continueth
not in all things which are written in the book of the law
to do them.' She had heard this fearful sentence fall from
the lips of her father, and from those of the 'holy Gifford,'
but hitherto they had seemed possessed of but little
meaning. Now they rung through her awakened soul in
awful notes of condemnation. How could she be accepted
of God? how restore herself to his favor? The more she
looked into her heart, the more fully she saw that she was
sold under sin. How could she relieve herself of this
fearful bondage? She must do something to reconcile her
to an incensed Jehovah, who is 'angry with the wicked
every day, and who cannot look upon sin with the least
degree of allowance.' In her deep anguish she forgot that
'Christ hath redeemed us from the curse of the law,
being made a curse for us. 'Come unto me all ye that are
weary and heavy laden, and you shall find rest for your
souls.' She heard the voice of his Spirit thus calling her;
'but how could she come unto him, wretched and sinful as
she was? She must wait until she could feel that she had
a right to receive.'

Mary was sitting alone in the room which looked out
upon the street. She was pale and haggard, and the traces
of mental anguish were visible in the downcast countenance. Her head rested upon her hand. Her whole attitude was expressive of deep thought and sorrow; no one
looking at her for a moment could mistake this. Her hair
hung loosely over her shoulders. Sighs escaped her heaving
bosom, and ever and anon the big tears would gather in
her sightless eyes, and roll down her marble-like cheeks.
She was dressed as we have described her on the preceding
evening. The clean white three-cornered handkerchief
pinned over her dark tight-fitting boddice. She was
thinking on her lost condition.

The front door, which stood ajar, opened, and persons
entered. The sound of footfalls arrested her attention.
She was frightened, and turned to leave the room.

'Stay, child,' said a kindly voice. 'I have brought
William to see you. Don't be running off.'

Mary paused as she recognised the voice of Mrs. Dormer.
She looked confused. William was before her. Blushing,
she timidly held out her hand, as she heard the young man
and his mother approaching her.

'How do you do, Mary?'

It was the same manly voice, the same sweet intonations.
Mary's heart beat quick and high. The changing color of

her cheek—now a soft rose-hue, and then again so pale—bespoke her deep emotion. The young man took her by the hand, and led her to the seat she had just vacated.

Mrs. Dormer left to see Mrs. Brown.

The color was in William Dormer's cheek too, and a look of soft tenderness in his eye, as he gazed upon the fragile form and blushing face before him. But Mary knew it not. Yet the subdued tone, so tremulous, which voiced words of kind inquiry, spoke to her quick ear and sensitive heart far more readily than changing aspect could have done to the most perfect vision. It rolled in upon her soul in waves of sweet harmony, but was not potent enough to drive away the trouble of her heart.

She sat with downcast eyes and agitated frame, awaiting some remark from William.

'You can go home now, my child,' said Mrs. Brown, as she entered the room where Mary and William sat. 'You can go to see Mrs. Gaunt now, for William here knows where she lives, and his mother says he can go with you. I have just been telling her how you wanted to go last night, after meeting.'

'And do you want to go to Drury Lane, Mary?' asked William of her, as she sat with her face now bright with hope, upturned in the direction of Mrs. Brown's voice. 'The plague has broken out there, too.'

'Oh, then you must stay here in Southwark with us,' exclaimed Mrs. Dormer, whose eyes, riveted on the lovely girl before her, wore a look of deep solicitude.

'Please let me go,' said Mary.

The tone was so sweet and so beseeching, that the two old women could not interpose any farther objections.

'Please let me go now,' said Mary, in the silence that followed her earnest entreaty. 'William, will you take me now?' she asked, while her voice trembled. 'I must go to Mrs. Gaunt; she does not know where I am. Margaret cannot tell her, for she left me in the street.'

'Poor Margaret,' she added, as the thought of her companion flashed across her mind, 'I wonder if she got home?'

'Who, Mary?' asked William; 'Margaret Purdy?'

'Yes; she left me in the street yesterday. We got lost, and she said she would go and find somebody to take us home. I have not seen her since. I hope somebody took her back to Drury Lane.'

'We'll see when we get there,' replied William.

Mary tied on her bonnet to leave. The two good old women commended her to the care of God.

'We may never meet on earth again, Mary,' said Mrs. Brown, as she held the blind girl by the hand, while tears ran down her aged cheeks. 'But don't give up the good work which God's Spirit has begun in your young heart, and we will meet after a while in heaven. Go on, my child, and may God be with you.' Mr. Brown, who had just come home from visiting a sick brother, added his blessing to that of his wife and Mrs. Dormer, and Mary and William departed.

'God bless, thee, sweet child,' said the old man, as he looked after the child; 'God bless her, for her father's sake.'

'And her own, too,' added the wife; 'she is a darling girl.'

The two passed hurriedly on up High Street to the old bridge, the hollow sound of which filled Mary's heart with terror. They did not speak. Neither one seemed to know how to break the deep silence. Just as they crossed Fleet Street, a death-cart rolled before them, and the driver called out in a cold, hollow tone, 'Bring out your dead!' Mary grew suddenly pale, and grasped the hand of William more tightly. He drew her closely to his side, and, supporting her with one arm, quickened his already rapid pace.

They passed through Lincoln's Inn, deserted by its former occupants, and which was now become the rendezvous of the lowest classes of society, who sought lodgings in these comfortable quarters. Mary instinctively shrunk to her companion for protection, as she heard the low jests and vulgar oaths, mingled with the groans and cries of sorrow, which escaped from this motley assemblage of wretched beings.

William, entirely unconscious of what he did, in his great anxiety to protect Mary, dashed on into Lincoln's Inn Fields, then an open square and mostly unenclosed. When he found himself, he was going northward, in the direction of Holborn. Seeing his error, he turned back, and passed out to Drury Lane. Cries of 'Bring out your dead!' met them at every step. The plague was increasing in violence every day. But it had not reached its worst.

Mary was almost breathless through fright and fatigue when she reached Mrs. Gaunt's door. They found it closed. William, knowing Mrs. Gaunt's method of fastening her lock when she went out, passed round and opened the house for Mary's admittance.

They had not been long in before Mrs. Gaunt entered.

She burst into a flood of grateful tears when she beheld Mary.

'Poor child!' she exclaimed 'I thought you were lost. I was sure some evil had befallen you. Where have you been, Mary? I have been looking through town for you. Oh, you cannot tell, my poor child, how I have been troubled. I feared you had been cut off by the plague. Thank God, you are safe, my child! Where is Margaret Purdy? Her mother is almost distracted. Jane Sevelles said she saw you go off together, and we feared you had both fallen victims. Thank God! you are safe. But where is Margaret?'

Mary told her the whole story as best she could. When she came to where Margaret had left her alone in the streets, Mrs. Gaunt, unable to wait further, exclaimed—

'And haven't you seen her since, Mary?'

'No, ma'am, I never heard from her after that. Oh, it is so dreadful, if she is lost, Mrs. Gaunt.'

'I must go and see if she has got back. I pray that she has. Her poor mother is almost mad about her.'

Poor Margaret! Her mother's eyes shall never again in this world behold her. She is even now struggling with the fell monster, which heeds not a mother's piercing cries for her lost child, neither a mother's anguished prayer. A few hours more, and that daughter, so beloved, shall be an inmate of the charnel house with the many that have found an unmarked resting place.

Mrs. Gaunt returned, bringing Margaret's mother with her. Poor woman, she was wild to hear all Mary had to say, that she might discover, if possible, some clue to her lost daughter. But all her inquiries were vain. Mary could give her no reliable information. She did not know the streets of the great city by name, and she could not see to describe the way. The mother had to return to her desolate home heart-broken. She could gain no intelligence of her lost daughter.

'I must go home, Mrs. Gaunt,' Mary said to the good woman, as the two sat talking with William Dormer after the excitement had subsided. She spoke in a very earnest tone, which betrayed to Mrs. Gaunt's ready mind something more than the fear of the plague.

'What for, Mary?' she asked, 'you are not afraid, are you?'

'I want to see my father,' answered the girl, reddening with excitement. 'I must see him, Mrs. Gaunt.'

'Is anything the matter, Mary?' the good woman asked,

somewhat alarmed at the manner of the blind girl. She did not know but what the fever which preceded the plague was upon her. 'Are you sick, my child?'

'Oh, no, it is not because I am sick that I want to see him,' and she hesitated for a moment. 'But I must go home,' she added, 'and you must go with me. You must not stay any longer in this dreadful city. You will die if you do.'

'Well, I will die in my Master's cause, if I do, Mary; and he will give me my reward. It matters but little where, or how, I go.'

William pledged that his mother should accompany them. She had been desiring for a long time to go up to see her husband. It was arranged that they should set out the next day, provided they all lived.

William left to see his mother and tell her of the plan. Poor woman, she was delighted at the prospect of again beholding her husband. But she knew not all the good things in store for her, else would her heart have bounded with joy. Her prayers were about to see their fulfilment.

CHAPTER XXIV.

THE BAPTISM OF MARY.

MARY and her friends reached Bedford safely. Her first act was to find out her father and pour into his ear all her distress.

'Blessed be the Lord God Almighty,' he exclaimed as he listened to her words. 'Blessed be his holy name for this great favor which he has vouchsafed to me. Now I know that he is the Lord my Redeemer, and that he has heard the voice of my supplication.'

Tears of joy and thanksgiving streamed down his pale cheeks as he knelt beside his blind girl and prayed fervently that Christ Jesus would manifest himself unto her, 'chiefest among ten thousand, and the one altogether lovely.' He remembered how the thunders of Sinai had driven her soul to the very verge of despair; and as he gazed upon the worn cheek, and sad, suffering face of his dear child, his heart was almost broken with tender solicitude for her. Never did man pour into the ear of the Infinite Jehovah a more earnest supplication than did John Bunyan, as he knelt beside his blind sin-stricken Mary.

And his prayer did not long remain unanswered.

Jesus, full of compassion, bent from heaven to list the cry of his faithful servant, and to Mary he gave an answer of peace and joy. While the father was yet speaking, Jesus manifested himself unto Mary, a Saviour able and willing to save her from her sins. She cast herself upon him. It was all that she could do. And her sins which were as scarlet were made whiter than snow.

There was a meeting in the cottage home of Elstow. But the father was not there. The stony walls of the prison bound him. But many were present with whom he had prayed, and wept, and rejoiced. That holy man of God, Mr. Gifford, was there, who, from the time of his most remarkable conversion to the day of his death, 'lost not the light of God's countenance—no, not for an hour.' And neighbor Harrow and Goody Harrow were there. And the London friends were present, together with others of God's faithful followers at Elstow and Bedford.

To this pious assembly, met for the worship of God, Mary, with throbbing heart and beaming face, told what the Lord had done for her soul. Her story was a simple one, and clear and convincing. It was a joyous time to the despised disciples. Their hearts took fresh courage. The 'holy Gifford,' who had directed the steps of the father, when, faltering, and despairing, he was plunging on through the darkest night of that most wonderful experience, until he had found peace through faith in the blood of the Lord Jesus Christ, now welcomed into the little church the daughter who had become partaker of ' like precious faith.'

It was an Ebenezer for the little church at Elstow. God blessed the occasion, to the building up in faith and love of his afflicted saints, and also in sending conviction to the heart of William Dormer, who sat a silent but deeply interested spectator of the joyous scene.

While these scenes were transpiring at the 'cottage,' the prisoner in his noisome cell, like Paul and Silas at Philippi, was praying and praising God.

The morning dawned. That morning Mary was to be baptised. It was thus arranged that they might not be disturbed by the populace, or be informed against by those who sought their destruction. Through the live-long night the father, like the Psalmist, had ' communed with God from off his bed.'

The faint grey light of the morning found its way into the prisoner's cell. He arose and prayed. The sun, climbing up the hill-sides, was beginning to throw its first soft beams of glory over the earth.

The prisoner sat at his grated window. The light of hope and joyous expectation made radiant his care-seamed countenance. He had put on his best attire, for to him it was a holy day. His Bible rested on his knee. He had been reading its glorious promises, and meditating thereon until his soul was filled with joy ; until he could exclaim in all the freeness of undimmed faith, ' Abba, Father, my Lord and my God.' His Concordance and Book of Martyrs lay on a settle by his side. The rose-bush, which, to him, had been a beautiful companion ever since that fearful day when the prison door barred out all liberty, stood blooming beside him, sending forth upon the close, damp air of the cell the little fragrance that the morning breeze evolved. His long hair was thrown back from his expansive brow, and, dressed in the fashion of that day, fell over his broad and manly shoulders. With looks of deep anxiety he , peered through the heavy bars of the narrow window. The ' lilied Ouse ' was before him, its crystal waters softly murmuring their onward way to the sea. Years before he had been buried with Christ in baptism in these same waters.

The scene came vividly up before his imagination, and with electric rapidity he ran over the time which had intervened between that memorable occurrence and the present hour. And all along the way, in darkness and in light, he saw the hand of God dispensing to him inestimable blessings. But this was the greatest gift of all—his Mary saved from the horrors of a second death. ' What shall I render unto thee, O God, for all thy mercies unto me,' he exclaimed, as his heart bounded with rapture.

There is a peace and joy which the world knoweth not. It cannot give it, neither can it take away. That peace is found in believing in the Lord Jesus Christ.

Presently he saw a little company wending their way down the descent to the banks of the stream. He gazed most searchingly into their midst. Soon his eager eye discovered his darling Mary led by the pastor and neighbor Harrow. His Elizabeth and William Dormer were behind. He thought he saw a look of holy joy on the countenances of the beloved ones. His heart leaped within him. How he longed to take his Mary in his arms and send up praise and thanksgiving to Him who had washed her in his own blood.

But the prison walls bound him : he could not go ; and Satan came tempting him. ' O God, my God, thy will be done,' he exclaimed, as thoughts of his dreadful situation came rushing through his soul. 'I will not chafe nor murmur under thy dispensation. Give me needed strength.'

How soon was his praise turned to prayer. But a few moments before, his soul, filled with ecstatic bliss, was rehearsing his many blessings. Now he was struggling mightily with the temptations of Satan.

'The world, the flesh, and the devil!' What a combination against the child of God. Can he ever overcome this triple power? Yes. Thanks be to Him who giveth us the victory. He is able to conquer all foes, though their name be legion.

The disciples silently reached the river's bank. No song of praise and thanksgiving marked their steps. Their enemies were round about them, and they dared not betray themselves to evil men.

They selected a spot where they could be in full view of the gaol window. They could not see the prisoner, but they knew his look was upon them. They knelt, and the man of God prayed for the divine approbation on what they were about to do.

It was a beautiful and striking scene. A few downtrodden, despised followers of the Lord Jesus kneeling beside the crystal water in the gray of the morning dawn, to invoke his blessing upon an act emblematical of his burial and resurrection. What could have been more sublime and more touchingly interesting? Human eyes were not spectators. But the Lord of light, and shining angels, bent as witnesses above the hallowed spot, and in heaven was a record made of this act of faith and obedience.

The prayer was ended. Mary arose, and round her head was bound a white handkerchief. Her shoes were then removed; and, leaning on the arm of the pastor, Mr. Gifford, the two descended into the water, and there, in the name of the Holy Trinity, Mary was burried with her Lord and Saviour in baptism. As she arose, she said sweetly, 'Bless the Lord, oh my soul, and all that is within me bless his holy name.'

The prisoner gazed through the bars of the narrow window upon the solemn scene. His face was streaming with tears, but they were tears of holy rapture. His heart was leaping with emotions of gratitude and love, and words of thanksgiving and praise were on his tongue.

The sightless eyes, flowing with tears, were turned to heaven as the two moved towards the bank. No word was uttered. All was silent as the grave, save the rippling of the pearly stream.   One and another clasped her hand and pressed her to their bosom.

As the morning sun, rising above the hill-tops, burst in a flood of glory over the scene, the little company ascended the bank.

There was one heart in that assembly bowed to the earth under a sense of sin.

It was William Dormer.

God, through his Holy Spirit, had convicted him, and had shown him the exceeding sinfulness of sin,' and the justice of his righteous law.   But Christ was not formed within him the hope of glory—he had not yet beheld him as the way, the truth, and the life ; and his soul was sending up the cry continually, ' How shall man be just with God?' He was hoping to secure the divine favor by prayers and tears.   He must do something to recommend him to God.

Poor sin-sick soul, you can do nothing but flee to the arms of Jesus.   There, and there alone, is hope found.

And so William at last saw the way.   He had come— as all the saved before him had done, and all who shall be saved till the end of the world must do—to the arms of the Saviour.

And when, the next week, the little band again assembled under similar circumstances to witness the ordinance of baptism, there were other eyes than Bunyan's gazing through prison grates.

CHAPTER XXV.

BUNYAN'S PRISON EMPLOYMENTS.

BUNYAN was not an idler in prison.   His active mind must have something to do.   And, besides all this, he was compelled to work hard for the scanty dole on which a a wife and four children dragged out their sorrowful existence.   With his pincers, old pieces of brass, and tape, he managed to eke out a miserable pittance by working from dawn till dark.

We must remember that during the first two years of Bunyan's imprisonment he was permitted by the gaoler, over whom he soon acquired a wonderful influence, to visit his family, and to be present at the meetings of his brethren whenever he desired so to do ; and during this time we have no account of his having written anything

at all. Composition was to him a recreation. But as long
as he could find relief from the tedium of the prison in
visits to his family, and in communion with his beloved
brethren, he sought nothing beyond this.

How our hearts are touched with sympathy and sadness
as we hear the gaoler say to him after his weary walk from
London, ' Mr. Bunyan, I have received a command, sir,
which says you must no longer look out of the door.'
' God knows,' replied the astonished man, 'it is a slander
that I went to London to make or plot an insurrection.'
But his innocence was of no avail. The sentence must be
enforced. And Bunyan bade farewell to family and friends,
green fields, and the light of day.

From this time begins his literary labor ; and from this
year, 1663, until the time of his release early in 1673, he
wrote several books, among them his inimitable ' Pilgrim's
Progress.' If it had not been for the rigor of his sentence,
it is highly probable that Bunyan would never have
produced that work, which, next to the Bible, has been
the solace and guide of the Christian in all succeeding
ages.

God had a purpose in his incarceration—a purpose of
good to his people. And his people should praise him, that
he has so wonderfully provided for their spiritual wants.
How many a heart has been led into peace and joy by the
reading of the Pilgrim ; has had its faith strengthened, its
hopes revived, its zeal inspired, by following Christian as
he journeyed on towards the Holy City.

After a diligent search of old records, it has not been
found that, from early in 1663 until 1668, Bunyan was
ever permitted to go beyond the prison walls. His employment throughout these five dreary years were, as we have
said, the study of the Scriptures only, and tagging shoe
laces. It has been found from the records of the church-
book at Bedford, that he was, during the year '68, three
times appointed to visit disorderly church members. The
gaoler must have granted him privileges in the face of the
law and the Conventicle Act. His name appears in the
minutes of the church meeting in 1669, 1670, 1671.
During the latter year, and while yet in prison, he was
called to take the care of the church at Bedford and
ordained.

The record in the old church-book reads as follows : ' On
the 29th of August, 1671, the church was directed to seek
God about the choice of brother Bunyan to the office of
elder or a pastor, to which office he was called on the 24th

of the tenth month, in the same year when he received of the elders (or pastors) the right hand of fellowship.'

When, after his ordination, he was permitted through the clemency of his gaoler to meet with his flock, and sometimes with the brethren of other churches, thereby taxing his time greatly, and interrupting to some extent his literary pursuits, he did not cease to write. It had become to him a pleasurable and profitable employment. It was the only way he could reach the popular errors of the day. And we find him, in a few months after his ordination, sending forth from the prison that bold and decisive answer to Dr. Fowler's work on the 'Design of Christianity.'

The precise number of works written by him while in prison we have no accurate means of ascertaining. We know that there have been published of his productions sixty entire works—one for each year of his life; for he was just sixty years old when he died. Two of the sixty, 'Gospel Truths Opened,' and a 'Vindication' of it, were published, the one, four years, and the other three, before his imprisonment. Several works were written after his release from gaol in 1673, for he continued a close student up to the time of his death. Sixteen of his works were published after his death, which occurred in 1688, fifteen years after his pardon.

Thus we see that this good and great man, in all situations, was a worker in the vineyard of his Lord. Nothing deterred him from his great purpose, that of winning souls to Christ. His pulpit efforts were signally blessed. His itineracies through the adjoining counties were frequent, and greatly blessed in the spread of the kingdom of the Lord Jesus Christ. His maxim was, 'If I can pluck souls from the clutches of the devil, I care not where they go to be built up in their holy faith.' Of his trials and persecutions after he came out of gaol, we shall speak in a following chapter.

CHAPTER XXVI.

BUNYAN'S RELEASE—EMPLOYMENT.

TWELVE years of imprisonment! Twelve long weary years shut up in a town gaol! What thoughts of misery, of loneliness, and despair does it suggest? And all this

deprivation, all this suffering, because Bunyan *would
preach the gospel of our Lord Jesus Christ.* This was his
offence!—no other. What a comment on the spirit of that
age! What a proof of the power of the Prince of the air
working in the children of disobedience?

But the man of God had been patient in afflictions through
the grace of God, which strengthened him, and while his
body was pent up in chill, noisome walls, his soul feasted
on the ravishing glories of the unseen world. The candle
of the Lord shone round about, and made glorious the thick
darkness.

Day and night he had labored—for food for his wife and
little ones—and, above all, to show himself an approved
workman to God—one that need not be ashamed. The
morning dawn found him tugging with his pincers to tag
stay laces—the midnight hour beheld him with his Bible and
his pen, studying and writing that he might give spiritual
food to the children of God, and warn sinners to flee from
the wrath to come. He took great delight, too, in corres-
ponding with his brethren who were in like sufferings with
himself; and also to his 'spiritual children,' as he called
those of his own immediate congregation, and all those
who had been born to God through his instrumentality.

One morning as he sat by his narrow window, thinking
over the trials of his brethren, and what the little flock at
Bedford were enduring for Christ's sake, it came into his
head to write them a letter of consolation. And thus he
speaks:

'Children, grace be with you. Amen. I being taken from you
in presence, and so tied up that I cannot perform that duty,
that from God doth lie upon me to you, and for your further
edifying and building up in faith and holiness, yet that you may
see that my soul hath fatherly çare and desire after your spiritual
and everlasting welfare, I now once again, as before from the top
of Shinar and Hermon; so now from the Lion's den, and from
the mountain of the Leopard, do look yet after ye all, greatly
longing to see your safe arrival in the deserved haven . . . I
have sent you here enclosed [in his life] a drop of that honey that
I have taken out of the carcase of a lion. I have eaten thereof
myself, and am much refreshed thereby.'

Then, after calling to their minds what God had done for
them in times past, and bringing before them in strong yet
tender words their present afflictions, he appealed to them
to trust in God, because he himself had called them out of
the world; and had manifested himself to them as he had
not done to the world. He continues:

'Have you never a hill Mizar to remember ? Have you forgot the close, the milk-house, the stable, the barn, and the like, where God did visit your souls? Remember also the word, the word I say, upon which the Lord hath caused you to hope. If you have sinned against light, if you are tempted to blaspheme, if you are drowned in despair, if you think God fights against you, or if heaven is hid from your eyes, remember it was thus with your fathers, ' but out of them all the Lord delivered me.'

* * * * * *

' My dear children, the milk and honey are beyond this wilderness. God be merciful to you, and grant that you be not slothful to go in to possess the land.

' JOHN BUNYAN.'

Release came at length. The prison doors flew open, and the narrow, dark cell was exchanged for the sweet cottage home, and its loneliness and dreariness for the blissful society of a loved and loving wife and children. He was once again permitted to mingle with his brethren, and indeed to go in and out before them as an under-shepherd, having been ordained, as we have before said, in 1771, at least one year before his final release. This was a source of great joy and thanksgiving to him. He loved to *preach* Christ crucified, and point sinners the way to eternal life.

As soon as he came out from prison he immediately entered on his duties as pastor to the flock over which he had been called to preside. Beside this, he itinerated extensively in all the adjoining counties. It was his meat and his drink to spread the news of the glorious gospel of the Son of God. It was his custom to make an annual visit to London for the purpose of preaching and setting in order the things of the kingdom of his Master.

His fame everywhere preceded him. ' If a day's notice were given,' says Southey, ' that he was going to preach in London, the meeting house at Southwark at which he generally preached, would not contain half the people.' And his friend Charles Doe, in his Circular, says : ' I have seen, by my computation, about *twelve hundred* persons to hear him at a morning lecture on a working day in dark winter time. I also computed that about *three thousand* came to hear him to a town's end meeting house, so that half were fain to go back again for want of rooom ; and then himself was fain, at a back door, to be pulled almost over people to *get up stairs* to the pulpit.'

But while thus engaged in pastoral duties, and in extensive and useful itineracies, he was not unmindful of his pen, but devoted all his leisure time to study and to writing. He was not exempt from the enmity of those who hated him for his doctrine's sake, even after he came forth from the prison. He sometimes made narrow escapes from their fell pursuits. But as Doe beautifully says: 'It pleased the Lord to preserve him out of the hands of his enemies in the severe persecution at the latter end of the reign of king Charles, though they often searched and laid wait for him, and sometimes narrowly missed him.' This explains it all — unfolds the mysteries of all his hair-breadth escapes. 'The Lord delivered him out of the hands of his enemies.'

CHAPTER XXVII.

THE TALE OF LOVE.

THE two were walking home together from Bedford — William Dormer and the blind girl. She was now no longer the frail child. Womanhood had thrown around her maturer charms and more finished graces. It had been twelve years since William Dormer for the first time gazed on that sweet pensive face and delicate form. The face was changed, and the form had assumed womanly proportions, but the one had lost nothing of its charming loveliness, its depth and purity of thought and expression, nor the other the soft sweet grace which bespoke the sensitive nature within.

William was upon a visit to his father, and as was his custom he made the Elstow cottage his home. He had accompanied the family to Bedford church meeting. Bunyan was at liberty now, and as the loved pastor of the little flock at Bedford, he ministered unto them in holy things. The dark shadow which for twelve long years had brooded over that desolate home was now removed, and the sunshine of a father's love and a father's presence dwelt in glad beauty over that peaceful household.

It was a calm autumn evening, the one of which we speak. The mellow light of the declining sun fell in streams of heavenly glory along the highway and across the meadows though which their homeward pathway lay.

William led her gently by the hand, guiding her foot-steps from all danger, and looking on her with an earnest, tender gaze. They had lingered somewhat behind the father and mother as they turned from the highway into the meadow.

William had been speaking to her of the sufferings of his father in prison, and the mysterious providence that ' kept him there when others had been released. He spoke of the sorrows that dear old father had undergone before the hand of the law had laid its iron grip upon him. Two sons had been torn from his bosom to pour out their blood on the battle-field. Another, by a strange accident, had been deprived of his mind at the age of twelve, and imbecile, had lingered on for years, until at last death came to relieve him of his suffering. A daughter fair and beautiful, and the idol of the father's heart, had been stricken down by consumption in the opening of womanhood.

'I remember her well, Mary,' he said, 'my sister Jane. She was much like you, Mary, gentle, confiding, true. We all loved her.'

'She was not blind, was she, William?' asked the girl timidly, yet anxiously. She thought, perhaps, this sad misfortune had served to link the brother's heart the more closely to his lost sister; and if he had loved her the more fondly for this, why—ah! why not *her?*

'No, Mary, she was not blind; her eyes were the color of yours.'

'But she could see, William, and I cannot,' interrupted the blind girl, sadly.

William pressed the hand he held in his more tightly, and the tears rushed to his eyes as the tremulous words, so full of hopelessness, fell on his ears and pierced his heart.

'If she had been blind like you, I should have loved her the more fondly. She would have been dearer to me from her very helplessness.'

Mary started as he spoke thus. A new thought rushed through her mind. Could anybody be more lovely because they were blind? Surely William did not mean this. He must have mistaken her words. But how could she be deceived? Did he not say, 'She would have been dearer to me from her very helplessness?' Strange emotions, pleasurable in their excitement, filled her bosom. She might be loved by him, blind as she was. The thought lighted up with a bright hopeful expression the calm face. To be loved for her blindness, and that, too, by William Dormer! It was a happiness too great.

Mary did not speak. She could not trust her faltering

lips with words. Her hand trembled in William's. He perceived it, and instantly divined the cause.

'Do you think, Mary,' he asked, 'that no one can love the blind?'

'Oh, yes, I suppose they can, but I cannot tell why they should love them more *because* they are blind. It is such a sore affliction, William. But did you not say you could have loved your sister far better if she had been blind?'

'Yes, Mary, I did. And I must tell you that this is one reason why I have loved you so dearly. Your very blindness has won my heart, and I feel that through life it will be my greatest joy to be eyes to you—to guide and protect you.'

The maiden made no reply.

'I have loved you, Mary, since first we met—since first I saw you in the door of your own cottage home. You were a child then, and I a youth. I have passed through many scenes since, but never has your image been absent from my mind. I have cherished it day by day, and hour by hour, until it has become a part of myself. Long ago would I have asked for a return of affection, but I dared not under the circumstances. My father in prison, and my mother feeble and dependent, without any protector but me, and I poor, very poor, Mary. I could not tempt God. I could not make your situation worse than it was. But God in his wisdom has seen fit to take my kind mother from me. She has gone, and I am left alone. Unless you love me, there is no one else in the wide world to whom I can look for sympathy and affection. Tell me, Mary, will you be to me more than mother and sister—more than all the world beside? I have nothing to offer you but a loving heart; but, by the help of God, I will be to you a kind protector, a true friend, as long as life shall last. Tell me, Mary, will you trust yourself to my guidance and protection?'

The fountain sealed up in her bosom for long years was suddenly opened. She had never dared to dwell on the probable realisation of her fondly cherished hopes. But now that bliss was hers. She could scarcely realise that it was true. It seemed to her like one of those beautiful dreams that had come to her pillow in the night watches. And like those airy visions she felt it must pass away.

'You answer me not, Mary. Do you refuse my proffered love?'

William drew aside her hood to look at her. Her face was bathed in tears. She turned her darkened eyes to his,

He needed not words to tell him he was loved. He read it in every lineament of that burning face; in the radiant beamings of those sealed eyes, and the tremulousness of the parted lips. They were all telling, in their silent eloquence, a tale of true, abiding affection.

Mary was happy. The world seemed to her full of life and beauty. There was but one sad thought to mar her joy. She could never look upon him she loved. It was but a passing shadow. Why should she desire to see him with her natural vision, when every feature, every light and shade of that handsome face was imprinted on her soul?

CHAPTER XXVIII.

THE SEPARATION.

'Tis a cold winter night in December, 1674. The snow is driving fast across the fields. And the fierce blasts of the northern wind, as it comes rushing on in its fury, almost prostrate the traveller as, shivering from its keen breath, he gathers more closely around him his heavy cloak. The heavens are covered with dark, leaden clouds, which shut in every ray of moon or star. God help the poor mariner on the storm-tossed ocean, and the poor traveller on the wind-swept plain.

In the little cottage at Elstow, the family are gathered round the blazing hearth. Peace and comfort now reign within. For the father is there.

The day's labor is over. The simple evening repast has been served. 'Bunyan's Elizabeth' is sitting quietly by the fire with her sewing. A smile of deep happiness overspreads her motherly countenance. Mary is sitting beside the father, with her face turned to his, and lighted up with a radiant beauty which tells of the deep wells of joy within. Sarah is now no longer a child. She is tall, and her rounded proportions and laughing face show health and vivacity, rather than grace and sensitiveness. She is a complete contrast to the blind sister by her side, and yet they are both lovely girls. The younger children, John and Elizabeth, tired with the day's sports, lie sleeping on their little cot beneath the window—the same spot where years before, when Mary, yet a child, had dreamed that dream of William Dormer and the beautiful land. Thomas and Joseph are now large enough to take care of themselves, and as they depend on their own exertions for support, they have found themselves homes elsewhere.

Bunyan is telling his Elizabeth and the daughters of his late itineracy into Buckingham. He speaks with all the fervor of his soul, for that soul is filled with gratitude to God for his many mercies and rich blessings. How the females hang on his words! The sewing rests on the lap, while the wife's eyes are fixed on her husband's beaming face. Mary's hand is on her father's knee (she often rests thus), while her face is turned up to him that she may catch every intonation of that rich, full voice. Sarah's arm is on Mary's shoulder, and her face close to hers, while her large dark eyes and flushing cheek show that she, too, is all alive to her father's words and sentiments. Sarah, too, is a child of God.

The fierce wind raves and moans without. And as its loud, long wail sounds round the peaceful cottage, the inmates shudder. Thank God! they are all safely housed. But they remember that many a fellow creature may even now be perishing for want of shelter.

A rap is heard at the door. The father rises to open it. The stranger steps in.

It is William Dormer.

His expression is one of intense excitement. His voice meets the ear of Mary. She starts, and tears suddenly fall. She knows that voice, but it is dry and husky, as if fear and alarm had frozen up the life blood.

'I cannot stay,' says he. 'I came to bid you all adieu; they are even now on my track, and if they overtake me I know not what will be my end. I have no time to explain. But when I reach a place of refuge, I will send you word all about it.'

The family stood aghast. Mary sunk to a chair. Bunyan, with his usual courage and self-possession, was speechless.

'I have done nothing wrong. Only the vindictive vengeance of enemies.'

He moved to Mary's side, and throwing his arms around her, leaned her head upon his bosom, and spoke hasty words of comfort and promise of return. The poor girl was almost unconscious. She knew something dreadful had occurred, but could not tell what. She did not speak, for she had no power to do so. She remained as motionless as though life had forsaken that bowed form.

'You must not grieve thus, Mary; you shall hear all in a fortnight, God willing. Trust in him, my dear girl. It will all be well.' He smoothed back the hair from the marble temples, and gazed as though he would look out his soul on those chiseled features, now so still and motionless.

' Church matters ? ' said Bunyan.

' Yes,' was the hasty reply.

' Speak to me, Mary, before I go. I must haste, or I am gone.' He stooped again and kissed her. The kiss seemed to wake her to life. She raised her head and said, ' William, what is all this ? '

' William will explain, in good time, my dear child,' and the father supported her in his arms.

' But now he must be off. His cruel enemies are at his heels, and if he stays talking to us they may overtake him. It is all right, my Mary. Do not fear, but trust in God.'

William bade them all farewell, and rushed through the door.

The loud wailing wind drowned the noise of his footsteps in the crisp snow.

The angel of sorrow again overshadowed the little cottage at Elstow with his heavy wing.

CHAPTER XXIX.

SUSPENSE.

THE beautiful summer of 1675, full of life, and love, and gladness, was smiling over the earth. Traces of the three great calamities, the ' Plague,' the ' Great Fire,' and the ' Dutch Invasion,' which had spread much consternation and suffering throughout the metropolis, and, indeed, the whole realm, had measureably passed away ; and prosperity, as great as could attend a people ruled by an effeminate and dissolute sovereign, and an intriguing and cruel parliament, marked the nation, and gave to it some little promise of future good.

The king and his courtiers had retired to Hampton Court to escape the noise and heat of the city. The morals of Charles and the nobility were by no means improved. Calamities, the sudden and signal visitations of heaven, had had no effect in bringing these slaves of pleasure to their sober reason and the conscientious discharge of duty. Dissipation, profligacy, in a word, vices of the darkest dye, held dominant sway over the minds and hearts of all in authority. They were enslaved; the Prince of the power of the air led them captives at his will. They were heaping up wrath and indignation, not only for themselves individually, but for the nation at large.

'The kings of the earth set themselves, and the rulers take counsel against the Lord, and against his anointed.' 'He that sitteth in the heavens shall laugh; the Lord shall have them in derision.'

The Lady Castlemaine, now Duchess of Cleveland, was still the reigning beauty of the court; and the imperious will of this unprincipled woman was law to the weak-minded monarch. She dictated—he obeyed with a serviveness disgusting even to those as sunken in voluptuousness and vice as himself. When her demands exceeded even his magnificent bounds, as they sometimes did (for she was rapacious in her desires,) and the king, exasperated by her selfishness and tyranny, openly offended her and forbade her the court, her fits of violent rage and vulgar denunciation were the astonishment and dread of all who were witnesses of her frenzies. She had no parallel, even in that reign of unbridled passion and vituperation. And she never failed to accomplish her aim. The cowardly monarch could not withstand her arrogant will, and was sure, in the end, to come penitent and supplicating to her feet. She knew his weakness well, and she availed herself of it to carry her ends, in affairs of state as well as of court. A groaning country fully attested the dire misrule of a prince given to women, wit, and wine, rather than to wisdom, judgment, and righteousness.

But times were somewhat changed for the better, for the people of God, since the day that John Bunyan was condemned without a hearing to a prisoner's cell, and there held by cruel injustice. The laws were rigorous still, but the creatures of the government were not so eager to hunt out and drag to condemnation those whose only sin was claiming the right to worship God after the teachings of his holy word. And the tinker preacher, who was seized upon, dragged from the bosom of his family to a reckless bar, and from thence to a dungeon, merely because 'he would preach Jesus,' was now permitted to meet with his flock at Bedford, and in peace and comparative security break unto them the bread of life. The blood-hounds of the law had become sated, and the children of God were thereby exempt, for a time, from their fearful pursuit.

It was a calm, lovely day, in the summer of 1675,

Bunyan had been with his people, setting in order the things that pertain to the house of God, and expounding to them the Scriptures. His faithful Elizabeth, and Mary, and Sarah, had accompanied him. As they passed the old gaol on their return home, what visions of long, dull days, of heart - aching dread, and dark forebodings, and of weary night-watchings, when his soul was breaking with sorrow at the thought of the distresses of his suffering family, and of the fearful temptations of Satan, who would have led him to despair, flashed before the father's mind. There he had known agony—intense agony; and the remembrance of it was never to be forgotten.

But in all the evil there was a good. His trials had taught him to feel another's woe. They had prepared him to teach more fully the doctrines of the divine word. He had experienced, and, therefore, he could speak with confidence of the grace of God made manifestly sufficient in the darkest hour. God was a Father of infinite love and tenderness; this his soul knew full well. And there was no sorrow, no temptation among his people that he could not find a balm for, and a power against, in the blessed Scriptures.

He had now much to be thankful for, much for which to take courage and press on. The black night was passed, and to it had succeeded a bright day of joy and peace. But this day was not without its clouds. A shadow even now rested on his breast, and its darkening hues portended to his paternal love a future of blight and sadness.

Since that fearful night, when William Dormer had so suddenly entered the little cottage at Elstow to break to its fireside group the dreadful news of his hasty departure to the continent, Mary, the loved of her father's heart, had been drooping, even as the lily in whose stalk is lodged the fatal worm. Mary was greatly changed. Parents and friends observed it, and strangers looked on that pensive face and said, ' Ah, poor child; she is blind, and she feels it deeply.' Ah, no! It was not that the sunshine of heaven was sealed out from her vision. The sun of love was darkened in her heart; the sun, which, in its rising, had promised a long day of happiness.

Eight months have passed since that fearful December night, and no news has yet been received from the absent one. Postal arrangements were not, two hundred years ago, such as they are now. Neither was education as generally diffused as it is in this nineteenth century.

William Dormer could not write his own name when he left the shores of England for Holland.

The father saw the daughter, sinking, day by day, under her weight of sorrow and disappointment. He endeavored to buoy her up with hope. But love is tenacious of its own powers of discrimination and foresight. Mary had entire confidence in her father's judgment in all other matters save this. In everything else he was her strength. He pointed out to her the promises of God (he would not mock her with a calculation of human probabilities), and pleaded with her to rely on his faithful word. And by faith she did lay hold, to a great extent, on the rich and abundant consolations of the gospel, but she was weak human nature, and she faltered, even in her most earnest endeavors, and oftentimes she fell, faint and weary. For weeks she had hoped each day to hear from him she loved. But the winter had passed, and spring-flowers budded and bloomed, and birds sung sweetly to their mates 'neath the hawthorn hedge, and yet no tidings from him who was far away.

Mary essayed to hide her corroding grief, not that she would blush to make it known, but she would save her father the slightest pain. But a father's love was too detective for her most sedulous care; aye, long before she would admit to her own bosom the fearful truth, he had read it all too plainly in the clouded brow and sad face, in the languid step and smothered sigh. He knew, and could appreciate the intensity of her distress, for he was thoroughly familiar with the painful depths of her sensitive nature.

Bunyan felt that his poor blind Mary loved as but few beings ever love. The strength and intensity of her affection, which made her a new being in requited love, was now a consuming fire, scorching with worse than lava stream every hope, every enjoyment.

As Mary walked with her parents home from meeting, she was pensive and silent. As she crossed the old bridge, thoughts of him on whose arm she had so often leaned for safety as she trod its narrow footpath, came rushing over her soul with fearful power. He was associated in her mind with every step of the way from Bedford to Elstow. Often had they trod the road and the smiling meadows together.

The little company of pedestrians turned from the highway into the meadow—the meadow where William had first made known his love to Mary, *in words*, and where she had looked, even from those sightless eyes, a full, free answer to his avowal. How gloriously beautiful then—how desolate and meaningless now !

In one short year Mary had lived a lifetime of sorrow. How many even in fewer months, can tell the same sad tale.

CHAPTER XXX.

THE VISIT—NEWS FROM WILLIAM DORMER.

As the family of Bunyan sat at the twilight hour at the front door of their cottage home on the evening of the church-meeting day, of which we have spoken, they beheld a female approaching the house across the meadow. She advanced with weary step, bearing in her hand a bundle of clothes.

'I cannot tell who she is, Elizabeth,' said Bunyan, in reply to the question of his wife, at the same time straining his vision to peer out into the evening twilight. 'It may be one of the neighbor girls, coming to spend the night with us ; or perhaps some poor travelling sister who needs our help.'

'She will be welcome, then,' said the gentle wife, with her calm maternal smile, as she placed the little Elizabeth on her knee, and kissed the bright glowing cheeks of the child.

'It's not one of the neighbor girls, father,' said Sarah, who stood in the door and gazed out into the deepening gloom. 'It is some stranger, and yet it seems to me I have seen her before.'

Mary sat listening ; her head was slightly bent, and rested on her hand. Her face was very sad. Her thoughts were with William in his lonely wanderings. At Sarah's remark she started. A beam of intelligence lighted her face.

'It may be her,' she said involuntarily to herself.

By this time the female was crossing the little stile that led into the yard. It was too dark to recognise her features, even so near.

'Good evening to you, friends. I believe you do not know me.'

Mary sprung from her seat, and started forward to meet her.

'Mrs. Gaunt ! Mrs. Gaunt !' she exclaimed, 'I knew it

must be her!' and she threw her arms fondly about the
kind woman's neck, and burst into a flood of tears.

'We welcome you to our home, sister Gaunt,' said the
father, extending to her his hand. We are glad to see you
once more on earth. How is it with you?'

'Well, brother Bunyan,' the Christian woman replied,
'thanks to God. His mercy has brought me safely on my
way.'

Mrs. Bunyan greeted her with her kind, sweet smile and
pleasant words of welcome, and the sister in the Lord was
soon made to feel at home among his people.

A wholesome and refreshing repast was quickly served
for her by Sarah, who had now supplanted both her mother
and Mary in the management of household affairs.

While the visitor partook of their kindly cheer, she
spoke to them of her day's journey, and of the condition of
the brethren in London, and recounted to their eager ears
some of the trials and hardships the people of God had
undergone in the city.

Mary was anxious to ask her something of William
Dormer. Whether she knew why he had left the city, and
if he had ever yet been heard from; but she dared not
breathe his name. Her heart stood still with suspense, and
her cheek was white as Parian marble. She leaned eagerly
forward to catch every word, every intonation of Mrs.
Gaunt's voice.

'Oh, that she would mention William's name!—that her
father or mother would say a word about *him!*' She longed
to ask herself. Once she essayed to do so, but the words
choked in her throat, and she was silent.

'And William Dormer, too, is among the sufferers,'
remarked Mrs. Gaunt.

Mary started as if an electric shock had passed through
her feeble frame. She held her breath to hear. Her hand,
which rested on the head of little John at her side, shook
as if she had been suddenly seized with an ague. The little
fellow looked up amazed at her trembling.

'Have you any news of William, sister Gaunt?' asked
Bunyan, whose quick penetration had read the desires of
his daughter's heart.

'Yes, and good news, too. That is my principal business
to see you.'

'What is it! what is it, Mrs. Gaunt!' exclaimed Mary,
as she started from her seat and threw her arms violently
out before her. This was her habit whenever highly
excited. Her natural timidity and desire to conceal her

feelings gave way under the thought of hearing from William.

'He is well, and doing well,' replied Mrs. Gaunt hastily, to relieve Mary of her preying anxiety.

'And where is he, Mrs. Gaunt, in London?'

'Oh, no, Mary, you know he left there last winter—'

'Yes,' interrupted Bunyan, 'he called here last December, in his flight. But we thought perhaps he had come back again.'

'Oh, no, brother Bunyan, William cannot return to London—*now* at least,' she added, as she caught a glimpse of Mary's pale face by the rush-light. 'It would be death for him to come back at this time. The persons who have sworn to take his life are on the watch for him, and should he fall into their hands, it would be all over with the dear boy.'

A shudder seized the frame of Mary as she heard these fearful words, and a pallor overspread her face. She pressed her hand to her brow, as if to drive back torturing thoughts. A deep sigh escaped her bosom.

'The hand of God is in all this, my daughter,' said Bunyan to Mary. 'Trust the Lord Jehovah; he is everlasting strength, and he will order all things in wisdom and love to his children.'

'Tell us where William is now, sister Gaunt, and then tell us what was the cause of his having to fly. He had no time to do it when he was here, and we have never heard from him since.'

'William was in Leuwarden, a small place in the north of Holland, two months ago, and in good business. I met a man last week who had seen him, and talked to him. He says he looks well, and is doing well, and he is learning to write, that he may write a letter to Mary. He sent a great many messages by Mr. Leeber, to all his friends, and made him promise, when he reached London, to find me out, and deliver them all to me, that I might come and tell Mary. He said she must not give up; he would come back again just as soon as he could learn that the danger was over, and then they would be happy together. He sent word for me to tell her that he thought of her every hour he lived; she was ever in his mind, and he was looking forward to the time, with the brightest hopes, when he could come back to England and claim her for his own.

'And, Mary, you must not despair. God will bring it all right, my child; trust in him. You remember how he saved you in London from the fearful plague, and when

you were lost, and could not find your way, how he sent
deliverance to you. He has been good in times past. His
loving kindness has never failed you. Take courage, then,
and trust him for the future, for he is unchangeable, and
his tender mercy is over you still.'

'The Lord Jehovah is the strength of his people; he
will save them from all their distresses,' responded Bunyan
to the remarks of Mrs. Gaunt.

'But tell us, sister Gaunt, how was it that William had
to flee from London?' inquired Mrs. Bunyan, as she sat
hushing the little Elizabeth to sleep on her knee. 'We
have thought of everything in trying to account for it.
He had just time to tell us it was for religion.'

'I cannot give you all the particulars, sister Bunyan.
I was not in London at the time, having gone into Hertford
to see a sick sister of Mr. Gaunt's, who was in a dreadful
condition. When I returned some weeks after it took
place, I could not find any one who could tell me the
straight story. But it seems that William and the brethren
had met together in the little upper room, in Southwark,
when they were turned out and interrupted by a band of
desperate fellows, who have leagued themselves together
under the sanction of the officers of the law for the purpose
of interrupting all Nonconformist meetings. This dreadful
gang of outlaws broke into the room, and with horrid oaths
declared they would bring to trial every man, woman, and
child they could lay hands upon. William, together with
other young men present, took active measures to prevent
the execution of their cruel threat, and at last they were
able to drive them back and keep them at bay until the
aged men and women could make their escape through the
trap door. William was unfortunate enough in the desperate struggle to throw one of the young men down the
stairway and seriously injure him; and the whole band
then and there declared they would avenge their comrade
at the peril of their own lives. The insensible condition of
the fellow drew their minds from the attack, and the young
brethren got off. Two of them, who are known to members
of this company of desperadoes, made their escape with
William to Holland, and are with him in the same manu-
factory at Leuwarden.'

'But can't these outlaws be brought to justice?' asked
Sarah as she stood wiping the plates. 'Can't the law force
them to behave themselves?'

'The law sanctions their outrageous proceedings, my
child. The law will protect all who take part against Non-

conformists. These dreadful fellows act out the command
of the officers of law, and there is no hope.'

'But couldn't he come back and live in some other part
of England, Mrs. Gaunt?' asked Mary timidly.

'There is no hope now, my child,' replied her father,
looking tenderly upon her. 'We must trust in God to help
us. It is a trained band, and they have their accomplices
everywhere. Spies are they, and no man can live in England
and escape their eye. William must remain abroad until
God in his wisdom brings an end to the present state of
tyranny. Let us look to him for mercy and thank him that
William is safe.'

Mary spoke not. It was a deep trial to her soul, but
she had learned in the dark afflictions which had surrounded her way since she was eleven years old, to stand
still and murmur not. She must suffer, but not complain,
since the Lord is her God. She would learn entire submission to his will, and implore his grace to sustain her
in the darkest hour. William was prosperous and learning
to write; and she would hear soon from him again. And
then her father could answer his letters. Oh, what a
comfort! It was the glorious sunshine tinging the dark
cloud which had so long hovered over her.

The friends sat for some time conversing on subjects
that related to the Redeemer's kingdom. At length, the
Bible was brought, and the family and the Christian
guest gathered around the table, and the man of God,
by the feeble taper light, read the ninety-first Psalm.
'Lord, thou hast been our dwelling-place in all generations.'

As was his custom, Bunyan explained as he read, and
exhorted his family to trust in God because of his great
power and goodness. When he came to the sixteenth
verse, 'Let thy work appear unto thy servants, and thy
glory unto their children,' he addressed his remarks to his
blind daughter, and exhorted her to lean upon God, and
recognise his hand in all the events of her life.

In the prayer which followed, he commended each
member of his family by name to God. Affectionately
he spoke of the dear sister who, for the love of them,
because they were brethren and sisters in Christ Jesus,
had left her home to bring the glad news of the loved
absent one. 'Thy will, O Lord God of hosts, be done
with us as it is in heaven,' added the servant of God
fervently.

'It is a short and simple prayer,
　　But 'tis the Christian's stay,
Through every varied scene of care,
　　Until his dying day,
As through the wilderness of life,
　　Calmly he wanders on,
His prayer in every time of strife
　　Is still, " Thy will be done." '

That night Mary slept with her friend ; into whose ear she poured all her trials, her sorrows, and disappointments.

'These providences are dark, Mary, very dark, I know. We cannot read the mind of God only so far as he vouchsafes to make it known to us, but we must trust him. We must build on his own eternal promises, which he has given us in Christ Jesus. We are as babes; we do not know what is best for us, but our Father knows, and just what is for our good he sends, for he makes all things work together for good to his children. This has been my stay and support in the darkest hours of my pilgrimage. When my way has seemed hedged in, and I could see no escape, then the Lord himself has come and opened up a way of deliverance, and with his help I have journeyed on.'

'But do you think, Mrs. Gaunt, that William will ever come home. But oh, it is so hard to know that he is a wanderer in a far off land—and then, oh then, Mrs. Gaunt, if he should die ? '

'This would be very sad, Mary; but even if it should take place, we must trust in God.'

'Oh, tell me not of it, Mrs. Gaunt, my heart will break.'

'It is best, Mary, to be prepared for the worst. Death is before us all, and sooner or later it must come. And there is no way to meet it except by leaning on the arm of Jesus. He only can give us strength to say farewell to those we love.'

The young girl moaned. Her heart was well nigh breaking with apprehension. She turned to Mrs. Gaunt, and throwing out her arms, suddenly and with violence exclaimed—

'William is dead, Mrs. Gaunt; you know he is,' she said wildly, convulsively clasping her hand. 'Oh why did you not tell me ? ' and she shrieked with anguish.

'No, no, my child ; William is not dead. Do calm yourself. You are excited, Mary. I tell you he is not dead, but doing well, and God grant that he may soon come back to us.'

'God grant it ! ' responded the sobbing girl.

'I was only telling you, Mary, that it is always best, by firm reliance on God, to prepare ourselves for what may come, even the very worst. I was urging it upon you as a Christian duty. Do not misunderstand me, nor think I wish to deceive you.'

'And do you think I will hear from him soon?'

'I think you will. The young gentleman who saw him told me he was learning to write that he might send you a letter. It has been two months since he left Leuwarden, and you know, Mary, that William is very apt, and when he is doing anything for your sake, it will make him more earnest still to gain his end.'

'I will try to wait with patience. Maybe the letter will come after awhile. I hope it will not be long.'

'For your sake, Mary, as well as your own, I hope it will not be many weeks. William feels to me like a son; and my heart was sorely grieved when I got back to London from Hertford, and found what had been done, and that he was gone. But though I cannot tell for what purpose this has been done, I am constrained to say that it is all right.'

'Yes, Mrs. Gaunt, I *know* that it is all right, but it is so hard to *feel* it! *So hard,*' she repeated sorrowfully. 'If we could always be submissive to the will of God, we would have but little trouble here on this earth. I wish I could be willing to all these things, but I am so weak I cannot.'

'The flesh truly is weak, Mary. We cannot think a good thought unless the Spirit of God give it to us. We are but dust and wretched sinners in his sight, unless we are found in Jesus. Then we are heirs of heaven, and raised above angels and archangels. My trials have been great, Mary, and I do not know what is before me; but this I do know, that the deeper the affliction the nearer God is to us.'

Ah, how true was that utterance, 'And I do not know what is before me.' Devoted woman!—could she have drawn aside the veil which shut out the future, and looked down the current of years, she would have seen direct in her pathway a prison and a stake amidst piles of lighted faggots. God was even now preparing her for these, but she knew it not.

Thus the two talked of this world's trials and the sure protection of Jehovah to all his children until the night was far advanced. Mary was comforted. Her mind grew calm under the sweet words of the experienced Christian.

Mrs. Gaunt, through the persuasion of Bunyan (who saw that her society was a great stay to his poor blind Mary), remained until the autumn.

Ever ready to do good, living for her Master, and not to herself, she went about among the little flock at Bedford, everywhere dispensing comfort and joy. She visited the sick and distressed, and while she alleviated the ills of the body, she fed the soul on the bread of eternal life, and pointed the throbbing bosom to the fountain of living water. She talked to those concerned for the salvation of their souls, and directed the inquirer the way to Zion. She became as much respected and beloved in Elstow and Bedford, as she was in London.

During her stay at Elstow, Mary received a letter from William, full of encouragement and hope. He spoke of future joy, and bade her be strong and cheerful, for brighter days were yet before them. He set no time for his return to his native land. This he could not do. But he was trusting in God to open up a way for him to come back to the bosom of those he loved.

The hearts of the parents were made glad by the happiness of the daughter. The smile returned to her sweet face, and buoyancy to her step.

Alas! all earthly joys are as fleeting as the rainbow hue, or evening cloud of summer. A dark storm even now was lowering over the little cottage. Soon it would expend its fury on the peaceful inmates.

Bunyan had become too popular. The green-eyed monster, Envy, had marked him for his prey. And soon he was called to pass through another severe trial. God keeps his children in the furnace, but thanks to his holy name, Christ sits by as a refiner of silver. When they reflect his image perfectly, he will assuredly release them.

CHAPTER XXXI.

SOLILOQUY OF MR. LANE, THE PREACHER.

'He shall meet his reward if I live—that he shall! The impudent upstart dissenter! He shall never lord it over me after that manner. No, no; he must, and shall, be brought down. Ah, I'll manage it! I'll manage it!'

The speaker was a tall, lank man, with light hair, and

eagle face. And the fierceness of his dark eye was fearful
to behold.

As he spoke, he rose, and rapidly paced the room, like
one bent on some desperate purpose. He struck the
clenched fist of his right hand violently into the open palm
of his left, as if aiming a deadly blow at his victim. His
eyes flashed and darted, and his compressed lips spoke
more than his words, the deep vengeance of his heart.
His whole manner showed the highest state of nervous
excitability, and the expression of his narrow face told of
the most determined revenge. It was sad to see one who
professed to minister in holy things the subject of such
fiendish passion. One, too, who, when before his fellow-
men, affected the utmost charity and kindness. Those who
saw him mixing with the world would never have suspected that, behind the scenes, the man of such urbane
manner, such pleasant address, could act the part of a
demon.

He strode the room rapidly, muttering to himself words
of dark revenge. His eye sought glaringly every nook
and corner of the apartment, as if to spy out his hated foe.
' Ah, yes ! ' he spoke in a louder tone, as his malice grew
hotter by feeding on itself. ' Ah, yes! I'll make it tell
to his sorrow. He shall see what it is to interrupt me in
my own congregation ! I'll teach him to mind his own
business ! And this popularity which he has so unright-
eously won, I'll make the means of stabbing him to the
heart. Yes, I'll do it ! But I must lay my plan deep, lest
I be defeated.'

' Ah, it shall be a dear ride to him, that ride to Gamlingay ! I'll make it tell to his ruin. Little did he think,
as he rode along so proudly, that it was to his shame and
utter overthrow. He must have his locks shorn of their
strength. His Delilah shall be his betrayer.'

And a low, demoniacal chuckle rung through the room,
as he rubbed his hands together in savage ecstacy, and
smacked his lips in the excess of his joy, while his dark,
deep-set eyes twinkled with wild malicious delight.

He seated himself for a moment, and took his pen, as if
to sketch out a plan of procedure. But before finishing
one line he threw it aside, and commenced again his rapid
strides, at the same time speaking to himself in a low
guttural tone. His thin light hair was flung wildly back
from his contracted forehead, through the temples of which
the heated blood coursed vehemently. Ever and anon he
ran his hands through his hair, and pulled at it most

violently; then he would strike his head and rub his hands quickly over his face.

He was like one demented. A looker-on would have pronounced him a ready subject for a lunatic asylum. He was in truth a monomaniac on the subject of destroying his hated victim.

And what had his victim done to incur this insatiate malice? What?

He had preached the word of God in its purity with earnestness and power, and thereby won souls to Christ. And was this sufficient cause for revenge? Ah, yes; his malice thought it interfered with the popularity and selfish interests of the man who was determined to rule at all hazards. And this man, too, was a preacher of the word of God; one who went in and out before a congregation to break to them the bread of life, and to lead them in the way of truth and righteousness.

'But how shall I accomplish my purpose, and not destroy myself? How shall I ruin this wretch, this tinker preacher, and not betray myself? That's the question. How can I make that ride to Gamlingay tell to his utter disgrace? I must get a rumor abroad, that's the thing! Rumor always gains by the running. I have only to cast out a suspicion and bring that ride as proof of it, and set the thing agoing among my people, and my purpose is accomplished. But how am I to begin?

'Let me see; have I not heard some whisper against his character?' and he scratched his head as if to dig out of his excited brain something for his horrid undertaking.

'Ah, yes, I remember now,' and he struck his hands together and rubbed them in the excess of his delight. 'Ah, yes, that story I heard about him and one of his congregation! It was a matter of no importance, but it will serve my ends, and I will make it apply to this girl— this Agnes Beaumont. I've got him now! He cannot escape. "They that exalt themselves shall be brought low." Yes, he shall lick the dust, shall cower in disgrace; and instead of the praise of all men, he shall receive their contempt.'

'But stop—let me see. What shall I do if I am asked my authority? I must be ready to throw all responsibility from my own shoulders. It will never do for me to accuse him. Ah, no, it must never be known that *I* am his accuser. This would frustrate all my ends, and bring the disgrace on my own head.' He shrugged his shoulders, drew down his brow, stroked his hair, and rubbed his face violently with his hands, while every nerve in him twitched with the intensity of excitement.

'I must manage to have this part of my game played by some one else. It will never do for me to be suspected. Oh, no. I, William Lane, of Bedford, pastor of the large congregation at Edworth, must not be known in this matter. I will do the work for him, but it must be my management. Let me see—who will act for me? Can I not get some one to set this rumor afloat. If I can the thing is done, my aim is accomplished, this upstart preacher silenced for ever, and I shall never be suspected of any hand in it. That's it, that's it!' and he laughed aloud at the supposed feasibility of his own plan.

'But now for the man to carry this out,' said he, biting his lips, and running his hands rapidly through his hair. 'Who will be the man? I know of two or three. I'll approach them cautiously at first, and if the thing doesn't take with them, I'll try some one else. I know I can find a man. Yes, yes, I am sure of that—'

A rap was heard at the study door.

'Who can that be? I wonder if I could have been heard? I must not appear excited, lest I arouse suspicion. Where is my Bible? I must seem to be reading.'

He seized his Bible, and laid it open on the table beside his chair. Then he glanced into the little mirror that hung at the further end of his bookcase, smoothed his hair with his hands, and at the call of a second rap, moved slowly towards the door and opened it.

'Good morning, Mr. Farry, good morning, sir! happy to see you. Walk in, and be seated. How is your health this morning? Very glad to see you. But be seated.'

CHAPTER XXXII.

THE CONFERENCE BETWEEN LANE AND FARRY.

THE preacher drew a chair near the table, on which lay the open Bible, and motioned the visitor to it, at the same time drawing his chair round, so that they two, when seated, should be *vis-a-vis*, and very near together.

The guest was, in some respects, altogether different from the preacher. He was low, not thick-set, with very black hair and eyes, the expression of which showed calm thought and some decision of purpose. His forehead was broad, but not high; the reasoning faculties pretty well developed, while the moral were defective. His mouth was small, and there was about it a certain degree of rigidity, which showed inflexibility of will. He was a member of Mr. Lane's congregation, and a violent opposer of Bunyan.

The two had often together berated the man of God for an upstart and a seducer of the people; a braggart, who was turning the heads of everybody, and filling them with all manner of old-fashioned whimsies. They had agreed that, if his views obtained (and it seemed likely they would), their notions must be entirely subverted.

The visitor fidgeted uneasily on his chair, and his manner bespoke an unusual degree of agitation.

'What is the matter, Mr. Farry?' asked the preacher, 'you seem unusually uncomfortable this evening. Has anything occurred to disturb your peace? Has anything gone wrong in your business? I hope you have met with no misfortune.'

'Not at all, sir, not at all,' replied the visitor calmly. 'I was only agitated by the startling news that reached my ears a few minutes since. I cannot recover from it.'

'And what is that? do tell me; anything going wrong among our people? Is that tinker preacher at work again, upsetting all our plans?'

'Is it possible, sir, you have not heard the news of old Mr. Beaumont's sudden death?'

'Not a word of it, sir, not a word of it! I have been in the house all day, and have seen no one. But tell me! did he die in a fit, or what?'

'Poisoned, sir, poisoned!'

'Is it possible? By whom? Who could be so vile as to poison that worthy old man?'

'It is not known, but it is said that Agnes, his daughter, was the only one in the house with him at the time of his death.'

'You astonish me, Mr. Farry! Do you suppose, for a moment, that the daughter would take the life of her father? What object could she have in view? What could have induced her to commit the foul deed?'

'It's hard to tell,' replied the lawyer, looking cautiously around him, 'what could make a child poison her father. I do not think she could have done it of her own accord. I have known Agnes Beaumont a long time. Once I had a thought of making her my wife, and I cannot believe she would have done this abominable deed unless she had been instigated to do it. I—'

'But is it a fact that the old man is dead, and was poisoned?' interrupted the preacher.

'No doubt of it at all. I have seen the corpse. He went to bed last night as well as could be, and before midnight he was dead.'

'Is it possible! And you say that only his daughter was with him in the house?'

'Yes.'

'Well, that is suspicious, truly. But why did she do this horrid thing?'

The lawyer drew his chair up more closely, and casting a prying glance around the room, to be assured that no one could hear, he uttered, in a half whisper:

'I suspect that preacher Bunyan for having a hand in it.'

'What!' said Lane, springing from his chair, and rubbing his hands together, while an expression of fiendish delight passed over his face. 'What! do you think that Bunyan really had a hand in it?'

'I would not be the least surprised.'

'Nor I. Hasn't there been a suspicion about him and this girl for some time? Last Saturday, I, myself, saw her riding behind him into the lower end of Gamlingay. And she sat as close to him as could be, and he was in earnest conversation with her.'

'Did you see this yourself? May be you were mistaken.'

'Oh, no, I cannot be mistaken. I saw them both, and spoke to them. I know Agnes Beaumont well.'

'And was no one with them, Mr. Lane?'

'Her brother and sister-in-law were on another horse some distance behind, so that they could not hear what the two were talking about.'

'And you saw that yourself?'

'I did, sir, I assure you; and I then thought of all that had been whispered into my ear. It is strange, sir, it is strange. And now that the girl's father is dead of poison, and that, too, so soon after, it looks very suspicious, very suspicious indeed.'

'Strange, sir, strange,' interrupted the lawyer. 'It is confirmation strong of what I have just said, that the wretch must have had a hand in the poor old man's death.'

'To-day is Wednesday, and you say he died last night, before midnight; and it was only last Saturday morning that I saw them. The deed could not have been done sooner. Ah, that man! that wretched man! Not content with ruining the daughter, he must poison the father. He certainly will be sunk in the deepest pit of disgrace, sir. His sins have overtaken him at last. Ah, what will become of his fair name now?'

'And is this matter much talked about?' he asked of his visitor eagerly.

'The old man's sudden death is spoken of everywhere; but no one that I know of suspects Bunyan and the girl.'

'But the world must know of it, Mr. Lane. Poor girl! she is to be pitied; but that infamous wretch, who led her astray, and then incited her to take her father's life, he ought to be hung. He deserves the execrations of all mankind. Let his name go forth to the world as the destroyer of virtue and a murderer. He deserves the faggot and the stake, and my word for it, he shall catch it yet.'

'But how can we prove these things, Mr. Farry?'

'Send for the Coroner, and let him examine the body. I am sure it already shows marks of poison. Did this morning when I was there.'

'Yes, yes, just so—no doubt of it; must be so, from all you have told me. And that wretched *tinker* is at the bottom of it. He'll get his dues now. But have you spoken of your suspicions to any one?'

'Not yet. I thought I would come and see you, and know what you had to say about the matter before I went too far.'

'Right, right. The world must know it. That scoundrel must be shown up. He has imposed upon us long enough. And the only way for him to be caught is to ferret the matter out. You send for the Coroner immediately, before the poor girl has time to escape, and I do not doubt but that you can get the whole story out of her at once. Scare her a little. But perhaps it will be better to take her by herself first, and get her to tell it all, and then take it down in writing. Our aim must be to catch that man. We don't care so much about the poor creature. He made her do it all. You see, Mr. Farry, we must manage this matter well, that that vile offender may be brought to justice. Yes, yes, we'll have him now. He can't escape this time!'

'And do you think it will be best to see Agnes, and get her to confess her crime?'

'Undoubtedly. Get her to tell all Bunyan had to do in the matter. He is the chief offender. And the sooner it is looked into, the better.'

'I will see to it this very evening!' exclaimed the lawyer, rising to go.

'Yes, do. But look here, Farry, whatever you do, don't you mention *my name* in it. Keep me clear. You must guard me as you would your own life. Don't forget this— it is an important point. It would not do for me to know anything about it. People might say it was envy, because that wretch is more popular just now than I am. Do you hear, Farry? Don't mention me, for your life.'

'I'll watch your interests; don't doubt me,' and the lawyer closed the study door, while his instigator remained within to gloat over his vile machinations, and the prospect of the disgrace of one whom he hated merely because he was good and God had blessed his efforts to spread the Redeemer's kingdom on earth.

'Yes, now 'tis done,' he repeated triumphantly, as the door closed behind his accomplice. 'Ah, yes, the matter is at work! A wretch and a murderer! I would not give a farthing for his reputation, even if he gets off with his life. He'll think he had better have stayed in prison and moped over his books, than to have come out to meet this. (Conscience whispered, Perhaps the man is innocent. What right have you to believe him guilty?) Innocent or guilty, what matters that to me? Let him be prostrated; he is a vile wretch, any way; the world ought to be rid of him. He ought to be sent out of the way of all genteel people, any way, with his old worn-out notions, and his great outcry against sin. We have no use for such preachers. *I* heartily despise them. But who would have believed it possible that things *could* have worked so to my hand? I'll show him what it is to interfere with *me!*' and the Rev. Mr. Lane smiled, stroked back his hair, and rubbed his hands together in anticipation of a result he had for a long time most ardently desired.

CHAPTER XXXIII.

BUNYAN'S GREAT TRIAL.

WITH a heavier heart than he had ever known before since God, through Christ, had spoken peace to his soul in the forgiveness of his sins, did John Bunyan, of Elstow, tread the highway and meadows between Bedford and his cottage home on that evening of the 12th of December,

1678. He had that day gone to Bedford for the purpose of buying little necessaries for his family. There he had met Mr. Wilson, the pastor of Hitchen, who, with tears and sorrow, had told him of the rumors against him just beginning to spread through his neighborhood.

'God knows I am innocent of these things, brother Wilson,' replied Bunyan, when he had finished his sad disclosures. 'It is the work of some enemy, who seeks my ruin. And I cannot tell what any one has against me. Surely, I have suffered enough to disarm even the cruelest foe. God knows it is hard to be thus evil spoken against, but it is sweet to know that you are not guilty. Surely I am a man of much sorrow; I am persecuted, sore-persecuted, down-trodden. God knows when my sorrows will end.'

The servant of God, Mr. Wilson, of Hitchen, tried to comfort the poor, distressed man.

'These things are very grievous, but they do not come upon us without the knowledge of God, my brother. He permits them for some wise purpose, which we cannot now see. They are for your good, and for the honor and glory of his name, though we cannot now see how it is possible. Our strength is so weak, we are so feeble in faith, that we cannot build on the promises of God, as it is our privilege to do. Man cannot do to you anything without the permission of God. The hearts of all men are in his hands, and he turns them whithersoever he will. It is all right, brother Bunyan, though hard to bear. May God give you grace to endure it.'

'Ah, it is hard! Imprisonment is nothing to it. My brethren then knew I was suffering for righteousness' sake, and I had their sympathies and their prayers; but maybe the Evil One will put it into the heads of some of them to believe these things. I do not mind the world, brother Wilson, but oh, to be suspected by my brethren! those with whom I have taken sweet counsel—this is more than I can bear! O God! why am I thus afflicted?' he exclaimed, in insupportable anguish. '"Is there no escape from the net of the fowler?" Shall I be devoured by the enemy!'.

'God is true, brother Bunyan, God is true. Look to him.'

'Yes, I know God is true; but man is so false, so deceitful! When shall I be delivered from them that seek to destroy me?'

'Our path is marked out before us, my brother. Our

Father who knows the end from the beginning, sees it all the way along, even before we, as pilgrims, enter upon it. He puts in our way just what is best for us. Sometimes he puts sickness; sometimes the death of our loved ones; sometimes bodily afflictions, disease, loss of property; sometimes imprisonments, and sometimes the persecutions of calumniators. He does it all. There they are in the narrow path that we have to walk in, just where they ought to be for our good. And we cannot jump over them; we cannot get round them. We cannot shut our eyes and remain ignorant of them. We have to go straight along through them, and sometimes we have to get the heaviest burden, and tread the narrowest, rockiest way, before we can be made to look to the hill from whence our strength cometh. We have got to kiss the hand that chastens us, before our stripes are healed. It is God's way, and it is good and righteous. These very trials you are enduring now will drive you more closely to the cross; will make you cling there, and your soul will feed on Jesus and his promises. You can live above the world, my brother, even while it frowns upon you.'

' I would glorify God in all I do, but I cannot see how this is to make for his honor and glory.'

' It may serve, in after years, to give consolation to some poor brother, when he is called upon to go through the same strait. God will bring you out if you are innocent. Truth is a part of his nature, and he will defend it to the end.'

' I am innocent! God knows I am innocent! I could not do these things for all this world. But how am I to show my innocence? I see no way of escape. You tell me this poor old man was poisoned, and that his daughter Agnes has done it; and the people say I must have had a hand in it, because I have misled her, and she rode behind me last Saturday to Gamlingay. I took pity on her, poor child, and let her ride behind me because she was so longing to go to meeting. I did not want to do it, but I found her at her brother's, and she begged me to give her a seat, for she could not walk through the snow, and her brother had no horse for her to ride. I talked to her about the things of God all the time, riding along with her brother and sister, who were on the same way. I wonder who could have been so wicked as to turn that into mischief? We did not meet any one on the way but neighbor Harrow's son, and old brother Pipes, and their children, and I am sure none of these would have told such a dreadful tale on me.'

'Yes, I did,' he added after a moment's pause, 'yes, I saw Mr. Lane, just as we were passing through the town's end ; and I remember now, he looked at me hard and long ; but he spoke in a friendly manner. I wonder if he would do me this great harm ! I know he is not very kindly disposed to me, but surely he could not lie like this. Do you know who was first heard to speak of this matter, brother Wilson ? Who says that they saw Agnes riding behind me to Gamlingay ?'

'I do not know. I only heard that this is the rumor, and I have come to you to let you know it, that you may meet it as you think best.'

'I must leave it in the hands of God. I don't know how to set myself about proving my innocence. If I am attacked, I will defend myself as well as I can. I must cast my burden on God, and leave it to him, for I am in a narrow strait, and sore pressed. Pray for me, brother Wilson. Ask God that all my afflictions may redound to his glory and my good. I would be like a weaned child in his hands. O God, pity me, and help me !'

With words of Christian love and comfort, these two tried soldiers of the cross solaced each other. They parted. The one to go to his happy family, over which no visible shadow rested ; the other, with bowed spirit and tried faith, to find his way to those whom he loved, and to whom he must communicate the dire intelligence which was well nigh breaking his heart.

Behold him, as with bent form and down-cast eye he treads the narrow path that leads to the loved ones of his bosom, over whom a cloud of fierce anger is darkly gathering. Hear him, as he sighs in agony of soul.

'O God, Jehovah, deliver me from mine enemies. They that seek after my life lay snares for me, and they that seek my hurt, speak mischievous things, and imagine deceits all the day long. O God, my God, how long shall mine enemies prosper—how long shall they who seek my ruin triumph ? My ways are all known to thee. Thine eye takes notice of them all. And thou, O Father, knowest I am innocent of those sins they wickedly lay to my charge. Shall I be put to an open shame ? Shall disgrace come upon my poor wife and children, and their name be cast out as evil ? Unless thou come to my help, O God, my foes will sweep me from the earth. Vain is the help of man. Unless thou interpose to save me, my life shall be swallowed up. My way is dark before me ; my strength faileth. I perish without thee.'

Thus did Bunyan cry unto God for succor, as he trod his dreary way homeward from Bedford. Never before had the world seemed so dark to him. ' He looked, and there was no one to pity ; he cried and there was no one to help.' How should he escape the snares they had laid for him ? Suppose Agnes should implicate him ? What if Satan should tempt her to lay the crime at his door ! Could she have had designs upon him, on Saturday, when she insisted so earnestly on riding behind him to Gamlingay ? And did she really poison her poor old father ? Surely, Agnes would not do this. He had known her since she was a child—a baby on her mother's knee, for she was younger than his Mary ; he, too, had listened to her account of her passing from the reign of sin and Satan into the glorious liberty of the children of God, and he felt that he could not be mistaken with respect to the truth of her change. Nor could he believe that God would suffer one of his children thus to fall. Then he thought of David and his grievous sin, and then looked in upon his own heart, and remembered his many sore temptations and his weakness ; and when he recalled all these, he felt afraid, lest this great evil had overtaken the poor girl. And if she could do this, would she not accuse him as her instigator, in order to escape punishment herself ?

Then there arose before his vivid imagination the shameful trial, the prison, and the gibbet. And then the darker picture, of a disgraced, suffering family. And as he dwelt upon the contemplation, the scene grew darker and darker, until his soul was ready to burst with agony. God's Holy Spirit seemed to forsake him, and he was left for a while to the sorest temptations.

Ah, how black was that hour ! The concentrated intensity of the Saviour's suffering, as he hung on the cross, was that God had forsaken him. How fearful, then, the moment, when poor, frail man feels that the loving kindness of God is clean gone. Have we not need to pray every hour, ' Take not thy Holy Spirit from us.'

Bunyan's life seemed a rayless void as he approached his cottage home. No pleasure in the past, no promise in the future.

His Elizabeth observed his changed appearance, and inquired its cause.

' You must be sorely troubled, my husband. I have never seen you look so since you came from prison.'

The poor man knew not what to say. How could he tell her that he was accused of two of the foulest crimes ? It would prostrate her, as it had done him. And yet how could he keep it from her ear? She must know it in a little while, and she had better hear it from his own lips.

The two walked into the close, that they might withdraw from the family, and there Bunyan broke to his trembling wife the horrid story. She shuddered, and gasped for breath, as she listened. She felt, with all the intensity of her nature, what must be the consequences to her husband, and herself, and children. She believed her husband was innocent; she *knew* that he was. But how was he to prove it? And even if he did prove it, there would still be many ready to believe him guilty.

She wept as if her heart would break. She knew every tear and groan but added to her dear husband's already insupportable weight of sorrow; yet her heart must burst if she did not give vent to her emotion. She could not speak; she could not think. She could only feel, God alone knows how deeply. And, poor man, what comfort could he give? He could only assure her of his innocence, and of this she was entirely satisfied.

God himself supports, but we are unconscious of his presence. He sees us through the dark cloud, when our darkened eyes can catch no glimpse of him. He himself suffers his children to be brought to these extreme straits, that he may manifest his own power in rescuing them from death. He will cause himself to be known, in that he saves his children from the fire and flood of persecution.

'We have no helper but God, my husband,' said the wife, as soon as she could command her voice, 'and if he does not come to save us, we are lost, for our enemies are set upon our destruction, and there seems to be no way of escape for us.'

Almost miraculously, as is oftentimes the case, Bunyan rose from the depths of distress, into which he had been plunged by the recital of Mr. Wilson, into the consoler and supporter of his wife. He must plead the promises of God that she might be kept from despair, and in thus doing they became his food and his strength.

The way for Christians to lose their troubles, is to undertake for God with another who is distressed and cast down.

'Let not sorrow overwhelm you, my Elizabeth,' he said to the weeping wife. 'God himself will deliver us. He is a sovereign God, and he stands pledged for the safety of his people. He oftentimes brings them into deep waters, that are ready to swallow them up; but then he verifies his immutable promise, 'When thou passest through the waters, I will be with thee.' He will always provide a way of escape for his people. Remember the children of Israel at the Red Sea. Who could see any help for them? And yet God delivered them with the right arm of his power, and overthrew their enemies. He gave victory to the armies of Israel when they cried unto him. He has never failed to save his people. And, you know, my Elizabeth, he has brought us through wonderful trials. Let us trust his grace and love to bring us safely through this strait.'

'But how could they be so wicked as to lay this thing to your charge?'

'Mine enemy hath done it.'

'Oh, how shameful! Who could be so vile? What enemy have you that owes you such a grudge?'

'I know of but one, Mr. Lane, the preacher. If he has not done this thing, I know not who has. I cannot say it is he. We must wait patiently, looking to the Lord to unfold it, and show me clear of the charge.'

'Oh, the wicked man! how could he do such a shameful thing?'

'He thinks I am in his way, Elizabeth. I am fearful he is proud and ambitious, and seeks his own good more than he does the honor of Christ. But we must wait until he makes himself seen. If he has done it, it will be found out. He cannot keep it hid always. God will bring it to light.'

Thus did Bunyan endeavor to console his heart-broken wife, by pointing her to God's immutable justice and love. And when they gathered that night around the altar of prayer, their faith was strengthened. They could cast their care on Jesus, for they felt that he cared for them.

The man of God pleaded for grace to sustain him under the trying conflict which he saw was just before him. With tears and groans he cried for help. He knew there was no eye to pity, no arm to save, but that of Jesus; and to his right arm he trusted to bring salvation, and rescue his servant from the den of lions.

It is a dark hour, an hour of fierce trial. 'How long, O Lord, how long?

CHAPTER XXXIV.

MR. WILSON'S VISIT TO BUNYAN.

THE pastor at Hitchen, Mr. Wilson, having heard the reports against Bunyan's character vouched for by men of

seeming respectability, determined, in his own mind, to
ride over to Elstow, to talk to Bunyan on the subject,
hoping to find out the truth of the matter. He felt a
deep interest for his friend, and a greater anxiety for the
cause of Christ, which was suffering because of the
malicious slander.

As he rode slowly along, and pondered the matter, his
fears increased. Circumstances were dark, very dark,
against his brother minister. There seemed to him great
cause for suspicion. Yet he hoped it might all prove
false, and he was too just to condemn him without a full
hearing.

It was Thursday evening, two days after the sudden
and fearful death of old Mr. Beaumont. That morning
Mr. Wilson had met Farry, the lawyer, at Baldock Fair,
who had told him the whole story, but would not give his
authority, although he asserted that it was of the most
respectable character. He informed Mr. Wilson of the
intention of a few persons to have the body of the old man
thoroughly examined before it was interred, repeating his
opinion, that there was no doubt about his having been
poisoned by his daughter, and that she was prompted to do
the deed by Bunyan.

'I cannot think so, Mr. Farry,' said the troubled man,
as the lawyer concluded his remarks. 'There must be
some mistake about it. I cannot believe that brother
Bunyan would be guilty of such an inhuman act. I have
known him ever since he came out of prison, and I have
always believed him to be a man of God.'

'You may rest assured, Mr. Wilson,' replied the
malicious lawyer, 'that the first charge is true. I got it
from one whose word could not be doubted. And as to the
circumstances of the old man's death, I will vouch for
them. He died of poison, and yourself must admit that
it looks very black against preacher Bunyan. The body is
to be examined, and then the whole matter will be decided,
and the guilty one will receive a just reward. But I must
bid you good evening, sir; for I must be off for Mr.
Hatfield, the Mayor. The old man's son wishes him to
come out this evening and examine the body. He has his
suspicions, though he has never breathed them to his sister,
but treats her very kindly. Good morning, Mr. Wilson,
good morning.'

With pain and sorrow the preacher turned his steps
homeward. Suppose it should be decided that old Mr.
Beaumont had met his death by unfair means; then the

conclusion from all the premises must be, that Bunyan was an accomplice of the daughter. What disgrace would such a revelation bring to the cause of Christ! How the enemies of truth and righteousness would triumph, and Zion mourn because of her reproach!

He unbosomed his fears and distresses to his wife; told her of his determination to go over to Elstow and learn from Bunyan himself the truth of the whole affair.

'I would go to see Agnes first, but she is in deep trouble, poor girl, and the surgeon will be there this evening to examine the body, to see if he can find any traces of poison. I will wait until after that is decided before I go to see the poor child.'

With painful foreboding, the pastor at Hitchen rode over to see his brother minister. He had confidently believed Bunyan's innocence when the rumors first reached his ear, and it was not until Farry, the lawyer, had so fully assured him that it must be so, that his opinion began to be shaken. Farry stood well in the community. He was regarded as a clever man, though somewhat avaricious, and so clearly did he set forth the guilt of the daughter, and the necessary participation of Bunyan, that it was difficult to explain the mystery without implicating him.

Bunyan received the visitor with a sad countenance. For the last few days these dreadful accusations had met him at every turn. Neighbor Harrow had just left, after laying the whole story before him in its most exaggerated form. He had declared his innocence and trust in God to the kind old neighbor, who, in his plain, artless manner, recommended him to the throne of grace.

The two walked out into the close, and seated themselves on the stile, and, in tender tones and gentle words, Wilson made known to Bunyan his fears that he must at least be greatly injured by the report, for the evidence, from what he had heard, was strong against him. He then repeated Farry's story.

'God knows I am innocent of these foul slanders,' said Bunyan, as his friend concluded his recital. 'I have not misled that girl, nor did I instigate her to poison her father, if it be true he is poisoned.'

'Did she ride behind you to Gamlingay, last Friday, to meeting?'

'Yes, she did; but it was not my seeking. She had no beast, and wanted very much to go. I objected to her sitting behind me, but she made such ado about not going, that finally I said she might go behind me, there, but I could not bring her back.   And I told her brother this, at whose house I found her.'

'Did you meet any preacher on the way?'

'As I told you the other day, we met Lane just as we were entering the town's end. We didn't meet any other.'

'How did he look when he saw you?'

'I did not observe anything remarkable in his appearance at the time, but since this vile slander has been told me, I now think he appeared well pleased, and laughed as he spoke.'

'Was the girl riding with both arms around you, and were her brother and sister far before?'

'No, the girl never put her arms around me; she only held on to my cloak, and when the road was good she did not hold on at all. And what they say about her brother and his wife being far before, is false. They were right by my side, for I said to them, just after Lane had passed, that he seemed to be in most excellent humor, and I had heard he was a forcible speaker. The woman said she did not like his looks, and she had never heard him in service. I remember these things distinctly, and Agnes' brother and sister know them to be true.'

'And when did you see her before?'

'Not since I preached with you at Hitchen, last August. I used to go frequently to her brother's, and sometimes I would call at her father's, as I passed to and fro; but Farry, the lawyer, has taken a grudge to me, and has filled up the poor old man's mind with prejudices against me, until I could not go any longer, perceiving my visits were not pleasant.'

'But suppose they should conclude that the old man was poisoned, and Agnes did it, what explanation will you make then that will clear you of this infamous accusation? Let me tell you, my dear brother, that things are dark, very dark.   But if you are innocent, and I hope you are, God "will bring forth thy righteousness as the light, and thy judgment as the noonday;" thy enemies shall see it, and be confounded.'

'I am innocent, that God knoweth, and I look to him to deliver me.   He hath hedged me in; he hath afflicted my soul; he hath torn me in pieces.   But I know that his promises are sure.   I know that he loves his Israel, and though he sorely chastiseth me, yet shall I not be destroyed; though he slay me, yet will I trust him, for his loving kindness and tender mercy can never fail towards the people of his choice.'

'It is good to have such faith, brother Bunyan. I am made glad to see you feed on the precious promises. If Christ is for you, who shall triumph against you? Hold to your integrity, and you shall never be ruined. And rest assured, my brother, I will give you all the aid and comfort I can; and if it should be found that the poor girl has been guilty of murdering her father, I will use all endeavors to show that you had no part in the matter. But I must tell you, my dear brother, that it will go far to bring trouble to you.'

'I have an understanding of this matter. I know I must suffer for a time, even if this poor creature is found clear; but if I suffer for righteousness' sake, I must take it gladly. My heart has been well nigh torn in twain to think of bringing infamy on my wife and children; but thanks be to God, I have gained somewhat of a victory over my fears. This morning, while in prayer, Christ came to me in his precious promises, and strengthened me by his might, until I can now say, I will not fear what man can do unto me. "In all their afflictions he was afflicted." Christ did not forget the purchase of his blood, neither will he suffer them to be put to an open shame.'

'It rejoices my heart, brother Bunyan, to see you so built up in the gospel. Oh, the strengthening grace of Almighty God! How it enables us to rise above the afflictions of this life, and to bask in the glories of that which is to come! I came to you with a burdened heart. I was weak, and I feared that perhaps you had sinned. But thank-God, I now know you are guiltless of this great transgression! And I shall pray for you,' he added, while the tears streamed down his cheeks; 'pray God he will support you, and deliver you from those that set snares for your feet.'

The two brethren embraced each other, then knelt and prayed.

'To-morrow I will see Agnes, and hear from her the whole story; and I will come and tell you the result of the examination. If it is found that she has been wrongfully accused, then will your innocence be proven by hers. But if she should be found guilty, then, my brother, we must be prepared for the worst. Good bye. God bless you, and enable you and sister Bunyan to trust him, never faltering.'

CHAPTER XXXV.

THE town of Edworth was in a state of great excitement, as the Mayor, accompanied by two or three friends, departed to examine the body of old Mr. Beaumont. All business was forgotten; all other topics swallowed up in this one. Never had there been anything so momentous before the minds of the villagers since poor old Mr. Deckworth had drowned himself in a small stream hard by, some twenty years before.

'Trifles light as air' were now 'confirmation strong as words of Holy Writ' against the accused ones. Each one could remember something that he or she had seen or heard, which was brought forward to show the certainty of their guilt.

He had died very suddenly, and under very peculiar circumstances. Rumor, with her thousand tongues, caught up the story, and now it was everywhere asserted as a fact, beyond all doubt, that he was poisoned by his daughter Agnes, and that preacher Bunyan had instigated her to do it, and had furnished her with the poison. What food for the vicious appetites of the preacher's enemies! They caught up the tale, and with trumpet-tongue sent it through the land.

'I must rest in my innocence,' said Bunyan, as one and another asked him what he would do. God knows I never dreamed of this wicked deed they lay to my charge.'

Wrapped in the twilight gloom, Lane sat alone in his study, musing over the success of his plan. Could any one have beheld him, they would have seen a wilder intensity of the eye than was even his wont, and a smile of Satanic enjoyment playing over his skinny face.

'I shall be revenged. To-morrow it will all be known,' said Farry, aloud, as he rode in the dusk of the evening toward Lane's. 'Little did I think, two years ago, when that proud creature refused my offered hand, that I should so soon have it in my power to revenge myself. "Revenge is sweet,"' he said, while his face assumed a demoniacal expression. 'The surgeon's engaged, and he will do a sure work. The plan is sure. To-morrow! — oh, to-morrow!'

'It looks well! Caught at last! He'll not trouble me again. "How is the mighty brought low!"' he muttered, using words of Holy Writ to express his delight. 'I thought I would bring the soaring eagle down! And he will not know the archer that stopped his upward flight! I have managed well! I have got Farry between me and danger. I have played a bold game. I have run a great risk. But it is successful. I am winner!'

The surgeon who was called made his examination of the body carefully, and with evident design to detect poison, if any lurked there. Not that he had any desire to implicate the poor girl, but there was an agreement between him and Farry, in which the lawyer promised to reward him handsomely if he would be the means of bringing the murderers (as he denominated Agnes and Bunyan) to justice. He applied all his tests, and observed with the greatest minuteness the result of each. But no evidence of poison was to be found; and such was his decision.

When the report was made to Farry, he burst into a paroxysm of rage, declaring, 'the scoundrel had not done his *duty*. He knew the old man had come to his end by foul means. All the neighbors knew it. And the law should not be cheated in that way. He would have a coroner and jury the next day. That body should never be buried until the truth was brought to light. The wretches should be exposed.'

Thus he raved and railed, as he strode across the floor of Lane's study.

The two held a consultation. Farry immediately left to execute their purpose. He never rested until the Coroner and jury were made acquainted with his story, and the necessary steps taken towards a second examination on the morrow.

The morrow was Friday. The morrow came. At an early hour the Coroner and jury left Gamlingay, and arrived at the house where the corpse lay. The prosecutor did not make his appearance. He had stationed himself at the nearest house in the neighborhood, that he might readily learn the result of the inquest. The Coroner and jury entered the house.

Beside the fire, surrounded by some Christian friends, who had come out from Gamlingay to pray with and comfort her in this hour of anguish, sat the victim of Farry's revenge, her heart stayed on God, and her countenance lighted up with that peace which passeth understanding. Who knows but that God may permit the devil and his tools to triumph? Suppose she should be called upon to pass through fire! Ah! should she? How fearful the

thought, as it rushes through her heart! But she stills
her rising fears. 'When thou passest through the fire, I
will be with thee.' It is enough. She can rest on that
sure promise, and dread no harm.

The Coroner approaches her to question her respecting
her presence in the house at the time of her father's death.
Calmly and unblanchingly she answers all interrogatories.

The men look hard upon her, and pass on to the back
room, where the corpse lay. She trembles not. Resting
on the arm of her heavenly Father, she feels secure. She
alone, of all the company present, is calm. Sighs burst
from melting bosoms, and tears course down from eyes all
unused to weep. Looks of fearful dread are exchanged,
and glances full of pity and sympathy fell on the sweet
countenance of Agnes, which, as they witness her composure, are exchanged to looks of wonder.

The Coroner and jury gather round the dead body. The
pall is removed. There rests the form of him they have
all known for years, whose face in death bore the livid hue
of strangulation. Why shake their heads? There has
been foul play they think. The windows are opened for
better light, and the examination is begun. Carefully and
slowly they proceed from point to point, from test to test.
Their fears and doubts vanish. Their work completed, they
pass through the room and go out. Not a word is spoken.
But hearts beat high with throbbing fears as they move
slowly along. Each one is anxious to ask, but no one
dares.

Agnes is sent for. The Coroner administers the oath
and commences to question her. Firm in the strength of
the Lord, and supported by his grace, she responds clearly,
and without the least hesitation, to every question. She
confronts her accuser, who has been sent for to answer to
the charge, without the least trepidation.

After this is done, she retires, and they proceed to return
a verdict. Their friends wait for it with longing, fearful
hearts. At last it comes.

'*Not guilty.*' The sound is caught up, and passes from
lip to lip. 'Thank God!' bursts from many a relieved
bosom. The noble girl is as unmoved under the acquittal as
she had been under the accusation. She had trusted to God
to bring forth her innocence, and he had signally done it.

Her false accuser skulks away from the presence of
honorable men, the fires of revenge burning the more
intensely in his bosom because of his defeat.

CHAPTER XXXVI.

AGNES BEAUMONT'S STORY.

Mr. Wilson attended the burial. He asked of Agnes a candid recital of the truth of the dreadful story which he had heard against her.

'Tell me, child, the truth, that I may be able to refute the base slander. Begin at the beginning and give me the detail.'

'I will tell you all. And to the truth of the most of it, my brother here can bear witness. He saw and heard much that occurred between me and my dear father.'

'This day a week ago, you know a church meeting took place at Gamlingay. About a week before I was much in prayer, especially for two things. One was that the Lord would incline the heart of my father to let me go, the other request was that the Lord would go with me, and that I might enjoy much of his presence at the table; that as in many times past it might be a sealing ordinance to my soul.

'The Lord was pleased to grant me my requests. Upon asking my father the day before, he seemed unwilling at first, but I pleaded with him, and told him I would do all the work in the morning before I went, and would return home at night. Finally, my father consented. Friday being come, I prepared everything to set out. My father inquired who carried me? I told him I thought Mr. Wilson of Hitchen, as he told my brother the Tuesday before he should call. My father answered nothing.

'I went to my brother's and waited, expecting to meet you there, but you did not come, and it cut me to the heart, for I feared I should not go, and I burst into tears, for my brother had told me his horses were all at work and that he could not spare one, save the two that he and my sister were to ride on, and I could not walk thither, the snow was so deep.'

'And what did you do, Agnes?' inquired the old pastor, touched with her simple story.

'I waited with many a longing look and with a sorrowful heart. Oh, thought I, that the Lord would put it in the heart of some person to come this way. Thus I still waited with my heart full of fears. At last, quite unexpectedly, brother Bunyan came. The sight of him caused a mixture of both joy and grief. I was glad to see him, but afraid he would not be willing to take me up behind him; and how to ask him I knew not. At length I desired my brother to do it, which he did. But when my brother asked him, Mr. Bunyan answered roughly, "No, I will not carry her."

'These words were cutting to my heart, and made me weep bitterly. My brother, seeing my trouble, said to him, "Sir, if you do not carry her you will break her heart." But he answered, "I will not carry her. Your father will be grievous angry if I should."

' "I will venture that," said I.

' At length after much entreaty, he was prevailed upon to take me. Soon after we set out my father came to my brother's, and asked the man whom I rode behind. They said Mr. Bunyan. When my father heard this his anger was greatly inflamed. He ran down to the close, thinking to overtake me and pull me off the horse, but we were gone out of his reach. I had not rode far before my heart began to be lifted up with pride at the thought of riding behind this servant of the Lord; and I was pleased if any one looked after us as we rode along.

' But my pride soon had a fall, for on entering Gamlingay we were met by Mr. Lane, who knew us both. He looked at us very hard as we rode along. And I do believe he raised this vile scandal, though God knows it is false.'

' And did brother Bunyan bring you home, Agnes?'

' Oh, no, sir! That brother, here, very well knows.'

' No, she did not return behind him, but rode behind a girl who lives half a mile from father's.'

' And how did you get from there home? Did you see brother Bunyan again that day?'

' No, sir, I did not see him again till Sunday, for I did not go to meeting on Saturday. The girl set me down at sister Pruden's gate, from whence I hastened home through the dirt, having no pattens, hoping to be at home before my father was in bed. On coming to the door I found it locked, with the key in it. There was no light in the house, and my heart began to sink, for I perceived what I was about to meet with. It was usual for my father to take the key out of the door and give it me from the window. I stood trembling. At length I called out "Father, father." "Who's there?" he answered. I said, "It is I, father, come home wet and dirty. Pray let me in."

' "I'll not let you in," he said harshly. "Where you have been all day, you may go at night. A pretty hussy, indeed, to ride behind that man Bunyan. You knew well enough it was against my will for you to have anything to do with that vile tinker. How did you dare to disobey me. Let you in, indeed! You shall never come within these doors any more unless you will promise me never to go after that man again." I begged, and cried, and pleaded with him to let me in.

'"Begone, I tell you, unless you'll promise me you'll never have anything to say to that wretch. Begone, or I'll rise and put you out of the yard. Do you hear me?"

' I then stood silent awhile, and the thought pierced my mind. What if I should come at last, and the door be shut, and Christ should say unto me "Depart"?

At length, seeing my father refused to let me in, it was put into my heart to spend that night in prayer. I would have gone to my brother's, where I could have had a good supper and a warm bed. No, thought I, I will go into the barn, and cry to heaven that Jesus Christ would not shut me out at the last day, and also that I might have some fresh discoveries of love to my soul. I am naturally of a timorous temper, and many frightful things presented themselves to my mind, as that I might be murdered before morning, or catch my death of cold. Yet one Scripture after another gave me encouragement. These came into my mind :—" Pray to thy Father which is in secret, and thy Father who seeth in secret shall reward thee openly." " Call upon me and I will answer thee, and show thee great and mighty things which thou knowest not." '

' And did you indeed pass the night in the barn, Agnes, that cold, bitter night?'

' I did sir, truly. No sooner was I in the barn than Satan again assaulted me. But having received strength from the Lord, and his word, I spoke out saying, " Satan, my Father hath thee in a chain ; thou can'st not hurt me." The Lord, after this, was pleased to keep all my fears from my heart. He was with me in a most wonderful manner. It froze hard that night, but I felt no cold, although the dirt was frozen on my shoes in the morning.

' While I was engaged in prayer and meditation in the barn, that Scripture came with mighty power on my mind, "Beloved, think it not strange concerning the fiery trial which is to try you."

' When the morning appeared, I peeped through the cracks of the barn to watch my father's opening the door. Presently he came out and locked it after him, which I thought looked very dark, apprehending from this that he was resolved I should not go in. But still that word, Beloved, sounded in my heart. He soon came into the barn with a fork in his hand, and seeing me in my riding dress, he stood still before me.

'"Good morning, father," said I pleasantly to him. "I have had a cold night's lodging here, but God has been good to me, else I should have had a worse."

'"It is no matter for you, you disobedient girl."

'"Will you let me go in, my father? I want to get off these dirty clothes. I hope, father, you are not still angry with me."

'"Begone out of my sight. I will not let you in; go and stay where you were on the yesterday," and my father went about foddering the cows. I followed him about, entreating him to forgive me and let me into the house. But the more I entreated him, the more his anger rose against me.

'"I tell you, hussy, you shall never enter my house again unless you will promise me not to go to meeting again as long as I live. Will you promise that?"

'"I cannot promise you that, father," I said gently; "my soul is of too much worth to do it. Can you, in my stead, answer for me at the great day? If so, I will obey you in this demand, as I do in all other things."

'But my father would not hear me, but kept asking me to say I would never go to meeting again as long as he lived, which I dared not do. At last some of my brother's men were come into the yard, and seeing my case, reported, when they went home, that their old master had turned Agnes out of doors. When brother heard this, he came to father, and endeavored to prevail with him to become reconciled to me. But father grew more angry with him than with me, and at last refused to listen to him. My brother then said, "Go home with me, sister; you will catch your death with cold." But I said, "No, brother, I will still plead with my father."

'I continued to follow him about the yard, taking hold of his arm, and crying, and hanging about, saying, "Pray, let me go in, father; pray, let me go in. I am so cold." I now wonder how I durst be so bold, my father being of a hasty temper, insomuch that his anger has often made me glad to get out of his sight, though he was a good-natured man when his passion was over. But I could not prevail, and growing cold and faint, I went and sat down on the door-step. But my father kept walking about the yard, and I soon saw that he did not intend to enter the house while I was there. And I did not want to keep him in the cold, so I went to my brother's house and obtained some refreshment and warmth.

'About noon my sister and I came home to entreat my father. We found him in the house, and the door locked. We went to the window, to speak to him.

'"Now, father," said my sister, "I hope your anger is over, and you will let sister in. Do be reconciled to her. She did not wish to offend you."

'"I will not let her in. She must go where she was, and find somebody else to take care of her. No doubt that tinker-preacher, Bunyan, will do it. She shall not have a penny of mine as long as I live, nor when I die, either. I would sooner leave my substance to strangers, than to her. Begone, begone, I tell you! You need not think to win me by your crying. Out of my sight!"

'My sister durst not speak a word more, my father was so mad. His threats were cutting and made my heart sink. "What will become of me?" I said; "to go to service and work hard is a new thing to me, who am very young. What shall I do?" Then these words were very seasonable and comforting: "When my father and mother forsake me, then the Lord will take me up."

Perceiving my sister's strong pleadings were all in vain, I asked my father to give me my Bible and pattens.

'"You shall have nothing from this house. You shall not have a penny, nor a penny's worth, as long as I live, nor when I die. Get you away, I tell you. I won't listen to you."

'I then went home with my sister, weeping bitterly, and withdrew into her chamber, where the Lord gave me hopes of a better inheritance. Oh, now I was willing to go to service, and to be stript of all for Christ! I saw that I had a better portion than that of silver and gold, and I was enabled to believe I should never want.

'Towards night I again felt inclined to go to my father. I concluded to go alone this time, since he was so angry with my brother and sister. When I reached the door, I found it partly open, and the key being on the outside, and my father within, I pushed the door gently, and was about to enter, which my father perceiving, ran hastily to shut it, and had I not hastily withdrew, one of my legs had been between the door and the threshold. I would not be so uncivil as to lock my father in his own house. But I took the key, intending, when he was gone, to venture in and lie at his mercy. After a while he came and looked behind the house, and seeing me standing in a narrow passage between the house and the pond, where I stood close up by the wall, he took me by the arm, saying, "Hussy! give me the key quickly, or else I will throw you into the pond." I immediately resigned it with silence and sadness. I could not contend any longer with my father. He was all cruelty. I went down the close to a wood-side, with sighs and groans, and a heart full of sorrow, when this scripture came again into my mind: "Call upon me, and I will answer thee, and show thee mighty things which thou knowest not." The night was dark, but I kept on to the wood, where I poured out my soul in many tears. Then that word also greatly comforted me: "The eyes of the Lord are upon the righteous, and his ears are open to their cry." And that was also a wonderful word at this time: "In all their afflictions he was afflicted."

'I staid so long in this place that it gave great concern to my brother and sister, who had sent one of their men to know if my father had let me in; and understanding that he had not, they went about seeking me, but could not find me.'

'And what did you do, Agnes?' asked the pastor, moved to tears by her touching recital.

'I spread my case before the Lord, and determined to go to my brother's, for I felt that I could not yield to my father's request, if I begged my bread about the streets. I was so strongly fixed in my resolution, that I thought nothing could move me. Yet, alas! like Peter, I was a poor, weak creature, as you will presently see.

'The next morning, which was Sunday, I said to my brother here, "Let us call on father as we go to meeting." But my brother said this would only provoke him the more, and we forbore. As we went along to meeting, brother said to me:

'"Sister, you are now brought upon the stage to act for Christ. I pray God to help you to bear testimony for him. I would by no means have you consent to my father's terms."

'"No, brother," I confidently answered; "I would sooner beg my bread from door to door." I felt that nothing could move me from my determination to cling to Christ, let it cost me what it would. While I sat at meeting, my mind was hurried, considering my case. On our way home, I proposed to my brother to call on our father. He repeated his admonition to me, though I felt I stood in no need of his counsel in this particular. He talked to my father mildly, pleading with him to be reconciled; but my father would not hear, and bade my brother to go home. I told him to go. "Not without you." I will come presently, I said, and my brother left.

'After my brother was gone, I pleaded with my father. "Father," I said, "I will serve you in anything that lies in my power. I only desire liberty to hear God's word on his own day. Grant me this, and I'll ask no more."

'My father looked at me hard. "Father," continued I, "you cannot answer for my sins, or stand in my stead before God. I must look to the salvation of my own soul, or be undone for ever."

' "Promise me you will never go to a meeting again as long as I live, and I will let you in the house, and provide for you as my own child. But if you don't do this, you shall never have one farthing from me."

' "Father," said I, trembling, "I dare not say so; my soul is of more worth than all else, and I dare not make you such a promise."

' "Begone, then, from my sight, hussy," said he, his rage greatly enkindled. "Unless, you promise me this, I shall know well enough what to do. Promise me you will never go to meeting again while I live. Promise me this, and all shall be right. What do you say? answer me quickly. If you now refuse to comply, you shall never be offered it more, and I am determined you shall never come within my doors again as long as you live."

'I stood crying. Those terrible threats almost took my life. "What do you say, hussy?" said my father, "do you promise or not?"

'At last I answered, "Well, father, I will promise you never to go to meeting again as long as you live without your consent." Whereupon he gave me the key, and I went into the house.

'In a little time my father came in, and behaved with affection. He bid me get him some supper, which I did. He also told me to come and eat with him, but it was a bitter supper to me. Now, thought I, I must hear the word no more.

'Monday came, and he still was kind to me. He told me with tears, how much troubled he was for me the night he shut me out of doors, insomuch that, he could not sleep; adding, it was my riding behind John Bunyan that made him angry.

'The greatest part of the next day being Tuesday, I spent in weeping and prayer, fearing I had denied Christ.

I humbled myself before the Lord for what I had done, and begged of him that I might be kept by his grace from denying him and his ways for the future. And blessed be his name, before night he brought me out of this horrible pit, and set my feet upon a rock, enabling me to believe the forgiveness of all my sins, by sealing many precious promises home on my soul.'

'And was this the day your father died?'

'Yes, sir; he died on Tuesday night, though he was as well all day as usual.'

'I am convinced, Agnes, that you and brother Bunyan have been shamefully scandalised. I see now there is no truth in the first vile rumor that met my ear. You are both as innocent as babes. God help you to bear it, and may he bring forth your righteousness like the light, and your judgment like the noonday. Trust in him. He can never forsake thee. I am convinced your sister is innocent,' he said to Agnes' brother, who had sat with his face bathed in tears during her plain but touching story. 'But tell me, poor child, if you can, something about your father's sickness and last moments. Did he repent of his sins? I wish to know, too, that I may give the truth when asked.'

At the thought of her father's death, the poor girl burst into a flood of tears, and it was some minutes before she could sufficiently regain her composure to proceed. She finally calmed herself and proceeded.

'My father was as well as usual this day, and ate his dinner as heartily as ever I knew him. He would sometimes sit up by candle-light while I was spinning, but he now observed it was a very cold night, and he would go to bed early. After supper he smoked a pipe, and went to bed seemingly in perfect health. But while I was by his bedside laying his clothes on him, those words ran through my mind, "The end is come, the end is come; the time draweth near." But I could not tell what to make of them.'

'As soon, therefore, as I quitted the room, I went to the throne of grace, where my heart was wonderfully drawn forth, especially that the Lord would show mercy to my father, and save his soul, for which I was so importunate that I could not tell how to leave pleading; and still that word continued on my mind, "The end is come." Another thing I entreated of the Lord was, that he would stand by me, and be with me in whatever trouble I had to meet with, little thinking what was coming upon me that night and the week following.

'After this I went to bed, thinking on the freedom which God had given me in prayer; but had not slept long before I heard a doleful noise, which at first I apprehended had been in the yard, but soon perceived it to be my father. Being within hearing, I called to him, saying, "Father, are you not well?" He said, "No, I was struck with a pain in my heart in my sleep, and I shall die presently." I immediately arose, put on a few clothes, ran and lighted a candle, and coming to him, found him sitting upright in his bed, crying to the Lord for mercy, saying, "Lord, have mercy upon me, for I am a poor, miserable sinner! Lord Jesus, wash me in thy precious blood!" etc. I stood trembling to hear him in such distress, and to see him look so pale. I then kneeled down by his bedside, and, which I had never done before, prayed with him, in which he seemed to join very earnestly.

'This done, I said, "Father, I will go and call somebody, for I dare not stay with you alone." He replied, "You shall not go out at this time of night; do not be afraid," still crying aloud for mercy. Soon after, he said he would rise and put on his clothes himself. I ran and made a good fire, and got him something hot, hoping that it might relieve him. "Oh," said he, "I want mercy for my soul! Lord, show mercy to me, for I am a great sinner! if thou dost not show me mercy, I am undone for ever!" "Father," said I, "there is mercy in Jesus Christ for sinners; the Lord help you to lay hold on it." "Oh," replied he, "I have been against you for seeking after Jesus Christ; Lord, forgive me, and lay not this sin to my charge!"

'I desired him to drink something warm, which I had for him; but his trying to drink brought on a violent retching, and he changed black in the face. I stood by, holding his head, and he leaned upon me with all his weight. Dreadful time, indeed! If I left him I was afraid he would fall into the fire; and if I stood by him, he would die in my arms, and no one person near us. I cried out, "What shall I do! Lord help me!" Then came that scripture, Isa. xli, 10, "Fear thou not, for I am with thee; be not dismayed, I am thy God; I will help thee, yea, I will uphold thee," etc.

'By this time my father revived again out of his fit of fainting, for I think he did not swoon away; he repeated his cries as before, "Lord, have mercy upon me, for I am a sinful man! Lord, spare me one week more! one day more!" Piercing words to me! After he had sat awhile, he felt an uneasiness in his bowels, and called for a candle to go into the other room. I saw him stagger as he went over the threshold; and making a better fire, soon followed him, and found him on the floor, which occasioned me to scream out, "Father, father!" putting my hands under his arms, lifting with all my might, first by one arm, then by another, crying and striving till my strength was quite spent.

'I continued lifting till I could perceive no life in him, and then ran crying about the house, and unlocked the door to go and call my brother. It being the dead of night, and no house near, I thought there might be rogues at the door, who would murder me. At last I opened the door and rushed out. It had snowed in abundance, and lay very deep. Having no stockings on, the snow got in my shoes, so that I made little progress, and at the stile, in my father's yard, stood calling to my brother, not considering it was impossible for any one to hear. I then got over, and the snow-water caused my shoes to come off, and running barefoot to the middle of the close, I suddenly imagined rogues were behind me, going to kill me. Looking back in terror, these words came into my mind, "The angel of the Lord encompasseth round about those who fear him;" which somewhat relieved me.

'Coming to my brother's, I stood crying dismally under the window, to the terror of the whole family, who were in their midnight sleep. My brother started from bed, and called from the window, "Who are you? What's the matter?" "O brother," said I, "my father is dead; come away quickly!" "O wife," said he, "it is my poor sister; my father is dead!" My brother ran immediately with two of his men, and found our father risen from the ground, and laid upon the bed. My brother spoke to him, but he could not answer, except one word or two. On my return, they desired me not to go into the room, saying he was just departing. Oh, dismal night! Had not the Lord wonderfully supported me, I must have died, too, of the fears and frights which I met with.

'My brother's man soon came out, and said he was departed. Melancholy tidings! But in the midst of my trouble I had a secret hope that he was gone to heaven; nevertheless, I sat crying bitterly, to think what a sudden and surprising change death had made on my father, who went to bed well, and was in eternity by midnight!

'The rest you know, sir. Pray God that I may have grace to do his will—to bear this hardness as a good soldier

of the Lord Jesus Christ.   O Mr. Wilson, pray for me, and
for him they have so falsely accused.   He is as guiltless as
I am.   God knows he had not seen my poor father for
months, and he never said a word to me about him as he
went to Gamlingay.'

The old man was convinced.   He knelt and prayed with
the sorrowing brother and sister, commending them to the
all-sufficient grace of God, and to his care and protection.

CHAPTER XXXVII.

DEATH OF CHARLES II.

IT was Sunday evening, the 1st of February, 1685.   Charles
and his court are at Whitehall, surrounded by all the
luxury and frivolity which ever characterised that dissolute
sovereign, and his lascivious courtiers.   The scene was one
of unusual gaiety.   The claims of the Sabbath were disregarded.   Immortal beings had forgotten their immortality,
and sported with their eternal interests as lightly as with
their most trifling gewgaws.   The obligations of religion,
of morals, yea, of decency, were set aside that men might
indulge, even to satiety, vice and disgusting immoralities.

The king, with many of the ladies and gentlemen, were
gathered in the large hall of the palace.   Around tables,
heaped with gold, drunken courtiers sat at cards.   Strains
of soft, amorous music were wafted on the evening air.
Hilarity and mirth reigned uninterrupted throughout the
palace.

Suddenly the king complained of feeling unwell.   A
great sensation followed the announcement.   But as his
health had been somewhat feeble for the last few months,
the consternation soon passed ; and while the king, unable
to partake of supper, retired to rest, the revellers returned
to their sports.   That night he slept but little, but as was
his wont, he rose early the following morning.   Scarcely,
however, was he risen from his bed, before his attendants
observed something very unusual in his appearance.   His
eyes had a wild strange expression, and when he strove to
speak, it was found his words were incoherent and his
ideas disconnected.

The alarm was given, and soon spread throughout the
palace.   As was the custom in that day, several persons of
rank had assembled to witness the king's morning toilet.

They observed with great fear the changed manner of the monarch, who, seemingly unconscious of his situation, was making ineffectual attempts to laugh and converse in his usual gay maner. Soon his color changed; his face grew black, his eyes assumed a fixed look. He sprung from his seat, sent forth a piercing cry, staggered, and fell. Fortunately, before reaching the floor he was caught by the Earl of Salisbury, who, with others, bore him and placed him on a bed, where he lay insensible. Medical aid was summoned. Bleeding was decided upon as the surest relief. But it was ascertained there was no lancet about the palace, and the king's arm was speedily opened with a pen-knife. The blood ran copiously, but Charles remained unconscious.

The news of the king's illness was speedily borne from tongue to tongue, until it filled the city. All classes forsook business, and thronged the ways to Whitehall to inquire for the sovereign's health. So great was the rush that the gates, which ordinarily stood open, were compelled to be closed. Yet many were admitted whose faces were familiar to those in attendance, and soon the galleries, and halls, and chambers, were filled with anxious inquirers for the king's condition. Physicians were called in immediately. The king was bled freely; his head cauterized with a red hot iron, and a disgusting salt, extracted from human skulls, was applied to his nose and forced into his mouth. These horrid remedies had the effect of restoring the king to consciousness, but his situation was regarded as one of imminent peril.

He continued to improve, slightly, up to Thursday morning, February 5th, and the *London Gazette* announced to eager thousands that the king was deemed out of danger by his attending physicians. The news spread like an electric shock through the city, and the most enthusiastic demonstrations of joy were made. The church bells were rung, loud acclamations of delight went up from myriad tongues, preparations were made for magnificent bonfires; every evidence of joy was given that a people idolizing a sovereign could give.

On the afternoon of the same day, it was understood that the king had grown worse. It was said his physicians had but little hopes of his recovery. Great was the consterna-tion created by this information. Sadness overspread the metropolis. The idol of the nation was dying.

The king suffered the most horrid agony. He said he felt as if a fire was burning within him. It was frightful to witness his tortures: The queen, who had watched him assiduously, fainted at the sight of his sufferings. Charles himself displayed a fortitude which was remarkable.

He was exhorted to prepare for his end, but he seemed to give but little heed to the warning. His apathy with regard to death was striking. At length Archbishop Sancroft spoke to him plainly. 'It is time to speak out,' said he, addressing the king; 'for, sire, you are about to appear before a Judge who is no respecter of persons.'

The king gave no heed to the advice, but remained unmoved. The Bishop of Bath, whom Charles respected above all other prelates, then approached the bedside of the dying monarch, and exhorted him to prepare for the solemn event before him. His pathetic and touching appeals moved the hearts of many who heard him to tears; but, his words failed to affect the king.

His indifference to spiritual matters was alarming and unaccountable. Some 'attributed it to contempt of devout things;' others 'to the stupor which often precedes death.'

The Duchess of Portsmouth was the only one who seemed to understand the condition of the king's mind. She was possessed of the dearest secrets of his bosom. She knew the king was a Roman Catholic in sentiment. Sending for the French ambassador, Barillon, she made known her secret to him, and besought him to convey intelligence immediately to the Duke of York, the king's brother.

James was in the bed-chamber, where the ambassador found him. He had been so much occupied with the affairs of state, setting in order all things preparatory to his accession, that the condition of the king's spiritual matters had been entirely overlooked by him. When he received the message, he started from his chair. He felt, for the first time, his heinous neglect of the sacred duty he owed his dying brother. His conscience smote him. But how to effect the desired end was the question now to be solved. It would not do to make the king's views public. James's safety and popularity required secrecy. Several plans were spoken of in a whisper, but all were rejected as not being feasible.

James, who was, and had always been, an uncompromising Roman Catholic, determined, at all hazards, to carry out his principle. Waving aside the crowd who continually thronged the sick chamber, he stooped down over the dying form of the king, and whispered something into his ear.

'Yes, yes, with all my heart,' answered Charles, so as to

be heard by many present, his face lighting up with a
pleased expression.

'Shall I bring a priest?' asked the Duke.

'Do, brother; for God's sake, do; and lose no time!'
replied the king, earnestly. 'But no,' he added, after a
moment's pause, 'you will get into trouble.'

'If it costs me my life, I will fetch a priest,' answered
the Duke.

Charles smiled approval.

But it was a difficult matter to find a priest to perform
the service, even for the dying king. The law forbade any
one to receive a proselyte into the bosom of the Roman
Catholic Church. It was regarded a crime punishable with
death. After much effort, one was found, however, who
was willing to undertake the dangerous office. It was
John Huddleston, a Benedictine monk, who had, with great
risk to himself, saved the king's life after the battle of
Worcester. He was willing to peril his life a second time
for his monarch. But then there arose another difficulty.
The poor monk was so unlearned that he did not know
what was necessary to be said on the occasion. This
obstacle was obviated, however, by his obtaining some
instruction from a Portuguese ecclesiastic, and John was
privately conducted up the back stairs by Chiffinch, a
confidential servant of the king.

The Duke, in the name of the king, commanded all
present to leave the room but the Earl of Teverst and the
Earl of Bath.

The room was cleared, the physicians withdrawing with
the others. A solemn silence reigned throughout the
chamber of death. The small back door, which communicated with the stairway, was cautiously opened, and the
monk introduced. By way of concealment, a cloak had
been thrown over his shoulders, and a long flowing wig
covered his shaven head.

The Duke led him to the bedside of the king. 'Here,
sire,' he said, 'this good man once saved your life; he now
comes to save your soul.'

'He is welcome,' faintly answered the king.

Kneeling low beside the bed, the monk listened to the
whispered confession of the king. When this was ended,
he pronounced in solemn tones, the absolution. He then
administered the extreme unction. The king passed
through the ceremony with evident satisfaction.

'Will you receive the Lord's Supper?' asked father
Huddleston of the king.

'Surely, if I am not unworthy,' replied Charles.

The host was introduced. The dying monarch strove to rise and kneel before it. But he was too far gone.

'Be still, sire,' commanded the priest, 'God will accept the humiliation of the soul, and not require that of the body.'

The king obeyed. Slowly, and with uplifted eyes, the priest approached the bedside, bearing in his hand the consecrated wafer. The king looked upward, as if to ask a blessing on what he was about to do. The Duke and the Earls stood round him. The sacrament was administered. The king could not swallow it, but seemed to choke in the effort. Some water was procured, and given him, which enabled him to accomplish his purpose.

All had been done that the church required.

The doors were thrown open, and again the chamber of death was filled with the anxious crowd.

'Bring me my children,' said Charles, after he had become somewhat composed, 'I want to bless them.'

They were assembled around his bedside. In tones of parental tenderness he spoke to each one. His words were low and broken, but they reached the hearts of the weeping group.

During the night the king could not sleep. He motioned to his brother to come near him. James obeyed the summons.

Gazing on the Duke with a look of peculiar tenderness and earnestness, he whispered, 'Take care of the Duchess of Portsmouth, and her boy. I leave them to you. And do not let poor Nelly starve.'

The queen, who was unable to watch with him, sent to implore his pardon for any offence she might have given him. As he received the message, he looked up with great concern. 'She asks my pardon! Poor woman; I ask hers with all my heart,' he replied.

The night wore on. The king was unable to obtain only short snatches of sleep. Those around his bed saw that life was fast waning. As the morning light began to steal into the chamber, the monarch turned his head and said to one of his attendants, 'Pull aside the curtain, that I may once more see the light of day. And the little clock which stands at my back must be wound.'

'I have troubled you much,' he said to the watchers, who had been with him through the night, 'but I hope you will excuse me. I have been a most unreasonable time dying, but you must pardon me.'

These were the last words he uttered. Soon his speech failed him, and before ten his senses were gone. He lay with his eyes closed. His breathing was scarcely perceptible. No attempt was made to revive him, for it was evident that his last moments had come. Two hours more, and Charles passed away without a struggle or a groan.

Thus died one whose life had been one continued scene of folly and vice, and whose reign had been marked with the three most awful visitations that had ever befallen the English nation—the plague, the great fire, and the Dutch invasion. But the English nation mourned for a monarch, who, though given to every vice, yet possessed for them a stronge infatuation, with his pleasant manners and good hearted familiarity.

CHAPTER XXXVIII.

MONMOUTH'S INVASION.

No sooner was Charles dead and James elevated to the throne, than wild, unsettled spirits, both in England and on the Continent, began to propose that the Duke of Monmouth should return from his banishment and assert his claim to the throne. It had long been believed by the common people that Charles had been secretly married to Lucy Waters, of whom the Duke was the offspring, and that the marriage contract was kept in a certain black box, which was known to have been preserved with great care by the king. This was regarded as a strong point in the case, and with more zeal than judgment and discretion, those who had become truly attached to the Duke of Monmouth, during his stay in England, because of his advocacy of religious toleration, now urged him to contest his uncle's claim to the crown.

Monmouth, on leaving England, had repaired to Holland, where he was regarded with great favor by the Prince and Princess of Orange. At court he was always received with the kindest and most flattering attentions. Thus he passed many years of his life, always indulging the hope that he would be forgiven and recalled by his father. But when it was announced to him that Charles was dead, and the Duke of York had ascended the throne, he relinquished all hope of the crown; and knowing that his presence at the Dutch court would necessarily bring trouble to Holland, he retired to Brussels. Here the overtures which had been made him while at the Hague, were repeated, and certain considerations urged upon him with such vehemence, and such plausibility, that he was at length induced to indulge the project. As soon as it was known that invasion was being considered, Monmouth found himself overwhelmed by offers of assistance from all classes of exiles. All were willing to rally round his standard, for having been exiled for the part they had taken in religious matters, they hated James intensely. Moreover, they were tired of banishment, and willing to attempt a return to their native land at all risks. All classes of fugitives flocked to the standard of Monmouth. Among these was William Dormer, who had, for years, been longing for an opportunity to return to his native land.

Secret negociations were carried on between the malcontents in England and Scotland, and the refugees, until, their plans being consummated, Monmouth and his forces sailed from Amsterdam, and landed off the coast of Lyme on the morning of the 11th of June, 1685.

Monmouth's first act on landing was to kneel down and return thanks to God for his protection. As soon as it was known for what purpose he had returned, the enthusiasm of the populace became uncontrollable. 'A Monmouth! A Monmouth! The Protestant Religion!' was shouted in wild acclaim by myriad tongues, and the cry spread from hamlet to hamlet, from village to village, until it had gone out through the length and breadth of the land.

An inflammatory manifesto was read before the people of Lyme, and then sent around throughout the realm. In it was declared that the Duke of York had burned down London, strangled Godfrey, had cut the throat of Essex, and had poisoned the late king. James was declared a 'mortal and bloody enemy; a tyrant, a murderer, and a usurper.' Vengeance was declared against him as the foe to liberty, and it was determined never to return the sword to the scabbard until just punishment should be meted out to him.

Wherever Monmouth went, he was hailed as the friend and guardian of liberty. In the western counties, the great mass of the population were Roundheads. From the days of the Lord Protector they had despised kingcraft most intensely. Besides this, many of them were Dissenters, who had suffered in the horrid persecutions of the late reign. These were, to a man, for Monmouth, for they regarded him as a good Protestant, and an enemy to Popery.

At every step hundreds rallied under the standard of the Duke. In less than twenty-four hours after he had landed at Lyme, he found himself at the head of fifteen hundred men.

Monmouth marched from Lyme through Devonshire to Taunton, which he entered without opposition. Here he was received with the most enthusiastic demonstrations of joy and loyalty. The doors and windows of the houses were adorned with plumes. Each man that appeared in the streets wore in his hat a green bough, the badge of the Duke's cause. A company of young girls, bearing a beautifully embroidered flag, marched out to meet him. The lady who headed the train presented him with a small Bible. He received it in his most agreeable way, and remarked so as to be distinctly understood, ' I come to defend the truths contained in this book, and to seal them, if it must be so, with my blood.'

Royalists hastened to arms. Several skirmishes between king James's men and king Monmouth's forces took place, one party conquering to-day, the other to-morrow. Monmouth gained some decisive victories. Elated with his success, he marched towards Bridgewater, which he reached on the 22nd of June. His army now consisted of about six thousand men, and but for the want of arms and ammunition could have been increased to double that number. Scythes, and other articles of husbandry, were called into requisition, but the demand could not be met, and hundreds had to return to their homes because they could not be provided with arms. The Mayor and Aldermen of Bridgewater came out to meet the Duke, clad in their insignia of office, and walking before him, proceeded to the High Cross, and there proclaimed him king.

Monmouth was elated with his success. He determined to march to Bristol, but was thwarted by the king's men, and they directed their steps towards Frome.

Among those who had come over from Amsterdam with the Duke, and attached himself to his cause with unflinching fervor, was William Dormer. After arriving in England he had longed to leave the army and hasten to Bedford. But his confidence in the Duke's success, and his loyalty would not permit him to act thus treacherously. He had been engaged in every skirmish that had yet taken place, and he fondly hoped a few more battles would place Monmouth in possession of his just claims, when he hoped to fly to Mary, and in peace and quiet pass the remainder of his days.

He had sent her word by a messenger, whom he had met in Lyme, of his arrival and his intentions. How her heart beat with joy as she heard the cheering words! A few weeks more, and she would listen to William's voice, and feel the pressure of his kind hand. Then he would leave her no more. She took the note he had written her, after her father had read it to her, and placed it next her bosom. It contained a lock of hair—a simple memento of his constant love.

After Monmouth's flattering reception in Bridgewater, he moved on with his enlarged army towards Bristol. His object was to seize that place before any of the king's soldiers could come to its protection. It was garrisoned only by the Gloucestershire train-bands, under the command of Beaufort, whom Monmouth believed to be but a poor general. But Beaufort was far-sighted and resolute. Instead of being drawn away by the feint which Monmouth prepared to deceive him, he remained in the city, with his men drawn up under arms, declaring, 'he would burn it down himself, rather than see it occupied by traitors.'

Monmouth rested through the afternoon of the 25th of June at Keynsham bridge, only a short distance from Bristol. His intention was to make a descent upon the place under cover of night; but his plans were thwarted by the arrival of the king's troops, and he was compelled to abandon his design for the present.

After several propositions to advance, all of which seemed impracticable, it was decided by the insurgents to return to Bridgewater, Monmouth having been informed that quite a large army favorable to him was there being put under arms.

When William Dormer heard of the proposed retreat, his heart sunk within him. As long as they were advancing towards London, he feared no danger, shrunk from no responsibility. He was nerved to action by the thought of soon again beholding her whom he loved with an ardent, undying affection. As they retreated, he was spiritless and dejected. His comrades rallied him on his sad appearance, and endeavored by jest and song to rouse his flagging courage. He was a great favorite. His manly, upright spirit, and agreeable manner, won for him friends wherever he went. His companions in arms painted to him a bright future. When king Monmouth triumphed over all foes, he would bestow upon them and him offices of impor-

tance for their good services. But it was in vain that they
thus endeavored to arouse him by picturing to him future
emolument. William Dormer could not cast away his
dark disappointment. It was to him a fearful foreboding.

On the 6th of July, the last engagement worthy the name
of a battle was fought near Bridgewater between the insurgents and the king's troops, in which the latter were
victorious, Monmouth and his army being totally defeated.
Many of his men were taken prisoners, while he, with
Buyse, Grey, and a few other prominent friends, fled in
disgrace from the scene of conflict, and were finally overtaken and brought to justice.

Many of the prisoners were executed immediately; others
were gibbeted on the following day, and others were thrown
into prison to rot in irons. A few of the soldiery escaped
to the woods and marshes. Among this latter class was
William Dormer, whose left hand had been shot through
during the engagement. He made his way, as best he
could, towards Bedford, suffering the most severe pain from
his wound, which had now become highly inflamed from
exposure. Wearied with his travel, and faint from the
misery he had endured, he halted on the fourth day at a
little cottage on the outskirts of Oxfordshire. A peasant
woman received him kindly. She was the half sister of a
Dissenting minister, who had suffered imprisonment for his
faith. She prepared for him a pallet of straw, dressed his
wound, and, together with her husband, insisted that the
poor fugitive should remain with them until he was able to
proceed on his journey.

'But you will bring trouble upon yourselves,' answered
William to their entreaties. 'If the officers know you are
harboring me, your lives may be the forfeit.'

'God will take care of us, replied the man. 'We are here
away from the world, and I do not see that there is any
danger. Beside, it is a part of our religion to feed the
hungry and bind up the wounds of the suffering; we are
willing to leave the rest with God. So, my friend, if you
will stay, you are welcome.'

William's hand was fast improving. The poultice of
green herbs made by the poor peasant woman drew out the
inflammation, and the salve she prepared healed it. In a
few days he was sufficiently strong to pursue his way.

He returned his hearfelt thanks to the kind strangers
who had saved him from wretchedness and death,
and bidding them farewell, set out upon his rugged path
towards Bedford. His heart was filled with grateful emo-

tions, and beat high with joyful anticipation. In three days more, God willing, he would be with Mary. Then his trials would be at an end. No longer fearing discovery and capture, he ventured into the highway with the hope of gaining some assistance on his way.

It was towards the evening of the day that he had left the peasant's hut. He was walking along as rapidly as his impaired strength would permit. His mind was busy with the past and future.

He heard the sound of horses' feet coming up in great haste behind him. He turned to look. They were the king's men. Before he could take a second thought they were upon him, and he was their prisoner.

CHAPTER XXXIX.

A STRANGE MEETING.

THE sun was gilding, with the glorious beams of morning, roof, and turret, and spire of the great city of London, throwing his radiance, like a sea of molten gold, across the noble Thames. It was the morning of the 28th of July, 1685, about two weeks after Monmouth's disastrous defeat.

A small frigate was seen about sunrise ascending the Thames. No one gave it particular heed, for it was by no means an unusual sight. Slowly it passed up to the landing.

Suddenly the guns poured forth their hideous bellowings, which resounded far and wide, and shook, as it were, the very foundations of the city. The people were astonished. What was there in that little frigate to cause such rejoicing? She soon landed. From tongue to tongue the news spread with electric speed. Soon the guns sent forth another loud, long peal. And the people caught up the strain, 'Long live the king! Death to the rebels!' was echoed in jubilant strains from multitudes of commingling voices.

And what was the cause of this great demonstration and rejoicing? What? That little vessel contained those who had fought for England and the Protestant religion now to expiate their crime on the scaffold. And the mad multitude send up shouts of loud acclaim that their fellow-men are to suffer and die.

But there were sad hearts in London when it was made

known who the prisoners were. Aged eyes wept bitter
tears, for the grandfather and grandmother have loved
Benjamin and William from their earliest years. The
mother, whose sad face tells that she has not forgotten to
mourn over the loved one lost, and the young, and frail
sister, whose heart is knit to the brothers by ties of
strongest love, weep in anguish over their sad fate.

The vessel lands. On the quay stands a group of
unhappy mourners. It is the aged William Kiffin and his
wife, and the mother and sister of the two young Hewlings.
Strainingly they gaze, as Captain Richardson, with his
aids, is seen on deck. They advance, holding in custody
two young men, one about twenty-two years of age, and
the other scarce twenty.

Oh, affecting sight to greet the eyes of loving ones!

Their noble forms are loaded with irons, and the
manacles on their wrists clash and rattle as they move
along. The sister screams, and rushes forward to clasp
her brothers in her arms. But the guards motion her back.
She dare not approach. Shrieking, she falls to the earth.
The young men smile, and lift their eyes to heaven as they
exchange glances of recognition with their grand-parents
and mother. The old man's heart is breaking. He has
nursed these children from their mother's breast, and he
loves them with more than a father's love. They are the
only sons of their father, whom God took to himself while
they were yet babes. Oh, it is trying. But respect must
be had to those in command, and the mourners can only
stand aside and wring their hands in anguish.

The young men are nothing daunted. They have fought
for liberty and religion, and their faith is in God. They
know in whom they have trusted, and are willing, yea,
rejoice to bear suffering for his name.

They move on towards Newgate, conducted by the
soldiers; for though the best blood in the land flows in
their veins, they are to be treated with all the ignominy
and cruelty of common felons. The massive bars spring
back to give them entrance. The hootings and mad
acclaims of the multitude fall on their ears.

There is a company of the king's men at the gate,
awaiting its opening. In their midst is a prisoner bound
with cords, but not loaded with irons. He is pale and
emaciated, and stands with trembling form.

The prisoners pass in. Just as they enter, they look at
each other. The brothers recognise the pale, worn face of
the other prisoner

It is William Dormer.

'Great God! and are you too here, William!' exclaims Benjamin Hewling. The guardsman strikes him on his mouth, and bids him be silent. It is an insult hard to brook by the spirited young man. But he remembers that his Master had been smitten and beaten. And following his example, he opens not his mouth.

The young Hewlings and William Dormer had often seen each other in the meetings of the Dissenters. They had met around the communion table of their Lord and Master. They had met on the battle-field, and fought side by side for the cause for which they were now to sacrifice their lives. They now met, prisoners, at Newgate. They should meet once more—before the throne of God. William Dormer smiled sadly as he returned the young man's recognition. He cared not for himself. His faith in God was firm, and he could meet death unflinchingly. But Mary! Ah, his heart bled for her! He dreaded the shock to her delicate nature. For her sake he prayed for liberty.

'William, my child, my poor, dear William!' exclaimed a female voice, and the form of an elderly woman was seen rushing towards the prisoner.

'Stand back, woman!' said one of the soldiers, pushing her back with his sword.

'Oh, let me speak to him once more, my poor child! I have not seen him this many a year. Kind sir, let me speak to him this once.'

The soldier gave back sullenly, and Elizabeth Gaunt rushed forward, and folded William to her bosom. The young man clasped her in his arms, and the two wept aloud. Neither could speak. Even the hard-hearted soldiers were touched by the scene, and tears started to the eyes of those unaccustomed to weep.

At length William found voice to speak. 'Mrs. Gaunt, Mary, Mary! Oh, tell me about her.'

'Well, my child, I saw her last week.'

'I shall never see her again. Give her this,' and with his bound hands he took from his bosom a note which the soldiers had permitted him to write after he was captured.

'She shall come down to see you, William. I will go for her myself.'

'But we will remain in London only a few days. They are going to take us to Dorchester for trial. Could I see her once more I could die happy.'

'Come, get away, woman!' said one of the brutal men,

' you have been there long enough, whining over that rebel.'

Mrs. Gaunt did not heed his words, but continued to talk to William. The soldier tok her arm rudely, and bade her 'be gone!'

' I'll see you again, my boy, before you go to Dorchester. They let *me* come here to visit the sick.'

The soldier motioned her to the gate. A moment more, and she had disappeared without the walls.

The prisoners were conducted to their gloomy cells, where they were lodged, still manacled with irons. But as in the case of Paul and Silas, God was with them in the dungeon, and they were enabled to sing and give praises unto him. Oh, the exceeding love of God, which enables his children to bear all things for his sake!—cruelty, imprisonment, shame, disgrace, death itself. His grace *is sufficient*. Who that has tasted his love can ever doubt it?

CHAPTER XL.

THE VISITORS.

THE next morning, at an early hour, there stood before the great eastern gate of the prison a man and two females, craving entrance. The women were dressed in deep mourning, and veiled closely. Their forms were bowed with grief. They scarcely lifted their heads. The old man's face bore the marks of recent sorrow. His silver locks hung over his shoulders, giving to him a highly venerable appearance.

They had been standing some time in waiting before the turnkey to the outer gate appeared. He eyed them closely. Then looked at the carriage, with its driver and handsome span of noble bays—then sullenly opened the massive portal, and bade them walk in. They were wholly unused to prison scenes, and the dark, fierce countenance of the porter, and frowning walls of the gloomy prison, filled their hearts with dreadful shuddering.

They halted in the court before the inner door to await its opening. While they stood thus, Captain Richardson, who had taken charge of the young men before they landed from the frigate, came up, and in a rough tone accosted them.

' Who are you, and whom do you want to see?' he asked gruffly.

'We wish to be permitted to see the young men who were put in prison yesterday—the Hewlings.'

'And who are you?'

'The mother and sister of the boys, and their grandfather, who has watched over them from their cradle.'

'Have you any permission to see the boys, old man?'

'I have obtained none, presuming I would be admitted. Can you not, sir, give us leave to enter?'

'Well, I suppose I could,' answered the officer, tauntingly, without making any movement towards doing so.

'We shall be glad to get in, sir. The ladies do not like to stand here exposed.'

'Well, it's no use deceiving you any longer, old man. You can't go in.'

'Oh, pray, do let us in!' exclaimed the mother, most beseechingly. 'My poor boys! My dear children! Oh, do, sir, let me see them!'

The man made no reply, but looking sneeringly at the suppliant.

'Do permit us to go in, sir; you have the authority to do so. It will break my poor daughter's heart if she is denied the sight of her boys.'

'Her boys are rebels of the worst character. I tell you, they are criminals, and their friends cannot see them.'

'For God's sake, sir,' ejaculated the sister, lifting her veil, and looking at him most beseechingly. 'Oh, do let us see my poor brothers. We do not wish to say anything to them but what you can hear, the whole world can know. Oh, do let us in, I pray you!'

Tears streamed down her face while she spoke, and the mother's sobs were heard above her words. The old man wept like a child.

It was a scene to melt a heart of stone. But the officer remained untouched. He appeared to delight in the misery before him, and replied roughly:

'They are rebels, lassie, against our most gracious king, and the laws of this most glorious land; and have forfeited all claims to compassion. You cannot go in. They must be punished for their evil doings. And I will keep them in close confinement until they have their trial.'

'They fought for the liberty of this land—for freedom to worship God,' replied the woman, drawing herself up to her noblest height, as if to resent the indignity that had been offered her in the words of the brutal captain. 'They have done what they believe to be right—what the nation will one day see is right; and if they must be cruelly punished for it, God will stand by them, and avenge them on those who shamefully use and abuse them.'

The old man felt it was of no avail. Even entreaties were naught to reach that savage nature. Yet, he would make one more effort.

'No, I tell you. There is no hope; so be gone.'

The two females wept aloud. The old man groaned, and taking the females by the hand, the three moved to the gate, and passed out.

'Curse that old Kiffin!' muttered Richardson, as the gate closed upon them. 'The old dog! he ought to be hung himself. He has done more for these devilish religionists than all the other men in London besides. He gives them money, and influence, and respectability. I am glad that I had it in my power to cross him. I felt sorry for the young lassie. She is a fair, buxom girl; but the rebel boys must be punished, and these sanctimonious preachers too.'

The little company had scarcely reached the carriage, which stood without the gate, before another female, altogether different in her aspect, applied for admittance. She acted as one used to the place. She scarcely asked to enter. The porter threw open the door, and she walked in with a calm, steady step. In her hand she held a porringer of broth. Beneath her arm was a loaf of bread, and in a reticule or bag she carried cloth and a salve, to dress the wounds of the poor prisoners.

Captain Richardson was yet standing in the court-yard when Mrs. Gaunt entered. He was accustomed to her daily visits, and could have no pretext for refusing her now, else the savageness of his present mood would have driven her thence.

'What do you want, woman?' he asked, as if delighted to torment her with questioning.

'I come to-day, as is my wont, to see the sick, and administer to their necessities.'

'And what do you expect to make by it?'

'Nothing, except the gratification it gives me to know I am doing my duty.'

'And what have you got there in your saucepan? Do you feed the prisoners as well as bind up their wounds?'

'A little broth, sir, for that poor man who lost his leg in the battle, and who, poor creature, is in almost a dying condition. He can't live many days, sir. He has been shamefully neglected. His limb is all inflamed, and I do believe, if he had not had some of this good salve that I bring with me, it would have mortified days ago.'

'Well, go in with your broth and salve. Let the poor wretches do the best they can, for their time is short. A few weeks more, and all who outlive their wounds will be dangling from the gibbets.'

The gaoler gave the woman admittance. She passed along her usual round, after the conductor, bestowing comfort and joy wherever she went. When she had finished her visits to those whom she daily attended, she asked if there were any more prisoners.

'Three new ones got in yesterday.'

'And are they sick?'

'One of them looks ailing; he is as white as your cap, and can hardly get along.

'Show me his cell.'

The man led her through a dark passage which terminated at the extreme rear of the building. Stopping before a low, narrow cell, he withdrew the key from his pocket, and unlocked the iron-grated door. The prisoner started from his low stool in the corner. Mrs. Gaunt spoke. She knew William would recognise her voice.

'Who is this poor man whom you have placed in such miserable lodgings?'

At the sound of the familiar voice, William started and came forward. He knew that caution was necessary, so he made no further manifestation of joy.

'I don't know what his name is. All I know is that he is one of the rebels, and got caught for his pains.'

'And can't he be put in a more comfortable place than this? It is cruel to keep him in this dark, damp cell to rot. Go and bring the keeper here, Mr. Nardley, and let's see what can be done for him.' The man turned the key in William's cell door, and made off to obey Mrs. Gaunt's command.

'William,' said the good woman, as soon as the man's footfall died away. 'William, my poor child, how do you do?'

'Well in *mind*, thank God, but my body is yet a little feeble. I was shot in the battle, and although the wound has healed, I have not recovered from the effects of it.'

'And you never can, here in this place, without light and air. But you are comfortable in mind, my child. God is with you in the dungeon, speaking peace and comfort to your soul, and bidding you to "fear not them which can kill the body only."'

'Yes, Jesus speaks sweet consolation to me. I am at

peace with him, and in him. My only distress is Mary.
I think of her night and day. I dreamed of her last night,
an angel, who came to me in this low, dark place, and said,
" Fear not, William, I am with you, and Christ our blessed
Lord is with you." And I thought she gave me a cup of
refreshing water, and bathed my throbbing temples, and
rubbed my chafed hands. And more, Mrs. Gaunt. I
thought those dark eyes were unsealed, and such a look as
she gave me! Oh, I have never seen anything so like
heaven! I was delighted and awoke, and for a moment I
could not think it was a dream ; I put out my arms to
bring her to me, but they met only the empty air. Then I
knew that I had been dreaming, for the heavy tramp of the
watchman's step was the only sound I heard, and no ray of
light lit up the horrid darkness of this loathsome place. I
tried to sleep again. I hoped to dream. But I could not.
My thoughts would not rest.'

'Poor child! when we get to that better land, there will
be no such disappointment, William. We shall not dream
there, for there shall be no night.'

'And it will not be long, Mrs. Gaunt, before I get there.
My days are fast drawing to a close. The law knows no
relenting in a case like mine. The Hewlings and I are
doomed.'

'It may be, William, that you can be pardoned.'

'Never, never, my dear woman. The gibbet is my lot.
But I die in a glorious cause. If I did not leave Mary
behind, and you, my more than dear mother, I would not
hesitate a moment. I am ready now to go.'

'Something tells me, my dear boy, that I shall not be
long behind you ; possibly I may go first. These are times
of persecution, and sword, and flame, throughout the land,
and I cannot hope long to escape. I belong to the despised
sect, and my deeds must become known. I try to do my
Master's will, to aid him, in the persons of the disciples,
when sick and in prison, and to minister to them a cup of
cold water in his name. When this thing comes to the ears
of those in authority, why, then I must suffer. But I'll
trust my Saviour, and go on.'

'Will you go to see Mary, Mrs. Gaunt, and tell her all?
You can break the sad news to her better than any body
else could. Oh, if I could see her once more!—could once
again hear her sweet voice, I should have nothing more to
wish for.'

'You shall see her again, God willing. I will go for her,
and bring her down here, if you stay long enough in this

gaol; and if they move you away, I'll go with her to where they lodge you.'

'They are going to take the young Hewlings and me to Dorchester, to try us; but I do not know when.'

'I'll find that out, and then I'll determine what to do.'

Just then steps of the guide and keeper were heard in the corridor.

'I sent for you, Mr. Nardley, to see if you cannot give this poor man a better cell. He will die here before his trial comes off.'

'Yes, Mrs. Gaunt, I think we can, though we are very full. I'll book him at better lodgings. I am glad you spoke to me about it. It is a shame to let our fellow-men suffer when there is no need for it.'

Mr. Nardley was a kind-hearted man. It was through his influence that Mrs. Gaunt had been permitted to visit the gaol, and attend on its suffering inmates.

The keeper and assistant went to look for a better cell, and again William Dormer and Mrs. Gaunt had opportunity for a word or two. It was arranged that Mrs. Gaunt, if possible, should find out from the keeper whether the prisoners were to be tried in London, or sent to the West, and at what time their trial should take place. The rest was left to her wisdom to plan and execute.

'I may not be back to-morrow, William. There is a poor sick sister near me, who needs my attention. She cannot live long, perhaps not beyond two days; and then, if it seems best, I will go to Bedford for Mary. I would not build you up on a false hope. As you say, the law knows no mercy. Trust in God, and he will bring to pass whatever is best for you. This world is a scene of trial and disappointment. You do not know, my poor boy, about this as I do. But we will not talk about its cares now, but think of better things. I must see the Hewlings before I go, if they will let me. The keeper is coming. She grasped his hand.

'This poor man will do well, Mr. Nardley, if he can have a comfortable cell. He has no fever, and good food and quiet sleep will be all he will need, together with a little exercise. The assistant told me of two other prisoners; can I see them?'

'They are doing well, Mrs. Gaunt, and Captain Richardson has commanded that nobody shall see them.'

'Who are they?'

'They are grandchildren of Rev. Mr. Kiffin, and were put in here for taking up arms against the government.

You know Captain Richardson hates the Dissenters, and he delights to punish them. He will not let their mother and sister see them.'

'How do the youths appear?'

'Very well, madam. I heard them singing and praying this morning in their cells, as I passed round.'

'Are they in the same cell?'

'Oh, no, ma'am; Captain Richardson had them put in different parts of the building. He said the miserable wretches should know no mercy.'

Mrs. Gaunt went speedily from the prison to the house of the sick sister. She found her in the agonies of death. Her mind was calm and collected, and she was enabled to praise God amid the most intense sufferings with which her body was racked.

'I go to Jesus,' were her last audible words.

Mrs. Gaunt spent the night with the family, performing the necessary duties preparatory to consigning the body to the grave. She remained the next day to the funeral—saw the body deposited in its narrow bed. She went with the bereaved husband and children to their now desolate home, prepared everything for their comfort, and then sought her own little cottage to commune with God and have her spiritual strength renewed.

That night about twelve o'clock she heard a low rapping at her front door. She arose, threw on her clothes, and went to see what it meant.

'For God's sake take me in, sister Gaunt. They are on my heels to bring me to the scaffold.'

'And who are you, man?' she asked.

'John Burton, one of the Nonconformists who took up arms to fight for the faith. But you know we were conquered, and I am trying to flee from England with my little family, for if I am overtaken I shall certainly perish on the scaffold.'

'Where are your wife and children, man?'

'I have but one child, a daughter, and she and my wife are here with me.'

'I cannot turn away him that asks for shelter,' the good woman answered. 'Come in, come in!'

She showed them to bed and retired.

The next day she made ample provision for them, bidding them to keep within doors until she returned, which would be in two or three days.

She then set out on her journey to Bedford, and did not rest till she reached there. She unfolded the sad news to the family as gently as she could. Poor Mary! it appeared her heart would break when she heard of her lover's condition. She knew he belonged to the defeated army, whose disastrous conflict had reached her ears. But amid all her suspense she had this ray of comfort, 'Perhaps William had again escaped to Holland!'

But now the worst had come. There was no longer any hope. William must die. She bowed beneath the fearful intelligence like the lily before the rushing storm. She sat as one stupified. Her father and mother and Mrs. Gaunt endeavored to draw her mind away from her trouble to feed on the promises of Christ. But grief had absorbed every other feeling and emotion. She heard their words, but they made no impression.

She only knew that William Dormer must die.

She consented to go to London. Indeed, it was the only thing that seemed to arrest her attention. Preparations were made, and the next day Mary and her father set out with Mrs. Gaunt for the city. They travelled as fast as they could. The roads were in good condition, and at night-fall they reached their destination.

CHAPTER XLI.

THE MEETING BETWEEN MARY AND WILLIAM DORMER.

WITH trembling step and faltering heart, Mary Bunyan set out with Mrs. Gaunt, on the morning after her arrival in London, to visit the prisoner.

But few words were spoken as the two hurried along the crowded street toward the prison. Mary clung closely to her friend for protection from the jostling crowd. Mrs. Gaunt had not forgotten the poor sick man, to whom she had for some time ministered daily. She carried with her a bucket of broth, and her salve and lint.

'Are we almost there, Mrs. Gaunt?' asked Mary, timidly, her voice trembling with the dread that pressed upon her heart.

'We will be there before long, Mary; it is a good walk from my house. Are you tired, child? Perhaps I walk too fast for you.'

'I do feel tired, Mrs. Gaunt, for I did not sleep much last night; but we will hurry on and get there as soon as we can. I do not love to walk these crowded streets.'

Just then a carriage passed, driving in the direction of the prison. The occupants, an elderly man and a young female clad in deep mourning, recognised Mrs. Gaunt. They bade the driver halt, and calling to her, asked her and her friend to ride. She gladly accepted the invitation, not so much for herself as for Mary, whose pale, sad face and faltering step attested her weariness. Old Mr. Kiffin and Miss Hewling did not need to be introduced to Mary. They immediately knew her to be the blind daughter of the beloved Bunyan. Mary spoke with a faint voice as Mrs. Gaunt called the name of her friends, and then drew herself timidly into one corner of the carriage. She did not wish to converse.

'You are on your daily mission of good, sister Gaunt,' said the old man in a kind tone, in which there was a blending of sorrow.

'Yes, I want to do what little I can to relieve the dreadful sufferings of the poor unfortunates. It is but little, but I remember a cup of cold water, given in the name of my Master, will not fail of its reward.'

'Poor creatures! they need your words of comfort and your kind ministrations. These are dark times for us, sister Gaunt. God is dealing with us very severely. William Dormer is to you as a child; and my poor boys, God knows how I love them!' and the old man heaved a deep sigh painful to hear.

At the name of William Dormer, Mary started and reddened. She turned her head towards the window to escape observation. Tears started to her sightless eyes, but she dashed them away. She did not wish to betray her secret. The sister of the two young Hewlings wept aloud.

Mrs. Gaunt made no reply to the remarks of the old man. She did not wish to protract a conversation which could only give pain. But the old man's heart was too full of his deep trials to remain silent. He must speak.

'And they will not let me see my poor dear boys. I have been twice and they refused. It is hard, hard to bear. I thought we would go again, Hannah and I; maybe we may be successful this time. But there is not much hope. Their hearts are made of iron, and they delight in cruelty.'

Just as the old man finished his sorrowful remark, they turned into a wide street that led to the prison grounds. As they did so, a volley of railing and cursing met their ears. Looking out, they beheld a most painful scene. Four

poor wretches, pale, and ready to faint from wounds and
starvation, loaded with irons, moved slowly on towards the
gaol, their emaciated forms scarcely able to bear the weight
of the chains and manacles which their furious persecutors
had heaped upon them. And because they could not proceed faster, they were lashed, and cursed, and goaded on.

Shudderingly the occupants of the carriage turned away
from the revolting spectacle. No remark was made. It
needed no comment. Well it was for Mary that she could
not see it. She heard the taunts and curses of the infuriated crowd, and her whole body shook with dread.

They reached the outer gate of the prison, and alighted.
As soon as the porter saw Mrs. Gaunt, he opened the gate,
and she and Mary passed in. He looked suspiciously on
the other two as they followed.

The company reached the second gate, and knocked for
admittance. As the heavy door swung open on its creaking
hinges, Mary shuddered. Remembrances of the old gaol at
Bedford and her father's sufferings rushed across her mind,
and filled her soul with horror.

The four passed in, and were met by one of the prison
guards, who eyed from head to foot the three new person-
ages. Mrs. Gaunt had so long been accustomed to pass in
and out, that all the attendants, and many of the inmates,
had come to know her well.

' Who is this you have with you, Mrs. Gaunt ? ' the man
asked, as Mary clung to the arm of the good woman.

' A poor blind friend of mine, who has come with me in
a morning walk.'

' The blind can do no harm,' he muttered to himself,
' pass on.'

Mrs. Gaunt and Mary proceeded towards the door. The
two were about to follow them.

' Your name, sir,' said the man, with something of polite-
ness in his manner. ' Have you permission to enter ? '

' My name is William Kiffin, and I have no authority to
enter. But I hope you will suffer me to do so. I have
two dear boys here that I wish to see, if it is but for a few
moments. Do suffer me to go in,' he added, most imploringly.

' I will see, sir.'

The man turned into a little office. He was gone but a
moment.

As he emerged from it, another officer followed. Instantly the old man recognised him as the captain who had
taunted him so shamefully a few days before. He knew all

hope was gone now. He read in the eye of his brutal tormentor a savage delight in his power to torture. Yet he would ask.

'We wish to see the Hewlings. Can we do it?'

'If you have permission, sir,' replied the officer, with a cold, derisive scorn.

'I have no permission. But cannot you suffer me to enter?'

'No, I cannot. The command is that you shall not see the rebels. And now I tell you, old man, you need not come again. This is the second or third time you have troubled me, and if you do it again, it will not be well for you. How did you get thus far on your way?'

The old man made no reply to this insulting question. Mrs. Gaunt, who had listened at the door until her friends could be answered, saw the hopelessness of the case, and turned to add her entreaties to those of the old man. But she could not be heard.

'Get you along, old woman, or I will turn you out. But who is that you have got with you?'

'A blind friend, whom I brought out for the walk.'

'Blind! ha, ha. Well, go in, go in!'

'Will you not suffer us to go in this once?' implored the young girl.

'No, I tell you; you shall not go in. It is not worth your while to stand here asking, for I tell you again, it has been forbidden, and there is no hope.'

The old man stood irresolute. The young girl wept bitterly.

'Oh, do let us enter!' she sobbed out. 'Just this once! I pray you, sir, let us see my poor brothers! Oh, for heaven's sake, do!'

'I tell you, I cannot do it. My instructions forbid it, and it is useless for you to ask.'

Still the old man pleaded. He felt that he must once more see the darlings of his heart, and hear from them the dealings of God with their souls. But the harsh man was inexorable.

While they were thus parleying, the door opened, and the four captives marched in.

'Get you gone, old man! See, here is more for me to do. I tell you, I will not let you in. So be off, and do not waste my time. Ah, ah,' he added, as if gloating in his diabolical work. 'And so they have caught some more of these devilish fellows!'

The old man wept like a child, as he turned to pass out.

The maiden leaned on his arm, while stifled sobs burst from her bosom. The door closed behind them. They never entered it again.

Mrs. Gaunt and Mary entered the narrow, dark passage that led to the cells of the prisoners. With frightened tread and suppressed breath, Mary glided noiselessly along behind her friend. She did not dare to speak.

Mrs. Gaunt dressed the wounds of the poor old man, as he lay on his pallet of straw in the large room where the sick were kept. She handled him as tenderly as a mother, yet the poor sufferer groaned with intense pain. She then gave him a little broth.

He looked up into her face, and thanked her. 'Not here long, good woman,' he said feebly. She was aware of this. A few hours more must terminate his sufferings.

'Willing to go?' she asked.

'Yes, yes.'

'Well, then, all is well.'

He smiled faintly, and repeated her words, 'All well, all well.'

She passed round among the other sick, giving a cup of water to one, a drink of broth to another, and in various ways soothing their pains, always speaking a word of consolation.

'Let me see the young man that came in a few days since.'

'Which? one of those two brothers?'

'No, his name is William Dormer.'

'Yes, yes,' and the old man opened the door and gave her directions how to proceed. He did not go with her, for just then the attending physician came in, and he had to remain to answer his questions with regard to the patients.

As they were groping their way along the dark aisle, they met one of the prison attendants.

'Show us to William Dormer's cell, will you, if you please,' Mrs. Gaunt asked.

The man answered kindly, and led the way.

'Do you wish to go in and see the prisoner?' he inquired, as they stopped in front of the cell.

'We should like to do so.'

The young man, who had known Mrs. Gaunt for many years, opened the cell door. She entered.

'Does this young woman wish to go in too?'

Mrs. Gaunt replied in the affirmative.

'I suppose it will be no breach of the regulations, as she is with you, Mrs. Gaunt.'

Mary followed.

William had arisen from his low stool at the first sound of Mrs. Gaunt's voice. He could see the two forms, and knew one was Mary's. As she entered, he sprung forward. 'Mary!' 'William!' were the only words that were heard, as he clasped the trembling form and pressed it to his bosom.

Not another word was spoken as they stood locked in each other's embrace. The keeper looked on amazed. Mrs. Gaunt, overcome, sunk on the low stool beside her.

Tears of joy streamed down Mary's cheeks, as she leaned on the breast of him she loved. It was happiness to hear him once more call her name, and feel his warm breathings on her cheek.

William seated her tenderly on his low bed, and sat beside her, placing his arm around her, and pressing her to him. He gazed in her face by the dim light, and as he did so, he marked the changes sorrow had made. He kissed her burning cheek and beating brow again and again.

'I may not see you more, Mary, my dear, dear Mary, and I cannot be formal now.'

'Oh, my William, say not this to me!' she exclaimed, as she started from her seat, impelled by the intensity of her emotion.

'I do not know, Mary. We must not hope for too much. Our persecutors are fierce and cruel.'

'Oh, William, I cannot bear the thought!' the agonized girl exclaimed, as she lay sobbing on his bosom.

It was a fearful rack to the poor prisoner. He would freely have yielded up his life, could that but have saved the loved one from suffering.

'We must try, my dear Mary,' he said, speaking in a cheerful soothing tone, 'to say, as did our blessed Master, "Not my will, but thine, be done."'

'Yes,' interrupted Mrs. Gaunt, 'the Lord is good and infinite in wisdom. He knows what is best for us his poor children. Oh, that he will give us all his grace, that we may say, "Even so, Father, for thus it seemeth good in thy sight." Our ways are in his hands. He ordereth our footsteps, and he hath a purpose in all the trials he sends us. They work out, my children, a far more exceeding and eternal weight of glory for us. Let us trust him at this dark hour, as we have always done. He will not leave nor forsake us.'

These words of her friend served somewhat to soothe Mary. She raised her hand, and seeking the face of William passed it carefully over it, as if to impress on her mind for ever every lineament of that loved yet unseen face. When she reached the long, stiff beard, she started with surprise, and withdrew her hand suddenly, but then replaced it, and traced again every feature. It was a simple act, yet so touching, that the guide turned aside to hide his starting tears.

'Leave us alone with William for a little while, won't you, sir?' Mrs. Gaunt asked of the man.

The man bowed assent, and strode up the narrow passage.

'Let us talk of the goodness of God, my children,' said Mrs. Gaunt, as the dull heavy footfalls died out in the distance. 'We will not dwell on the future, except to ask his guidance and care. We will praise his holy name for what he has done for us in the past. He has led us, my boy, through many trials, and now he has permitted us to meet once more on earth. And although we are surrounded by affliction and trials, yet his presence is near.'

'Yes, God has been kind to me,' replied William, 'and I would call upon all within me to bless and magnify his great name. He can make a prison a palace, of a truth. I have never had more spiritual enjoyment in my life than I have had since I came into this prison.'

William sat with his arms around Mary, while she leaned her head trustingly on his bosom. With the other hand he held the thin, pale hand of the trembling girl. He gazed upon her darkened face, so pale and grief-marked, with a look of indescribable earnestness and love. The strong man within him bowed, as he thought of what she had suffered for him, and the tears coursed each other silently down his face. Could he but have this gentle, loving being with him always, he would care naught for his prison.

How beautiful to see two such loving hearts cling to each other with tenderness and constancy, increased a thousand fold by the gloom and trials that surrounded them. Yet how painful to know, that that gloom and those trials should know no brightening, and no cessation, until the grave should close over the pulseless bosoms of those who had loved through danger and separation, and would love on to the last.

The three spoke of the past and the present. What was to be, they dared not look out upon. Each endeavored to be cheerful, for the sake of the others. Their words were more of thankfulness and comfort, than of hope.

Thus they sat and conversed for some time, Mary all the while leaning on the bosom of William. She did not often speak. It was happiness enough for her to lie and listen to the tones of his manly voice, as they gushed forth, softened in their accents by love. After some fifteen or twenty minutes had elapsed, the footsteps of the conductor were heard approaching. The two friends knew it was the signal for their departure, and Mrs. Gaunt, giving William some words of consolation, and promising to come the next day and bring Mary with her, rose, and gathered up her bucket and reticule of salve and bandages. Mary clung to William as long as she could. Her heart misgave her about seeing him on the morrow.

Mary put up her hand as before, and passed it slowly over William's face. As she did so, her sightless, streaming eyes were turned to his. He stooped over and kissed her again and again. A second command was given. She tore herself from him, and with one wild shriek, passed out into the passage.

When Mary reached Mrs. Gaunt's she was prostrate. She fell on the low bed like one lifeless—one whom grief had deprived of consciousness. Her father, who knew it was useless for him to accompany them to prison, and who, during their absence, had gone out to visit a friend of his, Mr. Strudwick, had not yet returned.

John Burton, his wife and daughter, were yet there, but did not dare to move from their hiding-place. Mrs. Gaunt endeavored to arouse Mary. But all her efforts were unavailing. A dead stupefaction had seized her, which rendered her incapable, body and mind, of any action. Her father was greatly distressed to find his daughter in such a fearful condition. But he knew the only cure was repose. A stimulating draught was administered, after which she sunk into a quiet slumber.

Poor William! we will not look back into his dreary prison cell. It were torture to do so. God alone knows the anguish of his true heart, as he sat there through the long weary hours of the night, thinking of his beloved Mary, and the death which inevitably awaited him.

About midnight, as he was thinking, his reflections were interrupted by a confused noise in that portion of the prison where he lodged, and footsteps and sounds were heard approaching his cell door. A light flashed in upon him. His door was unlocked, and the gruff voice of Captain Richardson bade him follow him. William threw his clothes about him and did as he was commanded. When he reached the court-yard, he found other prisoners assembled, among whom he recognised the faces of the two Hewlings. Without a word of explanation, they were marched out of the prison yard, and placed in wagons, which bore them rapidly away. They did not know but it was to the scaffold.

CHAPTER XLII.

THE SEARCH.

WHILE these scenes were transpiring at Newgate, the little family of Mrs. Gaunt slept sweetly. Mary, overcome by fatigue and sorrow, had fallen into a profound slumber. Mrs. Gaunt lay beside her. Bunyan, having committed all to the keeping of God, slept soundly. The fugitives were apart, in a back room, enjoying rest in their fancied security.

Suddenly Mrs. Gaunt was aroused from her slumbers by a fierce knocking at her front door. She threw on her dress, and went to seek the cause.

'Another poor soldier of the cross,' she said to herself.

But alas! no. It was the officers of the law, in search of John Burton.

'We come in the name of the king and the laws of our land, to search your house over for one of the rebels, whom we hear you have secreted,' said one of the officers, as soon as she had opened the door.

'But you will not disturb a poor, peaceable, unprotected woman, sirs?'

'Away with you! let us in. We are after the vile rebels.'

'But wait until I can get you a light,' said Mrs. Gaunt, turning round to go to her kitchen. She wished to arouse Burton and his family, and bid them escape.

'No, we'll not wait. We've got a light here. You can't deceive us, you old hag. We know well enough that fellow is here, and we'll have him, too,' and the speaker swore violently.

They forced themselves in. Burton and his wife had

been aroused by the noise when it was first heard at the
door.   They sprung from their beds, awoke the daughter,
who, like her parents, had slept in her dress, and climbing
out over the back fence, made good their escape, and were
soon lost in one of the narrow streets of that part of the
city.   They had barely time to elude their pursuers.   And
had it not been for the management of Mrs. Gaunt,
who led the officers to every other room first, and caused
them to search thoroughly, they would have been overtaken.

They were elated with joy when they entered the room
where Bunyan lay.   'Here is the rascal!' exclaimed the
foremost man.   'We have caught him napping.   Come,
let's take him before he wakes up.   Come, come!'

'You are mistaken, friends,' said Bunyan, rising, and
looking the man in the face by the light of his lantern.
'I am a peaceable citizen.   But tell me, for whom do you
search?'

'For that vile rascal, John Burton.'

'You will not find him here,' said Bunyan calmly, who
had seen from his window the fugitives leap the fence.

With imprecations and cursings the officers passed on to
search the out-buildings.   Their rage knew no bounds
when they found they were defeated of their prey.

Swearing vengeance against all rebels, and calling on
high heaven to visit them with most horrid torture if
they did not find out and bring to justice 'the wretch,
John Burton,' they left the house.

CHAPTER XLIII.

THE ARREST.

WHAT a wise providence that the day of our death is
hidden from us.   Life were one continually dread, else.

Mrs. Gaunt arose, and went about her morning work as
usual, feeling grateful to God that he had enabled one of
his servants to thwart the rigor of the law.   She prepared
her pot of broth, and gathered together her lint and
bandages.

Soon after their humble breakfast, she and Mary set
out for the prison.   Mary was stronger than on the preceding day, having been much benefited by her night's
sleep.   Bunyan walked out into the city to seek the house
of Mr. Kiffin.

The hope of again being beside William Dormer, and listening to his voice, gave Mary new life. On the two hastened. They reached the prison and entered uninterrupted. Mrs. Gaunt found the poor man, whom she had so long tended, had died during the night, and now lay ready for the grave. But there were others there that claimed her care and kindness, for there was at that time great suffering at Newgate. She dealt out her broth, dressed the wounds of the poor soldiers, and after having seen that all were as comfortable as her limited aid could make them, she and Mary went to seek William Dormer's cell. Just as they gained the landing beyond the hospital room, they encountered Mr. Nardley. He spoke to them very kindly.

Mrs. Gaunt asked to be shown to William Dormer's cell.

'He is not here, Mrs. Gaunt. He and the Hewlings left at midnight, for Salisbury.'

Mary fell like one suddenly deprived of life. Mrs. Gaunt stood for a moment in consternation. Recovering her senses, she bade Mr. Nardley run for some water. With superhuman strength she lifted Mary and placed her in the fresh air. Her face was as white as the spotless handkerchief which covered her beautiful neck. Her eyes were closed, and she gave no signs of life. For a moment Mrs. Gaunt feared she was dead. But undoing her dress, she found that her heart still pulsated, though slowly.

'For God's sake, Mr. Nardley, run,' she exclaimed, as she heard the guard approaching. 'Call Mr. Draper, he is in the sick room. My poor child will die unless she is relieved.'

Mr. Nardley hurriedly obeyed her instructions, and in a few moments the physician was beside the prostrate girl. He applied restoratives, and rubbed and chafed her hands and temples. It was some time before Mary gave any signs of returning life. Slowly she opened her eyes and motioned her lips. Mrs. Gaunt bent over her to catch the sound. 'William' was the only word she could understand.

'Take me from here, Mrs. Gaunt,' she faintly whispered, 'I shall die.'

Dr. Draper, who was through with his morning visit, proposed to take the two females home in his carriage, which offer was gladly accepted by Mrs. Gaunt.

When they reached the door of Mrs. Gaunt's cottage, the blind girl was able to walk to her bed. Bunyan was awaiting his daughter's return, having concluded to take Mary with him to see his old friend, Mr. Kiffin. He was horror-struck at her changed look. He clasped her in his arms, and placed her on the bed, and bent over her with all the tenderness of his heart, chafing her hands and smoothing back the hair from the clammy forehead.

As soon as she slept, he stole away to ask of Mrs. Gaunt the cause. She told him all.

'Ah, poor William!' he exclaimed, as she concluded her recital, 'and my poor child! she will never recover from this stroke. God is going to visit me again with trial. May he give me grace to bear me through, and to glorify his name in all my afflictions.'

He had but finished speaking, when the sound of loud voices was heard at the door, and in a moment more, two men entered the front room.

'Is this Mrs. Elizabeth Gaunt?' one of them asked, approaching the terrified woman.

'Yes, that is my name.'

'By the authority of this good commonwealth I arrest you, Mrs. Gaunt, for harboring rebels.'

She spoke not, but stood gazing at the men who addressed her, as one bewildered.

'Who gave you information, men, against this poor woman?' asked Bunyan.

'John Burton, his wife, and daughter, whom she has harbored these past three days.'

Bunyan remonstrated and entreated. But the hard-hearted men remained unmoved.

'We don't let such birds loose, I tell you, old man, and you needn't stand there talking. Come, come, woman, there's no time to be lost. Get on your hood, and come along, or else we'll take you as you are.'

Mrs. Gaunt obeyed. She saw any opposition was useless. Commending Bunyan and Mary to God, she bade them farewell, and left with the officers.

She was hurried before the tribunal, questioned, and sent to Newgate. In less than four hours after she and Mary left the prison with Dr. Draper, she was an inmate of the cell William Dormer had occupied.

CHAPTER XLIV.

'OH that I could go, father—that I could once more hear his voice!' was the burning exclamation of Mary as she fell upon the bosom of her parent.

They had been speaking of William Dormer's removal West, in order to his trial.

The obstacles in the way of such an undertaking were very great. Besides, there was no assurance that the father and daughter would reach Salisbury before a trial had taken place, and probably an execution. This was the father's apprehension, but he did not name it to his poor blind child. Her weight of grief was now overwhelming, he would not add another pang.

Bunyan had not encouraged Mary in her oft-repeated wish. But now that he fully understood how earnest was her desir e, he hesitated no longer.

'And you shall go, my child, and may God grant his blessing,' he said, while he strained the weeping girl to his breast, and the tears coursed down his face. 'I will go with you, my daughter. We must do what we can, and leave the result with Him who ordereth all things according to his wisdom. And we must lose no time, my child. It will not do to delay.'

Necessary preparation was hastily made, and Bunyan and his blind girl set out on their journey.

Long and weary were the miles over which they passed on their journey westward. But the hope of once more meeting William buoyed up Mary under the arduous travel. This gave courage to her heart, and strength to her feeble step, as on and on they went.

On and on they went, 'neath the scorching rays of an August sun. Mary felt no fatigue. The father endeavored all the while to stay the heart of his daughter in the precious promises of the gospel, thereby to prepare her for whatever might await her in the future. But the state of her mind was such that she could not lay hold on these words of eternal life and love. She could not think ; she could only hope and fear alternately. The father believed that there was but little prospect for William's acquittal, and he could not raise expectations which he felt must assuredly fail.

Ah! it was a heavy task for a loving father's heart. But Bunyan recognised that it was God who afflicted, and was still.

They had had a fatiguing day, sometimes riding, and then again finding their way on foot, striving by all possible means to hasten onward. They were now near Salisbury. Mary was seated beside her father in a small wagon, into which they had been asked by the kindness of a peasant, who, observing the weary condition of the sightless girl, and understanding whither they were bound, offered to take them to their destination.

Bunyan longed to enter into conversation with the peasant. He wished to ask him the news of the place—whether the prisoners had been taken to Salisbury, and if there had been any executions. But he dared not do it, lest, if the intelligence should be adverse, Mary might sink under it, away from any means of assistance. And the poor girl's heart was busting to ask, but she feared to do so.

They had rode in silence for some distance, each engaged in thought, when suddenly Mary laid her hand on her father, and turning her sealed eyes up to his, exclaimed:

'Father, do you think William is yet alive?'

'I can't say, my child, but I will ask this man. He will be likely to know.' And elevating his voice, he addressed the driver:

'Do you know whether any prisoners have reached Salisbury from London?'

'Yes, there were five brought down here last week.'

'And are they in prison?' asked Bunyan, tremblingly.

'They are still there, for they haven't yet had their trial. I heard to-day, as I came through the town, that they were all to be taken to Dorchester to be tried there.'

'They haven't had a trial then?' remarked Bunyan, in a manner as indifferent as he could assume. His heart was filled with joy to know that William yet lived.

'No, not yet.'

'Thank God!' Mary exclaimed, involuntarily rising from her seat. She felt that William could yet live. She would plead for his life, and surely, they could not resist her earnest appeals.

'Look to God in thankfulness,' said her father to her. 'It is a grant of mercy, my child, that William still lives.'

Then, turning to the man, he asked:

'When are the prisoners to be taken to Dorchester for trial—did you say?'

'In a few days more; may be to-morrow. I don't know

certainly, but they told me in Salisbury this morning it would be soon. All the town was in excitement, sir, when these rebels were brought in. The people wanted to hang them without a trial, and it was hard to keep them from it, I tell you.'

The heart of Mary sunk, and her cheek blanched as these words fell on her ear.

'There is but little hope then,' she said to herself, while her heart almost ceased its beating at the dreadful thought.

The father made no further remarks, and again the two were silent.

'Take us to the inn, friend, if you please,' said Bunyan, in reply to the peasant's inquiry.

The man nodded assent, and soon he landed them before the door of a heavy old building bearing the sign of the 'Cross and Dragon.'

Mary shuddered, as, seated in the large front-room of the inn, she heard the loud voices of the inmates of the tap-room in a discussion with regard to the fate of the prisoners. Some contended they would be hung without any possibility of escape; others declared that they ought to be burnt at the stake; others, that they should be gibbeted, and hung as malcontents. Various were the opinions expressed as to the manner of their execution, but all concurred in the opinion that they deserved death. There was much excitement—each man striving to be loudest and most violent in his denunciations of the rebels.

Bunyan sought the face of his Mary. It was very pale. For a moment he knew not what to do. To stay there was torture to her. She was too faint to walk in the streets. Where to find security from the angry voices he knew not. At last he resolved they would venture into the room to see if he could by any means put an end to the matter. Even his stout heart hesitated to take the step. It was a dangerous one, for infuriated men are always unreasonable, and their indignation was greatly increased by large potations from the ale-jug. He rose, reached the door leading into the tap-room—hesitated. Just then a noise attracted his attention at the further end of the room. He turned to look. Two female figures, clad in deep mourning, entered. He eyed them closely for a moment. Yes, it must be them; he could not be mistaken. He approached them. The foremost one started back in surprise as he stood before her.

'And it is surely you, brother Bunyan?' she said, in a tone of wonder. 'Pray tell us why you are here?'

He thought of his poor, suffering child. He knew her sensitiveness, and forbore a direct answer; but leading them forward, he introduced them to Mary. She looked up, surprised, while a faint hue overspread her pale cheek.

It was all understood. No further question as to the presence of the two parties was necessary.

'We go to prison to see my brothers,' the younger female said, in a sweet sad voice. ' We have not seen William and Benjamin since they were made prisoners.'

'And can you gain admittance?' asked Bunyan eagerly.

'We are not sure, brother Bunyan,' answered the mother. ' We have not yet made an effort. But we hope the Lord will prosper us. It would be hard for my darling boys to die without my seeing them once more.'

'We will go with you, sister Hewling. We want to see our friend, William Dormer. Come, my child,' he said, taking hold of Mary's hand, 'can you walk to the gaol?'

'Oh yes, father,' she answered. They were the first cheerful words she had spoken since she had heard of her lover's capture.

They asked the way to the prison, and were told it was situated not far distant from the inn.

The four started, and they had no difficulty in finding the object of their search. Since the prisoners had reached Salisbury, the old gaol had been a point of intense interest to every villager, from the oldest to the youngest.

It was the 30th of August, 1685—now nearly two centuries ago—that this little company of the sorrow-stricken children of God sought, mid the damp and noisomeness of the prison, those who were to bear testimony, even unto death, of their love to Christ Jesus and his glorious gospel. The sun was descending the western horizon as they passed along the streets of the old town of Salisbury. Their appearance attracted the attention of the villagers, and various were the surmises as to who they were. It was evident they were burdened with some great grief. The deep mourning of two of the females, the pale sad face of the blind girl, and the bowed head of the father, all betokened this—and prying curiosity dared not so far intrude itself as to ask the cause of their sorrow.

They reached the prison, and made their request known. There was hesitation and consultation. The hearts of the applicants grew faint as they stood waiting for an answer. At length a man dressed in the garb of a prison-officer appeared, holding in his hand a bunch of old keys, and told them they might enter.

With shuddering, the females followed the steps of the man along the dark and narrow passage which conducted them to a little yard, around which the prison cells were built.

'You want to see the prisoners that came down from London last week, do you?' said the coarse rough man, stopping suddenly before a row of narrow cells and turning squarely round upon the visitors.

'Yes,' Bunyan replied. 'The three young men.'

'Were two of them brothers? I believe they are in here—and the other is farther on. Do you wish to see all of them?'

'We want to see the two brothers. This young lady here, in black, and myself,' replied Mrs. Hewling.

'Well, you must see them one at a time. Then come in here and see this one, while this old man and girl go to the other cell. But I can't tell what she wants to go for— she can't see when she gets there,' and he looked on Mary with his little grey eyes most contemptuously.

The door swung back; the females entered. There on a low couch, by the faint rays of light struggling through the closely barred window, they beheld the form of the son and brother.

'Benjamin!—William!' the mother exclaimed, falling upon his neck and bursting into a flood of tears.

'My mother!—my sister!' It was the voice of William, her youngest son.

'Oh! William, my dear brother!' And the sister, too, fell weeping on the neck of the prisoner.

'Weep not, my dear mother; and you, my dear Hannah, dry your tears. I suffer for God, and he hath most abundantly rewarded me in the bestowment of his grace and comfort to my soul. I can glory in my afflictions, for Christ doth manifest himself to me in a most precious manner.'

'And your poor brother Benjamin! William, how is he?'

'Weak in body, mother, for we suffered much while we were in Newgate, and on our way here, being loaded with heavy irons; but, thank God, he is happy in mind— entirely resigned to his will, saying: "Life or death— anything which pleaseth God—what he sees best, so be it."'

'When did you see him last, my son?'

'Only a short time ago, mother, in the court-yard. We are allowed a half-hour, morning and evening for exercise, and then we talk over these glorious prospects to each other, and try to strengthen one another in our most holy faith.'

'Blessed be God, for this great mercy,' exclaimed the mother and sister, growing composed under the calm words of the prisoner.

'And is there any hope for you, my boy?'

'But little in this life, mother. I do not believe we shall be pardoned. But there is all hope of the life to come; for there joy and eternal blessedness await us at the right hand of God.'

They remained a few moments longer in conversation, when the turnkey appeared and told them they must now see the other young man, if they wished to, for it was late, and they could not stay much longer.

Bidding William an affectionate farewell, with the hope of seeing him again on the morrow, they followed the turnkey to the older brother's cell.

They found him, as William had said—calm, yea, rather joyous, that he was counted worthy to suffer.

While we leave the mother and sister with the prisoner, let us follow Mary and her father to the cell of William Dormer.

Clingingly Mary held on to her father as they proceeded along the narrow alley to the cell of the lover. They reached it. The man applied the key, and the ponderous bolt flew back.

'A man and lassie from London wish to see you, prisoner,' said the man, gruffly.

Bunyan entered and accosted William. He immediately recognised the voice, and returned the salutation. Then, springing forward, 'Mary!' he exclaimed and caught her to his bosom.

For a minute all was silent, save the weeping of the lovers as they stood folded in each other's arms.

The man locked the door and left them to themselves.

As soon as the first passion of grief was over, Bunyan tried to calm the prisoner and Mary by engaging them in conversation. He did not allude to the probable results of a trial. He knew that the bleeding heart of his Mary could not bear it. He inquired into William's physical and spiritual condition, and gave to him the encouragements of the Word of God, which had been to him such a solace when imprisonment enwrapped him in its gloom, and death stared him in the face.

Mary sat beside William—her hand rested in his, and

her sweet, sad face, now so pale and worn with grief, was turned, with a look of deepest love and sympathy, up to his. He gazed upon it—now so changed—and the tears gathered in his eyes and coursed down his manly cheek.

'My dear Mary,' he said, 'the hand of God is heavy upon us. But whom he loveth, he chasteneth. We must not forget that God is good, though he deals so mysteriously with us.'

'That is the true view of the case, William,' responded the father. 'God's ways are hid in the infinite depths of his wisdom, and we cannot find him out by searching. Our business is to know that he is God and be still.'

Mary could not speak, she could only weep. She did not see how it could be best that William should die. Her heart rebelled against the thought. How could she ever submit? 'My grace is sufficient' was not her stay 'mid her agony. It was a sore temptation.

William asked for Mrs. Gaunt. Bunyan had to break to him the sad story. He wept like a child as he heard of the sufferings of one whom he loved as a mother.

'These are times of sore visitation, brother Bunyan,' he said. I don't know what to think. It seems as if the hand of God is turned against his people. Surely Mrs. Gaunt is a good woman, and deserves to be rewarded here if ever a woman did.'

'Say not, William, that the hand of God is against his children,' replied the man of God. 'We must know that "all things," whatever they may be, whether tribulation, or persecution, or death, work together for the good of his people. In eternity we shall know it all. Now we must trust and pray that he will keep us pure and unspotted from the world, and make us willing to bear all things for his name.'

The three knelt, and Bunyan led in prayer. From the depths of his tried soul he poured out a petition before the throne of the Great Mediator for grace, and support, and submission to the Divine will. Then with words of encouragement and comfort he spoke to William and Mary, and entreated them to prepare for the worst.

Mary's whole frame shook with fear as the thought of death came up before her. Her father saw it would not do to pursue the subject.

There was a pause. Mary raised her thin, pale hands, and passed them gently over William's face, scrutinising with intensest accuracy every feature.

'Changed, changed,' she murmured to herself, as if unconscious of what she did.

'Yes, Mary, changed in appearance, but not in heart.'

She turned her face to his. It was beaming with love. He never forgot that look. Sleeping or waking, that sad face with its love look was ever before him. 'Oh, could he but live for her!' was the unheard ejaculation of his heart. 'Yet not my will, Father, but thine.'

A step was heard. They knew its meaning. Bunyan rose, and commending William to God bade him farewell, promising to return the next day.

Mary threw herself weeping upon his neck. He could not speak. The turnkey opened the cell door and asked the visitors to depart. Mary uttered a wild shriek as she tore herself from William. Her father caught her in his arms and bore her from the cell.

'Only once more, father, let me hear his voice and feel his breath upon my cheek.'

The father looked at the gaoler. Great tears were in his eyes. He asked not permission to return, but led his daughter back through the door into the cell.

Mary passed her hand once more over William's face and leaned on his bosom, then taking his hands in hers she held them close and long.

Unobserved she drew from her bosom a small pair of scissors, and passing her hand to his head she quickly severed a lock of chestnut hair. It was the work of but a moment.

'It is all I shall have left, William,' she said. Then bidding him farewell, she turned to her father, who bore her from the prison.

They never met more on earth. Once again Mary heard his voice. It was in reply to the questions of the Judge.

CHAPTER XLV.

THE TRIAL.

WOULD that we could throw a veil over the dark page of history which now follows. Would that the rage of the persecutors could have been satisfied with the punishment already inflicted. But they were insatiable, and nothing but death could answer their cruel desires.

The prisoners were removed in a few days from Salisbury

to Dorchester, there to be tried. Ah, what mockery to call such a farce a trial. The case had been heard, the jury instructed, verdict rendered, and sentence of death passed, before the prisoners were arraigned at the bar. What hope, then, for life?

Repeated efforts were made by the friends of William Dormer, to gain access to him during his stay at Dorchester, both before and after the trial, but all in vain. The hard hearts of those who had authority would not relent. They gloated on the misery they were inflicting.

The 8th of September came. It was the day of trial for William Hewling and William Dormer and others, Benjamin Hewling having been sent to Taunton.

At an early hour the room was filled. There sat the judges, with iron brows and adamantine hearts. The hour of trial came. The prisoners, in their prison garb, with pale faces and emaciated frames, bearing on their hands and ankles the marks of the heavy irons with which they had been bound, were marched in under guard and seated on the prisoners' bench. Their calm, collected mien, their pleasant, yea, joyous countenances, their wasted bodies, all conspired to enlist for them the sympathies of the by-standers.

To all questions addressed to them they answered with cheerful voice, in no way endeavoring to extenuate their conduct. Every effort was made to induce them to express regret for their past course. But they would not. Politely and respectfully they replied that they had done what they believed to be right in the sight of God. They had fought for the interest of England, thereby endeavoring to secure to her religious freedom.

When asked if they would repent their crime if opportunity offered, they answered they could not fail at all times to discharge what they conscientiously believed to be their duty, and were they placed at liberty they would never hesitate, God being their helper, to do what they believed to be right.

This reply so exasperated the mob that many of them cried out, 'Away with them! Away with them to the block! They deserve to die.'

But none of these things daunted them. They counted not their lives dear. They were willing to make any sacrifice for Jesus, the Great Captain of their salvation.

Just after the trial had commenced, and while the prisoners were being asked general questions, a commotion was observed near the entrance door. Soon an elderly man

was observed, supporting on his arm the frail form of a
lovely girl, followed by two female figures clad in deepest
mourning. Making their way through the crowd, they
proceeded up the aisle or open way, until they stood just
behind the prisoners' bench.

They were Bunyan and his daughter Mary, and the
mother and the sister of the Hewlings. One by one the
prisoners were tried personally. They all bore the same
witness.

Finally, it came to William Dormer's turn. He stood up
when commanded, and looked the Judge in the face. His
replies, like the others, were characterised by calmness and
adherence to his cause. He knew not as yet that she whom
he loved listened to his every word.

'Prisoner, have you anything to say in extenuation of
your crime against our most gracious king and the good of
this realm?' asked the king's attorney, a short, thick set
man, with piercing eye and countenance fierce with hate.

'I have nothing,' answered William Dormer, unmoved,
his eye fixed steadily on his cruel interrogator.

'And won't you say you are sorry for what you have
done?' The attorney's voice rose with his anger until he
could be heard all over the house.

'I cannot say I am sorry. That would be to lie before
God and these people.'

'What, you don't mean to say, you rebel, you, that you
acted right, and would do the same thing over again?'

'This is my belief,' and William stood erect with steadfast gaze. Not a muscle of his face moved. He stood in
conscious integrity, and neither the frowns of the Judge
nor the hisses of the people could intimidate him.

'Well, then, you must meet your fate,' retorted the
infuriated attorney, delighted that it was in his power to
be revenged.

A short, stifled moan burst from the blind girl. The
father urged her to leave, but she could not. With that
strange fascination of dread which often seizes the human
heart, she remained riveted to the spot.

'Take your seat.' The prisoner obeyed. The next prisoner
came forward. It was William Hewling, the last of the
number tried that day. The same round of questions
was put to him, and the same answers received as before.
No menaces, no fear of death, could cause to hesitate for a
moment these brave soldiers of the cross of Christ. They
knew the Captain of their salvation, and they entrusted all
into his hands, feeling assured that he would bring them off

conquerors and make them triumphant over all their foes.

Low, subdued weeping was heard in that part of the room where the friends of the prisoner sat. The jury retired after having received instructions from the judge.

After a few moments' consultation they returned with a verdict of ' *Guilty.*' The judge commanded the prisoners to stand up before him. He then, in a manner of solemn mockery, pronounced the sentence of condemnation upon each of the young men before him.

A loud shriek was heard as he called the name of William Dormer. Mary had fainted and fallen from her seat. Her father, with the assistance of another, took her up and bore her to the court-room.

William had heard the voice and recognised it. He turned ; all that his eye met was the lifeless form of Mary borne through the crowd. A heavy groan burst from his heart.

Deep and solemn was the feeling throughout that large assemblage, as the prisoners, so youthful yet so firm for the right, were conducted from the stand to the prison. Groans were heard throughout the house, and many a tear of pity flowed from eyes that had long been dry.

CHAPTER XLVI.

THE EXECUTION.

POOR Mary ! All hope was now gone for ever, and her heart bowed beneath its weight of anguish never again to rise. Her sensitive nature had received a shock from which it could never recover. Her father saw it and was sad. Surely the chastening hand of God was ever upon him. From the depths of his distress he cried out in the bitterness of his spirit, ' How long, O Lord, how long ? ' He had suffered greatly from want, from imprisonment, from persecution, calumny, and yet all these seemed light afflictions compared with the great sorrow which he saw was ready to burst over him. He prayed as he had so often done before, ' Father, thy will, not mine, only let me have thy grace and presence near.'

Mary was borne from the court room to the inn, where she received all attention from her father and the kind landlady, Mrs. Summers. As soon as she was sufficiently

recovered, her father proposed to her to leave for Bedford.
But she would not consent.

'O father, dear father, let me stay,' she pleaded in her
sweet earnest voice. 'Oh let me stay until all is over. It
may be I can get to see him once more, and if I could I
would die in peace. Father, let me stay.'

The tender heart of the father could not deny her
request. He knew the hard-heartedness of those who
held William in confinement would for ever bar the
prison doors against them, but he would not undeceive his
daughter.

'It will be but a few days until all is over, but if it will
be any gratification to you, my child, we will stay.'

'Do, father, do,' was all the prostrate girl could say.

The father watched over his frail child with all the
anxious solicitude of his great and loving heart, assisted
by Hannah Hewling, whose tenderness to Mary on this
occasion was never forgotten by Bunyan. Mrs. Hewling left
Dorchester to return to London the morning after the trial,
hoping to effect something with the king in behalf of her
condemned son. The sister remained behind to solace and
comfort him.

On the second day after the trial, and three days before
the execution, Mary was strong enough to leave her room.
She insisted on being carried to the prison where William
was. Her father assured her it was useless to make application for admittance, as he had been twice refused on the
previous day. But she urged her suit with such earnestness, that, to gratify her, he consented. Trembling from
feebleness she stepped into the carriage which stood in
waiting for them at the door. When they reached the
prison-gate they were encountered by a fierce, savage
looking man, who told them they could not get in.

'Just this once, sir, this once,' pleaded Mary.

'No, I tell you, you cannot get in. I have my instructions,
and I dare not. It's no use for you to stand there asking
me. I would lose my head if I disobeyed orders.'

'Oh let us see some officer—some one who has authority
to let us in,' said Mary, in the agony of her soul.

'It's no use, I tell you, it's no use. The laws are strict,
and can't be disobeyed. You can't get in.'

Bunyan knew not what to say. He saw the futility of
making farther effort, yet how could he tell his daughter
there was no hope?

'Oh! can't we get in?' said the poor, blind girl, in a
tone of despair.

'No! I tell you, no!' And the man turned round and walked away.

Mary fell into the arms of her father as one suddenly deprived of life. He bore her to the inn.

Two days after this event, William Dormer, William Hewling, and two others, were removed from Dorchester to Lyme for execution.

The 13th of September, 1685, came—that day so long remembered in the west of England as being the day on which 'the young Monmouth rebels' met their sad fate with so much courage and brave resignation.

The sun rose bright and beautiful. It mourned not over the sad scene. Nature was calm and peaceful. The serene, smiling heavens, and the beautiful, quiet earth, gave no intimation of sympathy with the sad and sorrowing hearts of her children.

At an early hour the gibbet was erected. Throngs assembled from every part of the street to witness the dreadful scene. It was a dreadful picture thus to see men, women, and children, gathered together to gaze on a spectacle so revolting.

The prisoners, shaven and attired in clean garbs, emerged from the prison gate-way under the escort of a guard of armed soldiers.

Their youthful appearance—their calm, yet courageous bearing—their expression of joyous resignation, all conspired to excite for them the deepest admiration.

Lamentations and cries of sorrow burst from the multitude as they moved onward towards the fatal spot. But none of these things moved those youthful witnesses for the truth as it is in Christ Jesus. Their minds were fixed on heaven and heavenly things. By the eye of faith they were gazing on the unseen glories of that blessed state of rest, on which they were so soon to enter. Christ was with them. He, the Elder Brother, who had gone before to prepare for each a mansion, had now sent for them that where he was they might be also.

They reached the scaffold. The hangman stood ready to do his dreadful work. The first who suffered was William Dormer. When he reached the platform he stood for a few minutes to address the multitude, who hung eagerly on his words. He assured them of his willingness to die—of his firm belief that he died for the cause of religious liberty, and the best weal of his unhappy country. He declared his strict adhesion to his principles, and his firm faith in the promises of God, exhorting his fellow sufferers not to waver or falter, for God would stand by them to give them strength. He then besought the multitude to look to the Lord Jesus Christ and be saved. His countenance was radiant with the truths he taught. It was evident that he had no fear. The crowd wept audibly.

Kneeling, he spent a few moments in prayer, in which he commended his spirit to God, earnestly supplicating that he would stand by those who this day were to witness for him with their blood, and to bless those, who, like the maddened Jews, knew not what they did.

The cap was adjusted—the rope placed—a moment more, and William Dormer was in eternity.

William Hewling was next to suffer. He had seen but nineteen years. His exceedingly youthful appearance and bold, courageous faith, awoke for him a lively interest. Many wished he could be spared so awful a fate. But he answered them that he would not exchange situations with any one in this world. ‘I would not stay behind for ten thousand worlds!’

Like William Dormer, he knelt and prayed for his enemies, and for the presence of God to support him and his friends. Then, rising from his knees, he exclaimed: ‘Oh, now my joy and comfort is that I have a Christ to go to!’ And with a sweet smile on his countenance, he willingly submitted to his fate.

The three remaining prisoners were soon dispatched. The work of death was over. The crowd dispersed. A record of this day's proceedings was made on high.

CHAPTER XLVII.

DARKNESS GATHERS.

‘Man, born of woman, is of few days and full of trouble.’—JOB.

THE arrow had found its mark. It had pierced the heart of the victim, never to be removed until death should end the suffering.

Mary and her father remained at Dorchester until after the execution of William Dormer. She would have it so. The father knew it would prove a fearful trial to his child, as the exaggerated descriptions of the death-scene must necessarily meet her ears; but she pleaded with such earnestness he could not refuse. She wished to know all—

even the very worst. To her mind dread reality was preferable to torturing suspense. Bunyan endeavored to sustain her with the promises of the eternal God, but in her present state of nervous excitement it appeared impossible for her to lay hold on them. She knew that God's dealings with her were wise and good; but oh, to feel submissive to his will, when that will deprived her of the dearest object earth contained—it was hard—too hard for her feeble faith.

And how often it is thus with us. How often faith grows so faint that we cannot look up, nor beyond the present evil. We feel forsaken of all—and help there is none. We fear our Father hath forgotten us, and earth and hell have leagued against us. But God hath not forgotten to be gracious. Our Elder Brother, ' touched with a feeling of our infirmities,' is near, and when the waters gather round us, when we are ' ready to perish,' his hand, though unseen, supports us still, and delivers us from the swelling flood.

' It is all over now, father. I can do no more, and we must go home,' said Mary to her father, after the first violent shock, consequent upon the intelligence of William Dormer's death, had passed away.

And the two made ready and set out on their sorrowful return.

The light of love and hope had gone out in Mary's bosom, and life was now far darker to her once bright and happy heart than was ever the outer world to her sealed eyes.

She did not murmur. Her grief was too deep for complaint. Her voice, once so cheerful, had sunk into a sad monotone, which pierced her father's heart to hear. The rose had faded from her cheek, the sweet smile died out from her lips, and her step, once so light and buoyant, had become heavy and sluggish. Sighs proceeding from the pent-up agony of her bosom escaped her whenever she thought there was no one near to listen.

For the sake of her dear father, whom she knew suffered so intensely on her account, she strove to hide her grief. But oh, how vain the effort. It had written itself in unmistakeable lines on every lineament of her lovely face —in every movement of her fragile form.

The father looked upon her as day by day she listlessly traced the long and weary way to Bedford, and his heart was seized with dreadful forebodings. From the dawn of her being she had been his earthly idol. He had loved her for her very helplessness, which had caused her to cling so closely to him. He had seen her struggles to support the family during his imprisonment, and while she was yet scarce twelve years of age. He had watched her development into womanhood with feelings of deep gratitude to God for such a precious gift; and then when God, according to his purpose, and of his sovereign love and mercy, begat her a new life in Christ Jesus, the bond of union became stronger and dearer. Their souls were knitted together by indissoluble ties.

Bunyan had hoped and expected that Mary would survive him. He had been thankful when she made a selection of William Dormer, as a companion for life, for he felt that in him she would have a kind friend and noble protector.

But now William was gone. He had suffered an ignominious death, and the blow that laid him low had also reached the heart of his darling Mary.

How fully his bowed soul realised, as he trod the weary miles of his return, that man's days are full of trouble. Sorrow after sorrow had fallen upon him since the time he had forsaken the world to follow Jesus. 'In the world ye shall have tribulation.' It is the inheritance of the children of the Most High.

On the fourth day after the setting out from Dorchester, they reached the little cottage-home at Elstow. The mother and Sarah could scarcely refrain from an exclamation of surprise as they beheld the changed appearance of Mary. They bore her to a seat (for she was weary and worn), and ministered to her comfort. They needed not to question The sad tale was too plainly told in that pale, meek face, and that hopeless voice. Joseph came in from his day's engagements. He was startled as he beheld his sister, and would have questioned as to her altered looks, but his father motioned him to be silent. The little ones around the hearth-stone looked on — their childish hearts filled with wonder and mystery as they beheld the strange sad scene.

No questions were asked in Mary's presence. Not the most distant allusion was made to the painful subject. They would spare the fading lily each rude blast. But eye spoke to eye the language of the heart, and that language was one of deep, dark dread.

The evening meal was spread and silently dispatched. There rested over that once glad household a feeling of sad foreboding. It was the hushed stillness which precedes the fearful storm.

Evening closed in. Around the altar of prayer the afflicted family gathered. As once before, when sorrow encompassed him, the man of God read the ninetieth psalm: ' O Lord, thou hast been our dwelling-place in all generations. Before the mountains were brought forth, or ever thou hadst formed the earth and the world, even from everlasting to everlasting, thou art God,' etc. When he had finished reading, Bunyan made a few remarks on the immortality of God, his nature and promises, and exhorted his little family to trust Him who was the same for ever, knowing no variableness nor shadow of turning.

A hymn was sung, but Mary did not join in singing. She sat as was her wont beside her father, her hand resting on his knee ; but her lips were sealed, and her pale face wore a look of hopeless agony. They bowed around the altar. Once, during the fervent prayer, allusion was made to the scenes just passed through. A low sob burst from Mary's aching bosom. A moment more and all was still, save the father's pleading voice.

Be firm, and trust in God, my child,' was all the father could say, as he imprinted the good-night kiss on the marble brow. The mother and Sarah accompanied her to bed, their hearts breaking to see the poor girl's sufferings, and they longed in some way, if possible, to alleviate them. Every little kindness that their anxious hearts could suggest was bestowed, and at another time their deep solicitude and kindly offices would have been repaid by many a sweet smile and grateful word—but now Mary could not smile. It was to her a sacrilege, and words of thanks a very mockery.

The mother, after seeing the last offices performed necessary to render her comfortable for the night—bent over her pillow and imprinted a tender kiss upon her cheek. ' God bless you, my child,' she said, and turned away with streaming eyes.

CHAPTER XLVIII.

ELIZABETH GAUNT.

ERECT the stake ! Bring the straw ! Pile high the faggots ! See the cords are strong ! Bind the unhappy victim ! Let the loud shout of the infuriated multitude deafen the heavens while the work of death goes on.

Why all this fearful preparation ? Why this wild rush
of incensed people? Why this vast assemblage at Tyburn,
on October 23rd, 1685 ?

It is the execution-day of Elizabeth Gaunt. And for
what is she to die ? For this : She ignorantly harbored a
man, John Burton, who was accused of being engaged in
the Rye-house plot. A wretch, who, under the cloak of
Nonconformity, had gained shelter under her hospitable
roof, and then with that unparalleled meanness which
characterises the vile and cowardly, turned king's evidence,
and arraigned before the heartless Jeffries, the woman who
had saved his life and protected him and his family when
fugitives from justice. Base, ignoble creature ! Merciless
judge ! Infuriated rabble ! Day of fearful retribution !

See ! there she comes, guarded by those savage-looking
men. Her face is pale and wan, and her steps slow. She
has been above a month in prison, and no one has ministered to her as she was always wont to do to those in prison
who were hungry and naked. Like the great proto-martyr,
even the Lord Jesus, her mien is meek and humble, for
she bears within her bosom that same spirit which was
also in Christ Jesus. The jeers, and taunts, and gibes of
the crowd fall on her ear. She reviles not again, but
rather prays, ' Lord, lay it not to their charge.'

Slowly she moves along, wearing her prisoner's garb,
and on her head a clean, white cap. She heeds not the
multitude that crowd around her, each eager to catch a
glimpse of the unhappy victim. Her thoughts are with
God, to whom she commends her spirit, and whose forgiveness she seeks for those who are shamefully going to
put her to death.

' Make way! make way !' the guards shout as the wild,
restless mob close up the avenue leading to the fearful
stake.·

' Make way ! make way !' is repeated in fiercer tones of
command, and the prisoner under escort moves on through
the narrow aisle, made by the densely crowded ranks,
towards the heap of straw and faggots. Many there are
in that vast assembly moved to tears at her Christian
bearing, and the heavenly expression of fortitude which
marks her countenance, while others shout, in fiendish
malice, ' Let the traitor die! God save the king ! '

She reaches the stake, and, quietly folding her hands
across her bosom, submits, without a word of complaint, to
be bound thereto. The men perform their work with jests
and bursts of savage laughter. She heeds it not. She

looks to God for aid in this her hour of death. Her countenance is serene, over it there plays a look of heavenly light which strikes with awe the crowd of spectators.

The work of fastening is done. She speaks not, nor looks affrighted as the men approach the pile with lighted torches.

As they are about to apply fire to the heap she looks pityingly upon them, and the petition, ' Father, lay it not to their charge,' escape her lips. Then, casting a glance on the vast multitude of curious faces gazing upon her, ' Father, forgive them—they know not what they do!' she prays, and closes her eyes. The pile is lighted. Slowly it burns at first. But see! the straw and light wood have caught! Now the crackling flames mount higher and, higher. They have reached the hem of her garment. Already are her feet enveloped in the fiery sheet. Will the martyr cry for aid as the heat cinders her limbs? Ah, no! See her there—calm and collected--looking to Jesus.

How beautiful with divine trust is that placid face, which knows no contraction or writhing, though the flames have reached her waist and are every moment becoming hotter and hotter. What meekness in that attitude, fettered as is the poor, consuming body, and what heavenly pity in those eyes as they are bent on the eager mass about her.

Look! She moves. Has her stay failed her?—and is she striving to loose herself from her tortures. Ah, no! God's grace is sufficient. She is only adjusting the straw about her that the horrid work of death may be the sooner over.

The crowd gaze upon her, awe-struck. How is it that a timid woman can thus add to her tortures? Hear her answer: 'I can bear all things through Christ, who strengtheneth me.' Ah! this is it—Christ's right arm to support. His loving voice to whisper words of cheer. ' To-day thou shalt be with me in Paradise.' Hundreds weep at this manifestation of heavenly fortitude. But the martyr is alike insensible to their tears as to their jests and taunts. ' Behold I see,' said the martyr Stephen, ' the heavens opened, and the Son of Man standing on the right hand of God.' Has she not a glimpse of the same glorious vision?

Higher and higher ascend the raging fires, until soon the whole body is enshrouded in an intensely glaring, flame sheet. Tears of wonder and horror are streaming down the faces of the spectators. Such a sight has never before been witnessed by any present, for Elizabeth Gaunt is the first to suffer by fire during the reign of the wicked James.

Will she not now shriek and cry out with pain? See, the fires are all around. No. Not one word of complaint escapes her.

The three Hebrew children passed through the fires unhurt. The angel of the Lord was with them. And Elizabeth Gaunt went up to heaven from the faggot and the stake without betraying the least fear or suffering. The presence of the covenant angel sustained her.

A few moments more, and the work is done. The body, roasted and marred, is taken from the stake, while the affrighted spectators close their eyes in horror. She has witnessed for God, who is her everlasting portion, and now her spirit sings the song of Moses and the Lamb in the holy city—the new Jerusalem.

And did she leave no testimony behind save what she gave in her death? Let us turn from the stake to the prison-cell, in Newgate, where she was confined. Here is a folded paper, written by her own hand. Let us open and read:

'Not knowing whether I shall be suffered, or able, because of weaknesses that are upon me, through my hard and close imprisonment, to speak at the place of execution, I have written these few lines to signify that I am reconciled to the ways of my God towards me; though it is in ways I looked not for, and by terrible things, yet in righteousness; for having given me life, he ought to have the disposing of it, when and where he pleases to call for it. And I desire to offer up my all to him, it being my reasonable service, and also the first terms which Christ offers, that he who will be his disciple must forsake all and follow him. Therefore let none think it hard, or be discouraged at what hath happened unto me; for he hath done nothing without cause in all that he hath done unto me; he being holy in all his ways, and righteous in all his works, and it is but my lot in common with poor desolate Zion at this day.

'Neither do I find in my heart the least regret at anything I have done in the service of my Lord and Master, Jesus Christ, in securing and succoring any of his poor sufferers, that have showed favor, as I thought, to his righteous cause; which cause, though it be now fallen and trampled on, yet it may revive, and God may plead it at another time more than he hath ever yet done, with all its opposers and malicious haters. And therefore, let all that love and fear him not omit the least duty that comes to hand or lies before them, knowing that now Christ hath need of them, and expects they should serve him. And I desire to bless his holy name that he hath made me useful in my generation to the comfort and relief of many desolate ones; that the blessing of many who were ready to perish hath come upon me, and that I helped to make the widow's heart leap for joy.

'And I bless his holy name that in all this, together with what I was charged with, I can approve my heart to him, that I have done his will, though it may cross man's. The Scriptures which satisfy me are these: "Hide the outcasts; betray not him that wandereth. Let mine outcasts dwell with thee: be thou a covert to them from the face of the spoiler. Thou shouldst not have delivered up those of his that did remain in the day of distress." (Isa. xvi. 3, 4; Obad. 12, 13, 14.) But men say you must give them up, or die for it. Now whom to obey, judge ye. So that I have cause to rejoice and be exceeding glad, in that I "suffer for righteousness' sake," and that I am counted worthy to suffer "for well doing;" and that God hath accepted any service from me, which hath been done in sincerity, though mixed with manifold infirmities, which he hath been pleased for Christ's sake to cover and forgive.

'And now as concerning my crime, as it is now called; alas! it was but a little one, and such as might well become a prince to forgive. But he that shows no mercy shall find none; and I may say of it, in the language of Jonathan, "I did but taste a little honey, and lo, I must die for it"—I did but relieve an unworthy, poor, distressed family, and lo, I must die for it. Well, I desire in the lamb-like nature of the gospel to forgive those that are concerned; and to say, "Lord, lay it not to their charge!" But I fear he will not; nay, I believe, when he comes to make inquisition for blood, it will be found at the door of the furious judge, who, because I could not remember things through my daunted-ness (confusion) at Burton's wife and daughter's witness, and my ignorance, took advantage of it, and would not hear me when I called to mind that which I am sure would have invalidated the evidence. And though he granted something of the same kind to another, he denied it to me. At that time my blood will also be found at the door of the unrighteous jury, who found me guilty on the single oath of an outlawed man: for there was none but his oath about the money, who is no legal witness, though he be pardoned, his outlawry not being reversed, also the law requiring *two* witnesses in point of treason. As to my going with him to the place mentioned, namely, the Hope, it was by his own word before he could be outlawed, for it was about two months after his absconding. So that though he was in a proclamation, yet not for high treason, as I am informed; so that I am clearly murdered. And also bloody Mr. Atterbury, who had so insatiably hunted after my life, though it is no profit to him, yet through the ill will he bears me, left no stone unturned, as I have ground to believe, till he brought it to this, and showed favor to Burton, who ought to have died for his own fault, and not to have bought his own life with mine. Captain Richardson, who is cruel and severe to all under my circumstances, did, at that time, without any mercy or pity, hasten my sentence, and held up my hand that it might be given. All which, together with the great one of all (James II., who had just come to the throne, carrying on his brother's proceedings,) by whose power all these and multitudes more of cruelties are done, I do heartily and freely forgive as against me; but as it is done in an implacable mind against the Lord Jesus Christ, and his righteous cause and followers, I leave it to him who is the avenger of all such wrong, and " who will tread upon princes as upon mortar, and be terrible to the kings of the earth."

'Know this also, that though you are seemingly fixed, and because of the power in your hands are weighing out your violence, and dealing with a spiteful mind, because of the old and new hatred, by impoverishing and every way distressing those you have got under you; yet unless you can secure Jesus Christ, and also his holy angels, you shall never do your business, nor shall your hand accomplish your enterprise. He will be upon you ere you are aware; and therefore that you would be wise, instructed, and learn, is the desire of her that finds no mercy from you.

'ELIZABETH GAUNT.'

'P.S. Such as it is, you have from the hand of her who hath done as she could, and is sorry she can do no better; hopes you will pity, and consider, and cover weaknesses and shortness, and anything that is wanting; and begs that none may be weakened or stumble by my lowness of spirit; for God's design is to humble and abase, that he alone may be exalted in that day. And I hope he may appear in a needful time and hour, and it may be he will reserve the best wine till the last, as he hath done for some before me. None goeth a warfare at his own charges; but I may mourn, because I honor not more my God nor his blessed cause, which I have so long loved and delighted to serve; and repent of nothing but that I have served it and him no better.'

CHAPTER XLIX.

THE DEATH SCENE.

IN viewing life as it really is, aside from the gloss of the imagination, and the deceitful halo which earthly hope throws round it, we find more of sorrow than of joy. 'Man is of few days, and full of trouble.' This is the teaching of Holy Writ; the declaration of Him who created us; the sad, sad lesson of experience, which, sooner or later, all must know. And well it is for us, if we, as children, sit at the feet of Jesus to learn of him, so that when the storm shall come we shall find safe covert in his cleft side. The 'Lord uses his flail of tribulation

to separate the chaff from the wheat.' Happy is the man
who recognises his hand, and bows submissive to his
chastening rod.

> ' Frail flower! Earth's winds for thee too chill,
> Thou fadest here—to bloom in heaven.'

Throw open the windows! Let the glorious sunlight
of heaven look in upon the peaceful scene, and the rose
and hawthorn breathe their sweet fragrance round the
dying pillow.

The silver cord is loosing—the sands of life fast ebbing
away. Tread lightly! 'Tis a sacred, solemn hour. A
mortal is about to put on immortality—a captive to be
freed. A pilgrim stranger, who has long journeyed towards the heavenly city, is about to lay down the staff,
and exchange the tattered garments of earth for the
glorious vesture of heaven. Angels, on invisible wing,
are hovering over the scene. They wait to bear the ran-
somed soul, escaping from its house of clay, away from
earth—up, up, beyond the shining sun and the pale,
solemn stars, to the paradise of God. And as they wait,
they sing in sweet, soft strains that reach the dying ear,
choruses of heavenly melody. They sing of the pearly
gates of the New Jerusalem; its shining street; of the
' pure river of water, clear as crystal;' ' the throne of God
and the Lamb;' the ' tree of life;' of the redeemed clad
in robes of dazzling white; of cherubim and seraphim,
and God and the Lamb in the midst thereof. What
enrapturing strains! Wonder we that the sweet, calm
face, lights up with more than earthly beauty, and the
pale, quivering lips murmur, ' Come, Lord Jesus, come
quickly!'

The Master had called Mary Bunyan, and she had listed
his voice. So she went about putting her house in order,
that she might be ready for the change which awaited her.

She had been fading, through long weary months.
Ever since the fatal blow she had received in William
Dormer's death, the light of life had been waning. She
knew when the autumn flowers passed away that she had
looked upon them for the last time, and when ' merrie
Christmas' came with its sports and carols, and invited her
to its enjoyments, she turned not aside at its call of mirth;
she was journeying towards the heavenly city, with her
eye steadily fixed upon its ravishing glories. Could she,
for a moment forget them for the dull, cold scenes of earth?

Spring flowers bloomed. And nature, clad in all her gorgeous loveliness, enticingly wooed her to its banquet of beauty. But her pulse was slow now, and her step tottering, and she could only walk, supported by the arm of Sarah, across the little close in front of the house to the hawthorn beyond.

Her father saw with aching heart the slow and painful change. He did not deceive himself, as is often the case, with flattering hopes of the spring's recovering influences. He knew that his poor blind child, who had so bravely fought the fearful battle of life, was now about to lay aside the armor of warfare, to rest peacefully. And the mother, and sister, and brothers, too, were bowed beneath the fearful weight. Even the little ones had caught the fear, and their laugh was less ringing, and their footfall lighter, as they came into the presence of the pale, meek sufferer.

Frequent were the conversations of father and daughter on the subject of the approaching change. Bunyan spoke with unwavering faith of the promises of the gospel, and the dying girl's heart responded 'Amen.' The Spirit bore witness with her spirit that she was a child of God, an heir to all the promises.

It was a sweet fresh evening in May, that Mary, leaning on the arm of her faithful sister, walked to the hawthorn hedge, and seated herself beside it.

'O come, sister,' she said, in a sweet calm voice, 'for the last time to this little seat.' Her pale hand rested on the lap of Sarah, while the feeble head reclined against her bosom.

'O sister, you are not worse. What makes you talk to me so?' replied the loving girl. Yet her heart misgave her. She felt the sufferer's words were too true.

'I know it, Sarah, I know it. My days on earth are almost over. A few more hours of pain, and then I go away to Jesus.'

Sarah's heart was too full. She could make no reply. She pressed the invalid more tenderly to her bosom, while the tears streamed down her saddened face.

Bunyan came across the fields from Bedford, where he had been preaching. Approaching his daughters, he saw the change that had come over Mary.

'Come, children,' he said, 'we will go in. The air is getting damp, and Mary must not be exposed to it, lest she take cold.'

He gently raised her from her sister's bosom, and supported her slow, languid steps to the cottage door. She passed its threshold. It was the last time.

Gently the father placed her on her low cot, and tenderly he smoothed back the hair from her marble forehead, and chafed the attenuated hands, while the big tears stood in his sad, blue eyes.

Day by day fled by, until six were numbered. The dying girl suffered much, but no word of complaint escaped her. All that parental care and kind sympathy could suggest was done to alleviate her pain. The father was untiring in his watchfulness and attentions, and his words of heavenly instruction were a great stay to Mary's failing heart.

'Yes, yes, father,' she would say, as the old man would repeat to her the promises. 'I know these words are true. He will never leave nor forsake me. I once dreaded death, but now I find it has no sting. Jesus has removed it by suffering for me. I long to go to be with him, where I shall see him as he is. Father, don't you think I shall see in heaven?'

'Yes, my child, I do. There is no affliction there. You will look upon Jesus, for yourself; shall see him who died for you.'

'It is a glorious thought, father, that these poor eyes, that have so long been sealed, shall there see the King in his beauty. Oh, how I long to go! But I must wait patiently until my time comes,' she said, after a pause.

'It will not be long, my child,' said the father, in a broken voice.

'Not long, father. Already I seem to be going.'

The father took the motionless hand in his, and felt the thin wrist. It was almost pulseless. Grief filled his heart, but he heaved no groan, uttered no sigh. 'It was the Lord's doing;' and while he yearned over his first-born with all the tenderness and sympathy of his loving heart, he *knew that his afflicted child was on the verge of that heavenly glory which 'eye hath not seen.'

It was the morning of a calm, sweet Sabbath that Mary and her father thus talked. Cheerfully and beautifully she spoke of the rest on which she was so soon to enter. Her face brightened up, and her darkened eyes would turn heavenward, as she dwelt upon the joy that was just before her.

The day wore on, and with it wore away the life of Mary. Fainter and fainter grew her breath; feeble and yet more feeble, her life pulse.

The sun was low in the West. The sweet, fresh air of heaven stole in through the open windows. On a low cot, where the rays of the setting sun fell over the thin, wasted form, lay Mary Bunyan with closed eyes, her bosom scarcely moved by the slow, faint breath. The stricken family stood round. In silent grief they were awaiting the exit of the escaping spirit. All was hushed, solemn. No word was spoken. Each broken heart looked steadfastly on that loved form so soon to pass from their gaze for ever. Ah! it was a moment of sad trial, but it was also a time of humble submission.

The thin hand moves upward. The sightless eyes open, and turn to heaven. The pale lips murmur, 'Come, Lord Jesus, come quickly.' Then there steals over the palid countenance a smile of ineffable beauty. The hands fall motionless on the bosom; a gasp, a breath, and all is ended.

The wasted form is there. The spirit borne by angels up through the realms of ether, is ushered into the presence of the Great King. Now the poor blind girl sees even as she is seen, knows even as she known. A crown and a harp are given her, and she joins in the song of Moses and the Lamb.

Subdued weeping is heard throughout the room. The man of God kneels beside the inanimate form, and prays the blessing of God on himself and stricken ones.

The next day the neighbors and friends gathered in, and the remains of the poor blind girl were borne from the little cottage, and deposited beside those of her mother in the burying ground of the church at Elstow. From this sad event Bunyan never entirely recovered. It was a dark shadow all along his pathway until he, too, came to lie down peacefully in the silent tomb.

CHAPTER L.

A GLANCE AT BUNYAN'S LIFE AFTER HIS RELEASE FROM BEDFORD GAOL—HIS DEATH.

SIXTEEN years elapsed from the time of Bunyan's release to the time of his death. During this period he was a man of toil; not that he worked at his trade as a tinker—of this we have no evidence, but he was a laborer in the vineyard of the Lord.

As we have before said, Bunyan had been chosen pastor by the church at Bedford, 'to whose edification he had long administered,' more than a year before his imprisonment terminated. His confinement could not at that time have been as rigid as the law required. We are assured that he found a sympathising friend in the gaoler, and to this we must ascribe his privileges.

This pastorship continued uninterrupted up to the time of his death. But his labors were not confined to the people of his charge. He went 'everywhere preaching the gospel,' and that, too, at his imminent peril.

So severe were the enactments against Dissenters under the reign of the cruel James, that they were compelled to worship God under the cover of night, with sentinels placed round the building to give the signal of alarm if any stranger approached. Every precaution possible was resorted to, to elude the merciless grasp of the persecutor. Hymns were dispensed with entirely in their worship, and means were used to lessen the sound of the preacher's voice, as he exhorted his brethren to remain steadfast and immoveable.

Often the midnight hour found the people of God assembled in some lowly spot—some isolated dwelling, or the silent forests of Hitchen, to call upon the name of the Lord Jehovah, and supplicate his mercy. And oftentimes the first faint light of the grey morning dawn saw them returning to their homes, after having listened to the truth as it is in Christ Jesus from the lips of the beloved Bunyan.

Bunyan had oftentimes to disguise himself in the smock coat of a teamster, and thus attired, with a cartman's whip in his hand, he would be admitted through the back yard, and then through the kitchen door, and thus introduced to the little band of disciples, who eagerly received from him the bread of life. And sometimes, too, he had to escape thus disguised through back doors and windows, that he might not fall into the hands of his rapacious pursuers.

Bunyan's labors were not confined to his own immediate vicinity. He went on missionary work into the adjoining counties.

But Bunyan did not employ his time wholly in preaching. He wielded the pen of a ready writer, and devoted many of his hours, during the later years of his life, to authorship. He was sixty years old at the time of his death, and he produced sixty works, one for each year of his life. Many of these productions were written after he

left Bedford gaol. The number of them shows him to have
been a man of devoted energy to his undertakings. He
must have written both late and early thus to have given
to the world such a large collection of manuscript, in
addition to his work as pastor, and tinker, and preacher.
Beside all this, he had his family to take care of. In his
faithful Elizabeth he had a help-meet indeed; but Bunyan
did not choose to let the whole burden of domestic duty
rest upon her. He was still poor, though enabled, through
the frugality of his wife and his own industry, together
with the kindness of those to whom he administered in
spiritual matters, to enjoy a fair competence, thus being
relieved from the canker of poverty, which had so worn
upon his strong heart while he was in gaol.

His preaching was greatly blessed of the Lord. It was
of that practical, searching nature, that no one could
remain unmoved under his sermons. He did not gloss over
the truths of the gospel, thereby keeping men in carnal
security merely to please their sinful fancy, but spoke as
one who would declare the whole counsel of God—warning
sinners to flee from the wrath to come; arousing by earnest
appeals the careless professor, and building up in the most
holy faith the children of God.

He was also a peacemaker, a character that his great
goodness of heart and superior judgment admirably fitted
him for. And the last act of his life was one which
entitled him to that promise of the Saviour, ' Blessed are
the peacemakers, for they shall be called the children of
God.'

A father, residing at Reading, had become very greatly
displeased with his son, who lived in the neighborhood of
Bunyan. The son understood that his father was so highly
incensed as to be about to cut him off from any share in
his property. Knowing his father's unyielding disposition,
he feared it was too true. Not wishing to be thus unjustly
dealt with, and yet not daring to approach into the presence
of his injured parent, he hit upon Bunyan as the only
man likely to effect a reconciliation. Bunyan, with
that great desire for good which so strongly marked the
years of his eventful life, on hearing a plain statement of
the facts, readily undertook the case.

He visited the father, and by his earnest persuasions and
truthful representations of the demands of the law of
Christ, succeeded in effecting his object. The father not
only forgave his son, but reinstated him in his favor and
fortune.

Bunyan's work of reconciliation being accomplished, he set out to return home by way of London. It was in the month of August, 1688. A heavy, chilling rain fell throughout the day. But on he rode, anxious to reach the bosom of his family. He did not dream that he was nearer heaven than home.

Perhaps, with his own toil-worn pilgrim, he was enabled by faith to look on the Delectable Mountains, and dwell in the goodly land of Beulah, and have enrapturing visions of the New Jerusalem.

God oftentimes vouchsafes to his children joys and consolations of the most ecstatic character when all things earthly seem darkest and most opposed. He takes from us the support of the arm of flesh that we may learn to lean on him. And where can the child of God find such happiness as when, looking up, he can say with steadfast heart, Abba Father?

Late in the afternoon, Bunyan arrived at the house of a long-tried friend, a Mr. Strudick, grocer, of Snow Hill. His clothes were completely drenched with the rain that had been falling continuously through the day. His health had been somewhat poor for several months past, and soon after reaching his friend's house, he was seized with something like an ague fit, which continued to increase until he was forced to take his bed. Everything was done for his comfort and relief that love could suggest. But his indisposition continued to assume a more serious form, until a violent fever set up. He then felt that his days on earth were numbered, and so told his kind host.

Great anxiety was felt throughout the circle of his acquaintances in London when it was made known that he was ill, and many were the prayers that went up for his recovery. But God, who doeth all things well, had ordained otherwise. The Master had need of him. His poor pilgrim had been buffeted and tossed on the rough sea of life long enough. He had fought a good fight. He must now go up to receive his reward, even a crown of everlasting joy and glory.

And let us look at the worn soldier, as he lays aside his armor and prepares for rest. How does he bear himself, now that the battle is fought, the victory won? What is his hope and consolation in view of the great change through which he is so soon to pass?

We are told that ' his prayers were fervent and frequent; and he even so little minded himself as to the concerns of this life, that he comforted those that wept about him exhorting them to trust in God and pray to him for mercy and forgiveness of their sins, telling them what a glorious exchange it would be, to leave the troubles and cares of a wretched mortality, to live with Christ for ever, with a peace and joy inexpressible; expounding to them the comfortable Scriptures by which they were to hope, and assuredly come unto a blessed resurrection in the last day. He desired some to pray with him, and he joined with them in prayer, and his last words, after he had struggled with a languishing disease, were, "Weep not for me, but for yourselves. I go to the Father of our Lord Jesus, who will, no doubt, through the mediation of his blessed Son, receive me, though a sinner, where I hope ere long we shall meet to sing a new song, and remain everlastingly happy, world without end. Amen!"'

'Now while he was thus in discourse, his countenance changed, his strong man bowed under him; and after he had said, "Take me, for I am come unto thee," the Lord took him, and he ceased to be seen of men.

'But glorious it was to see how the open region was filled with horses and chariots, with trumpeters, and fifers, with singers and players on stringed instruments, to welcome the pilgrims as they went up and followed one another in at the Beautiful Gate of the city; and on it was written, in letters of gold, "Blessed are they that do his commandments, that they may have a right to the tree of life, and may enter in through the gates of the city."'

On the last day of August, 1688, at the age of sixty, the good man died. He was buried in Bunhill Fields, then in the suburbs of London.

All that now remains to mark the spot of his burial is an ancient square tomb, whose inscriptions have all mouldered away, save this simple one :—

MR. JOHN BUNYAN,

AUTHOR OF THE PILGRIM'S PROGRESS.

Obt. 31st August, 1688, *æt.* 60.

In three short years Elizabeth followed her faithful pilgrim to dwell in the celestial city, in the presence of her King and her husband for ever.

OTHER RELATED SOLID GROUND TITLES

In addition to the volume which you hold in your hand, Solid Ground is honored to offer many other uncovered treasure, many for the first time in more than a century:

THE STILL HOUR by Austin Phelps

MARTYRLAND: *Tale of Persecution of Scottish Covenanters* by Simpson

THE BACKSLIDER by Andrew Fuller

THE TRANSFIGURED LIFE by J.R. Miller

COME YE APART: *Daily Devotions from the Gospels* by J.R. Miller

CHILD'S BOOK ON THE FALL by Thomas H. Gallaudet

CHILD'S BOOK ON REPENTANCE by Thomas H. Gallaudet

CHILD'S BOOK ON THE SABBATH by Horace Hooker

THE FAMILY AT HOME by Gorham Abbott

THE MOTHER AT HOME by John S.C. Abbott

THE CHILD AT HOME by John S.C. Abbott

SMALL TALKS ON BIG QUESTIONS by Helms and Kahler

BIBLE ANIMALS *and their Lessons for Children* by Richard Newton

BIBLE JEWELS *and their Lessons for Children* by Richard Newton

THE KING'S HIGHWAY: *10 Commandments* by Richard Newton

HEROES OF THE REFORMATION by Richard Newton

HEROES OF THE EARLY CHURCH by Richard Newton

BIBLE PROMISES: *Lectures for the Young* by Richard Newton

BIBLE WARNINGS: *Lectures for the Young* by Richard Newton

THE SAFE COMPASS: *Lectures for Young* by Richard Newton

RAYS FROM THE SUN OF RIGHTEOUSNESS by R. Newton

LIFE OF JESUS CHRIST FOR THE YOUNG by R. Newton

FEED MY LAMBS: *Lectures to Children* by John Todd

TRUTH MADE SIMPLE: *Attributes of God for Children* John Todd

Call us at 1-205-443-0311
Send us an e-mail at sgcb@charter.net
Visit us on line at solid-ground-books.com

Printed in the United States
89785LV00003B/97-498/A